SHIP

CLIVE CUSSLER

with JACK DU BRUL

THE BERKLEY PUBLISHING GROUP
Published by the Penguin Group
Penguin Group (USA) Inc.
375 Hudson Street, New York, New York 10014, USA
Penguin Group (Canada), 90 Eglinton Avenue East, Suite 700, Toronto, Ontario M4P 2Y3, Canada
(a division of Pearson Penguin Canada Inc.)
Penguin Books Ltd., 80 Strand, London WC2R 0RL, England
Penguin Group Ireland, 25 St. Stephen's Green, Dublin 2, Ireland (a division of Penguin Books Ltd.)
Penguin Group (Australia), 250 Camberwell Road, Camberwell, Victoria 3124, Australia
(a division of Pearson Australia Group Pty. Ltd.)
Penguin Books India Pvt. Ltd., 11 Community Centre, Panchsheel Park, New Delhi—110 017, India
Penguin Group (NZ), 67 Apollo Drive, Rosedale, North Shore 0632, New Zealand
(a division of Pearson New Zealand Ltd.)
Penguin Books (South Africa) (Pty.) Ltd., 24 Sturdee Avenue, Rosebank, Johannesburg 2196,
South Africa

Penguin Books Ltd., Registered Offices: 80 Strand, London WC2R 0RL, England

PLAGUE SHIP

A Berkley Book / published by arrangement with Sandecker RLLLP

PRINTING HISTORY
G. P. Putnam's hardcover edition / June 2008
Berkley international edition / March 2009

ISBN: 978-0-425-22856-2

BERKLEY®
Berkley Books are published by The Berkley Publishing Group,
a division of Penguin Group (USA) Inc.,
375 Hudson Street, New York, New York 10014.
BERKLEY® is a registered trademark of Penguin Group (USA) Inc.
The "B" design is a trademark of Penguin Group (USA) Inc.

PRINTED IN THE UNITED STATES OF AMERICA

10 9 8 7 6 5 4 3 2 1

"A NEW CLIVE CUSSLER NOVEL IS LIKE A VISIT FROM YOUR BEST FRIEND."
—Tom Clancy

PLAGUE SHIP

Clive Cussler returns with a new novel in his *New York Times* bestselling *Oregon* Files, as Captain Juan Cabrillo and the motley crew of his high-tech spy ship take on their most extraordinary—and lethal—mission yet . . .

The *Oregon* is churning sea in the Persian Gulf, returning from a secret mission against Iran, when it comes across a cruise ship adrift at sea—with no signs of life. Cabrillo and his crew are shocked to find hundreds of bodies littering the deck, killed by an unknown virus. One lone survivor is recovered before explosions rip through the length of the ship, destroying any clues.

The answer lies within a mysterious cabal known as the Responsivists—a demented cult devoted to controlling the earth's population by any means necessary. They have found the means to their madness hidden in an ancient ship. And they are about to unleash their wrath on the human race.

And Cabrillo may already be too late to stop them . . .

THE *NEW YORK TIMES* BESTSELLING NOVELS OF THE *OREGON* FILES

SKELETON COAST • DARK WATCH
SACRED STONE • GOLDEN BUDDHA

"Ablaze with action."   —*Kirkus Reviews*

"Readers will burn up the pages."   —*Publishers Weekly*

"Fans of Cussler will not be disappointed." —*Library Journal*

continued . . .

PLAGUE

A NOVEL OF
THE OREGON® FILES

BERKLEY BOOKS   NEW YORK

Arguably the greatest transfer of wealth in human history occurred when the Plague swept through Europe and killed a third of its population. Lands were consolidated, allowing for a greater standard of living, not only for the owners but also for those who worked for them. This event was the single greatest contributor to the Renaissance and gave rise to Europe's eventual domination of the world.

We're Breeding Ourselves to Death:
How Overpopulation Will Destroy Civilization,
by Dr. Lydell Cooper, Raptor Press, 1977

PROLOGUE

A PALE HUNTER'S MOON HUNG ABOVE THE HO-
rizon so that its light threw dazzling reflections off the
frigid ocean. With winter not yet given way to spring, the sun
had yet to rise this year. Instead, it remained hidden behind
the earth's curvature, a faint glowing promise that crept along
the line where sky met sea as the planet spun on its tilted axis.
It would be another month before it would fully show itself,
and, once it did, it would not disappear again until fall. Such
was the odd cycle of day and night above the Arctic Circle.

By rights of their extreme northern latitudes, the waters of
the Barents Sea should be frozen over and impassable for
most of the year. But the sea was blessed with warm waters
cycling up from the tropics on the Gulf Stream. It was this
powerful current that made Scotland and the northern reaches
of Norway habitable, and kept the Barents free of ice and
navigable even in the deepest winters. For this reason, it was
the primary route for war material being convoyed from the
tireless factories of America to the embattled Soviet Union.
And like so many such sea routes—the English Channel or
the Gibraltar Strait—it had become a choke point and, thus, a
killing ground for the wolf packs of the *Kriegsmarine* and
shore-based *Schnellboots*, the fast-attack torpedo boats.

Far from random, the placement of U-boats was planned
out with the forethought of a chess master advancing his
pieces. Every scrap of intelligence was gathered about the
strength, speed, and destination of ships plying the North At-
lantic in order to have submarines positioned to strike.

From bases in Norway and Denmark, patrol aircraft
scoured the seas, looking for the convoys of merchantmen,
radioing positions back to fleet headquarters so the U-boats

could lie in wait for their prey. For the first years of the war, the submarines enjoyed near-total supremacy of the seas, and untold millions of tons of shipping had been sunk without mercy. Even under heavy escort by cruisers and destroyers, the Allies could do little more than play the odds of having one ship sunk for every ninety-nine that made it through. By being gambled so coldly, the men of the merchant marine paid as high a toll as frontline combat units.

That was about to change this night.

The four-engined Focke-Wulf Fw 200 *Kondor* was a massive plane—seventy-seven feet long, with a wingspan of nearly one hundred and ten feet. Designed before the war for Lufthansa as a passenger airliner, the aircraft had been quickly pressed into military duty as both a transport and a long-range reconnaissance platform. Her twenty-five-hundred-mile range allowed the *Kondor* to remain aloft for hours and hunt Allied shipping far from shore.

Used in an attack role through 1941 by carrying four five-hundred-pound bombs under her wings, the *Kondor* had taken some heavy losses and was now strictly employed as a reconnaissance plane, and remained well above Allied antiaircraft fire during their patrols.

The aircraft's pilot, Franz Lichtermann, chafed at the monotonous hours spent searching the trackless sea. He longed to be in a fighter squadron, fighting the real war, not loitering thousands of feet above frigid nothingness hoping to spot Allied shipping for someone else to sink. Back at base, Lichtermann maintained a high level of military decorum and expected the same from his men. However, when they were on patrol and the minutes stretched with the elasticity of India rubber, he allowed a certain amount of familiarity among the five-man crew.

"That should help," he commented over the intercom and jerked his head in the direction of the dazzling moon.

"Or its reflection will hide a convoy's wake," his copilot, Max Ebelhardt, replied in his customary pessimistic tone.

"With the sea this calm we'll spot them even if they've stopped to ask for directions."

"Do we even know if anyone's out here?" The question came from the crew's youngest member, Ernst Kessler. Kessler was the *Kondor*'s rear gunner and sat scrunched at the aft of the ventral gondola that ran the partial length of the aircraft's fuselage. From behind his Plexiglas shield and over the barrel of a single MG-15 machine gun, he could see nothing other than what the *Kondor* had already flown over.

"The squadron commander assured me that a U-boat returning from patrol spotted at least a hundred ships two days ago above the Faeroe Islands," Lichtermann told his crew. "The ships were heading north, so they've got to be out here somewhere."

"More likely, the U-boat commander just wanted to report something after missing with all his torpedoes," Ebelhardt groused, and made a face after a sip of tepid ersatz coffee.

"I'd rather just spot them, then sink them," Ernst Kessler said. The gentle lad was barely eighteen, and had harbored ambitions of being a doctor before he had been drafted. Because he came from a poor rural family in Bavaria, his chances of an advanced education were nil, but that didn't prevent him from spending his off-hours with his nose buried in medical journals and texts.

"That isn't the proper attitude of a German warrior," Lichtermann admonished gently. He was thankful that they had never come under enemy attack. He doubted Kessler would have the stomach to open fire with his machine gun, but the boy was the only member of his crew who could sit facing aft for hour after hour without becoming incapacitated by nausea.

He thought grimly about all the men dying on the Eastern Front, and about how the tanks and planes shipped to the Russians prolonged the inevitable fall of Moscow. Lichtermann would be more than happy to sink a few ships himself.

Another tedious hour dragged by, the men peering into the night in hopes of spotting the convoy. Ebelhardt tapped Lichtermann on the shoulder and pointed to his log. Although the fore gunner kneeling at the front of the ventral gondola was the official navigator, Ebelhardt actually calculated their flight time and direction, and he was indicating that it was time for them to turn and search another swath of open sea.

Lichtermann applied rudder and eased over the yoke in an easy turn to port, never taking his eyes off the horizon, as the moon seemed to swing across the sky.

Ernst Kessler prided himself at having the sharpest eyes aboard the aircraft. When he was a boy, he would dissect dead animals he found around the family farm to learn their anatomy, comparing what he saw to books on the subject. He knew his keen vision and steady hands would make him an excellent doctor. His senses, however, were just as adept at finding an enemy convoy.

By rights of his aft-facing station, he shouldn't have been the one to spot it, but he did. As the plane canted over, an unnatural glint caught his attention, a flash of white far from the moon's reflection.

"Captain!" Kessler cried over the intercom. "Starboard side, bearing about three hundred."

"What did you see?" The primeval thrill of the hunt edged Lichtermann's voice.

"I'm not sure, sir. Something. A glimmer of some kind."

Lichtermann and Ebelhardt strained to see in the darkness where young Kessler had indicated, but there was nothing apparent.

"Are you sure?" the pilot asked.

"Yes, sir," Kessler replied, forcing confidence into his reply. "It was when we turned. The angle changed, and I'm sure I saw something."

"The convoy?" Ebelhardt asked gruffly.

"I can't say," Ernst admitted.

"Josef, get the radio powered up," Lichtermann said, ordering the fore gunner to his ancillary position. The pilot added more power to the BMW radial engines, and banked the aircraft once again. Their drone became a bit sharper, as the props tore through the air.

Ebelhardt had a pair of binoculars pressed to his eyes as he searched the blackened sea. Rushing toward a possible contact at two hundred miles per hour, he should spot the convoy any moment, but, as seconds grew into a minute and nothing revealed itself, he lowered the binoculars again. "Must have been a wave," he said without keying the intercom microphone, so only Lichtermann heard.

"Give it a chance," Lichtermann replied. "Kessler can see in the dark like a damned cat."

The Allied powers had done a remarkable job of applying dizzying camouflage patterns to their freighters and tankers, to prevent observers from seeing the ships from the surface, but nothing could hide a convoy at night, since the wakes that formed behind the vessels burned white against the ocean.

I'll be damned, Ebelhardt mouthed, and then pointed through the windscreen.

At first, it was just a large patch of gray on the otherwise-dark water, yet, as they flew closer, the gray sharpened to become dozens of parallel white lines, as distinct as chalk marks on a blackboard. They were the wakes of an armada of ships, driving eastward as fast as it could. From the *Kondor*'s altitude, the ships looked as plodding as elephants traveling in a herd.

The *Kondor* flew closer still, until the moon's sharp glare allowed the crew to distinguish between the slower freighters and tankers and the slim wakes of destroyers set like pickets along each flank of the convoy. As they watched, one of the destroyers was making a fast run up the starboard side of the convoy, smoke pouring from her two stacks. When the destroyer reached the head of the convoy, it would slow again, and let the freighters pass it by, in what the Allies called an "Indian run." At the tail of the mile-long convoy, the destroyer would accelerate once again, in a never-ending cycle. In this way, it took fewer combat vessels to provide cover for the convoys.

"There must be two hundred ships out there," Ebelhardt estimated.

"Enough to keep the Reds fighting for months," the pilot agreed. "Josef, how's it coming with the radio?"

"I have nothing but static."

Static was a common enough problem, working this far above the Arctic Circle. Charged particles striking the earth's magnetic field were driven to ground at the poles and played havoc with the radios' vacuum tubes.

"We'll mark our position," Lichtermann said, "and radio in our report when we get closer to base. Hey, Ernst, well done. We would have turned away and missed the convoy, if it weren't for you."

"Thank you, sir." Pride was evident in the boy's response.

"I want a better count of the convoy's size, and a rough approximation of their speed."

"Let's not get so close that those destroyers open up," Ebelhardt cautioned. He had seen combat firsthand and was flying second stick now because of a piece of shrapnel buried in his thigh, thanks to antiaircraft fire over London. He recognized the look in Lichtermann's eye and the excitement in his voice. "And don't forget the CAMs."

"Trust me," the pilot said with cocky bravado, and wheeled the big plane closer to the slow-moving fleet ten thousand feet below them. "I'm not going to get too close, and we're too far from land for them to launch a plane at us."

CAMs, or Catapult Aircraft Merchantmen, were the Allies' answer to German aerial reconnaissance. A long rail was mounted over the bows of a freighter, and, with a rocket assist, they could launch a Hawker Sea Hurricane fighter aircraft to shoot down the lumbering *Kondor*s or even attack surfaced U-boats. The drawback to the CAMs was that the planes couldn't land back aboard their mother ship. The Hurricanes either had to be close enough to Great Britain or some other friendly area for the pilots to land normally. Otherwise, the plane had to be ditched in the sea and the pilot rescued from the water.

The convoy steaming below the Fw 200 was more than a thousand miles from any Allied territory, and even with the bright moon a downed pilot would be impossible to rescue in the dark. There would be no Hurricanes launched tonight. The *Kondor* had nothing to fear from the mass of Allied shipping unless it strayed within range of the destroyers and the curtain of antiaircraft fire they could throw into the sky.

Ernst Kessler was counting rows of ships when winking lights suddenly appeared on the decks of two of the destroyers. "Captain!" he cried. "Fire from the convoy!"

Lichtermann could just make out the destroyers beneath his wing. "Easy, lad," he said. "Those are signal lamps. The ships are sailing under strict radio silence, so that's how they communicate."

"Oh. Sorry, sir."

"Don't worry about it. Just get as accurate a count as you can."

The *Kondor* had been flying a lazy circle around the flotilla and was passing along its northern flank when Dietz, who manned the upper gun platform, shouted, "Incoming!"

Lichtermann had no idea what the man was talking about and was a beat slow in reacting. A perfectly aimed string of 7.7mm machine-gun rounds raked the *Kondor*'s upper surface, starting at the base of the vertical stabilizer and walking up the entire length of the plane. Dietz was killed before he could get a shot off. Bullets penetrated the cockpit, and, amid the harsh patter of them ricocheting off metallic surfaces and the whistle of wind through rents in the fuselage, Lichtermann heard his copilot grunt in pain. He looked over to see the front of Ebelhardt's flight jacket covered in blood.

Lichtermann mashed the rudder and pressed hard on the yoke to dive away from the Allied aircraft that had come out of nowhere.

It was the wrong maneuver.

Launched just weeks earlier, the MV *Empire MacAlpine* was a late addition to the convoy. Originally built as a grain carrier, the eight-thousand-ton vessel had spent five months in the Burntisland Shipyard having her superstructure replaced by a small control island, four hundred and sixty feet of runway, and a hangar for four Fairley Swordfish torpedo bombers. She could still haul nearly as much grain as she could before her conversion. The Admiralty had always considered the CAMs a stopgap measure until a safer alternative could be found. As it was, the Merchant Aircraft Carriers, or MACs, like the *MacAlpine*, were to be used only until England secured a number of Essex Class escort carriers from the United States.

While the *Kondor* loitered over the convoy, two of the Swordfish had been launched from the *MacAlpine* and flown far enough out from the fleet that, when they climbed into the inky sky to ambush the much larger and faster German aircraft, Lichtermann and his men never knew they were coming. The Fairleys were biplanes, with top speeds barely half that of the *Kondor*. They each carried a Vickers machine gun,

mounted above the radial engine's cowling, and a gimballed
Lewis gun in a rear-facing cockpit.

The second Swordfish lay in wait three thousand feet below the Focke-Wulf and was nearly invisible in the darkness.
As the *Kondor* dove away from the first attacker, the second
torpedo bomber, stripped of anything that could slow it, was
in position.

A stream of fire poured into the front of the *Kondor* from
the Vickers, while the second gunner leaned far over the rear
cockpit coaming to train his Lewis gun on the pair of BMW
engines attached to the port wing.

Coin-sized holes appeared all around Ernst Kessler, the
aluminum glowing cherry red for an instant before fading.
There had been only a few seconds between Dietz's scream
and the barrage that swept the underside of the *Kondor*, not
nearly long enough for fear to cripple the teen. He knew his
duty. Swallowing hard because his stomach had yet to catch
up with the plummeting aircraft, he squeezed his MG-15's
trigger, as the Fw continued to dive past the slower Swordfish.
Tracers began to fill the sky, and he aimed the 7.92mm weapon
like a fireman directing a stream of water. He could see a
circle of little jets of fire glowing in the darkness. It was the
exhaust popping around the Fairley's radial engine, and it was
there that he targeted the withering fire, even as his own plane
was continuously hammered by the British craft.

The arcing line of tracers converged on the glowing circle,
and, suddenly, it appeared as if the Allied plane's nose were
engulfed in fireworks. Sparks and tongues of fire enveloped
the Swordfish, metal and fabric shredded by the assault. The
propeller was torn apart, and the radial engine exploded as
if it were a fragmentary grenade. Burning fuel and hot oil
rolled over the exposed pilot and gunner. The Swordfish's
controlled dive, which matched the *Kondor*'s, became an
out-of-control plummet.

The Fairley winged over, spiraling ever faster, as it burned
like a meteor. Lichtermann began to level the *Kondor*. Kessler could see the flaming wreckage continue to drop away. It
suddenly changed shape. The wings had torn loose from the
Swordfish's fuselage. Any aerodynamics the mortally wounded
aircraft had possessed were gone. The Swordfish dropped

like a stone, the flames winking out when the wreckage plowed into the uncaring sea.

When Ernst looked up and across the fifty-foot trailing edge of the port wing, the fear he had been too distracted to acknowledge hit him full force. Smoke trailed from both nine-cylinder engines, and he could plainly hear the power plants were misfiring badly.

"Captain," he shouted into the microphone.

"Shut up, Kessler," Lichtermann snapped. "Radioman, get up here and give me a hand. Ebelhardt's dead."

"Captain, the port engines," Kessler insisted.

"I know, damnit, I know. Shut up."

The first Swordfish that had attacked was well astern, and most likely had already turned to rejoin the convoy, so there was nothing Kessler could do but stare in horror at the smoke rushing by in the slipstream. Lichtermann shut down the inboard engine in hopes of extinguishing the flames. He let the propeller windmill for a moment before reengaging the starter. The engine coughed and caught, and fire appeared around the cowling, flames quickly blackening the aluminum skin of the nacelle.

With the inboard engine producing a little thrust, Lichtermann chanced shutting off the outside motor. When he kicked on the starter again, the engine fired immediately, producing only an occasional wisp of smoke. He immediately killed the still-burning inboard engine, fearing the fire could spread to the *Kondor*'s fuel lines, and throttled back the damaged outside motor to save it for as long as he could. With two engines functioning properly and a third running at half power, they could make it back to base.

Tense minutes trickled by. Young Kessler resisted the urge to ask the pilot about their situation. He knew Lichtermann would tell him something as soon as he could. Kessler jumped and hit his head on an internal strut when he heard a new sound, a whooshing gush that came from directly behind him. The Plexiglas canopy protecting his position was suddenly doused with droplets of some liquid. It took him a moment to realize Lichtermann must have calculated the *Kondor*'s fuel load and the distance back to their base at Narvik. He was dumping excess gasoline in order to lighten the aircraft as much as possible. The fuel-dump tube was located behind his ventral gun position.

"How are you doing down there, Kessler?" Lichtermann asked after cutting off the flow.

"Um, fine, sir," Kessler stammered. "Where did those planes come from?"

"I didn't even see them," the pilot confessed.

"They were biplanes. Well, at least the one I shot down was."

"Must be Swordfish," Lichtermann said. "It appears the Allies have a new trick up their sleeve. Those didn't come off a CAM. The rocket-assisted motors would tear the wings clean off. The British must have a new aircraft carrier."

"But we didn't see any planes taking off."

"They could have seen us coming on radar and launched before we spotted the convoy."

"Can we radio this information to base?"

"Josef's working on it now. The radio's still picking up nothing but static. We'll be over the coast in a half hour. Reception should clear by then."

"What do you want me to do, sir?"

"Stay at your station, and keep an eye out for any more Swordfish. We're making less than a hundred knots, and one could sneak up on us."

"What about Lieutenant Ebelhardt and Corporal Dietz?"

"Didn't I hear that your father's a minister or something?"

"Grandfather, sir. At the Lutheran church in our village."

"Next letter home to him, have him say a prayer. Ebelhardt and Dietz are both dead."

There was no more talk after that. Kessler continued to stare into the darkness, hoping to spot an enemy plane but praying he didn't. He tried not to think about how he had just killed two men. It was war, and they had ambushed the *Kondor* without warning, so he shouldn't feel the creeping sense of guilt tingling along his nerves. His hands shouldn't be trembling and his stomach shouldn't be so knotted. He wished Lichtermann hadn't mentioned his grandfather. He could imagine what the stern minister would say. He hated the government and this foolish war they had started, and now it had turned his youngest grandchild into a killer.

Kessler knew he'd never be able to look his grandfather in the eye again.

"I can see the coast," Lichtermann announced after forty minutes. "We'll make Narvik yet."

The *Kondor* was down to three thousand feet when it flashed over Norway's north coast. It was a barren, ugly land of foaming surf crashing against featureless cliffs and islands. Only a few fishing villages clung to the crags and inlets, where natives eked a meager living from the sea.

Ernst Kessler felt a small lift in his spirits. Somehow, being over land made him feel safer. Not that a crash into the rocky terrain below would be survivable, but dying on the ground, where the wreckage could be located and his body given a proper burial, seemed so much better than the anonymity of dying at sea, like the British pilots he'd shot down.

Fate chose that instant to deal her final card. The outboard port engine, which had been humming along at half power and keeping the big reconnaissance plane in trim, gave no warning. It simply seized so hard that the propeller went from a whirling disc providing stability to a stationary sculpture of burnished metal that added a tremendous amount of drag.

On the flight deck, Lichtermann slammed the rudder hard over in an attempt to keep the *Kondor* from spiraling. The thrust from the starboard wing and the drag from the port made the aircraft all but impossible to fly. It kept wanting to nose over to the left and dive.

Kessler was thrown violently against his gun mount, and a loop of ammunition whipped around him like a snake. It cracked against his face, so that his vision went dim and blood jetted from both nostrils. It came at him again and would have slammed the side of his head had he not ducked and pinned the shining brass belt against a bulkhead.

Lichtermann held the plane steady for a few seconds longer but knew it was a losing battle. The *Kondor* was too unbalanced. If he had any hope of landing it, he had to equalize thrust and drag. He reached out a gloved hand and hit the kill switches for the starboard engines. They wound down quickly. The stationary propeller continued to cause extra drag on the port side, but Lichtermann could compensate, as his aircraft became an oversized glider.

"Kessler, get up here and strap in," Lichtermann shouted over the intercom. "We're going to crash."

The plane shot over a mountain guarding a fjord with a small glacier at its head, the ice dazzlingly white against the jagged black rock.

Ernst had his shoulder straps off and was bending to crawl out of the gun position when something far below caught his eye. Deep in the cleft of the fjord was a building constructed partially on the glacier. Or perhaps something so ancient that the glacier had started to bury it. It was difficult to judge scale in his brief glimpse, but it looked large, like some kind of old Viking storehouse.

"Captain," Kessler cried. "Behind us. In that fjord. There is a building. I think we can land on the ice."

Lichtermann hadn't seen anything, but Kessler was facing backward and would have had an unobstructed view into the fjord. The terrain ahead of the *Kondor* was broken ground, with ice-carved hillocks as sharp as daggers. The plane's undercarriage would collapse the instant they touched down, and the rock would shred the aircraft's skin as easily as paper.

"Are you sure?" he shouted back.

"Yes, sir. It was on the edge of the glacier. I could see it in the moonlight. There is definitely a building there."

Without power, Lichtermann had one shot at landing the plane. He was certain that if he tried it out in the open, he and his two remaining crew members would be killed in the crash. Landing on a glacier wouldn't be a picnic either, but at least there was a chance they could walk away.

He muscled the yoke over, fighting the *Kondor*'s inertia. Turning the plane caused the wing surfaces to lose lift. The altimeter began to spin backward twice as fast as when he was maintaining level flight. There was nothing Lichtermann could do about it. It was simple physics.

The big aircraft carved through the sky, coming back on a northerly heading. The mountain that had hidden the glacier from Lichtermann's view loomed ahead. He silently thanked the bright moonlight, because, at the mountain's base, he could see a field of virgin white, a patch of glacial ice at least a mile long. He saw no indication of the building Kessler had spotted, but it didn't matter. The ice was what he focused on.

It rose gently from the sea for most of its length before seeming to fall from a cleft in the side of the mountain, a near-vertical wall of ice that was so thick it appeared blue in the uncertain light. A few small icebergs dotted the long fjord.

The *Kondor* was sinking fast. Lichtermann barely had the altitude to turn the plane one last time to line up with the glacier. They dropped below the mountain's peak. The glacially shaped rock appeared less than an arms' span from the wingtip. The ice, which looked smooth from a thousand feet, appeared rougher the closer they fell toward it, like small waves that had been flash-frozen. Lichtermann didn't extend the landing gear. If one strut was torn off when they hit, the plane would cartwheel and tear itself apart.

"Hang on," he said. His throat was so dry the words came out in a tight croak.

Ernst had climbed from his position and had strapped himself in the radioman's seat. Josef was on the flight deck with Lichtermann. The radio's dials glowed milky white. There were no windows nearby, so the inside of the aircraft was pitch-black. At hearing the pilot's terse warning, Kessler bent double, wrapping his hands around the back of his neck and clamping his knees with his elbows, as he'd been trained.

Prayers tumbled from his lips.

The *Kondor* struck the glacier with a glancing blow, rose a dozen feet, and then came down harder. The sound of metal against the ice was like a train racing through a tunnel. Kessler was thrown violently against his safety straps but didn't dare uncurl himself from his seated fetal position. The plane crashed into something with a jarring bump that sent radio manuals fluttering from their shelves. The wing struck ice, and the aircraft began to spin, shedding parts in chunks.

He didn't know what was better, being alone in the hull of the plane and not knowing what was happening outside or being in the cockpit and seeing the *Kondor* come apart.

There was a crash below where Kessler huddled, and a blast of frigid air shot through the fuselage. The Plexiglas protecting the forward gunner's position had been blown inward. Chunks of ice that were being shaved off the glacier whirled through the plane, and, still, it felt like they were not slowing.

Then came the loudest sound yet, an echoing explosion of torn metal that was followed immediately by the rank smell of high-octane aviation fuel. Kessler knew what had happened. One of the wings had dug into the ice and had been sheared off. Though Lichtermann had dumped most of their gasoline, enough remained in the lines to make the threat of fire a very real one.

The plane continued to toboggan across the glacier, driven by her momentum and the slight downward slope of the ice. But she had finally started to slow. Having her port wing torn off had turned the aircraft perpendicular to her direction of travel. With more of her hull scraping against the ice, friction was overcoming gravity.

Kessler allowed himself a sigh. He knew in just moments the *Kondor* would come to a complete stop. Captain Lichtermann had done it. He relaxed the death grip he'd maintained since the shouted warning and was about to straighten in his seat when the starboard wing tore into the ice and was ripped off at the root.

The fuselage rolled over the severed wing and flipped onto its back in a savage motion that nearly tossed Kessler out of his safety belts. His neck whiplashed brutally, the pain radiating all the way to his toes.

The young airman hung dazed from his straps for several long seconds until he realized he could no longer hear the rasping scrape of aluminum over ice. The *Kondor* had come to a halt. Fighting nausea, he carefully unhooked his belts and lowered himself to the aircraft's ceiling. He felt something soft give under his feet. In the darkness, he shifted so he was standing on one of the fuselage support members. He felt down and immediately yanked his hand back. He had touched a corpse, and his fingers were covered in a warm, sticky fluid he knew to be blood.

"Captain Lichtermann?" he called. "Josef?"

The reply was a whistle of cold wind through the downed aircraft.

Kessler rummaged through a cabinet below the radio and

found a flashlight. Its naked beam revealed the body of Max Ebelhardt, the copilot, who had died in the first instant of the attack. Calling out for Josef and Lichtermann, he trained the light on the inverted cockpit. He spotted the men still strapped to their seats, their arms dangling as limp as rag dolls'.

Neither man moved, not even when Kessler crawled over to them and laid a hand on the pilot's shoulder. Lichtermann's head was back, his blue eyes unblinking. His face was dark red, suffused with blood pooling in his skull. Kessler touched his cheek. The flesh was still warm, but the skin had lost its elasticity. It felt like putty. He flashed the light over to the radioman/gunner. Josef Vogel was also dead. Vogel's head had smashed against a bulkhead—Kessler could see the blood smeared against the metal—while Lichtermann's neck must have been broken when the plane flipped over.

The rank smell of gasoline finally burned through the fog in Kessler's head, and he staggered to the rear of the aircraft, where the main door was located. The crash had crushed the frame, and he had to slam his shoulder into the metal to pop it open. He fell out of the *Kondor* and sprawled on the ice. Chunks of the fuselage and wing were strewn along the glacier, and he could plainly see the deep furrows the aircraft had gouged into the ice.

He wasn't sure how imminent the threat of fire was or how long it would be before he could safely return to the damaged *Kondor*. But with the wind chilled by the ice as it came down off the glacier, he knew he couldn't remain out in the open for very long. His best bet lay in finding the mysterious building he'd spotted before the crash. He would wait there until he was certain the *Kondor* wouldn't burn and then return. Hopefully, the radio survived the crash. If it hadn't, there was a small inflatable boat stored in the tail section of the plane. It would take him days to reach a village, but if he hugged the coastline he could make it.

Having a plan helped keep the horror of the past hour at bay. He just had to focus on surviving. When he was safely back in Narvik, he would allow himself to dwell on his dead comrades. He hadn't been particularly close to any of them, preferring his studies to their carousing, but they had been his crew.

Kessler's head pounded, and his neck became so stiff he could barely turn it. He took bearings on the mountain that hid so much of the tight fjord and started trudging across the glacier. Distances on the ice were hard to determine, and what had looked like just a couple of kilometers turned into an hours-long walk that left his feet numb. A sudden rain squall had drenched him, the water freezing on his coat flaking off in icy bits that crackled with each step.

He was thinking about turning back and taking his chances with the plane when his eye caught the outline of the building thrust partially out of the ice. As he got closer and details emerged from the dark, he began to shiver with more than the cold. It wasn't a building at all.

Kessler came to a stop under the bow of a huge ship, constructed of thick wood with copper sheathing and towering over his head, that had become trapped in the ice. Knowing how slowly glaciers moved, he estimated that for the vessel to be so deeply buried it had been here for thousands of years. It was unlike anything he'd ever seen. Even as that thought crossed his mind, he knew it wasn't true. He'd seen pictures of this ship before. There were illustrations in the Bible his grandfather used to read to him when he was a boy. Kessler had much preferred the Old Testament stories to the preachings of the New, so he even recalled the ship's dimensions—one hundred cubits long, fifty cubits wide, and thirty cubits tall.

"... and onto this ark Noah loaded his animals two by two."

CHAPTER 1

THE TIRED-LOOKING FREIGHTER HAD LAIN AT anchor off the busy port of Bandar Abbas long enough to arouse the suspicion of the Iranian military. An armed patrol boat was dispatched from the nearby naval base and streaked across the shallow azure waters toward the five-hundred-plus-foot ship.

The vessel was named the *Norego* and carried a Panamanian registry, if the flag hanging from her jack staff was any indication. From the look of her, she had been converted to container duty after serving her life as a general cargo vessel. Growing up from her deck like branchless trees were five cargo booms, three forward and two aft. Around them were stacks of brightly colored containers piled to just below her bridge windows. Despite the large quantity of containers, she sat high in the water, with at least fifteen feet of red antifouling paint showing below her maximum-load line. Her hull was a uniform blue, but looked as though she hadn't seen a new coat of paint in some time, while her upperworks were a mismatched shade of green. Her twin funnels were so darkened by soot that the original color was indeterminate. A trickle of smoke coiled from the stacks and hung over the ship in a pall.

Scaffolding of metal struts had been lowered over her fantail, and men in grease-smeared coveralls were working on the freighter's rudder bearing.

As the patrol craft approached, the NCO acting as captain of the nimble boat raised a megaphone to his mouth. "Ahoy, *Norego*," he said in Farsi. "Please be advised that we are going to board you." Muhammad Ghami repeated his words in English, the international language of maritime trade.

A moment later, a grossly overweight man wearing a sweat-stained officer's shirt appeared at the head of the gangway. He nodded to a subaltern, and the boarding stairs began to descend.

As they drew nearer, Ghami saw captain's epaulets on the man's shoulders and sourly wondered how a man of such rank could let himself go so badly. The *Norego*'s master carried a heavy gut that sagged ten inches over his belt. Under his white cap, his hair was greasy black with gray streaks, and his face was covered with stubble. He could only imagine where the owners of such a decrepit ship would find such a man to command her.

With one of his men standing behind the patrol boat's .50 caliber machine gun, Ghami nodded for another sailor to tie the rigid-hulled inflatable to the gangway. Another sailor stood close by, an AK-47 slung across his shoulder. Ghami checked that the flap over his holster was secured and leapt onto the boarding stairs with his second-in-command at his heels. As he climbed, he observed the captain try to smooth his hair and straighten his filthy shirt. They were futile gestures.

Ghami reached the deck, noting that the plates were sprung in places and hadn't seen paint in decades. Rust caked nearly every surface except for the shipping containers, which probably hadn't been on board long enough for the crew's lack of diligence to affect them. There were gaps in the railing that had been repaired with lengths of chain, and corrosion had eaten into the superstructure so much that it looked ready to collapse at any moment.

Hiding his disgust, Ghami snapped a crisp salute at the captain. The man scratched his ample stomach and made a vague gesture at the bill of his cap.

"Captain, I am Ensign Muhammad Ghami of the Iranian Navy. This is Seaman Khatahani."

"Welcome aboard the *Norego*, Ensign," the freighter's master replied. "I am Captain Ernesto Esteban."

His Spanish accent was so thick that Ghami had to go over each word in his head to make sure he understood. Esteban was a few inches taller than the Iranian sailor, but the extra weight he carried hunched his shoulders and curved his back so that he and Ghami appeared almost the same height. His eyes were dark and watery, and when he smiled to shake Ghami's hand his teeth were yellowed and crooked. His breath smelled like curdled milk.

"What seems to be the trouble with your steering gear?"

Esteban cursed in Spanish. "The bearing froze up. Fourth time in a month. The cheap owners"—he spat—"won't let me have it fixed in a shipyard so my men have to do. We should be under way by tonight, maybe in the morning."

"And what is your cargo and destination?"

The captain slapped one of the shipping containers. "Empty boxes. They're all the *Norego* is good for."

"I don't understand," Ghami said.

"We're transporting empty containers from Dubai to Hong Kong. Full containers get shipped in, unloaded, and pile up on the dock. We take them back to Hong Kong, where they are reloaded."

That explained why the ship was riding so high in the water, Ghami thought. Empty containers weighed only a few tons each. "And what do you carry on your return trip here?"

"Barely enough to cover our costs," Esteban said bitterly. "No one will insure us with anything more valuable than boxes of nothing."

"I need to see your crew manifest, cargo manifest, and the ship's registration."

"Is there some kind of problem?" Esteban asked quickly.

"I will determine that after I have seen your papers," Ghami said with enough menace to make certain the disgusting man complied. "Your vessel is deep in Iranian waters, and I am fully in my right to inspect every inch of this ship if I see fit."

"No problema, señor," Esteban said with oily smoothness. His grin was more grimace. "Why don't we step out of this heat and into my office?"

Bandar Abbas sat tucked in the tightest curve of the Strait of Hormuz, the narrow entrance to the Persian Gulf. Summertime temperatures rarely dipped below a hundred and twenty during the day, and there was little wind. The metal decking beneath the men's feet was quite literally hot enough to fry eggs.

"Lead the way," Ghami said, and swept his hand toward the superstructure.

The interior spaces aboard the *Norego* were as dilapidated as her outside. The floors were chipped linoleum, the walls bare metal with large swatches of peeled paint, and the fluorescent lights mounted to the ceilings buzzed loudly. Several of them flickered at erratic intervals, casting the narrow corridor in stark shadow.

Esteban led Ghami and Khatahani up a tight companionway with a loose railing and onto another short corridor. He opened the door to his office and gestured for the men to enter. The captain's cabin could be seen through an open door on the opposite side of the office. The bed was unmade, and the sheets that spilled onto the floor were stained. A single dresser stood bolted to the wall, and the mirror above it had a jagged crack running from corner to corner.

The office was a rectangular room with a single porthole so rimed with salt that only murky light came through. The walls were adorned with paintings of sad-eyed clowns done in garish colors on black velvet. Another door led to a tiny bathroom that was filthier than a public washroom in a Tehran slum. So many cigarettes had been smoked in the office that the stale smell seemed to coat everything, including the back of Ghami's mouth. A lifelong smoker himself, even the Iranian naval officer was disgusted.

Esteban jammed the bare wires of a desk lamp into an outlet next to his desk, cursed when they sparked but seemed pleased that the lamp came on. He eased himself into his chair with a groan. He indicated for the two inspectors to take the seats opposite. Ghami used a pen from his shirt pocket to flick the dried-out carcass of a cockroach from the chair before sitting.

The captain rummaged through his desk, coming out with a liquor bottle. He eyed the two Muslims and returned the bottle to its drawer, muttering in Spanish. "Okay, here's the manifest." He handed over a binder. "Like I said, we're carrying nothing but empty containers bound for Hong Kong." He set other binders onto the desk. "My crew's manifest. A bunch of lazy ingrates, if you ask me. So if you want to detain any of 'em, be my guest. These are the *Norego*'s registration papers."

Ghami thumbed through the list of crew members, noting their nationalities and double-checking their identity papers. The ship's complement was a mixed bag of Chinese, Mexicans, and Caribbean islanders, which jibed with the men he had seen working on the rudder. The captain himself was from Guadalajara, Mexico, had been with Trans-Ocean Shipping and Freight for eleven years and master of the *Norego* for six. Ghami was surprised to see that Esteban was only forty-two. The man looked closer to sixty.

There was nothing here to arouse suspicion, but Ghami wanted to be thorough.

"It says here you are carrying eight hundred and seventy containers."

"Thereabout."

"They are stacked in your holds?"

"Those that aren't deck-loaded," Esteban agreed.

"I do not wish to insult you, Captain, but a ship such as this was not designed to carry containers efficiently. I suspect there is room in your holds where contraband may be hidden. I wish to inspect all six."

"Until my steering gear's fixed, I've got nothing but time, Ensign," Esteban breezed. "You want to go over the whole ship, you be my guest. I have nothing to hide."

The office door was suddenly thrown open. A Chinese crewman wearing coveralls and wooden flip-flops jabbered excitedly at the captain in Cantonese. Esteban cursed and launched himself from his desk. His quick movements alerted the two Iranians. Ghami got to his feet, resting a hand on his holster. Esteban ignored him entirely and raced across the room as fast as his extra hundred pounds of flab would allow. Just as he reached the bathroom door, the plumbing made a throaty, wet gurgle. He slammed the door shut, and, a moment later, they could all hear the sound of water erupting like a geyser and splashing against the ceiling. A new, more pungent smell overwhelmed the cramped office.

"Sorry about that," Esteban said. "Seng here's been working on our septic system. I don't think he quite has it yet."

"If they're hiding anything," Seaman Khatahani whispered to his superior in Farsi, "I don't think I want to find it."

"You're right," Ghami replied. "There isn't a smuggler in

the Gulf who would trust this fat lout or his broken-down scow." Considering that smuggling along the Persian Gulf was a time-honored and noble tradition, Ghami wasn't being facetious. He addressed Esteban, "Captain, I can see that your hands are full with simply maintaining your vessel. Your paperwork appears to be in order, so we won't take up any more of your time."

"You sure about that?" Esteban asked, cocking a bushy eyebrow. "I don't mind giving you the nickel tour."

Ghami got to his feet. "That won't be necessary."

"Suit yourself." Esteban led them out of the office and back along the dim hallways. The glare of the afternoon sun was especially brutal after being in the dim confines of the ship. Backdropped against the hazy horizon behind the *Norego*, a twelve-hundred-foot supertanker was easing its way north-ward, where its holds would be filled with crude.

Ghami shook Esteban's hand at the head of the gangplank. "If your steering problem isn't corrected by morning, you must notify the Bandar Abbas port authorities. They may need to tow your vessel farther from the shipping lanes and into the harbor."

"We'll get this pig fixed soon enough," Esteban said. "She's tired, but there's still life in the old *Norego*."

Ghami threw him a skeptical look. He descended to the patrol boat and nodded to his crewmen when he and Khata-hani were aboard. The line was cast off, and the boat acceler-ated away from the tired freighter, its wake clean and white against the dark salty water.

Standing at the rail, Esteban made to wave at the Iranian vessel if any of her crew looked back, but it was as if they couldn't distance themselves from the *Norego* fast enough. The captain scratched his ample belly and watched the patrol craft vanish into the distance. When it was no more than a speck, a second man emerged from the superstructure. He was older than Esteban, with a fringe of thinning auburn hair wreathing his otherwise-bald head. He had alert brown eyes and an easygoing demeanor, and while he'd done a good job keeping himself in shape, a slight paunch pressed at his belt-line.

"The microphone in your office needs to be replaced," he

said without preamble. "You all sounded like cartoon characters sucking helium balloons."

The captain took a moment to pluck wads of medical gauze from behind his molars. The fleshiness around his cheeks vanished instantly. He then peeled off the brown contact lenses to reveal startlingly blue eyes. The transformation from a down-on-his-luck sea dog into a ruggedly handsome man was completed when he removed his cap and dragged the greasy wig from his head. His hair was naturally blond, and he kept it trimmed to a long crew cut. The stubble was his own, and he couldn't wait to shave it off, but that wouldn't come until they had cleared out of Iranian waters just in case he had to play Ernesto Esteban, master of the MV *Norego*, again. "Alvin, Simon, and Theodore, that's us," Juan Rodriguez Cabrillo said with a grin.

"I heard you had to hit the panic button."

There were hidden controls under the desk in the office that Cabrillo could use in a variety of situations. One of them summoned Eddie Seng, who'd been standing by to play the role of an ill-fated engineer, and activated a pump in the plumbing below the nonworking toilet. The pump made the commode erupt like a volcano. Chemicals added to the water furthered the illusion by creating a noxious smell.

"Ensign Ghami wanted to play Sherlock Holmes and have a look around. I had to discourage him," Cabrillo said to Max Hanley, vice president of the Corporation, of which Juan was the chairman.

"Think they'll come back?"

"If we're here in the morning you can bank on it."

"Then I guess we should make sure we're not," Hanley replied with a devilish look in his eye.

The two men entered the superstructure. Juan led them to a utility closet packed with mops, broom, and cleaning supplies that apparently had never been used. He worked the handles of a slop sink as though he were dialing a safe. There was a distinct click, and the back wall popped open to reveal a richly carpeted hallway beyond. Gone were the utilitarian metal walls and cheap linoleum. The hallway was paneled with dark mahogany, and chandeliers along the ceiling provided warm light.

Like the disguise Cabrillo had donned to fool the Iranian Navy, the *Norego* wasn't what she seemed. In fact, that wasn't even her name. By transposing the metal letters held to her bow and stern by magnets, the crew had created the *Norego* from her real name, *Oregon*.

Built originally as a lumber carrier, the vessel had plied the Pacific for nearly two decades, hauling Canadian and American timber to Japan and the other Asian markets. The eleven-thousand-ton freighter had served her owners admirably, but the ravages of time were getting to her. As with any older ship, she was nearing the end of her useful life. Her hull was starting to corrode, and her engines no longer worked as efficiently as when they were new. The owners placed advertisements in maritime trade magazines that they were interested in selling her for scrap, knowing their once-proud flagship would fetch a few dollars per ton.

At the time, Juan Cabrillo was starting the Corporation, and he needed a ship of some kind. He'd visited ports all over the globe, looking for the right one. When he saw pictures of the lumber hauler, he knew he'd found his freighter. He'd been forced to bid against three breaker yards, but he still managed to buy the vessel for far less than had he purchased a newer ship. He had no interest whatsoever with the vessel's cargo-hauling abilities. He wanted her for her anonymity.

The *Oregon* then spent the better part of six months in a covered dry dock in Vladivostok, going through the most radical refit in history. Without changing her outward appearance, the vessel was completely gutted. Her old diesel engines were replaced with the latest cutting-edge power plants. Using a process called magnetohydrodynamics, the engines employed supercooled magnets to strip naturally occurring free electrons from seawater to produce a near-limitless amount of electricity. That power was then fed into four aqua pulse jets that pushed water through a pair of gleaming vectored-thrust drive tubes at tremendous force. The technology had been tried on only a few vessels, and since the fire on an MHD-driven cruise ship called the *Emerald Dolphin* it had been banished back to laboratories and scale models.

At the speeds the vessel was now capable of, her hull had to be stiffened and reinforced. Stabilizing fins were added, and her bow modified to give her modest icebreaking abilities. Several hundred miles of wiring were run throughout the ship for her sophisticated suite of electronics, everything from military-grade radar and sonar to dozens of closed-circuit television cameras. Keeping tabs on the system was a Sun Microsystems supercomputer.

Then came the weapons. Two torpedo tubes, a 120mm cannon that used the targeting system from an M1A1 Abrams main battle tank. She sported three General Electric 20mm Gatling guns, vertical launchers for surface-to-surface anti-ship missiles, and a slew of .30 caliber machine guns for self-defense. All the weapons were cleverly hidden behind retractable hull plates, like the German K boats used during World War I. The .30 cals were tucked inside rusted oil barrels permanently affixed to the deck. With a flick of a button in the operations center, the barrels' lids would pop open and the weapons would emerge, fired remotely by gunners safely inside the ship.

Cabrillo added other surprises, too. Her aft-most hold was converted into a hangar for a four-passenger Robinson R44 helicopter that could be hydraulically raised to the deck. Concealed doors where she could unleash all manner of small craft, including Zodiacs and a SEAL assault boat, were at her waterline, while, along her keel, two massive panels opened into a cavernous space called a moon pool, where a pair of mini-subs could be launched covertly.

As for the crew's accommodations, no expense was spared. The passageways and cabins were as luxurious as any five-star hotel. The *Oregon* boasted probably the finest kitchen afloat, with a staff of cordon bleu–trained chefs. One of the ballast tanks along her flanks, designed to make the vessel appear fully loaded should the need arise, was lined with Carrara marble tiles and doubled as an Olympic-length swimming pool.

The workers who'd done the refit had thought they had been doing the job on behalf of the Russian Navy as part of a new fleet of covert spy ships. Cabrillo had been assisted in this ruse by the commander of the base where the dry dock was located, an eminently corruptible admiral whom Juan had known for years.

The money to start the Corporation and pay for the conversion of the *Oregon* had come from a hidden Cayman Islands bank account that had once belonged to an assassin-for-hire Cabrillo had taken care of for his former employer, the Central Intelligence Agency. Technically, the money should have reverted to the CIA's black budget, but Juan was given tacit approval to fund his enterprise by his immediate superior, Langston Overholt IV.

Cabrillo had been contemplating leaving the CIA for a short while when Saddam Hussein invaded Kuwait on August 2, 1990, and caught everyone at Langley completely unaware. Central Intelligence had fought the Cold War for so long that when the Berlin Wall came down and the Soviet Union imploded, they weren't ready for the regional flare-ups that Juan had known would follow. The Agency's corporate culture was too entrenched to see the looming danger. When Pakistan tested its first nuclear bomb, the CIA learned about it from news broadcasts. Cabrillo felt the CIA's inflexibility was blinding them to how the world was reshaping itself after so many years of being dominated by two superpowers.

Overholt never formally gave Juan permission to fund his own covert paramilitary company, the Corporation, but he, too, had understood that the rules were changing. Technically, Cabrillo and his crew were mercenaries, but while the money to fund their operation could never be traced back to the United States, Juan never forgot who allowed him to get his start. So it was on Overholt's behalf that the *Oregon* was sitting a couple of miles off Iran's coast, pretending to be something she was not.

Cabrillo and Hanley made their way to a conference room deep inside the ship. The meeting that Juan had been chairing when secondary radar had picked up the approaching patrol boat and prompted him to play Ernesto Esteban was still going on.

Eddie Seng was standing in front of a flat-panel television with a laser pointer in hand. Far from the hapless plumber he'd portrayed for the Iranians, Seng was a CIA veteran like Cabrillo. Because of his uncanny ability to meticulously plan and carry out missions, Eddie was the Corporation's director of shore operations. No detail was too small not to demand his full attention. It was his intense concentration that allowed him to spend much of his career under deep cover in China, eluding perhaps the most ruthless secret police in the world.

Seated around the large conference table was the rest of the Corporation's senior staff, with the exception of Dr. Julia Huxley. Julia was the *Oregon*'s chief medical officer, and she rarely attended mission briefings unless she was going ashore.

"So did you chase away the Iranian Navy with your breath?" Linda Ross asked Juan when he sat next to her.

"Oh, sorry." Cabrillo fished in his pockets for a mint to mask the smell of the Limburger cheese he'd eaten just before the sailors came aboard. "I think it was my bad English," he said in the horrible stereotyped accent he'd used.

Linda was the newly promoted vice president for operations. With her strawberry blond hair, long bangs that she was forever brushing away from her green eyes, and the dash of freckles across her cheeks and nose, Linda had a pixieish appearance. Her high-pitched, almost-girlish voice didn't help. However, when she spoke, every member of the crew knew to listen. She'd been an intelligence officer on an Aegis Class cruiser and left the military after being a staffer for the chairman of the Joint Chiefs.

Across from them sat the *Oregon*'s best ship handler, Eric Stone, and his partner in crime, Mark Murphy, whose responsibility was the vast arsenal of weapons secreted throughout the vessel.

Farther down the table were Hali Kasim, the chief communications officer, and Franklin Lincoln, a massively built ex-SEAL who was in charge of the ship's complement of former Special Forces operators, or, as Max called them, the "gundogs."

"Are you back, Chairman?" a voice from a speakerphone called. It was Langston Overholt, on a secure channel from Langley.

As founder of the Corporation, Juan maintained the title of chairman, and only one member of the crew, the elderly chief steward, Maurice, called him captain.

"Just keeping the natives from getting too restless," Cabrillo replied.

"There wasn't any indication that they are suspicious, was there?"

"No, Lang. Despite the fact we're only a couple of miles from the Bandar Abbas naval base, the Iranians are used to a lot of shipping coming in and out of here. They took one look at the ship, one at me, and knew we aren't a threat."

"There's a very narrow window in which to pull this off," Overholt cautioned. "But if you think we should delay, I'll understand."

"Lang, we are here, the rocket torpedoes are here, and the arms-export limitation talks with Russia are in two weeks. It's now or never."

While the proliferation of nuclear material remained the most critical problem facing global security, the exportation of weapons systems to less-than-stable governments was also a top concern for Washington. Russia and China were racking up billions of dollars in sales for missile systems, combat aircraft, tanks, and even five Kilo Class subs that were recently bought by Tehran.

"If you want proof," Juan continued, "that Russia is supplying the Iranians with their VA-111 *Shkval* torpedoes, we go in tonight."

The *Shkval* was perhaps the most sophisticated torpedo ever built, capable of reaching speeds in excess of two hundred knots because it cut through the water in a cocoon of air in the form of supercavitating bubbles. It had a range of seventy-five hundred yards, and was reportedly very difficult to steer due to its incredible speed, so it was basically a last-resort weapon to be fired from a crippled submarine in order to destroy its attacker.

"The Iranians claim to have developed their own version of the *Shkval* without Russian help, or so they say," Max Hanley said. "If we can prove the Russians gave them the technology, despite their protests to the contrary, it will go a long way in hammering them on reducing arms exports in the future."

"Or this could blow up in our faces if you guys get caught," Overholt said testily. "I'm not so sure this is still such a good idea."

"Relax, Langston." Cabrillo laced his fingers behind his

head, detected a little of the glue used to hold on his wig and carefully plucked it off. "How many jobs have we pulled off for you without a hitch? The Iranians won't know what hit them, and we'll be five hundred miles from the Gulf by the time they figure out we were in their submarine pen. And after they realize what happened, the first place they are going to look is the American Navy ships pulling interdiction duty up and down these waters, not a broken-down, Panamanian-flagged derelict with a bad steering bearing."

"Which reminds me, Mr. Overholt," Eddie said from the head of the room. "You will have our naval forces pulled far enough back from Bandar Abbas that any charge of American intervention by Tehran will prove fruitless?"

"There isn't an American ship within a hundred miles of the port," Overholt assured. "It took some doing to keep the Fifth Fleet brass from getting suspicions of their own, but we're set on that end of it."

Cabrillo cleared his throat. "Let's just do it. In twelve hours, we'll have the proof you need to take the Russians to task. We all understand the risks, but if they mean that the Kremlin's going to be forced to rethink selling arms to every mullah with deep pockets we have to go."

"I know. You're right," Overholt sighed. "Juan, just be careful, okay?"

"Count on it, my friend."

"Do you need me to stay on the line?" the veteran CIA officer asked.

"You know where to deposit the money once we're out," Juan replied. "Unless you want to know specifics of our operation, I think you should hang up."

"You got it." The line clicked dead.

Juan addressed the assembled officers. "Okay, we've been at this long enough. Are there any last-minute details that need to be cleared up before we adjourn?"

"The containers on deck," Max said. "Should we start breaking them down at nightfall or wait until you return from the navy base and we're under way? And what about the paint and the other camouflage measures?"

The stacks of containers littering the *Oregon*'s deck were so much window dressing, just another way for the crew to hide the nature of their ship. They could be folded flat and stored in one of her holds, altering her silhouette. The blue paint coating her hull and the green covering her upperworks was an environmentally friendly pigment that could be washed off using the fire-suppression water cannons mounted on the superstructure. Beneath the paint her hull was a patchwork of mismatched colors that looked as though they had been applied over a couple of generations of owners. That coating, however, was a radar-absorbing compound similar to the skin of a stealth fighter.

Metal plates had also been installed around key features of the ship to further distort her shape. A fairing over her bows that gave her a racier look would be removed. The twin funnels she was currently carrying would be dismantled and a large, oval stack erected to replace them. This funnel also acted as armor to protect her main radar domes, which were currently retracted into the amidships accommodations block. To further change her appearance, the ballast tanks would be flooded to make her look like her holds were loaded with goods.

In all, it would take four hours and the work of every crewman aboard, but, when they were done, the *Norego* would have vanished completely and the *Oregon* would be sailing innocently down the Persian Gulf, flying, ironically, the Iranian flag, because that was where the ship was actually registered.

Juan thought for a moment before answering, balancing risk versus reward. "Eric, what's the moon tonight?"

"Only a quarter," the ship's navigator and de facto weatherman said. "And the meteorological report calls for cloud cover after midnight."

"Let's leave everything in place until midnight," Cabrillo told his crew. "We should be back aboard by two A.M. We'll have a two-hour head start on the conversion work, but if something goes wrong we can put everything back quickly enough. Anything else?"

There were a few head shakes and a general rustling of papers as everyone got ready to leave.

"We'll meet in the moon pool at eleven hundred hours for final equipment checks. We launch the mini no later than eleven forty-five. If we're late, we're going to run into trouble with the tides." Cabrillo stood to get their attention. "I want it clear to all department heads, and especially to shore operations"—he looked pointedly at Eddie Seng and Franklin Lincoln—"that there can be no slipups. We've got a good plan. Stick to it and everything will go as smooth as silk. The situation in this part of the world is bad enough without mercenaries getting caught trying to steal a couple of rocket torpedoes."

Linc grumbled good-naturedly, "You all know I got out of Detroit to get away from my friends who were boosting stuff."

"Out of the frying pan . . ." Eddie grinned.

". . . and into an Iranian jail."

CHAPTER 2

YEARS OF WORKING WITH THE CIA HAD trained Juan to function on very little sleep over long periods of time. It wasn't until he'd founded the Corporation and purchased the *Oregon* that he developed the mariner's ability to fall asleep on command. After the boardroom conference, he'd returned to his cabin, an opulent suite more befitting a Manhattan apartment than a ship at sea, stripped out of his Captain Esteban costume, and fell into bed. Thoughts of the danger they'd be facing once the team was ashore kept him awake for less than a minute.

Without the need for an alarm clock, he awoke an hour before he was to report to the moon pool.

His sleep had been dreamless.

He strode into the bathroom, sat on a mahogany stool to remove his artificial leg, and hopped into the shower. With such a surplus of electricity, the *Oregon*'s water-heating system ensured that the lag time between turning the taps and a steaming shower was measured in seconds. Cabrillo stood under the near-scalding spray with his head bowed and water pounding his body. He'd accumulated a dozen lifetimes of scars over the years, and he vividly recalled the circumstances behind every one. It was the blunt pad of his stump that he thought the least about.

For most people, losing a limb would likely be a defining moment in their lives. And during the long months of rehab, it had been for Juan as well. But, after that, he barely gave it a moment's consideration. He had trained his body to accept the prosthesis and his mind to ignore it. As he'd told Dr. Huxley early on in his physical therapy, "I may be crippled, but I won't allow myself to be handicapped."

The prosthetic leg he'd worn throughout the day was designed like a human limb, with a covering of flesh-toned rubber to match his own skin color and a foot with toes that even had nails and hair to match those of his left foot. After toweling off, and finally shaving off the itchy beard, he went to his closet to retrieve a very different limb.

There was a section on the *Oregon* dubbed the Magic Shop, and it was overseen by an award-winning Hollywood effects master named Kevin Nixon. It had been Nixon, working in secret, who had developed what Juan called his combat leg. Unlike the natural-looking prosthesis, this one looked like it had been left over from the *Terminator* movies. Constructed of titanium and carbon fiber, combat leg version 3.0 was a virtual arsenal in itself. A Kel-Tek .380 pistol was secreted in the calf, along with a perfectly balanced throwing knife. The leg also contained a wire garrote, a single-shot .50 caliber gun that fired through the heel, and storage compartments for all manner of equipment Cabrillo might need.

Just fitting it over his stump and attaching a set of reinforcing straps helped Juan prepare himself mentally for the mission.

There were two reasons he'd started the Corporation. One, of course, was as a moneymaking venture. And, from that perspective, it had done better than his wildest dreams. Each member could retire with what they had earned in the years since joining, and Cabrillo himself could buy a small Caribbean island, if he so chose. But it was the second reason for forming his own security force that kept him at it long after a normal man would have hung up his guns. The need for such a group was so great that his conscience wouldn't allow him to stop.

In just the past year, he and the crew of the *Oregon* had broken up a piracy ring that had been targeting ships carrying illegal Chinese immigrants and using them as slave labor at a remote gold mine, and they disrupted an ecoterrorist's plan to steer a poison-laden hurricane into the United States.

It seemed that as soon as one job was complete there were two more equally deserving of the Corporation's unique abilities. Evil was running rampant all over the globe, and the world powers were stymied to prevent its spread by the very morality that made them great. Though they worked under the guidance of Cabrillo's own moral compass, he and his crew weren't hampered by politicians, of any ilk, who were more concerned with reelections than results.

As Juan was dressing, the chief steward knocked on the cabin door and entered quietly.

"Breakfast, Captain," Maurice said in his mournful English accent.

The steward was a veteran of the Royal Navy, having been forced into retirement because of his age. A rail-thin man with a shock of pure white hair, he carried himself ramrod straight, and remained unflappable no matter the circumstances. While Cabrillo himself could be a bit of a clotheshorse, nothing compared to the dark suits and crisp, white cotton shirts Maurice wore no matter the weather. In the years he'd been aboard the ship, no one had ever seen the steward sweat or shiver.

"Just set it on my desk," Juan called as he strode from the bedroom adjoining his office. The room was done in rich woods, with coffered mahogany ceilings and matching display cabinets for some of the curiosities he had accumulated over the years. Framed as the centerpiece on one wall was a dramatic painting of the *Oregon* pounding through a raging storm.

Maurice set the silver service on the desk, frowning at the affront. There was a perfectly appropriate dining table in a nook in the chairman's cabin. He removed the covers, and the smell of an omelet, kippers, and dark-roasted coffee filled the room. Maurice knew Cabrillo poured a small measure of cream in his first coffee of the day, so the steward had it ready by the time Juan plopped himself in his chair.

"So what's the latest on young Mr. Stone's Internet romance with the girl from Brazil?" Juan asked, and took a huge bite of egg.

Maurice was the shipboard clearinghouse for gossip, and Eric Stone's numerous cyberaffairs was his favorite topic.

"Mr. Stone is beginning to suspect that he and the lady in question might have more in common than he was first led to believe," Maurice said in a conspiratorial whisper.

Juan was opening the freestanding antique safe behind his desk as he listened. "That's not usually a bad thing."

"I am referring to gender, Captain. He thinks the lady may in fact be a man. Mr. Murphy showed me pictures he/she sent and proved they had been, how did he put it, 'photoshopped' to hide certain anatomical details.'"

Cabrillo chuckled. "Poor Eric. The guy can't even get lucky in a chat room."

He eased open the heavy door emblazoned with the name and logo of a long-defunct southwestern railroad. Nearly all the small arms kept aboard the *Oregon* were stored in the armory next to the soundproof shooting range, but Juan preferred to keep his guns in his office. In addition to the arsenal of machine pistols, assault rifles, and handguns, Juan also kept stacks of money from various countries, a hundred thousand dollars' worth of gold coins struck from four national mints, and several small pouches of uncut diamonds. There was a particular forty-carat stone that he kept separate from the others that had been the gift of the newly elected president of Zimbabwe in appreciation for the Corporation's efforts in releasing him from political prison.

"Dr. Huxley seems to have confirmed Mr. Murphy's suspicions by checking the facial ratios of the individual's face against norms for men and women." As Maurice continued, Cabrillo checked over a semiautomatic pistol, the only weapon he was taking with him. Unlike the rest of his team, he wasn't going in armed to the teeth.

He slurped the rest of his coffee and had another bite of omelet. Adrenaline was beginning to course through his veins and knot his stomach, so he gave the rich kippers a pass.

"So what's Eric going to do?" Juan asked as he got to his feet.

"Obviously, he's postponing his vacation to Rio de Janeiro until he can verify things one way or the other. Mr. Murphy thinks he should hire a private investigator."

Cabrillo scoffed. "I think he should drop this whole Internet thing and meet women the regular way, face-to-face, in a bar over too many drinks."

"Hear! Hear! One can't overstate the social lubricating abilities of a few cocktails." Maurice tidied Cabrillo's desk and hoisted the serving dish to his shoulder, a fresh linen napkin over his other arm. "We'll see you when you return."

That was as close as the steward would say to "Good luck."

"Not if I don't see you first," was Juan's customary reply.

They left the cabin together, Maurice turning right to return to the galley, Juan left. He took an elevator down three decks. The doors opened to a cavernous room lit with ranks of floodlights and smelling strongly of the sea. An overhead crane held the larger of the two submersibles the *Oregon* carried, a sixty-five-foot Nomad 1000. The blunt-nosed mini-sub could carry six people, including a pilot and copilot. Clustered near her three bow portholes were armored xenon lamps and an articulated manipulator arm with a grip that could rip steel. The Nomad was rated for a thousand-foot depth, almost ten times as much as her little sister, the Discovery 1000, hanging suspended in a cradle above it, and was outfitted with a diving chamber, so swimmers could exit the craft while she was submerged.

Beneath the submersible, crewmen had already pulled the deck grating away to reveal a gaping pit that went all the way to the *Oregon*'s keel. The outer doors were still closed, but pumps were filling the swimming pool–sized opening in preparation for the launch.

Linc, Eddie, and Max were already sliding black wet suits over their swim trunks. Scuba equipment for all of them had already been loaded into the sub. Linda Ross stood with her arms crossed over her chest, watching Max with amusement. Hanley had served two tours in Vietnam as a Swift Boat captain and no longer cut the dashing figure he once had. He was having a hard time stretching the suit over his paunch. He didn't normally accompany a team on a shore excursion; however, he was the best marine engineer in the Corporation, and everyone agreed his expertise could come in handy.

"Come on, old boy," Juan said with a grin, and patted Max's belly. "I don't recall you having this much trouble a few years ago."

"It's not the years," he moaned, "it's the pastries."

Cabrillo sat on a bench and, unlike the others, started to put a dry suit on over his clothes. "Linda, have you done your pre-launch checks?"

"We're good to go."

"And the cradle?"

"It's secure," Max answered for her with possessive pride. He'd designed it, and had overseen its fabrication in the *Oregon*'s machine shop.

Juan took a communications headset from an attending engineer and called up the Op Center. "Hali, it's the Chairman. How's it look out there?"

"Radar shows the normal procession of tankers heading in and out of the Gulf. There's a containership that pulled into Bandar Abbas's main dock about two hours ago, plus a handful of feluccas and dhows."

"Nothing from the naval base?"

"They're quiet. I've scanned all frequencies, and, other than normal blather between ships at sea, there's not much going on."

"I hope you're honing your language skills." It was a joke between the two. Hali Kasim was the son of Lebanese parents but couldn't speak a word of Lebanese or Arabic, one of four languages in which Cabrillo was fluent.

"Sorry, boss, I'm letting the translating algorithms of the computer do the work for me."

"Eric, Murph, you guys set to go?"

When Cabrillo was sending a team ashore, there were no better officers to have manning the ship's navigation and weapons systems than Stone and Murphy.

"Yes, sir," the two said in unison. Murph added, "We are locked and loaded and ready to be goaded."

Juan groaned. Murph's newest hobby was slam poetry, and, despite the crew's repeated assertions to the contrary, he thought he was a master of the edgy street genre. "Stand by for a comm check once we're secured in the Nomad."

"Roger that," Hali replied.

Linc and Eddie gathered up the waterproof bags containing their weapons and gear and climbed atop the mini-sub. They vanished into the hull through the small hatch. Max and Cabrillo followed them up, Juan giving the thick steel hull a superstitious slap before descending into the submersible. The ride to shore would take an hour, so they took their seats along the mini's flanks rather than cram half the team into the two-man dive chamber. All four of them would don their scuba equipment during the trip in.

Linda Ross wiggled her way past Juan and Max and took her place in the pilot's seat, a low-slung chair surrounded by banks of switches, dials, and computer monitors, their glow giving her face an eerie green cast.

"How do you read me, *Oregon*?" she asked after settling her own headset over her tousled hair.

"Five by five." Their communications system used 132-bit encryption and cycled through frequencies every tenth of a second, so the chance of intercept and decryption was zero.

The men in the back of the submersible also checked in. The dive helmets they were to wear had integrated ultrasonic transceivers to allow easy communications among themselves, the Nomad, and the *Oregon*.

"Okay, you can open her up," Linda ordered.

The lights in the moon pool were dimmed, so as not to show underwater, as the keel doors slowly hinged open. The mechanism that lowered the submersible was engaged. The mini-sub lurched suddenly and then began its stately descent. The warm Gulf water soon lapped against the portholes, before the vessel sank to its neutral buoyancy point. The clamps were disengaged, and the Nomad bobbed free.

Linda activated the ballast pumps, slowly drawing water into the tanks, and gently eased the sub out through the bottom of the *Oregon*'s hull. Though she had done it dozens of times, her motions were careful and deliberate. She watched the depth gauge and the laser range finder mounted on the top of the submersible, to ensure they had cleared the keel.

"Nomad is free," she said, when they were twenty feet below the hull.

"Closing the doors. *Oregon* over and out."

Linda descended another forty feet, until the seafloor was just a yard or two below the mini, and set her course for the Bandar Abbas naval base. She kept her speed to just above a crawl so the sound of the propellers churning the water wouldn't alert any attentive sonar operators in the area, although with the amount of traffic in the Strait of Hormuz it would be next to impossible to single out the whisper-quiet Nomad amid the acoustical clutter.

They were at risk of visual detection because the waters were so shallow, forcing her to leave off the external lights.

She would have to rely on the LIDAR system, or Light Detection and Ranging system, which used a series of reflected lasers to map out the terrain immediately in front of the sub. She would get them to the base by following the three-dimensional computer representation of their surroundings. The LIDAR could detect objects as small as a soda can.

"This is your pilot, up here in the cockpit," she called over her shoulder. "We will be cruising at an altitude of negative forty-eight feet at a speed of three knots. Our estimated arrival time at our destination is approximately sixty-two minutes. At this time, you may use approved electronics, and don't forget to ask an attendant about our frequent-flier program."

"Hey, Pilot, my peanuts are stale," Linc called up to her.

"Yeah, and I want a blanket and a pillow," Eddie added.

Max chimed in, "While you're at it, a double Scotch would hit the spot."

Listening to the banter over the next half hour, one would have never known they were about to infiltrate Iran's most heavily secured naval facility. It wasn't that they weren't aware of the risks. It was just that they were too professional to let that wear on their nerves.

But all that dried up with thirty minutes to go. The shore team started putting on their scuba gear, checking and rechecking each other's equipment as they went. When they were suited up, Juan and Linc slid their way into the phone booth–sized air lock. There was a hatch in the ceiling of the claustrophobic chamber that could be opened from the cockpit or from inside the air lock, but only when the pressure on each side of the armored door was equalized. To save time, Juan hit the controls that allowed seawater to slowly fill the chamber. The water was blood warm as it climbed up their bodies, pressing in on Juan's dry suit. Juan had to smooth out the wrinkles so the suit wouldn't chafe. Both men had to work their jaws to ease the pressure on their inner ears.

When the level was just below their necks, Cabrillo hit the button again. There was no need to put on their dive helmets until the last moment.

"How are you doing back there?" Linda's voice was tinny and distant through the helmet.

"Why is it I always get stuck in this thing with the biggest member of the crew," Juan cried theatrically.

"'Cause Max's belly's too big to fit in there with Linc, and Eddie would be squashed like a bug," Ross said.

"Hey, man, just be thankful I don't take a deep breath," Linc joked in his deep baritone.

"Chairman, the LIDAR is picking up the submarine pen's doors. We're about fifty yards away."

"Okay, Linda. Put us on the bottom to the right of the dry dock's entrance."

"Roger."

A moment later, the Nomad shuddered slightly as Linda settled it onto the sandy seafloor. "Powering down all nonessential equipment. Whenever you're ready."

"What do you say, big man?" Cabrillo asked Lincoln.

"Let's do it."

Juan put on his helmet, making sure the locking rings to keep the suit watertight were secure and that he was getting sufficient air from the tanks. Cabrillo waited until Linc gave him the dive signal for "OK" before opening the flood valve again. The water quickly rose to the air lock's ceiling. He doused the lights and hit another toggle to open the door.

The hatch swung upward, releasing a small amount of trapped air. The bubbles were silver-white in the gloom, but with waves lapping against the enclosed pier they wouldn't be spotted.

Juan hoisted himself out of the dive chamber and paused on the submersible's upper deck. Without lights, the water was as dark as ink. Cabrillo had grown up in Southern California and had been drawn to the sea for as long as he could remember. He graduated from skin diving to scuba diving and from body boarding to surfing in his early teens. He was as comfortable in water as a seal and was almost as powerful a swimmer. The darkness only enhanced the calm he felt whenever he dove.

Lincoln emerged from the Nomad a moment later. Juan closed the hatch, and together they waited for Eddie and Max to cycle through. Once they were all out of the submarine, Cabrillo chanced turning on an underwater flashlight, shielding the beam from the surface with his hand.

The Iranian submarine pen had been built by first excavating a six-hundred-foot-long, hundred-foot-wide trench from the ocean eastward into the desert. Over this, they erected a reinforced-concrete shell, supposedly eight feet thick and capable of withstanding a direct bomb hit. It had been built before the U.S.-led invasion of neighboring Iraq, and the Iranians must be well aware that some of the bunker busters in the American arsenal now could level the entire structure with a single hit. To the south and north of the dry dock sat the main piers of the naval base, while administration buildings, machine shops, and barracks sprawled for two miles inland.

On the seaward side of the pen were two massive doors that swung outward hydraulically. Inflatable bladders sealed the gap between the bottom of the door and a cement pad to keep water from flooding into the building. Short of explosives or a couple of hours with an acetylene cutting torch, the doors were impenetrable.

Cabrillo finned away from the doors, leading his team through the stygian realm. Every few moments, he would flash his light along the barnacle-encrusted seawall protecting the base from the ravages of the ocean. After fifty feet, the beam settled on what he had been searching for. There was a four-foot-wide culvert in the wall, a dark hole that fed the pumps to drain the dry dock. Careful to protect the light, he inspected the metal grille embedded in the concrete that prevented anything from swimming up the conduit. The steel was only slightly corroded, while the concrete maintained its integrity. It took him over a minute of careful inspection to spot the wires at the top and bottom of the six metal rods.

One way to protect against tampering was to rig the grates with motion detectors, but with so many curious fish in the Persian Gulf the alarms would sound almost constantly. The easier way was to run an electric current through the metal, and if the connection was ever cut guards would be alerted that someone had removed part of the grille.

Juan pointed the wires out to Linc, the Corporation's best infiltration specialist. Working mostly by feel, Lincoln rigged bypasses on three of the steel rods, using alligator clamps and lengths of wire to keep the current flowing. Next, he removed two squeeze tubes from his dive bag. He uncapped one tube

and applied a bead of a gray puttylike substance around the
ends of the bars. He then applied an equal amount of putty
from the second tube over the first.

Inert when separated, the two compounds formed a caus-
tic acid when combined. In less than a minute, the metal under the beads had been eaten away enough for Linc to snap
them free, his loose wires still keeping the circuit closed and
the alarms silent. He set the broken rods on the sand, making
sure he didn't touch the still-corrosive tips, and held the slack
wires apart for Max, Eddie, and Juan to slip through before
carefully sliding into the pipe himself.

Now that they were sheltered from prying eyes, Juan turned
up the intensity of his dive light, its beam forming a white ring
circling the curved sides of the conduit that seemed to retreat
with the pace of his advance.

A fast shadow suddenly lunged at him. He struck out
blindly as a darting shape passed him by. He caught sight of a
dorsal fin and the rapier tail of a baby shark before it vanished
behind him.

"Good thing we met him now and not in a couple of years,"
Eddie quipped.

Cabrillo needed a second for his heart to slow before continuing down the constricting pipe. He was jumpier than he'd
thought, and that didn't bode well.

The conduit fed into a large valve that would be in the
closed position if the dry dock was empty, but, in the two days
the crew had been watching the facility, they had seen no indication the Iranians had pumped out the sub pen since their navy's newest Kilo Class diesel-electric boat had been admitted.

The four men squeezed through the butterfly valve and
into the monstrous pump that could drain the pen. The impeller blades were made of bright ferrobronze that had been
bolted to the hub.

Juan had come prepared for bolts, and, in case the blades
had been welded, he carried a small torch. He pulled an ad-
justable wrench from a pouch on his thigh and attacked the
bolts. The angles were awkward, and the nuts had been
screwed in place by a pneumatic gun, so it took all his effort
to get each of the twelve bolts started. One in particular had
him straining so hard that pinwheels of color exploded be-

hind his tightly closed eyes. When the seal finally popped, the wrench kicked free, and Cabrillo sliced his hand on the scimitar-shaped blade. A small cloud of blood hung in the glow of his flashlight.

"Trying to get the shark to come back?" Max teased.

"So long as your big butt is between me and him, I'll be fine."

"It's not big, just well padded."

Juan finished with the bolts and set each of the eighteen-inch impeller blades aside. He had to unsling his scuba tank and wriggle beneath the pump's hub to make it through. He waited on the other side for the men to join him and slide their tanks back in place.

The pipe continued for another dozen feet before turning ninety degrees. Cabrillo shut off his light, and, after waiting a moment for his eyes to adjust, could make out a pale, watery corona coming from around the bend. He cautiously swam closer, and when he reached the turn he ducked his head around for a quick peek.

They had reached the dry dock. The light was coming from fixtures mounted on the tall ceiling. The low level told him that there was just enough illumination for guards to patrol the pen but not enough for a slew of technicians to be working on the Kilo. As they had anticipated, there wouldn't be more than a handful of men to subdue.

Cabrillo swam out of the pipe and dove down to stay along the concrete bottom, followed by Max, Linc, and Eddie. They made their way closer to the towering doors, where there was the least chance of there being guards. Juan checked their depth on his dive computer and held the men at ten feet for a minute, to allow the small amount of nitrogen bubbles that had accumulated in their bloodstream to dissolve.

With the patience of crocodiles emerging from a river in pursuit of prey, the four men approached the surface, hovering just below its silvery reflection in order to affix small periscopes to their helmets. Capable of magnifying starlight so that it shone as light as day, the third-generation optics of the scopes had to be dialed back a bit as they slowly searched every corner of the dry dock from the security of the water.

The dry dock was wide enough for two ships to be serviced side by side, and each edge of the sub pen was flanked with raised cement jetties that ran almost the entire length of the building. They were littered with equipment, barrels of lubricant, piles of gear under tarps, small electric golf carts to make moving around easier, and a trio of forklifts. At the far end was a raised platform that stretched the width of the building. Part of it was glassed in to make an office or observation room, and under it, on each side, were enclosed spaces for secure storage. There was also an overhead crane on rails that could reach any part of the covered dock.

Tied to one side of the pier by thick Manila lines was the ominous black shape of a Kilo Class attack submarine. The twenty-two-hundred-ton vessel had once been the most feared sub in the Soviet arsenal. When running on her batteries, the Kilo was among the quietest undersea hunters ever built and was capable of sneaking up on ships equipped with sophisticated passive sonar systems. She was fitted with six torpedo tubes, and could stay on patrol for a month and a half without replenishing.

The presence of the Kilos was seen as a provocation, given the fact that Iran had a history of sinking merchant shipping in the Persian Gulf. The United States and her allies had tried every conceivable diplomatic trick to prevent Russia from selling the Kilos to the Iranian Navy, but neither party could be deterred. Usually, the two-hundred-and-twenty-foot subs were stationed at Chāh Bahār in the Arabian Sea and not bottled up in the Gulf, but Overholt's intelligence indicated that this particular Kilo was being outfitted with the newly developed rocket torpedoes.

If the Corporation could prove the Russians illegally sold such a technology to Tehran, it would kill any deal Iran might be cooking up to acquire more subs, something they wanted desperately.

"So, what do you have?" Juan asked, after five quiet minutes of observation.

"I count six," Linc replied.

"Confirmed," Eddie said.

"Max?"

"Are you sure that isn't a guard catching a few z's on the

left there in what looks like a bundle of linens waiting to be put aboard?"

The men silently rechecked the location Max had indicated, straining to make out the shape of a man. The three breathed in sharply when what they had thought was just a shadow suddenly lurched up, peered around for a second, scratched under his arm, and lay back down.

"Good eyes, my friend," Juan said. "I won't tease you about wearing cheaters when you read a report ever again. So we've got four guards upstairs on the observation platform and the two over by the personnel exit door, plus sleeping beauty. Linc, Eddie, the second-floor gang's all yours. Max, extend that guy's nap for a while, and I'll have a go at the pair at the door." Cabrillo checked his watch. It was one o'clock in the morning. The chance the guards would be relieved before dawn was remote. "We've got one hour to be back aboard the Nomad if we are to make our three A.M. deadline, so let's get a little hustle on, shall we?"

The men sank back under the water and swam the length of the dry dock, Max stopping approximately where the one guard was sleeping and hovered just below the edge of the concrete dock in the dark shadow cast by the Kilo's hull. Eddie and Linc swam along the left side of the pier so they would emerge under a set of metal scissor stairs that rose to the second-floor balcony. For his part, Juan pulled himself from the water behind the cover of a stack of crates, a good hundred yards from the well-lit vestibule where a pair of bored guards watched a set of locked doors.

He silently stripped out of his scuba gear and dry suit. Beneath it, he wore the uniform of a captain in the Syrian Navy, right down to the tie and combat ribbons. The only thing out of place were the rubber dive booties he sported on his feet, but there wasn't much he could do about that. He buckled on his gun belt and set a cap on his head to cover his blond hair. He waited another minute for his men to get in position before boldly stepping around the containers and marching toward the guards.

He closed to within twenty feet before one of them became aware of his presence. The man snapped to his feet, looking around in bewilderment for a moment before remembering

he'd set his AK-47 on the floor next to the table he was shar-
ing with his partner. Juan kept coming as the man groped for
the weapon and came up with it pointed straight at Cabrillo's
chest. He growled a warning, as his teammate gained his feet,
his hands clutching an assault rifle of his own, though the
sling had tangled around his hands.

"What is the meaning of this challenge?" Juan asked
arrogantly in pitch-perfect Arabic. "I am Captain Hanzi Hourani, of the Syrian Navy, and a guest of your base commander,
Admiral Ramazani."

The two guards blinked at him before one said in halting
Arabic, "You are who?"

"Captain Hourani," Cabrillo snapped testily. "For the love
of the Prophet, I have been in and out of this building a dozen
times in the past week. Surely you know I am here to watch the
demonstration of your new miracle weapon, the torpedoes that
will drive the Crusaders out of our waters once and for all."

Juan knew the Farsi speaker was catching every three or
four words of his rapid-fire delivery, but it was the attitude
more than the words that were important. He had to get them
to believe he belonged here, despite the late hour. There was a
walkie-talkie on the table next to an overflowing ashtray,
plates of congealed food, and a rumpled heap of newspapers.
If they called base security, the jig was up.

"I lost track of time touring the submarine," Juan went on,
then gave a trace of an embarrassed smile. "That is not true. I
fell asleep in the captain's cabin, dreaming that it would be me
to strike the first blow against the American imperialists."

There was still wary suspicion in the guard's eye, but the
admission that a superior officer, though from a different
navy, could succumb to the same fantasies as they did put the
guard slightly at ease. He translated to his partner what Cabrillo had said.

It didn't seem to make much of an impression. He barked
at the first guard, gesturing with the barrel of his AK. The
Arabic speaker asked to see Juan's identification.

Juan withdrew a billfold and presented it to the senior of
the two. As the guard looked it over, Juan plucked a pack of
cigarettes from his breast pocket and lit up. The smokes were
Dunhills, a vastly superior brand to the cheap local tobacco

the men choked down, and he saw that both had noticed the distinctive flat pack. The guard kept the billfold and was turning to grab the walkie-talkie when Juan offered him the cigarettes.

He hesitated for an instant, so Juan thrust the pack closer.

"We must call the main security station," the younger guard told him.

"Of course," Juan said, jetting smoke from his mouth. "I thought you might enjoy a decent cigarette while they yell at you for not knowing I am authorized to be here."

Sheepishly, both men took a cigarette. Juan held the lighter for them. They only had time to exchange a look, following their first drag, before the fast-acting, narcotic-laced tobacco hit their nervous systems like a freight train. Both men crumpled wordlessly to the ground.

Cabrillo ground his cigarette into the floor with his foot. "Usually, boys," he said, crushing out the guards' smoldering Dunhills and tucking all the evidence into his pant pocket, "these things'll kill you. In your case, you'll be out for a couple of hours. However, I don't envy you when your superiors discover your dereliction."

The Corporation tried to keep their operations as nonlethal as possible. From the earliest planning stages of the mission, Cabrillo made sure the guards wouldn't die doing their job just because Russia was illegally selling advanced military equipment.

That isn't to say there wasn't a lot of blood on Juan Cabrillo's or the rest of his team's hands, but they wouldn't kill if it wasn't absolutely necessary.

Juan was just turning away when the metal door leading to the outside was thrown open and a lab-coated technician flanked by two soldiers strode in. They saw the two unconscious guards on the floor under the table and Juan's unfamiliar uniform. One guard brought his assault rifle up and shouted a challenge. The second said something to the first that Cabrillo didn't need to translate to "I'm going for help" before he turned on his heel and vanished into the night.

In a minute, all three thousand sailors and support personnel were going to be descending on the dry dock like a horde of berserkers.

CHAPTER 3

As THE SECOND GUARD WAS RACING FOR THE door, a speck of ruby light appeared on the first guard's weapon, followed an instant later by a silenced bullet that ripped the AK-47 from his grip amid a shower of blood from his mangled hand.

Juan didn't hesitate. Linc or Eddie had immobilized the man, from their position on the raised platform above, and Cabrillo knew they would have the stunned technician covered with their silenced Type 95 bullpup assault rifles. He wheeled and took off after the fleeing guard. He accelerated with each pace, driven by his most stubborn trait, his inability to let himself fail. The guard was disappearing into the darkened naval base, and, if not for his khaki uniform, Cabrillo would have lost him in the gloom. In eight steps, he'd cut the sentry's two-second head start to almost nothing, and, in another three, he lunged at the fleeing Iranian, grabbing the man around the knees in a tackle that would do a professional football player proud.

The two went down on the unyielding asphalt road. Juan had been protected by the guard's body, but the sentry hadn't been so lucky. His head slammed into the macadam with a sickening crunch, and their slide ripped his face open down to the muscle.

Cabrillo looked around quickly. There were a couple of darkened warehouses nearby, and, in the distance, he could see a four-story office building with a few illuminated windows, but he didn't think he'd been spotted. He whipped a pair of FlexiCuffs around the unconscious guard's wrists and hefted the man over his shoulder to jog back to the submarine pen.

When Cabrillo closed the door behind him, he saw that

Eddie had cuffed and gagged the technician. He was dragging him to the secluded corner of the entry vestibule where he'd already hidden the two drugged guards. Juan dumped his burden next to them.

"That shaved a few months off my life," he panted.

"Any chance someone saw you?" Seng asked.

"If you hear an alarm start wailing, you'll have your answer. Any problems upstairs with the others?"

"One went for his gun. Linc has stopped his bleeding, and if he gets to a hospital in the next couple of hours he'll make it. We wore face masks, and I was shouting in Mandarin, like we planned, and if those guys know their weapons they'll recognize the Chinese-made Type 95s."

"Coupled with the Czech ammunition we're using, that should keep them guessing."

Max Hanley sauntered over, a wry grin on his face. "You just had to make this harder than it already is, didn't you?"

"Come on, Max, if we didn't up the risk we wouldn't get the exorbitant fees we've all grown so accustomed to."

"I'll give up part of my cut next time."

"Any problem with your guy?"

"His nap will last well into tomorrow. Now, if you don't mind, let's go find those torpedoes."

In the first of the two large rooms under the elevated platform, they found a store of conventional Russian-made TEST-71 torpedoes, exactly like the ones the *Oregon* herself carried. It was in the second room, after Linc shot off the lock, that they found Iran's newest and most lethal weapon. The room was taken up with workbenches, diagnostic computers, and all kinds of electronic gear. In the middle of the space were two shroud-draped shapes that looked a bit like cadavers in a morgue. Max strode over to one and whipped off the sheet. At first glance, the torpedo sitting on the mechanized trolley looked like the TEST-71s except it lacked a propeller. He eyed the twenty-five-foot underwater missile, especially its radically shaped nose. It was this feature that created a bubble of air around the torpedo and allowed it to cut through the water with virtually no friction.

"What do you think?" Juan asked, approaching his second-in-command.

"It's exactly like the pictures I've seen of the Russian *Shkval*," the engineer told him. "Form follows function on something like this, meaning there are only a couple of designs that would lead to the supercavitation effect, but this thing is identical to the Russkies' fish."

"So they're helping the Iranians?"

"No doubt." Max straightened. "The proof's going to be in the design of the rocket motor, but, for my money, we've got them dead to rights."

"Okay, good. You and Eddie gather everything you can." Eddie was already at a computer terminal, jacking in a pirate drive that would siphon everything on the system. Linc was looking through log books and binders for anything relevant. Cabrillo turned to Franklin Lincoln, "You ready, big man?"

"Aye."

Max stopped Juan from leaving the room with a hand to the elbow. "One or two?"

Juan cast an eye at the two torpedoes. "In for a penny, in for a pound, let's take 'em both."

"You know they are most likely armed and fueled."

Cabrillo grinned. "So we'll take 'em carefully."

While Linc searched the upper platform for the mechanism that would open the main outer doors, Juan climbed up a ladder welded to one wall and walked along a catwalk to the overhead crane's control cabin. Familiar with all manner of cranes from his years at sea, he powered up the machine and started it trundling down the length of the building toward the head of the dock. As it slid back, a fiendish thought struck him, and he lowered the huge hook assembly. Weighing nearly a ton, and traveling fast enough that it had pendulumed back a couple of degrees, the hook was steered by Cabrillo toward the conning-tower dive plane of Iran's newest Kilo Class submarine.

The hook didn't have the momentum to rip the fin off, but the tear it left in the delicate steering control would mean the sub would remain in dry dock for the next couple of months.

When Juan finally had the crane in position, Eddie and Max had wheeled one of the three-ton torpedoes from the laboratory and out into the open. He lowered the hook, and they attached sling cables that the Iranians had thoughtfully left in place. When it was secure, Max shot Cabrillo a wave while Eddie went to retrieve his scuba gear.

Cabrillo lifted the torpedo from the trolley and backed the crane out over the water again, making sure to keep it well away from the Kilo. Twenty feet short of the doors, he lowered the weapon into the water, watching for the thick steel cable to slacken, indicating the torpedo was resting on the bottom. He eased off the controls when the line started to bow. Eddie had walked along the jetty, lugging his tanks, helmet, and regulator. He slid into the gear and stepped off the dock. Juan watched where Eddie's bubbles popped when they reached the surface, and, after a minute, Eddie's raised thumb rose through the roiling water.

Juan lifted the hook free and set the crane to return to the head of the dock once again, where Max had the second rocket torpedo in position. As the crane crawled along its rails, Juan could see Linc in the upper observation area. He was bent over a computer, working the controls for the outer doors. He must have found the right combination because lights started popping off until only a single one remained illuminated above Hanley. Cabrillo looked over his shoulder. In the distance, he could just make out one of the massive doors swinging outward. That would be Linda's signal to guide the submersible into the pen. The LIDAR system would pick up the torpedo resting on the bottom, and she knew to wait for word from Cabrillo if they were going to steal another.

Once the second torpedo was slung under the crane, Max joined Linc and together the two men carried the rest of their dive equipment, including Juan's scuba rig and dry suit, to the edge of the dry dock. They got ready to leave, while Juan positioned the crane to lower the torpedo into the water.

Once the torpedo vanished below the surface and the line went slack, he powered down the crane, reached under the small control panel and ripped out a fistful of wires amid a shower of sparks.

There was no conceivable way the Iranians wouldn't discover the theft, so the least he could do was make their job of putting the dry dock back in order as difficult as possible. Linc would have set a small explosive charge to disable the computer that controlled the doors and lights and rigged it to blow on a motion sensor. To further muddy the forensic waters, the explosives and trigger were of Chinese manufacture.

Remembering a detail he'd overlooked, Juan pulled the pistol from his holster and flicked it out into space, where it landed with a splash. It was a QSZ-92, the newest standard sidearm of China's People's Liberation Army. The Iranians would scour the dry dock for clues, trying to piece together who had infiltrated the base, and he was sure the pistol would be found. What they would make of the evidence, he wasn't sure, but it was fun to mess with their heads.

Rather than waste time laboriously climbing down off the crane, Juan scampered across the enormous I beam that spanned the width of the building. When he reached the cable spool, he gingerly wrapped his hands around the braided cable and lowered himself, hand over hand, until he was ten feet from the dim water, and simply let go.

Max was there with his equipment and helped Juan sling the tank over his shoulders and fit the helmet over his head.

"Linda, do you read?" Juan asked, treading water. Because his helmet was designed to work with the dive suit Linc had bundled in his arms, he wouldn't be able to use it once he was under.

"Roger, Chairman. Nice dive, by the way. From the splash, I score it a 9.2."

"Reverse double half twist with a full gainer," he deadpanned. "We've got two fish so start recovery operations while we cycle through the air lock."

"Affirmative."

The men could feel water swirl below them as Linda crept forward in the Nomad.

Without an effective dive mask, Cabrillo was guided by Linc down to the air lock, and he let the Chairman enter first. He wedged his considerable bulk through the tight opening, reaching over his head to secure the hatch. When an indicator on the wall turned green, he opened the valves that drained the chamber.

Cabrillo yanked off his helmet as soon as the level dropped below his chin. The air was cold and crisp, refreshing after an hour of breathing the chemically tainted atmosphere trapped in the dry dock. Despite the tight quarters, he managed to wriggle out of his tank without giving Linc too many bruises, so when the air lock was empty he was ready to join Linda in the cockpit.

"Welcome aboard." She threw him a saucy smile. "How'd it go?"

"Piece of cake," he said absently, sliding into the reclined seat in his wet Syrian Navy uniform. The computer monitor between them displayed a closed-circuit television shot from below the mini-sub.

The low-light camera slung under the Nomad showed Linda that the sub was slightly off center of the first torpedo. She made an adjustment so that one set of the curved grappling arms Max had installed were directly above the three-ton weapon. She hit a control, and the tungsten-steel claws curled around the torpedo and clamped it tight to the Nomad's belly.

Juan helped her by pumping out one of the ballast tanks to regain neutral trim. Linda eased the Nomad to the side, using its directional thrusters, a corner of her lip pinched between her teeth.

She cursed under her breath when the sub lurched past the torpedo. "Tide's coming in," she explained, and reversed power to back the submersible over her target.

A light on the air-lock control panel went from red to green. Eddie and Max were aboard.

For the second time, the Nomad drifted beyond the torpedo, forcing Linda to ramp up the power in order to fight the tidal waters swirling into the dry dock. The eddies and cross-currents played havoc with the little sub. Juan was confident that if Linda didn't think she could do it, she'd ask for his help. He let her do her job, and, on the third try, she vented air and set the submersible atop the second torpedo. She closed the claws around its tubular shape and dumped more ballast.

With a self-satisfied smile, Linda said, "Third time's the charm."

Juan extended the manipulator arm and used its dexterous fingers to gather up the four slings they'd used to move the torpedoes and stow them in a bin under the Nomad's chin. As soon as the arm was returned to its default position, Linda jammed the joystick hard over to rotate the Nomad in the dry dock. Signals from the LIDAR system allowed her to squeak through the partially open door and into the open water of the port.

Juan checked their battery status, their speed through the water, and speed over the bottom. He tapped the numbers into the computer to get an approximation of the Nomad's range. Behind them, his team was getting out of their wet suits and dressing in fresh clothes they had packed earlier.

With the tide coming in harder than they'd estimated, the little submersible would have just an hour of reserve power by the time they reached the *Oregon*. It was an uncomfortably close margin, and one Juan was going to make worse. He had a bad feeling about the Iranian response and wanted to put distance between his ship and the Strait of Hormuz.

"Nomad to *Oregon*," he radioed.

"Good to hear your voice, Chairman," Hali Kasim replied. "I take it everything went well?"

"Like stealing candy from a baby," Cabrillo said. "How's the reconfiguration going?"

"Like clockwork. The fairing over the bow is gone, the funnel's back to normal, and we've got a good jump on folding up the containers."

"Good. Hali, in about thirty minutes I want you to get under way, but take her out at about three knots." The Nomad was making four. "We'll make our rendezvous a little farther down the coast."

"That will put us pretty close to the shipping lanes," Hali pointed out. "We can't stop out there to pick you up."

"I know. We'll do the recovery on the fly." Surfacing the Nomad in the moon pool was dangerous enough, but doing it with the *Oregon* under way was something Cabrillo would only risk if he felt it was absolutely necessary.

"Are you sure about that?" Max asked, leaning into the cockpit.

Juan turned to look his old friend in the eye. "My right ankle is acting up." That was their code for the Chairman having a premonition. He'd had the feeling before accepting an assignment from NUMA that cost him his right leg below the knee, and in the intervening years both men had come to trust Juan's instinct.

"You're the boss," Max said, and nodded.

It took an additional two hours to reach the *Oregon*, as she slowly steamed away from the Iranian coast. The Nomad passed under the dark hull forty feet below the keel. The moon-pool doors were fully retracted and flattened against the hull, and red battle lamps within the ship cast the water in a scarlet glow. It was almost like they were approaching the gates of hell.

Linda slowed the submersible to match the *Oregon*'s sluggish pace, centering the craft beneath the opening. In a normal recovery, divers would enter the water to secure lifting lines to the Nomad, and it would be winched into the ship. Though making only three knots, it was too much of a current to dive safely in the moon pool's confines.

When she was comfortable with the speed, she dialed off ballast, pumping the tanks so slowly that the Nomad rose in fractional increments.

"Not to add pressure or anything," Hali called over the comm link, "but we have a turn coming up in less than four minutes." The shipping lanes within the Strait of Hormuz were so tight that any deviation was simply not tolerated.

"Yeah, that's not adding pressure," Linda replied, never taking her eyes off her computer screens.

She released more ballast, her fingers featherlight on the joystick and throttle. She made tiny corrections as the opening loomed larger and larger.

"You're doing great," Juan said from the copilot's seat.

Foot by foot, the gap narrowed until the Nomad was directly below the ship. They could hear the quiet hum of her revolutionary engines and the sluice of water through her drive tubes.

Linda slowed the Nomad a fraction, so that it drifted back to the aft part of the moon pool, the submersible's rear fins and propellers less than a foot from the opening. "Here we go," she said, and dumped the remaining hard ballast, a hopper loaded with a half ton of metal balls.

The Nomad popped up and broached the surface. Though roiled like a cauldron because the *Oregon* was making three knots, the water in the pool was motionless in relation to the submersible. The mini began to accelerate forward. Linda kicked on emergency reverse thrust as the little sub quickly crossed the pool, which was barely twice the sub's length. An inflatable fender that spanned the width of the pool had been lowered to the water's edge for just such a contingency. The sub hit it so softly that it barely compressed.

Pairs of feet slapped down on the top of the Nomad as technicians attached lifting lines to the submersible's hardpoints. Below them, the doors were already closing. Linda let out a relieved sigh, flicking her wrists to ease the cramping.

Juan patted her shoulder. He could see the strain in her eyes. "Couldn't have done it better myself."

"Thanks," she said tiredly. She cocked her head as if listening to a voice in the distance. "I think I hear my bathtub calling me."

"Go ahead," Juan said, sliding back off his seat and leaving a puddle on the dark vinyl. "You've more than earned it."

The team was waiting under the hatch when the Nomad was set onto its cradle and the outer lid popped open. Despite the fact he was still dripping on the nonslip floor, Juan let his team precede him out of the mini. A tech handed him a headset without being asked. "Eric, you there?"

"Right here, Chairman," Eric Stone said from his place in the Operations Center.

"As soon as the doors are closed, take us up to eighteen knots. How long before we clear the strait?"

"Two and a half hours, give or take, and it will be another fifteen hours to the rendezvous coordinates."

Cabrillo would have liked to have the torpedoes and all the technical information Eddie had pirated from the computer off the ship as quickly as possible, but the timing to meet up with the USS *Tallahassee*, a Los Angeles Class fast-attack submarine, had to be carefully coordinated to avoid spy satellites and the chance of a nearby ship spotting the transfer.

"Okay, thanks. Tell Hali to keep a sharp ear out for military chatter coming from Bandar Abbas. If he gets anything, wake me in my cabin."

"Will do, boss man."

Max was overseeing the removal of the rocket torpedoes from under the Nomad, working a chainfall himself to lower them onto motorized carts. Eddie had already placed the computer drive loaded with information into a waterproof hard case.

Juan slapped one of the weapons with his palm. "Five million apiece, plus another million for the information off the computer. Not bad for a day's work."

"You should call Overholt now so he knows we nabbed two of these babies and doesn't have a heart attack when he gets our bill."

"A shower first," Juan said. "Then I'll call him. You turning in?"

Max glanced at his watch. "It's near four-thirty. I think I'm going to stay up and help out with the rest of the work to put the ship back in order. Maybe enjoy a sunrise breakfast."

"Suit yourself. Good night."

THE TERM *POSH* originated during the time of the British Raj in India, when passengers booking ships to their imperial postings in Bombay or Delhi asked for portside cabins on the way to India and for starboard cabins on the return to England. This way, their rooms were always on the shaded side of the ship. Booking agents shortened "Port Out, Starboard Home" to POSH, and a new word entered the English language.

Cabrillo's cabin was on the port side of the *Oregon*, but the angle the ship sailed relative to the sun allowed light to stream through his porthole and made his suite swelter despite the air-conditioning. He woke bathed in sweat, momentarily disoriented about what had roused him until he heard the phone ring a second time.

He glanced at the big wall clock opposite his bed, as he yanked his arms free of the twisted sheets. It wasn't yet eight and already the sun was a torture.

He lifted the handset. "Cabrillo."

"Chairman, it's Hali. The jig is up."

Juan did some mental calculations as the news sank in. The *Oregon* would be clear of the strait by now but wouldn't have ventured very far into the Gulf of Oman. They were still very much within Iran's military sphere of influence.

"What's happening?" he asked, swinging his legs out of bed and running a hand across his crew cut.

"There was a burst of chatter out of Bandar Abbas about five minutes ago and then nothing."

Juan had expected this. It would take some time for the base commander to figure out what had happened and finally have the courage to report the theft to his superiors in Tehran. They in turn would have immediately told the naval base to stop using radios and nonsecure telephones and to switch to dedicated landlines.

During the first Gulf War, America tipped her hand to the world concerning her eavesdropping abilities. Using its satellites and ground listening stations, the NSA could listen in on or read virtually every telephone call, radio broadcast, fax transmittal, and any other form of communication with impunity. It was how our military knew exactly where to target Saddam Hussein's command and control facilities. In response to this overwhelming technological advantage, nations who saw the United States as a threat—namely, Iran, Syria, Libya, and North Korea—spent hundreds of millions of dollars building a network of landlines that couldn't be hacked or listened in on without a direct tap.

After those first frantic calls that the *Oregon* intercepted, the Iranians had switched to this system and denied Cabrillo a valuable source of intelligence.

"What did you get?" Juan asked.

"They reported a break-in at the dry dock, a small explosion that damaged the control room, and the theft of two whales."

"That's their code name for the rocket torpedoes," Juan said. "I think the Farsi word is *hoot*."

"That's what the computer said. After that, there was an order out of the defense ministry to switch to something they call 'the voice of the Prophet.'"

"That'll be their military communications lines." Juan clamped the cordless phone between his head and shoulder to free up his hands so he could dress. "Anything else?"

"Sorry, Chairman. That was it."

Cabrillo put himself in the Iranians' shoes and thought through what would come next. "They're going to close Bandar Abbas and reinspect every ship in the harbor. The Navy's going to be put on high alert, and they may try to stop vessels within fifty or so miles of the coast all along the Gulf of Oman."

"We're still within that radius," Hali told him.

"Tell the helmsman to get us the hell out. I'll be in the Op Center in two minutes. Assemble the senior staff." Although Juan's top people had been on duty until just a couple of hours ago, he wanted them manning the ship until they were well beyond Iran's ability to strike.

When Juan had designed the *Oregon*, a tremendous amount of effort went into the ship's Operations Center. It was the brain of the vessel, the nerve center from which everything could be controlled, from her engines and weapons systems to the fire-suppression sprinklers and communications. The room was as high-tech as the exterior of the *Oregon* was decayed. Dominating the front wall was a massive flat-panel screen that could show dozens of images at a time, from the battery of ship's cameras as well as feeds from her submersibles, the unmanned aerial ROV, and from cameras mounted on the Robinson R44 chopper. Sonar and radar images could also be flashed onto the screen.

The helm and weapons station was immediately below the flat panel, with Hali's communications console, Max Hanley's engineering station, and the principal sonar waterfall display ringing the darkened room. In the center of the Op Center was what Mark Murphy and Eric Stone had dubbed the "Kirk Chair." From the command position, Cabrillo could monitor everything happening on and around his ship and take over any of the other stations if necessary.

With its low ceiling and the glow from dozens of computer displays, the Op Center had the palpable buzz of NASA's mission control.

An exhausted Max Hanley was already in his chair when Juan strode in, as was Mark Murphy. Murph was the only member of the crew without a military or intelligence background, and it showed. Tall and gawky, he had nearly black hair that was long and unkempt, and he was trying to grow a beard, although, so far, his best efforts resembled an anemic billy goat's. He possessed the highest IQ of anyone aboard ship, having gotten a Ph.D. from MIT while still in his early twenties. From there, he had gone into systems development for a major military contractor, where he had met Eric Stone. Eric was working procurement with the Navy but had already planned on resigning his commission and joining the Corporation. During the two months the pair of them had spent on a still-secret long-range cannon for the Arleigh Burke Class destroyers, Eric had convinced Murph to join up as well.

Juan couldn't fault Murph's proficiency with the *Oregon*'s weapons systems. He just hoped for the day young Mr. Murphy would stop dressing in all black and playing punk music loud enough to shake barnacles off the hull. This morning found him wearing a T-shirt emblazoned with a pair of ruby lips. On the back it read THE ROCKY HORROR PICTURE SHOW. His workstation was littered with half a dozen empty energy drink cans, and Juan could see by the glassy look in Murph's eye he was mainlining on caffeine.

Cabrillo took his seat and adjusted the computer display at his elbow. A steaming cup of coffee materialized at his side. Maurice had approached so silently Juan never heard him coming. "I'm going to have to put a bell on you."

"To employ an overused cliché, Captain, over my departed corpse."

"Or dead body, whatever." Juan smiled. "Thanks."

"You're most welcome, sir."

Over the rim of his coffee, Juan studied the displays in front of him, especially noting the radar picture of the surrounding waters. The coast of Iran still showed at the top of the screen, at the radar's extreme limit, while around them countless ships were heading into and out of the Persian Gulf. From the size of the returns, he knew most of them were tankers, and the traffic seemed as thick as Atlanta at rush hour. Far to the south was a cluster of ships around one large vessel he guessed was an American aircraft carrier task force.

He checked their speed and heading, as well as the depth of the water under the ship. The bottom had dropped to four hundred feet, plenty deep enough for a lurking Iranian sub. But with the Americans so close, he was more concerned with a helicopter or aircraft assault, if they were linked to the theft somehow. A quick glimpse at the camera displays showed him that the *Oregon* looked as she should, with her single funnel, and decks devoid of containers. Her name was back to normal, though he noted the Panamanian flag still flew from her jack staff. A prudent precaution, because the Iranians wouldn't need permission to board a ship flying their ensign, as the *Oregon* normally did. The mast camera high atop one of the cargo derricks showed a tanker they must have passed recently less than a mile astern and a containership steaming along their track a half mile to the north.

"Hali, anything on sonar?"

"Except for the noise from eight ships within range that the computer's already scrubbed, there's nothing out here but us innocent merchantmen." He paused, as if to add something.

Juan saw his frown and said, "Tell me. No matter how small."

"About a minute after communications from Bandar Abbas went dead, there was a burst of transmission from the naval base at Chāh Bahār."

"Have you heard it since?"

Hali shook his head. "Just that one time."

Juan wasn't sure what to do with that piece of information, so he let it go for the moment. "What about aircraft or helos?"

"An ASW plane off the carrier to our south did a pass an hour ago, but nothing from our friends to the north."

Cabrillo relaxed slightly, and was beginning to think they might get away with it after all.

It was just as that thought entered his mind that Hali shouted, "Sonar contact! Bearing ninety-five degrees, seven thousand yards. Torpedo in the water. Damnit, he was waiting to ambush us, with his bow doors open and his tubes flooded."

There was more than five miles separating the ship from the incoming torpedo, so Juan knew he had more than enough time to get the *Oregon* out of danger. His voice remained calm. "Track it, Hali. Let's make sure we know where it's going before we react."

"Sonar contact!" Kasim cried again. "Second torpedo in the water, same bearing and range. I'm getting target extrapolation off the computer. The first fish is heading for the containership. I have her identified as the *Saga*, and she left Bandar Abbas twenty minutes before we did."

The tactical picture went from bad to worse.

"We're getting a warning from the carrier battle group," Hali called out. "They heard the shots and are launching aircraft."

"This is turning into a hell of a fur ball," Max said sardonically.

"Tell me about it," Juan muttered.

"Come on!" Hali shouted. "New contact. They launched a third torpedo. It's looking like a spread pattern targeting us, the *Saga*, and the tanker behind us, a Petromax Oil ULCC named the *Aggie Johnston*."

Had there been just the one torpedo tracking the *Oregon*, Cabrillo could have handled it. Maybe even two, if he could put his vessel between the second one and the ship it had targeted, but with three fish in the water his options had quickly run out. Either the *Saga* or the *Aggie Johnston* was going to take a direct hit. And with a full load of two hundred thousand tons of Gulf crude, there was no way he would let it be the supertanker.

"They just launched another," Hali said with disbelief in his voice. "That's four fish in the water. Range between the *Saga* and the first is down to six thousand yards. This last fish is going much slower than the others."

"It's lurking to see what the others miss," Max said. "And will go in to finish it off."

If one of the first three torpedoes missed or failed to detonate, this reserve salvo would be in position to destroy its intended target. Cabrillo was familiar with the tactic. He also had no defense against it. He was now thinking they would be lucky to get out of the Sea of Oman alive.

CHAPTER 4

THE MUGGER'S HAND WAS LIKE A VISE AROUND Jannike Dahl's mouth and nose. She couldn't breathe, and any effort to fight him off only made it seem worse. Wriggling against the restraint, she managed to draw a sip of air, barely enough to stave off the blackness threatening to engulf her. She twisted one way and then the other, only to have the hand inexorably stay with her.

She had seconds before unconsciousness overcame her, but there was nothing she could do. It was like drowning, the most terror-filled death she could ever imagine, only it wasn't a cold water's embrace that would take her life but the hands of a stranger.

Jannike fought one last time, a desperate lunge to break free.

She came awake with a wet gasp, her head and shoulders lifting from the bed only to be dragged back by the sheets and blankets covering her. The clear plastic cannula feeding pure oxygen into her nose had wrapped itself around her throat, choking her as much as the asthma attack she was suffering.

Filled with the chilling aftereffects of the nightmare that always accompanied an attack when she was asleep, Janni groped for the inhaler on the bedside table, dimly aware that she was still in the ship's hospital. She placed the mouthpiece between her lips and fired off several blasts of medicine, drawing in the Ventolin as deeply as her fluid-filled lungs would allow.

As the medicine relaxed her restricted airways, Janni was able to inhale more of the drug and eventually calm the most acute symptoms of the attack. It didn't help that her heart was still racing from the nightmare or that she had dislodged part of her cannula so only one nostril was getting oxygen. She readjusted the plastic tube and felt the immediate effects. She glanced at the monitor over her bed and saw her oxygen stats start to rise immediately. She smoothed her sheets and settled deeper into the inclined bed.

This was her third day in the dispensary, the third day of being alone for hours on end, bored out of her mind and cursing her lungs' weakness. Her friends had stopped by regularly, but she knew none of them wanted to stay. Not that she blamed them. Watching her gasp like a fish and suck on her inhaler wasn't a pretty sight. She hadn't even had the strength to let the lone nurse change her sheets and could imagine what her body smelled like.

The curtain around her bed was suddenly drawn back. Dr. Passman moved so softly that Janni never knew he had entered the recovery room. He was in his sixties, a retired heart surgeon from England who had given up his practice following his divorce and had signed on to be a shipboard doctor with the Golden Cruise Lines to enjoy a more peaceful life and to deny his ex-wife half of the salary he had once made.

"I heard you cry out," he said, looking at the monitors rather than his patient. "Are you okay?"

"Just another attack." Janni managed a smile. "Same as I've been having for three days now." She then added in her lilting Scandinavian accent, "It wasn't as bad as before. I think they're passing."

"I will be the one making that determination," he said, finally looking at her. There was concern in his eyes. "You're as blue as a berry. My daughter has chronic asthma, but not like you."

"I'm used to it." Jannike shrugged. "I had my first attack when I was five, so I've been dealing with it for three-quarters of my life."

"I've been meaning to ask, are there other members of your family who have it?"

"I don't have any brothers or sisters, and neither of my parents had it, though my mother told me her mother had it when she was a little girl."

Passman nodded. "It tends to run in families. I would have

thought being at sea and away from pollution would have reduced your symptoms."

"I had hoped so, too," Janni said. "That's one of the reasons I took a job waitressing on a cruise ship. Well, that and
to get out of a small town with nothing to do but watch fishing
boats come in and out of the harbor."

"You must miss your parents."

"I lost them two years ago." A shadow passed behind her
dark eyes. "Car accident."

"I am sorry. Your color's coming back," Passman said to
change the subject. "And your breathing seems to be getting
easier."

"Does that mean I can leave?" Janni asked.

"'Fraid not, my dear. Your oxygen saturation level is still
below what I would like to see."

"I suppose it doesn't matter to you that today is the crew's
social," she said with a trace of disappointment. According to
the clock on the far wall, the party was only a few hours away.

The dance was the first opportunity for the younger members of the ship's hotel staff to cut loose a little since the
Golden Dawn had left the Philippines two weeks earlier. It
was to be the highlight of the cruise for the waiters, waitresses, maids, and off-duty crew, which happened to be composed of some devilishly handsome Norwegians. Janni knew
some of the younger passengers were going to attend as well.
It was all anyone had been talking about for a week.

"No, it doesn't," the doctor said.

The door to the small hospital ward opened, and, a moment later, Elsa and Karin, Janni's best friends on the *Golden
Dawn*, swept into the room amid a cloud of perfume. They
were from Munich, a couple of years older than Janni, and
had spent the past three years working for the cruise line.
Elsa was a pastry chef, and Karin worked the same dining-
room shift as Jannike. They were dressed to kill. Karin wore
a black dress with spaghetti straps that accented her ample
chest, while Elsa wore a tank dress and, from the lack of lines
under the clinging fabric, nothing else. Both were heavily
made up and giggly.

"How are you feeling?" Elsa asked and sat on the edge of
Janni's bed, ignoring Passman.

"Jealous."

"You aren't well enough to come to the party?" Karin scowled at the doctor as if it were his fault Jannike's asthma wasn't in check.

Janni pushed her damp hair off her forehead. "Even if I was, I wouldn't stand a chance the way you two are dressed."

"Do you think Michael will like it?" Karin pirouetted.

"He'll die for it," Elsa told her friend.

"Are you sure he's coming?" Janni asked, caught up in gossip despite the pain constricting her chest. Michael was one of the passengers who sat at the table they served, a Californian with blond hair, blue eyes, and a body honed from a lifetime of exercise. It was generally agreed by the female staff that he was the best-looking guy on the boat. She also knew that Karin and Michael had made out on more than one occasion.

Karin smoothed her dress. "He made sure to tell me himself."

Passman cut into their conversation, "It doesn't bother you he's a Responsivist?"

She shot the doctor a look. "I grew up with four brothers and three sisters. I don't think not having children is such a bad idea."

"Responsivism is more than not having children," he pointed out.

Karin took it as an insult that she didn't know what the group who had chartered the ship believed in. "Yes, it is also about helping humanity by making family planning an option for millions of third world women and reducing the burden our population places on the earth. When Dr. Lydell Cooper founded the movement in the nineteen seventies, there were three billion people in the world. Today, there are twice that many—six billion—and the rates aren't slowing. Ten percent of all humans who have ever lived, going back a hundred thousand years, are alive right now."

"I saw the same informational placards they have placed around the ship," Passman said archly. "But don't you think Responsivism goes beyond social consciousness? For a woman to join, she has to agree to have her fallopian tubes tied. It sounds to me more like, well, a cult."

"That's what Michael said people tell him all the time."
With the stubbornness of youth, Karin felt she had to defend
her crush's convictions. "Just because you don't know all the
facts doesn't mean you can dismiss what he believes."

"Yes, but surely you see . . ." Passman let his voice trail
off, knowing that whatever argument was put forth would
stand little chance against a twenty-something girl with raging hormones. "Actually, you probably wouldn't. I think you
two should let Jannike rest. You can tell her all about the
party later." He left Janni's bedside.

"Are you going to be okay, *Schnuckiputzi*?" Elsa asked,
touching Janni's thin shoulder.

"I'll be fine. You two have fun and I want lurid details tomorrow."

"Good girls don't kiss and tell," Karin said, and grinned.

"In that case, I don't expect either of you to be good
girls."

The two Germans left together, but Karin returned a second later. She eased up to the head of the bed. "I want you to
know that I think I'm going to do it."

Janni knew what she meant. She knew that Michael was
more than a passing crush for her friend, and that apart from
kissing a few times he had spent hours talking to her about
his beliefs.

"Karin, that is way too big of a step. You don't know him
that well."

"I've never really wanted kids anyway, so what's the big
deal if I have my tubes tied now or in a few years."

"Don't let him talk you into it," Janni said as forcefully as
her weakened body would let her. Karin was nice, but not the
strongest person Jannike had ever met.

"He didn't talk me into it," she dismissed too quickly. "It's
something I've thought about for a long time. I don't want to
be worn out at thirty like my mother was. She's forty-five now
and looks seventy. No thanks. Besides," she said with a bright
smile, "nothing will happen until we dock in Greece anyway."

Janni took Karin's hand to emphasize her point. "This is a
decision that will affect the rest of your life. Give it some
more thought, okay?"

"Okay," Karin said, as if to a parent.

Janni gave her a quick hug. "Good. Now, go have some fun for me."

"Count on it."

Their perfumes lingered long after the girls were gone.

Janni's face was scrunched in concentration. The ship wasn't due to dock in Piraeus for another week, giving her hope that she and Elsa could talk Karin out of her decision. One of the prerequisites for becoming a Responsivist is being sterilized. A vasectomy for men and a tubal ligation for women. It was part of their code to agree to not add more children to an already-overpopulated planet, a dramatic first step that was difficult, expensive, and, in later years, impossible to reverse. Karin was too young for that just so she could bed a good-looking guy.

She drifted off to sleep, and when she awoke a few hours had passed. She could hear the muffled rumble of the ship's engines but could hardly feel the calm rocking of the Indian Ocean swells. She wondered how Elsa and Karin were enjoying the party . . .

Jannike woke again an hour later. She hated being in the hospital. She was lonely and bored, and, for a moment, considered grabbing her old clothes from under the bed and sneaking up to the ballroom for a peek. But her body just wasn't up to it and again she closed her eyes.

She heard a crash the instant before the mugger wrapped his hand around her throat again and started to squeeze.

Jannike flashed awake, reaching for her inhaler just as the door to her room opened in a blaze of light from the office beyond. Stricken by the asthma attack, she wasn't sure what she was seeing. Dr. Passman staggered into the room. He wore a bathrobe and his feet were bare. It looked like the front of the robe and his face was covered in blood. Jannike sucked greedily on the inhaler, blinking to clear her eyes of sleep.

Passman made an obscene cawing sound, and more blood dribbled from his mouth. Janni gasped. He took two more faltering steps, and it seemed the bones of his knees dissolved. He fell back, and his body hit the linoleum floor with a wet smack. Janni saw that wavelike ripples traveled the length of his body, as though his insides had been liquefied, and in seconds he was surrounded by a viscous moat of his own blood.

She clutched her sheets tighter, drawing on the inhaler as she began to hyperventilate. Then another figure came into her room. It was Karin in her little black dress. She was coughing violently, wet, racking convulsions that spewed blood in a bright spray. Janni screamed through her own coughing fit, terrified at what she was seeing.

Karin tried to speak, but all that came out was a watery gargle. She stretched out with her arms in a supplicating gesture, her pale fingers reaching for Jannike. Janni hated herself for recoiling back to the far side of her bed, but she could not will herself forward. A crimson tear escaped the corner of Karin's eye and left a thick red streak down to her jaw where it dripped, blooming like a rose when it pattered against her chest.

Like Passman seconds earlier, Karin could no longer support herself. She tipped backward, making no move to break her fall. When she hit the floor, it was as though her skin didn't exist. Blood exploded everywhere as Karin's body came apart, and in the instant before Jannike Dahl went into catatonic shock she was certain she was going insane.

CHAPTER 5

JUAN CABRILLO STUDIED THE TACTICAL DISPLAY on the forward bulkhead of the Op Center for a few seconds, time he knew he didn't have but needed to take anyway. Three of the four torpedoes fired from the Iranian Kilo Class sub were fanning out and tracking toward their targets, while the sonar showed the fourth had slowed so much that the computer gave only its approximate location.

There were less than two miles separating the containership *Saga* from the first torpedo, while the two-hundred-thousand-ton supertanker *Aggie Johnston* had another mile-and-a-half cushion. The third torpedo was coming straight for the *Oregon* at more than forty knots.

Cabrillo knew the *Oregon* could take a direct hit, thanks to the reactive armor along her hull that exploded outward when struck by an incoming torpedo and negated the detonative forces, though it would likely damage critical systems. He could also dodge the incoming fish, using the *Oregon*'s superior speed and maneuverability, but the overshooting torpedo then would home in on the *Saga* as a secondary target and seal her fate. There was simply no way for him to protect the two merchantmen and the *Oregon*, especially with the reserve torpedo lurking out there.

He was dimly aware of Hali Kasim sending a radio alert to the two ships about the inbound torpedoes, not that there was anything they could do. A ship the size of the *Aggie Johnston* had a pathetically large turning radius, and needed five miles to stop from her current cruising speed.

"I'm tracking two fast movers off the carrier," Mark Murphy said from the weapons stations. "I suspect they're S-3B Vikings, antisubmarine warfare planes armed with either

Mark 46 or Mark 50 torpedoes. That Kilo is going to have a real bad day starting in about ten minutes."

"Which is five minutes too late for us," Eric said.

"Hali, what's the range to the fish tracking us?" Cabrillo asked.

"Six thousand yards."

And for the *Saga*?"

"Thirty-two hundred."

Cabrillo straightened in his chair, his decision made. It was time to roll the dice and see what happened. "Helm, increase speed to forty knots, put us between the *Saga* and the torpedo headed for her."

"Aye."

"Wepps, open the ports for the forward Gatling and target that fish, slave your computer to the master sonar plot, and you might need the targeting reticle from the crow's nest camera."

"Just a second," Mark said.

"Mr. Murphy." Juan's tone was sharp. "We don't have a second."

Murph wasn't listening. He was engrossed with something taking place on a laptop computer he had jacked into his system. "Come on, baby, learn it, will you," he said anxiously.

"What are you doing?" Cabrillo asked, leaning over to compensate for the *Oregon*'s sharp curve through the water.

"Teaching the Whopper a new trick."

Whopper was what he and Eric Stone called the *Oregon*'s supercomputer, having stolen the name from an old Matthew Broderick movie about a young computer hacker who breaks in to SAC/NORAD and almost starts a nuclear war.

"We don't need new tricks, Wepps. I need that Gatling online and spooled up."

Murph spun around in his seat to look across the room at Max Hanley, who was engrossed with his own computer. "I don't think this is going to work."

"Keep at it, lad," was all Max said.

"You two mind telling me what's going on?" Juan asked, looking at each man in turn.

"Yes! Yes, yes, yes," Mark crowed, jumping up from his chair and pumping his fists over his head. He began typing furiously, not bothering to sit again, his fingers flying over the keyboard, as dexterous as a classical pianist's. "Logarithm's lining up, targeting's coming online. The onboard computer's in sync with ours. I have full control."

"Of what?"

Mark glanced at him with a fiendish grin. "We're about to have ourselves a whale of a time."

Cabrillo blanched and spun to glance at Max. Hanley looked as inscrutable as a Buddha statue. "You can't be serious," Juan said but knew his second-in-command was. "You do know the last time the Russians tried to fire one of those things it blew a hole in the side of the *Kursk* and killed all one hundred and eighteen aboard? And this one's an Iranian knockoff, for the love of God."

"There's a thousand yards between the *Saga* and the torp," Linda Ross said. With communications swirling among the freighters, the American battle group, and the fast-approaching ASW aircraft, she had taken over the sonar station so Hali Kasim could concentrate on the radios.

"Just giving you an option, Chairman," Max said broadly.

"Don't 'Chairman' me, you crafty old bastard."

Juan studied the tactical display again, noting the *Oregon* was about to slip between the incoming torpedo and its intended target. Because of the water density they needed to be directly in front of the torpedo if they were to have any realistic chance of hitting it. By the time they got into position, there would be less than five hundred yards between them and the weapon barreling in just ten feet below the surface.

From the camera on the loading derrick, Cabrillo could see the wake line of the incoming torpedo, a faint disturbance in the otherwise tranquil water. It was approaching at better than forty knots.

"Wepps, we need to take it before it dives for the keel."

"Tracking," Murph said.

Eric Stone slid the *Oregon* into position, using her athwartship thrusters and a heavy blast from the magnetohydrodynamics on full reverse, to place them directly in the path of the torpedo.

"Permission to fire," Juan said.

Mark tapped a few keys.

Outside, along the *Oregon*'s flank, the armored plate over the Gatling redoubt slammed open and the six-barrel gun shrieked, a string of foot-long empty shell casings arcing from the mechanism in a continuous blur. A plume of smoke and flame erupted from the ship as a second's-long burst from the 20mm machine cannon arrowed across the water. Just ahead of the onrushing torpedo the sea came alive, shredded by hundreds of depleted uranium shells. Gouts of water flew in the air as the slugs bored a hole in the ocean amid a cloud of steam.

The Russian-made TEST-71 torpedo, packed with over four hundred pounds of explosives, roared into the path of the Gatling gun. With enough water forced out of the way by the continuous stream of fire, four of the kinetic rounds hit the weapon dead center. The warhead exploded, sending a series of concussion waves racing across the sea, while, at the epicenter of the blast, a column of water rose eighty feet into the sky before gravity overcame inertia and the entire plume crashed back into the chasm.

Though located in the heart of the ship and well insulated from the outside, the crew heard the detonation as though it were thunder crashing directly overhead.

Juan immediately turned to Max. "That bought us about thirty seconds. Convince me."

"Their torpedoes are all wire guided. If we can cut them loose, they should go inert. Not even the Iranians would let fish run around in these waters without some sort of control."

"What do you propose?"

"Isn't it obvious? Sink the damned Kilo."

Juan looked at the tactical display again. He saw the red flashing lights indicating the two inbound American S-3B Vikings, as well as the track lines for the three remaining torpedoes. The reserve fish was beginning to accelerate toward the *Oregon*, while the primary weapon targeting her had altered course for interception.

"You sure it'll work?" he asked without looking back.

"'Course not," Max told him. "It's an Iranian copy of an already-flawed Russian weapon. But my crew worked through the night adapting the number one tube so we can fire it, and Murph seems to have the software worked out, so I say go for it. If it works as advertised, it'll take out the three torpedoes long before they reach their targets."

"Murph?"

"Whopper has it pegged, Chairman. I can control it as best as it can be controlled, but it's mostly an aim-and-hope kind of weapon. At two hundred knots, it's pretty damned hard to steer anything."

Cabrillo would either kiss Max and Murph in a few seconds or curse them in hell. "Helm, turn us bow on to the Kilo. Wepps, open outer door for tube one. Match bearings and shoot."

Foam creamed off the *Oregon*'s bow as Eric Stone brought the ship around, digging her deep into the waves, to give Murph his shot.

"Stoney, another two points to starboard," Mark asked, and Eric goosed the thrusters to maneuver the ship so she was pointed directly at where the Kilo had fired the spread of torpedoes. "Linda, she hasn't moved, right?"

"No. She's just sitting there paying out wires to guide her school of fish," Ross replied and took off the passive sonar headphones she'd been wearing.

That was the last piece of information Mark needed. He keyed the launch control. With a blast of compressed air powerful enough to make the freighter shudder, the modified tube shot the rocket torpedo out through the hull door at nearly fifty knots, fast enough for its specially designed nose cone to create a high-pressure bubble of air around the whole weapon. Just as its onboard computer detected the torpedo was slowing, its rocket kicked on with a deafening roar and its stabilizer fins flicked open.

The Hoot, or Whale, rocket torpedo sliced through the ocean in an envelope of supercavitated bubbles that eliminated the deadly drag of having to bull its way through the water. In essence, it was flying, and quickly accelerated to two hundred and thirty knots. Its wake was a boiling cauldron of steam.

The image from the topside camera showed that the sea was being ripped apart by a perfectly straight fault line that began at the *Oregon*'s bow and grew at four hundred and twenty feet per second.

"Look at that mother go!" someone exclaimed.

"Range to target?" Juan called.

"Three thousand yards," Linda said. "Make that twenty-six hundred. Twenty-two hundred. Two thousand yards."

"Mr. Murphy, be ready with the autodestruct," Juan ordered.

"You don't want to sink the Kilo?"

"And cause a bigger international incident than we're already looking at? No, thank you. I just want to ring their bell a little bit and cut the guide wires spooling out of the sub's bow."

"How close?"

Juan checked the tactical display, gauging distances between the torpedoes targeting the *Aggie Johnston* and the *Oregon* and the ships themselves. The *Johnston* was less than thirty seconds from having her hull split open by a direct hit. He watched the line of the rocket torpedo cutting across the flat panel, moving so fast that the computer needed to recycle the image every second. He had to make sure to damage the Kilo enough so she couldn't fire another spread but not to so cripple her that she sank.

"One thousand yards, Chairman," Linda called out, although Juan could see the numbers on the screen blurring backward for himself.

There was less than two hundred yards now separating the *Johnston* from the torpedo hunting her. The vectors and speeds involved were complex, but Juan had a handle on it all.

"Wait for it," he said. If he detonated the rocket too early, there was a chance it wouldn't cut all the wire. Too late and the Kilo's crew of fifty-three were going to die.

"Wait for it," he repeated, watching the Hoot arrow through the sea and a faint line of disturbed water approaching the supertanker's exposed flank.

One torpedo was fifty yards from its target, the other, three hundred, but their relative speeds were so vastly different that they would reach their objectives at precisely the same instant.

"Now!"

Mark hit the button that sent an autodestruct signal to the

torpedo's onboard computer. The warhead and remaining solid rocket fuel blew a fraction of a second later, sending an erupting geyser of water into the air and opening a hole in the sea that was fifty feet deep and equally as wide. A stunning concussion wave radiated from the explosion. It hit the *Oregon* bow on, but hammered the side of the *Aggie Johnston* so that the massive ship heeled slightly to port.

With the explosion's acoustical onslaught reverberating through the sea, it made passive sonar signals impossible to detect. Cabrillo focused his attention on the topside camera shot of the Petromax supertanker. She rolled ponderously back to an even keel. He continued to watch her for a moment before a smile crossed his lips. There was no explosion from a torpedo slamming into her hull. Max's plan had worked. The wires coiling out from the Kilo to guide her fish had been cut, and the weapons immediately shut down.

"Linda, tell me the instant you hear anything," he ordered.

"Computer is compensating now. Give me another few seconds."

Hali turned in his seat. "Chairman, the pilot of one of the S-3B Vikings wants to know what just happened."

"Stall him," Juan said, his focus still on Linda, who sat as still as a statue, her right hand clamping the sonar headphones tightly to her head while in front of her tendrils of light floated down the sonar system's waterfall display.

She finally looked over at him. "No high-speed props sounds, so the three remaining torpedoes are dead and most likely on their way to the bottom. I hear machinery noises from the Kilo and alarms coming from inside the hull. Wait . . . Okay, it's pumps and . . . they're blowing ballast." A bright smile bloomed on her impish face. "We did it! They're on their way to the surface."

A round of cheers and applause reverberated through the Op Center, and even Max's bulldog face cracked into a grin.

"Nice job, everybody. Especially you, Mr. Murphy, and you, too, Max. Tell the team who installed the rocket torpedo and modified the tube to expect a little something extra in their next paychecks."

Although each member of the crew shared in the Corporation's profits on a sliding scale, Cabrillo delighted in handing out bonuses for work above and beyond. It was part of the reason he engendered so much loyalty, though mainly that came because he was the best natural leader any of the people under him had ever worked for.

"Look at that!" Eric Stone gasped.

On the main display, he had shifted the camera view to show the spot of ocean where the Kilo had launched its ambush. The water boiled like a maelstrom, and, in the center of the disturbance, a blunt object rose from the sea. As the bow of the Iranian sub emerged, they could see her hull plates were buckled, as if she had run full speed into a seamount. The normally convex nose was dimpled in the center, the result of the rocket torpedo exploding sixty yards in front of her.

The craft continued to surface, bobbing on waves of her own creation. As it steadied, Stone zoomed the camera in on the damaged hull plates, the *Oregon*'s computer automatically compensating for the ship's motion so the image remained rock steady. Air bubbled up from around the torn metal—not much, but enough to indicate the Kilo was taking on water. Hatches on her conning tower and her fore and aft decks were thrown open and a stream of men poured out of the crippled sub.

"You getting anything from them, Hali?" Juan asked.

"General distress calls, sir. Their pumps are barely keeping pace with the flooding. They are requesting assistance from the naval base at Chāh Bahār. Her captain hasn't ordered them to abandon ship, but he wants all unnecessary personnel on deck in case they founder."

"Are they asking for help from any ships in the area?"

"Negative, and I doubt they will."

"Agreed. Firing at civilian freighters without warning violates about fifty international treaties."

"And what do you call what we did back at Bandar Abbas?" Max asked, just to tease.

"Petty larceny," Cabrillo dismissed, "punishable by a fine and a couple hours of community service."

Just then, the pair of S-3Bs off the American aircraft carrier streaked over the *Oregon* and flew less than a hundred feet off the surface of the ocean as they roared down the Kilo's length. Sailors dove flat on the decks as the jet wash ripped across their uniforms.

"Chairman, the pilot of the lead Viking still wants to talk to you," Hali said. "And I'm getting an official request from the carrier that we remain in position. It's a Commander Charles Martin, aboard the *George Washington*."

"Pipe it over," Juan said, and settled earphones over his head and adjusted the integrated microphone. "This is Juan Cabrillo, master of the MV *Oregon*. What can I do for you, Commander?"

"Captain Cabrillo, we would like to send over a contingent of men to debrief your crew about what just occurred. The captains of the *Saga* and *Aggie Johnston* have already agreed. A helicopter can reach you in twenty minutes. The guided missile cruiser *Port Royal* will be there in two hours if you don't have facilities for landing a chopper."

"With all due respect, Commander Martin, none of my crew saw anything. I myself was asleep, and the watch stander on duty is blind in one eye and can't see out of the other."

Martin's voice sharpened. "Captain, I needn't remind you that coalition forces operating in these waters reserve the right to inspect all shipping entering or leaving the Persian Gulf. I call this a request out of courtesy, but it is an order. You will remain where you are and prepare to be boarded."

Juan understood the pressure the Navy was under to interdict potential terrorists from using the Gulf as a highway for weapons and fighters, but there was no way he was going to let them inspect the *Oregon*. Corrupt officials in foreign ports could be easily dissuaded from searching the scabrous freighter, but this was not the case with the U.S. military.

"Could you please stand by?" Juan requested. He covered the mike with his hand and called over to Hali Kasim. "Get Overholt on the horn. Tell him what's going on, and have him get these guys off our back. Eric, set a course bearing one hundred and five degrees, and make our speed eighteen knots." He took his hand away from the microphone. "Sorry about that, Commander. We can't land a chopper on the *Oregon*, so you'll have to send a boarding party from the *Port Royal*."

"Very well, Captain. Plan on our arrival at about eleven hundred hours."

"We'll leave the light on for ya," Juan drawled, and ended the call. He glanced around the Op Center. "Anyone want to bet? Twenty bucks to the person who guesses the closest."

The crew knew immediately what he was referring to.

"They'll call back in ten minutes," Hali opined.

"Five," Linda said.

"They're going to have their hands full for a while." This from Mark Murphy. "He won't notice we're under way for at least a half hour."

"I'm with Linda," Eric said. "Five minutes. We'll split the twenty."

Juan looked over at Max Hanley. "Care to venture a guess?"

Max studied the acoustic tile ceiling for a moment, then leveled his eyes on the Chairman. "Right about now."

"Holy crap," Hali cried. "He's right. Martin's hailing us again."

"Put him through," Cabrillo ordered.

"Captain Cabrillo, consider this your final warning," Commander Martin said. Juan could hear through the clipped speech that the officer's teeth were clenched. "If you do not stop immediately, I will order the circling Vikings to open fire on your ship."

Cabrillo didn't doubt Martin's sincerity. But he was also tired of dealing with the man. "Commander, an Iranian submarine just took a potshot at a fully loaded supertanker. I'm not going to wait around for them to come after us. I will be clear of your interdiction sphere before you arrive and there isn't much you can do about it."

"You will—" Martin's voice suddenly cut out. He came back on the line thirty seconds later. Juan couldn't quite place the new tone in his voice. Awe? Fear? Respect? Some combination of all three? "Captain, you are free to leave the area at your own discretion."

Cabrillo wondered who Langston had gotten to make the call. It had to be the commander in chief for Naval Operations for the Indian Ocean or one of the Joint Chiefs. Whoever it was, it was nice to have some pull in Washington.

"I thought you'd see it our way. Thank you and good luck. By the way, the Iranian Kilo's taking on water, so if you want a look inside her I suggest you hurry. *Oregon* out."

A meaty hand appeared under Juan's chin. He pulled his wallet from his pant pocket and slapped a twenty-dollar bill into Max's palm.

Max sniffed the money as though it were a fine cigar. "Like taking candy from a baby."

"Doesn't surprise me you know what that feels like." Cabrillo stood. "Nothing like a little naval battle before breakfast to make you hungry. Navigator, what's our ETA at the rendezvous site?"

"Not until midnight," Eric replied.

"Okay, I'll want senior staff on watch, so shuffle your schedules as needed. I have to go call Langston, thank him for his help, and then explain why we're only delivering one rocket torpedo." As he made to leave the Op Center, he grabbed the twenty from Max's hand. "For costing us that second torpedo, you still owe the Corporation four million, nine hundred ninety-nine thousand, nine hundred and eighty bucks."

CHAPTER 6

THE SALT TANG OF SEAWATER STRUCK DR. JULIA Huxley as soon as she opened the door to the ballast tank that doubled as a swimming pool. Because of the way the *Oregon* was configured, it was more of an Olympic-length lap pool, measuring one hundred and sixty-four feet long, but it was only two lanes wide, and flanked by a narrow catwalk tiled in pale marble that was striped with nonskid adhesive tape. The lighting was a mix of fluorescent and incandescent bulbs that gave the illusion of sunshine. The walls were of matching tile, and were a constant source of concern for the cleaning crews, because when the tank was filled to ballast down the ship the glossy marble was inevitably smeared with algae.

Though not much of a swimmer herself, Hux knew the four basic strokes. Freestyle was the speed stroke, breast was for endurance, the backstroke was a quirk of the body's buoyancy in motion, and the butterfly was the power stroke. It took an incredible amount of strength for a swimmer to haul his arms and upper torso completely out of the water, arch to launch himself forward, and pull himself through the water. She paused at the head of the pool to watch the lone swimmer flying down his lane doing the butterfly. He moved as if he were born to swim, with long, fluid movements, and not a bit of energy wasted, his body sawing up and down like a porpoise, as his arms broke free, with barely a splash with each stroke.

When she looked closer, she noticed waterproof weight bands clamped around his wrists, to make the workout even more difficult. To her way of thinking, this went beyond exercise and leaned toward masochism. Then again, she hadn't used the ship's fitness center for a while and tended toward yoga to keep most of the unwanted pounds off her curvy frame.

She had long gotten over how well Juan had adapted to losing his leg. He never let it stop or even slow him. Like everything else in his life, he took it as a challenge to be conquered.

Cabrillo made a crisp flip turn at the far end of the pool and powered his way toward her, his blue eyes obscured by a pair of goggles, his mouth opening wide for every breath. He must have seen her, and knew his time alone was coming to an end, because he suddenly accelerated, pouring on the power to finish the last part of his swim as though it were a sprint.

As the ship's doctor, Hux knew everything about the crew's medical status, and she would have sworn Juan was half his age by the way he swam.

He reached her in a froth of water that spilled onto the landing and forced her back to save the Gucci loafers she was wearing with a pair of khakis and a simple oxford shirt. Over that, Julia sported her ubiquitous lab coat. He slapped the edge of the pool and looked up at the big timer's clock on the wall behind her.

"Damn, I'm getting old," he said, and stripped off his goggles and the weights from around both wrists.

"Could have fooled me." Julia tossed him a towel as he heaved himself from the water in one fluid motion.

"I've been down here for thirty minutes," Juan said, running the thick towel over his body. If he felt self-conscious wearing a Speedo in front of her, it didn't show, but with his physique there was nothing to be embarrassed about. "Five years ago, I could have done at least fifteen more laps."

"And five years ago, I didn't have crow's-feet. Get over it," she said with a smile that revealed the tiny lines at the corners of her eyes were laugh lines and not a sign of impending dotage.

"What do they say, 'youth is wasted on the young'?"

"I have a feeling you didn't waste much of yours, Juan Cabrillo."

He chuckled but didn't deny it. "You aren't dressed for a swim, so you didn't come down here to work off that excellent beef Wellington we had for dinner. What gives?"

A look of concern darkened Huxley's face. "We have a little problem. Well, it's actually Max's problem, but I think it should affect all of us."

Julia wasn't a trained psychologist, but her medical background and calming demeanor made her the ship's de facto counselor.

Cabrillo draped the damp towel over his shoulders and gave Hux his undivided attention. "Talk to me."

"He got a call this evening from his ex-wife."

Juan interrupted, "There are three to choose from. Which one was it?"

"Lisa. Number two. The one in Los Angeles he had the kids with. He didn't give me all the details, but his ex thinks their son has been kidnapped."

Juan didn't react for a couple of seconds. None of Max's wives knew what he did for a living. Like most of the crew, Hanley told his family that he was a sailor working for a small shipping company, so Cabrillo didn't think the abduction could connect back to his work for the Corporation, but he couldn't discount the idea. They had made a lot of powerful enemies over the years. He finally asked, "Have there been any ransom demands?"

"No, not yet. She thinks she knows who's behind the kidnapping but has gotten nowhere with the LAPD or FBI. She wants his help getting the kid back."

Max's son would be about twenty-two or twenty-three by now, Juan recalled. His daughter was a few years older, a newbie attorney doing environmental law. Kyle Hanley hadn't lasted a year in college and had been drifting around L.A.'s counterculture scene ever since. He'd been busted a couple of times for minor drug possession, but Juan thought he'd done a stint in rehab two years ago and had remained clean. Though they'd been divorced for a few years before Juan had founded the Corporation, he remembered meeting Max's second wife on a couple of occasions. Max had assured Cabrillo that she had once been a loving, wonderful woman, but something had changed her into a shrewish paranoid who accused him of infidelity while it was she who was having affairs.

Max had done the best he could with their children's upbringing, paying far above what the divorce decree called for in terms of alimony and child support. Their daughter had turned out to be a bright, ambitious woman but their son, Kyle, was one of those people who believed life owed him, and no matter how he was approached he rebuffed any offers to help him find his way.

Juan knew that Max would do anything to help the kid, and he suspected why his second-in-command hadn't come to him directly with his problem. Had he done so, Juan would have offered the full services of the Corporation to rescue Kyle, and Max would never ask for that kind of favor. "God, he can be stubborn."

"He said the same about you," Hux replied. "He wouldn't even consider coming to you with this because he was sure you'd demand he take your help. He told me in no uncertain terms that this was his problem, not the Corporation's, and that he'd handle it on his own."

Cabrillo expected no less, but that didn't mean he wasn't frustrated by Hanley's pigheadedness. "What's his plan?"

"As soon as we transfer the torpedo, he's going to ask you to divert the *Oregon* to Karachi, the nearest city with an international airport where he can catch a flight to Los Angeles. After that, he wasn't too sure."

Juan checked his watch. They were due at the rendezvous coordinates in two hours. Once they finished up, they could reach Karachi in about twenty hours. The Corporation's Gulfstream jet was in Monaco in preparation for their next mission. Although he could get the plane to Pakistan's largest city in time, he believed flying commercial would be faster. It would mean leaving behind weapons and other contraband that wouldn't make it through airport security, but he had enough contacts in L.A. to get what they might need so he wasn't too concerned about that.

He had a mental list of questions, but he would wait to talk to Max directly.

The ship's onboard computer flipped the lights in the pool area on and off a couple of times. Juan had programmed it to alert him the rendezvous was coming and to finish up his swim. He slipped on a terry robe and a pair of flip-flops. Hux walked with him as they exited the pool. He made certain to securely dog the waterproof hatch. "I'll talk to him tonight and make sure he sees the error of his ways," he said.

"That's why I brought this to you. Max can't go it alone." It was clear Julia was relieved, though there wasn't much doubt Juan would help his best friend.

"Thanks, Hux. One day, Max's obstinacy is going to get him into trouble, but not this time."

AN HOUR AND A HALF LATER, a freshly showered Juan Cabrillo strode into the Operations Center. Stone and Murphy were in their chairs at the helm and weapons control. Hali sat at the communication's station, while Linda Ross covered the sonar suite. Unlike during their escape from Bandar Abbas, there was a relaxed feeling in the room. Transferring the remaining rocket torpedo from the *Oregon* was going to be a relatively straightforward job. When Max entered a few minutes later, the atmosphere seemed to chill by a couple of degrees. He went straight to the engineering console without a word to anyone.

Juan slid out of his chair and approached him.

"I don't want to hear it," Hanley said, not looking up from his computer monitor.

"We'll lay in a course for Pakistan as soon as we're done, and I'll get someone on buying us plane tickets. In the morning, you and I are going to sit down together and figure out our next move." Max glanced up at Cabrillo and was about to protest. Juan held up his hand. "Our next gig is a straightforward eavesdropping job. Linda and Eddie can handle it without us."

"This isn't your fight," Max said.

"Like hell, it isn't. Someone kidnapped a member of your family. To me, it's the same as if they'd taken one of my parents. I would expect nothing less than your help, so don't expect me not to be here for you."

Max paused a beat before saying, "Thanks, Juan."

"Don't mention it." He returned to the command chair, the matter settled. "Linda, anything yet?"

"Negative, but there's still twenty minutes to go."

"Okay. Max, everything set on your end?"

"The torpedo's up on deck in a sling and a technician is standing by the derrick controls."

"Hali, anything on radar or over the comm channels?"

"No, sir. We're in about the deadest spot you can find in the Indian Ocean. I haven't seen or heard from another ship in about eight hours."

The rendezvous was to take place far from conventional shipping lanes to avoid detection from freighters and tankers, and, in an area devoid of much sea life, that would attract commercial fishing vessels. The timing of their operation coincided with a gap in satellite coverage, just in case anyone was looking down from above.

Fifteen minutes trickled by before Linda called out, "Contact. I've got machinery noises almost directly below us, four hundred feet down. Ballast tanks are being purged." She washed the noise picked up by the passive sonar through the computer to cross-check the sound with a loop of tape provided by Overholt. "Confirmed. It's the USS *Tallahassee*, making for the surface."

"Very good," Juan said. "Helm, keep sharp. You dent that sub, you bought it."

Another few minutes passed as the Los Angeles Class fast-attack submarine climbed up from the depths, rising so slowly that she was dead silent from more than a couple miles away. Eric Stone had split his computer display so he could watch the sonar returns as well as the *Oregon*'s GPS coordinates, to make certain the sub wouldn't crash into the underside of the hull. It was the responsibility of the crew aboard the *Tallahassee* to hold their position stable relative to the freighter. Any corrections would come from Eric's controls.

"One hundred feet and fifty," Linda said. "Her ascent is slowing. Slowing. Leveling off at one hundred."

"She's holding about two hundred yards off the port beam," Eric said.

"Slide us over so she'll surface within fifty yards, please, Mr. Stone."

Eric punched up the bow and stern thrusters to shove the eleven-thousand-ton ship laterally through the water, placing her exactly on her mark, and reactivated the dynamic positioning system so the computer would hold them steady.

"She's coming up again. Ten feet per minute."

"Very good, Sonar. You have the conn."

"I have the conn," Linda repeated. Juan got up and went to the elevator in the back of the Op Center, joined a second later by Max. Together, they rode up to the *Oregon*'s bridge. As soon as the floor hatch opened, they could feel the sultry night air.

The ramshackle bridge was pitch-black, but both men were so familiar with their ship they didn't need light to make their way aft to a set of stairs that would take them to the main deck. Outside, the stars shone with particular brilliance because the sliver of moon had yet to rise.

Over the port rail, the inky water began to grow agitated as the three-hundred-and-fifty-foot submarine neared the surface. Her conning tower appeared first, and then the vessel seemed to grow as she shed water, fore deck and long aft deck emerging, as well as her stiletto rudder. She came up on an even keel so slowly that there were hardly any waves. She rode low in the water, menacing in her silence, like a sea monster basking on the surface.

Juan had a handheld walkie-talkie and brought it to his lips. "Mr. Stone, ballast us down about fifteen feet. I want our decks to be lined up a little closer."

Eric acknowledged, and a moment later the pumps that filled the tanks spooled up and the *Oregon* began to settle deeper in the water.

"Deck crew, get those fenders over the sides." Juan's order was met with a frenzy of activity, as men lowered thick rubber bumpers down to just above the waterline. Unlike the old truck tires they used in port partly as disguise, these were modern cushions, and could take a tremendous amount of pressure before failing.

Over on the *Tallahassee*, part of her deck just fore of her sail began to articulate upward, emitting the faint red glow of battle lights. This was the loading port for the twenty-four Mk 48 ADCAP torpedoes the boat could carry. For this mission, she was carrying less than a full complement of the Advanced Capability weapons in order to accept the Iranian rocket torpedo, which was sitting on the *Oregon*'s deck on a wheeled trolley. The cases of captured computer information were secured to the torpedo.

Cabrillo keyed his walkie-talkie again. "Okay, Helm, shove us over using the thrusters, twenty-five percent power."

"Twenty-five, aye."

The *Oregon* began to move toward the waiting submarine, creeping slowly enough to let the water she was pushing dissipate rather than rock the *Tallahassee*. Several officers watched from the sub's conning tower, using night vision binoculars.

"Ease off, Mr. Stone," Juan ordered, judging distance and speed with an expert eye. The ships were less than twenty feet apart. "Very good, now, ten percent opposite side."

Water frothed at the thruster ports as Eric used them to stop the ship with only ten feet separating them from the submarine.

"Hold us here, if you please," Juan said over the scrambled channel.

"Nice piece of ship handling," a voice boomed from the *Tallahassee*'s conning tower.

"Thank you," Juan called back. "Are you ready to receive the package?"

"I was led to believe there were two packages," the sub's captain shouted.

"Slight change of plans, following a dustup this morning in the Sea of Oman."

"How'd it work?"

"Believe it or not, flawlessly."

"Very well. We're ready. Our satellite window closes in four minutes forty seconds."

Juan turned to the technician waiting next to the derrick controls. Though the crane looked like it was ready to topple at any moment, it was rated to lift seventy tons. Slack was taken up, and the sling cradling the rocket torpedo rose off the deck. Other men were standing by with guide ropes to prevent the weapon from spinning as it was lifted clear of the railing. The long boom rotated on its axis to swing out over the waiting submarine, where sailors stood by to receive the torpedo.

One of the sailors guided the lift using universal hand gestures, rotating his finger downward to call for more cable as the weapon came down into their waiting hands. They locked it into the boat's autoloader and unstrapped it from the cradle. The lead sailor spun his hand over his head to indicate the torpedo was free and they could recover the crane. No sooner had it vanished into the hull than the large door began to close.

"Stow the derrick," Juan ordered, before calling down to Eric Stone: "Helm, edge us away, twenty percent power, and pump us dry. Make ship ready for a high-speed run, and steer us best possible course for Karachi."

"I thought we were going to Monaco." This from Mark Murphy. It was clear in his voice he was looking forward to a few weeks at the opulent principality abutting the Riviera. Maurice had told Juan that Murph had even requisitioned a tuxedo from the Magic Shop so he could play James Bond in Monaco's fabled casino.

"Don't worry," Juan assured him, "you are. Max and I have other plans."

Hali Kasim's voice cut through the line. "Radar contact, Chairman. Just came on the scope at a hundred miles out, bearing due east."

"Track it, and keep me posted." Juan cupped his hands to his mouth to shout over to the *Tallahassee*'s captain, as the *Oregon* put more and more distance between the two vessels. "We just got a blip on radar. It's east of us, and the range is pretty extreme, but you guys might want to do your Houdini act and vanish."

"Roger that, and thank you." The captain waved. "We saw her on our approach. The read from the passive sonar sounds as if she's derelict, and we caught nothing on any of our sensors, no radar emissions or radio. Not even an automatic distress signal. Obviously, we couldn't investigate, but you all might want to. If she's abandoned, it could mean a pretty hefty salvage fee."

"We might just do that," Juan said, intrigued. He could leave a prize crew on her to sail to Karachi while the *Oregon* went ahead. "Any idea how big she is?"

"By the sound of waves lapping against her hull, my chief

sonar man estimates about the same size as your ship, five hundred and fifty feet or so."

"Thanks for the tip, Captain. We might just check her out."

"Good luck, *Oregon*." With that, the last of the men disappeared down the conning tower hatchway.

Moments later, spray erupted around the sub's ballast tank inlets as seawater rushed in and expelled the air trapped inside. A gout of froth boiled at her stern as her reactor directed power to her single, seven-bladed screw. The tail planes sank below the calm ocean surface and a wave began to stream over her bows. She sank swiftly, vanishing into her natural realm, and leaving behind a bare ripple that quickly dissolved as though the massive boat had never existed.

"Rotten way to make a living." Max scowled. Though not exactly claustrophobic, Hanley wasn't fond of confined spaces.

"Linc has done a couple of stints on fast-attack subs in his SEAL days. Says they're nicer than a lot of the hotels he's stayed in."

"Linc's cheap. I've seen the places he goes for. Hourly-rates-available, clean-sheets-extra kind of joints."

Wind started to blow as the *Oregon* accelerated eastward. In a few minutes, the magnetohydrodynamics would have them going so fast that standing on the deck would be like facing into a hurricane. The deckhands had finished securing the crane boom, and the trolley had been returned to the torpedo room.

"What do you say, Max?"

"What do I say about what?"

"The derelict out there. Do we stop and take a quick look-see or hightail it to Karachi?"

Max led Cabrillo into the protection of a stairwell, where he could light his pipe. "Kyle's been missing since the day before yesterday. My ex thinks she knows who he's with—some group of friends she doesn't care for—which makes me think this isn't as big a deal as she's making it. It'll take us at least twenty-four hours to get to L.A., once we reach Pakistan, so losing an hour investigating a ghostship isn't going to matter much."

"You sure?" Juan asked, blinking rapidly because hot ash from Max's pipe whipped across his face.

"Sorry." Max tapped the pipe over the side. "Yeah. It'll be fine."

"Eric, you read me?" Juan asked into the walkie-talkie.

"Right here."

"New course. Get us over to that ship at best possible speed. Track down Gomez and have him prep the Robinson." George "Gomez" Adams was a matinee-idol-handsome chopper pilot who'd gotten his nickname after using his charms on a South American drug lord's wife, a woman who bore a striking resemblance to Carolyn Jones, the actress from the old *Addams Family* television show. "Tell him I want a UAV on the launch rail as soon as we're in position. If need be, you can fly it."

Eric couldn't fly a real plane to save his life but played enough flight simulator games to easily handle the *Oregon*'s remotely operated drones.

Cabrillo asked, "What's our ETA?"

"Little over two hours."

"Put yourself down for a bonus if you make it in two."

CHAPTER 7

By the light of the stars smeared across the night sky, she looked like a wedding cake, multiple tiers rising higher and higher, a delicate balance of form and function. Yet to the men and women in the Op Center studying the feed beamed back by the flying drone, she also looked like a ghostship.

Not a porthole was lit, nothing stirred on her deck, even the bar of her radar transmitter was stationary.

Cresting waves slapped against her long white hull, hitting her as if she were as immutable as an iceberg. Thermal imaging off the drone's IR camera showed that her engines and funnel were cold, and while the ambient air temperature in this part of the Indian Ocean hovered near the high eighties the gear was sensitive enough to detect body heat. They saw none.

"What the hell happened here?" Linda asked, knowing there couldn't possibly be an answer.

"Gomez, buzz the deck," Juan ordered.

George Adams sat at a workstation at the rear of the Op Center, his slicked-back and brilliantined hair shimmering in the dim neon glow of his computer. He ran a finger across his pencil mustache and eased the joystick forward. The UAV, nothing more than a commercial radio-controlled airplane fitted with powerful cameras and an extended transceiver, complied with his command, diving down toward the cruise ship lying dead in the water thirty miles east of the hard-charging *Oregon*.

The crew watched expectantly as the tiny aircraft arced out of the sky and ran along the ship's starboard rail, the camera tracking along her deck. For several long seconds, it was quiet in the room, each person absorbed with what they were seeing. It was Cabrillo who finally broke the silence.

He keyed his communications pad. "Medical to the Op Center. Hux, we need you now!"

"Are those what I think they are?" Eric Stone asked in a hushed whisper.

"Aye, lad," Max replied, equally subdued. "Her deck's littered with bodies."

There had to be a hundred corpses on the deck, sprawled in twisted shapes of agony. Their clothing fluttered with the breeze. Adams zoomed in on the open deck around the ship's swimming pool, where it seemed as if every guest at a party had simply collapsed, the area was strewn with dropped dishes and glasses. He tightened the camera's focus as he slowed the UAV to narrow in on one passenger, a young woman in a dress. She lay in a pool of her own blood. It looked as though everyone was.

"Did anyone notice the ship's name?" Mark Murphy asked.

"Golden Dawn," Juan told him, all thoughts of salvage and prize money driven from his mind.

Mark concentrated on his computer, calling up everything he could get about the ship as the others stared transfixed at the grisly tableau.

Julia Huxley rushed into the Op Center wearing pajama bottoms and an oversized T-shirt. Her feet were bare and her hair was a gnarled mess. She carried a medical case that she kept in her stateroom. "What's the emergency?" she asked breathlessly.

When no one answered, she looked up at the screen holding their attention. Even for a seasoned medical professional, the carnage arrayed around the deck of the cruise ship was appalling. She visibly blanched, before composing herself with a subtle shake of her head. She approached the monitor and cast a critical eye at what she saw. The low light and unsteady UAV made it difficult to discern details.

"It doesn't appear to be trauma," she said. "I'd say they were struck by some kind of fast-acting hemorrhagic virus."

"Natural?" Max asked.

"Nothing in nature strikes this swiftly."

"They didn't have the time to send out a distress signal," Juan remarked, to back up Hux's assessment.

Julia turned to him. "I need to get over there. Take some samples. There is biohazard gear in the medical bay, and we can set up a contamination station on deck."

"Forget it," Juan said. "There's no way I'm letting you get some virus anywhere near this ship." Julia made to argue but Cabrillo wasn't finished. "We'll do decon on a tethered Zodiac inflatable and then sink it. Eric, take over the UAV from George. Gomez, get down to the hangar and finish prepping the chopper. Mark, go roust Eddie, get yourselves a couple of pistols from the armory, and meet us in the hangar. Julia, do you need a hand?"

"I'll get an orderly to help me," she said.

"Okay. Bring a couple extra bio-suits in case there are any survivors." Cabrillo was already on his feet. "I want to be in the air in twenty minutes."

The *Oregon* reached the stricken *Golden Dawn* a minute short of Juan's deadline. Because of the Robinson's weight limitations, it would take two trips to ferry everyone and their equipment to the cruise ship. Eric had scouted the liner from the drone and determined the best place for them to land was on top of the bridge. It was the largest area on the ship that was free of the dead. Though the chopper wouldn't land directly on the *Dawn*, George Adams was kitted out with a rebreathing orange biohazard suit like the rest of them, and two of Julia's staff were prepping a hose on deck, fed from a tank of powerful bleach concentrate, to disinfect the chopper prior to its touching back down.

Juan was taking no chances. The crewmen who would tow the Zodiac over with the ship's SEAL assault boat would go through a similar drill. Because whatever agent had wiped out the passengers and crew of the *Golden Dawn* wasn't natural, he knew they were looking at a case of intentional terrorism and murder on a mass scale. He was concerned not only about the virus itself but was already thinking ahead to the people responsible.

He held out his hands to Julia so she could duct-tape where the suit's tall gloves meshed with the sleeves. She then secured the back zipper with more of the silver tape. The airflow off his tank was steady, and the carbon scrubbers were activated. He had three hours before he needed to be out of the suit.

"Move slowly and deliberately," Julia was telling them over the integrated communications net as she worked. "Plan out everything before you do it. Avoid running. These suits are your life. If the pathogen is airborne, a tiny tear could leave you exposed."

"What happens if I do rip the suit?" Mark asked. His voice quavered.

Murph had been on a few shore operations, but he was clearly uncomfortable going over to the *Dawn*. Cabrillo wanted him with them to check the cruise ship's computers and learn exactly where she had been in the past few weeks.

"I'm going to leave extra lengths of tape on all of your suits. If you get a rip, tape it up immediately and contact me. The suits have a positive air pressure, so, if you're quick, you should be okay. Don't move from where you are, because I will need to examine whatever it is that cut you."

She worked on Eddie next, looking over every square inch of the rubberized fabric before taping the seams. He, Mark, and Cabrillo had gun belts slung around their waists. The protective gloves made working the triggers difficult, but there was no way Juan would let them go over unarmed.

"Any time, Chairman," George said from the Robinson's open cockpit door. A stack of gear was on one of the nimble little helicopter's backseats.

Juan tried to shout at a nearby technician but couldn't be heard through the hazmat suit. He strode over and hit the button that would activate the hangar elevator. Overhead, the two sections of rear deck hatch folded open as the lift eased upward on four hydraulic rams. He secured the helo's back door once Julia was inside and swung around to the copilot's seat.

Eddie and Murph backed away to give George some room before he fired the engine. After warming up the helicopter for a couple of minutes, he engaged the transmission to start the main rotor turning. The Robinson bucked and wobbled, as the blades built speed, until it had generated enough force to lift them free.

The ride stabilized as he brought the chopper up vertically

and then peeled away from the *Oregon*. There was a half mile
of open ocean separating the two ships. Below, Juan spotted
the wake of the SEAL boat and the little Zodiac bobbing behind it. There was a large loading door just above the *Golden
Dawn*'s waterline used when the cruise ship was being provi-
sioned. They would tie off the Zodiac there and return for
their bleach shower.

The *Dawn* had beautiful lines, Cabrillo thought as they
approached. She was slightly shorter than his ship, but with
seven decks of cabins and suites she was much taller. Her bow
had a nice racy curve to it, and she had a classic champagne-
glass fantail. Her single funnel, just aft of the pool, was raked
back, giving the impression that she was cutting through the
water. As the Robinson crossed over the *Dawn*'s stern, Juan
could just make out the Golden Cruise Lines' logo, a cascade
of gold coins, on the smokestack.

Adams brought the Robinson to a hover over the wheelhouse, making sure he had enough room to stay well away
from the mass of antennas and radar dishes. The confining
suit couldn't diminish his skills as a pilot. He lowered the
chopper to within two feet of the deck and kept it there as
though it were tethered.

"Good luck," he said as Juan threw open his door and
jumped clear, instinctively ducking low.

Julia opened her own door and handed out the crates of
medical gear, the rotor downwash rippling her suit. Juan set
each on the deck and caught Julia as she jumped free. He
closed the door and slapped the chopper's flank. Adams instantly lifted away to get Murph and Eddie.

"I want to get down to the sick bay right away," Julia said
when the noise from the Robinson faded enough to use the
radios.

"No. We're going to wait here for George to come back. I
want Eddie with you at all times while you're looking
around."

Julia knew Juan was right. He wasn't being protective because she was a woman. He was being protective because she
was the only doctor within a thousand miles. If something
happened to them while they were out here, it would fall to
her to find a cure.

The helo returned in less than ten minutes, her underside still wet from being hosed with bleach. Juan and Julia positioned themselves on the stairwell down to the flying bridge to give George room. Eddie and Mark jumped simultaneously from the chopper, and Gomez took off again. This time, the Robinson would be thoroughly scrubbed down, and left on deck in case the boarding team got into trouble.

"How you doing, Mark?" Juan asked.

"Little creeped out. I'm starting to regret playing those video games about laboratory accidents that create armies of zombies."

"Want me to stay with you on the bridge for a few minutes?"

"I'll be okay." His tone indicated he wanted to accept the Chairman's offer, but pride was getting the best of him. Eric Stone and the rest of the team in the Op Center were listening in on their conversation, so there was no way he'd show any weakness.

"Good man. Where did you say the *Dawn* came from?"

"The Philippines," Murph said. "From the cruise line's database, I learned she's on a charter from Manila to Athens for some self-help group."

"Check her logs and computer memory. Find out if she's made any stops and, if so, where. Also, see if there's mention of anything unusual happening during her run. It should all be there. Julia, you know where to go and what you're looking for. Eddie, stay with her and give her any help she needs collecting her samples."

"Where are you going to be?" Eddie Seng asked.

"We've got three hours of air, so I'm going to search as much of the ship as I can." He clicked on one of the flashlights they had brought and made sure he had a couple of spare batteries in a pouch at his back.

Cabrillo led them down the stairs and onto the wing bridge. At the far end of the narrow promenade, hanging eighty feet above the ocean, was a set of controls for a harbor pilot to maneuver the cruise liner into port. The door that gave entry to the bridge was closed. Juan pulled it toward him and stepped into the high-tech room. With the power off and the batteries for the emergency lights apparently drained, the bridge was nearly pitch-black. Only the glow of the stars and moon shone through the big windows, rendering everything in murky shadow.

Juan played the beam of the light around. He spotted the first body in less than two seconds. Julia added her torch to the illumination as she moved past him. Mark had a video camera held up to his visor. The corpse wore the uniform of a ship's officer, white trousers, and a white shirt with dark shoulder boards. His head was turned away from the team, but even with the uncertain flashlight beams they could see the skin of his neck was a sickly shade of white. Julia knelt at his side and gently turned the body over. The man's face was smeared with blood, and his torso had been lying in a lake of it. Dr. Huxley performed a quick examination, grunting to herself with each discovery.

As she worked, Mark Murphy was searching for the backup electrical system, and, in a moment, several lights came up and a few computer monitors flickered to life. There were three other corpses on the bridge, two men in utility uniforms and a woman wearing a cocktail dress. Cabrillo surmised that she had been the guest of the officer who was showing off the bridge when they were struck by whatever pathogen had swept through the passengers and crew like wildfire. The other two crewmen had been standing watch.

"Well, Hux?" he asked before she had finished her grisly task.

"It's possible it was a gas attack of some sort, but with so many of the victims out on deck my money's on a new form of hemorrhagic fever, but more powerful than anything I've ever heard of."

"Like a super Ebola virus?" Eddie asked.

"Faster and more lethal. This has a hundred percent mortality. Ebola Zaire, the worst of the three strains, is about ninety percent. The blood isn't black, which leads me to believe it didn't pass into his gastrointestinal tract. Judging by the spray patterns, I'd almost say he coughed it all up. Same with the woman. However, there are other things at work here." She gently lifted the officer's arm. It was as rubbery as a tentacle. "The bones have decalcified to the point they have almost dissolved. I think I can press my finger into his skull."

"That's okay," Juan said before she gave a demonstration. "Any idea what we're dealing with?"

She stood and used a disinfecting wipe to clean her gloves. "Whatever it is, it's an engineered virus."

"You're sure?"

"Absolutely. For no other reason than this bug kills its host too quickly to be natural. Like any other living organism, viruses are biologically compelled to reproduce themselves as often as possible. By destroying its host in a matter of minutes, it doesn't have much time to transfer itself from one person to the next. An outbreak of this stuff in the real world would die out as quickly as it flared up. Even Ebola takes a couple of weeks to kill its victims, leaving enough time for family members and neighbors to catch it. Natural selection would have killed off this bug a long time ago." She looked him in the eye, so there was no mistaking her meaning in the next sentence. "Someone made it in a lab and unleashed it on board this ship."

Juan was torn by pity for the poor men and women who were on the *Golden Dawn* when the virus was set free and rage at those who perpetrated the attack. It was the fury in his voice that carried the strongest over the radio. "Find what you need to nail them, Hux."

"Yes, sir." His tone compelled her to salute, even though such actions were almost unheard of for the crew of the *Oregon*.

Juan turned on his heel and strode aft through a doorway leading into the ship.

The hallway beyond was thankfully empty, and the cabins he peered into were vacant. Judging by the dress of the young woman on the bridge and the other passengers they'd observed from the UAV and chopper ride in, he assumed there had been a large party under way and that most cabins would be empty. When he finished his sweep of the officers' accommodations, he opened another door that led into what the cruise industry called the hotel section of the ship. Though not as opulent as some modern cruise vessels, the *Golden Dawn* sported her fair share of polished brass and plush carpets, done in accents of pink and teal. The sound of his own breathing was all he heard as he reached a balcony overlooking an atrium that sank four decks to a marble floor. Without lights, the towering foyer was like a dingy cave. The flashlight beam momentarily flashed off the windows of specialty boutiques down below, making Juan think he'd seen movement.

He was jumpy and took a deep breath to calm himself. There were bodies strewn all around the atrium, each of them settled in a repose of agony. Some lay on the staircases as if they'd sat themselves down to await death's embrace while others had simply collapsed where they were. As he circled down the wide steps that ringed the foyer, Cabrillo saw where a six-piece orchestra had been. Five of the tuxedoed musicians had simply fallen over their instruments, while only one had tried to get away. He'd made it less than a dozen feet from his bandmates before he had succumbed to the virus.

There were hundreds of stories to tell from the dead: a man and woman clinging to each other as they died, a waitress who'd taken the time to set her tray of drinks on a side table outside a bar before she fell, a group of young women still close enough to each other for him to tell they were getting their picture taken, though there was no sign of the photographer, just his expensive camera lying in pieces on the floor. He couldn't see inside the glass-enclosed elevator that linked the decks because the panes were painted with blood.

Juan continued on. The hazmat suit and recycled air could protect him from the environment, but nothing could shield him from the horror. He had never seen mass murder on such a scale, and, if not for one hand curled around the flashlight and the other clutching a pistol, he knew they would be trembling uncontrollably.

"How's everyone doing?" he called over the communications net, more to hear a human voice than any need for a progress report.

"Eddie and I are en route to the ship's hospital," Julia replied. The transmission was garbled by interference from the ship's steel construction.

"I'm about to enter the engineering spaces. If you don't hear from me in thirty minutes, get Eddie to come find me."

"Copy that."

"Murph?"

"With just backup power, the computer's slower than my first PC on dial-up," Mark said. "It's going to take me a while to retrieve what we need."

"Keep on it. *Oregon*, do you read?"

"Affirmative," a voice replied. Static made it difficult to tell who it was, but Cabrillo assumed it was Max Hanley. Juan had never thought to upgrade the suite's radios from the ones that came standard from the manufacturer. A rare oversight he was paying for now.

"Anything on the scopes?"

"We're all alone, Juan."

"If anyone shows up, tell me right away."

"You got it."

The door in front of Juan was labeled CREW ONLY and was secured with an electronic lock. With the power out, the lock had automatically disengaged, so he pushed it inward and started down a corridor. Unlike the passenger spaces, decorated with wood paneling and elaborate lighting, this passage was painted a plain white with vinyl tiles on the floor and boxy fluorescent fixtures on the ceiling. Bundles of color-coded piping conduits ran along the walls. He passed small offices for stewards and pursers as well as a large dining hall for the crew. There were a half dozen more victims here, either slumped over tables or lying on the floor. As with all the others Juan had seen, he noted that they had coughed blood in copious amounts. Their final moments must have been excruciating.

He passed by one of the ship's gleaming kitchens, which now resembled a slaughterhouse, and an industrial-sized laundry room with twenty washing machines that looked as big as cement mixers. He was aware that certain ethnic groups dominated the service sectors of the cruise industry and wasn't surprised to see the laundry gang was Chinese. It might seem a racist stereotype, but, in this case, it was true.

He kept on, looking for and finally spotting a heavy door marked ENGINEERING/NO UNAUTHORIZED ADMITTANCE. Beyond the door was a small vestibule and a second soundproof hatch. He ducked through, and descended three flights of stairs, before emerging in an auxiliary room off the main engine room. His light revealed a pair of generators sitting side by side and banks of computer controls. A massive sliding door aft led to the engine room. Dominating the cavernous space were two huge engines, each the size of a commercial truck. He laid a hand on one engine block. It was stone cold. The *Golden Dawn* must have been without power for at least twelve hours for it to have cooled to the ambient air temperature. Overhead, the engines' exhaust pipes merged into a plenum and funnel that would rise all the way to the main smokestack.

Unlike the hundreds of other engine rooms Juan had been in, he didn't feel the palpable power, the sense of strength and endurance that these engines were capable of. Here, he felt nothing but the chill of a crypt. He knew if Max was with him, his engineer's pride would require him to refire the diesels, just to give them life again.

He tried his radio, calling to Hux, then Mark, and finally the *Oregon*, but interference returned nothing but static. Juan quickened his pace, training his light over the equipment for any sign of something out of the ordinary. He passed through another watertight door and found himself at the ship's sewage treatment plant. He moved on. Beyond was another set of idle generators and the *Dawn*'s desalinators. Using a technique called reverse osmosis, the water treatment system drew in seawater and extracted almost one hundred percent of the salt, rendering it safe enough to drink. This one machine provided water to the galleys, the laundry, and every bathroom aboard the vessel. Of the two places he could think to introduce a deadly virus and make certain it affected everyone aboard, this was number one. He would search for the second—the vessel's air-conditioning units—later.

Cabrillo spent ten minutes examining the desalinator, borrowing a tool kit from a nearby workbench to unbolt inspection ports and peer inside. He saw no evidence of tampering or recent maintenance. The bolts were all stiff, and the grease felt gritty, even through his protective gloves. There was nothing at all to indicate that a foreign object, like a bunch of vials of toxin, had been injected into the plant.

The explosion came without warning. It rumbled someplace aft of the engine room and sounded deeper within the ship. And even as the sound faded, another blast rocked the

Golden Dawn. Cabrillo stood, immediately trying to raise his team on the radio net, when a third explosive charge detonated.

One second, Juan was standing over the desalinator and, the next, he was halfway across the room, his back a flaming sheet of pain from being slammed into a bulkhead. He fell to the deck as another rumbling detonation hit the ship. The blast was well forward of his position, and, yet, he could feel the overpressure wave sluice through the engine room and press him to the floor. He staggered to his feet to retrieve his flashlight, which had been flung ten yards away. As soon as his fingers curled around the light, some sixth sense made him turn. There was motion behind him. Even without electricity, the ship's gravity-powered watertight doors functioned flawlessly. The thick metal plates began to slide down from the ceiling to cover the open hatchways.

A new sound struck the Chairman, and he whirled in time to see a wall of white water erupt from under the deck through grates that gave access to bilge spaces below the engine room.

A fourth explosion rocked the *Golden Dawn* and made the entire ship rattle.

As he ran for the descending watertight door, Juan knew that whoever had poisoned the passengers and crew had placed scuttling charges to hide the evidence of their crime. There was something significant in that, but now wasn't the time to worry about it.

The water welling up from below was already to his ankles when he ducked under the first door, with four feet to spare. Hampered by the protective suit, he ran as best he could across the next room, passing the sewage plant without a glance, his feet splashing through the rising water. His breathing wheezed in his ears and taxed the suit's filters.

The next door was already a mere two feet from slamming into the deck. Juan put on a burst of speed and dove flat, sliding through the water so it foamed over his faceplate. His helmet hit the bottom lip of the door. He twisted under it, pressing himself flat as he moved, wriggling to get by without ripping the suit. He could feel the weight of the door pressing down and he lurched as hard as he could, pulling his chest

and upper legs through. He tried to roll away, but the solid
gate continued to drop. In a desperate gamble, he cocked one
leg and wedged his foot between the door and the sill.

The door weighed at least a ton, so Cabrillo's artificial foot
delayed its descent for only a second but it bought him enough
time to yank his other leg clear.

The pulverized limb remained jammed under the door and
allowed a curtain of water to surge into the main engine room
unchecked. It also held Juan helplessly pinned, because, no
matter how he tried, he couldn't free the prosthesis.

Cabrillo was trapped in the engine room of a doomed ship,
and, no matter how he fiddled with his radio dials, he got
nothing but static.

CHAPTER 8

MAX HANLEY DIDN'T NEED HALI'S FRANTIC cry to tell him a series of explosions had struck the *Golden Dawn*. He could see the bursts of white water erupting in sequence along the cruise ship's side on the *Oregon's* main monitor. It looked like she'd been struck by torpedoes, but he knew that was impossible. The radar scopes were clear, and sonar would have detected the launches.

As the smoke cleared, Eric zoomed the low-light camera in on one of the damaged areas. The hole was easily big enough for a person to walk through, and seawater was cascading into the breach at a staggering rate. With four identical punctures along her waterline, there were too many compartments flooding to save the ship, especially without power going to her bilge pumps. He estimated that she would founder in less than an hour.

Max tapped his communications console. "George, get your butt back in the whirlybird and get over to the *Dawn*. A series of scuttling charges just went off, and our people are in trouble."

"Copy that," Gomez Adams replied instantly. "Do you want me to land over there?"

"Negative. Hover on standby and await further orders." Max changed channels. "*Oregon* to Cabrillo. Come in, Juan." Static filled the Op Center. Hali fine-tuned the transceiver, searching in vain for the Chairman's signal, but he couldn't find it. "Julia, are you there? Eddie?"

"I'm here," a voice suddenly boomed over the loudspeakers. It was Mark Murphy. He was still in the *Golden Dawn's* wheelhouse and had better reception. "What just happened? It sounded like explosions."

"It was," Max replied. "Someone's trying to sink the ship, and, from what we can tell over here, they're going to succeed."

"I've barely started on the downloads."

"Pack it in, son. Gomez is on his way to you. Hightail it out of there as soon as you can."

"What about Juan and the others?" Murph asked.

"Have you been able to reach them on the radio?"

"No. Juan cut out about twenty minutes ago when he went down to the engine room."

Hanley suppressed a curse. That was about the worst location to be when the explosives went off. "What about Eddie and Hux?"

"They fell off the net a couple minutes later. I'll tell you one thing, Max, the radios in these suits are getting upgraded as soon as we're back."

"We'll worry about that when the time comes," Max said, although he'd been thinking the exact same thing. He studied the image relayed to the monitor and saw that the *Dawn* was settling fast. Her lowest row of portholes was less than three feet from going under, and the ship had developed a slight list to starboard. If he sent Murph out to search for the rest of the team, there was a good chance the weapons specialist would become trapped in the vessel. She was sinking pretty evenly now, but he knew the ship could lurch downward at any second. He would just have to trust that the others would make their own way out.

"Mark," he called, "get aboard the chopper as soon as you're able. We'll have you stay on station, searching over the ship for when the rest reach the upper deck."

"Roger that, but I don't like it."

"Neither do I, lad, neither do I."

AFTER ONLY A QUICK GLANCE at a ship's schematic, Eddie Seng led Julia unerringly to the *Golden Dawn*'s small hospital, located on level DD, well below the main deck. With his help, she had gathered blood and tissue samples from a number of victims on the way.

"You're holding up pretty well for someone who isn't a

medico," Hux had told Eddie when she was working on the first of the victims.

"I've seen how Chinese interrogators leave their prisoners after extracting whatever information they think the person had," Eddie had said in an emotionless monotone. "After that, nothing much bothers me."

Julia knew of Seng's deep-cover forays into China on behalf of the CIA and didn't doubt he'd seen horrors far worse than anything she could imagine.

As she had suspected, there was a trail of bodies leading down the corridor toward the dispensary, men and women who had had just enough time after falling ill to go to the one place they thought they could find help. She took samples here as well, thinking that something in their physiology gave them a few minutes other victims had been denied by the pathogen. It could be an important clue at finding the cause of the outbreak, since she was holding little hope of finding any survivors.

The hospital door was open when they arrived. She stepped over a man wearing a tuxedo lying across the threshold and entered the windowless antechamber. Her flashlight revealed a pair of desks and some storage cabinets. On the walls were travel posters, a sign reminding everyone that handwashing was a crucial step in reducing infections aboard ship, and a plaque stating that Dr. Howard Passman had received his medical degree from the University of Leeds.

Julia played her light around the adjoining examination room and saw it was empty. A door at the far end of the office led to the patients' rooms, which were little more than curtained-off cubicles, each containing a bed and a simple nightstand. There were two more victims on the floor here, a young woman in a tight black dress and a middle-aged man wearing a bathrobe. Like all the rest, they were covered in their own blood.

"Think that's the doctor?" Eddie asked.

"That would be my guess. He was probably struck by the virus in his cabin and rushed here as fast as he could."

"Not fast enough."

"For this bug, no one is." Julia cocked her head. "Do you hear that?"

"In this suit, I can't hear anything but my own breathing."

"Sounds like a pump or something." She pulled back one of the curtains surrounding a bed. The blanket and sheets were crisp and flat.

She went to the next. On the floor next to the bed was a battery-powered oxygen machine like those used by people with respiratory problems. The clear-plastic lines snaked under the covers. Julia flashed her light over the bed. Someone was in it, with the blankets pulled up over their head.

She rushed forward. "We've got a live one!"

Huxley peeled back the blankets. A young woman was sound asleep, the air tubes feeding directly into her nostrils. Her dark hair was fanned over the pillow, framing a face with pale, delicate features. She was bone thin, with long arms and slender shoulders. Julia could see the outline of her clavicles through her T-shirt. Even in repose, she'd obviously gone through an ordeal that had taken its toll.

Her eyes fluttered open, and she screamed when she saw the two figures in space suits hovering over her bed.

"It's okay," Julia said. "I'm a doctor. We're here to rescue you."

Julia's muffled voice did little to calm the woman. Her blue eyes were wide with fear, and she backed up against the headboard, drawing the blankets over herself.

"My name is Julia. This is Eddie. We are going to get you out of here. What's your name?"

"Who . . . Who are you?" the young woman stammered.

"I'm a doctor from another ship. Do you know what happened?"

"Last night, there was a party."

When the woman didn't continue, Julia assumed that she was in shock. She turned to Seng. "Break out another hazmat suit. We can't take her off the supplemental oxygen until she's in it."

"Why's that?" Eddie asked, tearing open the hazmat suit's plastic wrap.

"I think it's why she survived and no one else did. The virus must be airborne. She wasn't breathing the ambient air but drawing oxygen from the hospital's oh-two system, and, when that went down, she started using this portable unit here."

Julia looked back at the girl. She estimated her age to be early twenties, either a passenger traveling with her family or a member of the crew. "Can you tell me your name, sweetie?"

"Jannike. Jannike Dahl. My friends call me Janni."

"May I call you Janni?" Julia asked, seating herself on the bed and holding the flashlight so Janni could see her face through her suit's faceplate. Jannike nodded. "Good. My name is Julia."

"You are American?"

Just as Julia opened her mouth to respond, a deep bass sound filled the room. "What was that?"

Eddie didn't have time to tell her it was an explosion before a second, closer blast echoed through the ship. Jannike screamed again and yanked the covers over her head.

"We have to go," Eddie said. "Now!"

Two more blasts rocked the *Golden Dawn*. One of them detonated a short distance from the ward, knocking Seng to the floor and forcing Julia to use her body to shield Jannike. A light fixture crashed from the ceiling, its fluorescent bulb shattering with a loud pop.

Eddie got to his feet. "Stay with the girl." He ran from the room.

"Janni, it's okay. We'll get you out," Julia said, and drew down the blankets again. Tears coursed down Jannike's smooth cheeks, and her lower lip quivered.

"What is happening?"

"My friend is checking it out. I need you to put this on." Julia held out the protective hazmat suit. "We have to do it very carefully, though, okay?"

"Am I sick?"

"I don't think so." Julia had no idea until she could run some tests, but there was no way she was going to tell the frightened girl that.

"I have asthma," Janni told her. "That's why I was here in hospital. It was a bad attack that the doctor couldn't control."

"Has it passed?"

"I think so. I have not used my inhaler since . . ." Her voice trailed off.

"But you stayed on the oxygen?"

"I saw what happened to Dr. Passman and to my friend,

Karin. I thought maybe it was something they had breathed, so I kept using it."

"You are a brave and resourceful girl. I think you saved your life by doing that."

Knowing she had done something to help herself gave Jannike a bit of confidence, and hope that she would get off the ship alive.

Eddie jogged back into the room. "The blast wrecked the hallway about twenty yards from here. We can't go back up the way we came."

"Is there another way?"

"We better hope so. I can hear the lower part of the ship flooding."

WATER SURGED UNDER the jammed door like a rising tide, and, if not for the protection of his hazmat suit, with its own air supply, Cabrillo would have drowned. After a few minutes struggling again to free his crushed prosthesis, he lay back and let the sea roar over him, as it rapidly filled the main engine room. The swell was already a foot and a half deep, and rising by the second.

Juan's only consolation was that the rest of his team hadn't ventured this deep into the *Golden Dawn* and would be able to escape relatively easily.

During his earlier examination of the engineering spaces, he hadn't seen any victims of the virus, or whatever had been unleashed on the ship, telling him that the vessel had been running on automated mode, with just two men on the bridge and no one down here to monitor the power plants. With no one to infect, he wondered, how long would the pathogen remain in the air? Hux might have an idea, but this was a new virus, even for her, so, at best, she could make only a calculated guess.

The air conditioners had been shut down for a while, letting dust and microbes settle. Had enough time elapsed? Cabrillo could only hope so, because he knew that by lying in the torrent of rising water and thinking about it, he was just putting off the inevitable.

He worried his right arm free of his sleeve and snaked it

down across his chest to his right leg. He took a handful of cloth from the bottom of his pants and yanked it upward over his artificial limb, giving him access to the straps that held it in place. With practiced fingers, he released the straps and popped the slight vacuum seal that held the leg to his stump. He felt an immediate measure of freedom after detaching the limb, although his suit remained pinned beneath the door.

Now for the hard part. Juan reached over his shoulder to crank up the airflow in his suit and felt it balloon out against its seams. He carried three things on him at all times. One was a cigarette lighter, although all he smoked was an occasional cigar; the other two were a compass, no bigger than a button, and a folding knife. He pulled the knife from his pocket and opened the blade with one hand. He had to lie in a fetal position to reach as far down his pant leg as he could, fighting the weight of water still pouring in from under the door.

The knife was as sharp as a scalpel and sliced though the protective hazmat suit with ease. Air began to gush from the slit, and, for a moment, was able to hold back the force of water trying to exploit the cut, but the suit soon began to fill. Juan worked faster, slicing through the material in a race to free himself before he was overwhelmed by the flood. He was lying on his side, and the water pressed against his face forced him to turn his head and try to raise himself a couple of inches without losing track of where he was cutting the suit.

His new position was too awkward to allow him to work efficiently, so he took a deep breath and lay flat again, torquing the blade around his calf, to keep cutting away the trapped suit material. His lungs screamed for air, but he ignored his body's needs, working with preternatural calm despite the danger. He tried yanking himself free, but the tough plastic cloth wouldn't tear. He tried again with the same results. Now he had to breathe, so he heaved himself upright to clear his helmet of water, but there was too much pressure. The helmet wouldn't drain.

Cabrillo's lungs convulsed, allowing a trickle of bubbles to escape his lips. It was like suppressing a cough, and the corresponding pain in his chest was an unnecessary reminder that his brain was starving for oxygen. He was already becoming light-headed. He pulled savagely at the suit and felt it tear slightly, but it wouldn't give completely. Juan tried to force himself to calm down, but survival instincts were overwhelming any sense of logic. He bent down yet again to work the knife, though this time he hacked at the suit in a frenzy, all the while pulling against it with his last bit of strength.

Without warning, he tumbled back. Either he had completely cut away the boot portion of his suit or it had ripped. He rolled onto his knees and pushed himself from the floor, feeling the water drain from the suit through the rent in its fabric. Fearful of exposing himself to anything, he allowed himself only a tiny sip of air, barely enough to clear the creeping shadows that filled his mind.

He stood, letting the rest of the water that had filled his suit to sluice down his body and out. With seawater surging under the door, Juan couldn't stand steady on one leg, so he hopped a couple of feet to a workbench. Leaning against it, he quickly tied off the shredded remains of the suit, making the tightest knots he could. He dialed down the airflow when the suit became rigid. He was sure a little would leak through the cut, but, with positive pressure on the inside, he didn't think anything could enter. In all, his exposure had been nominal, and having spent nearly all of his exposure time under water he was confident that he would be okay.

That was until he remembered he was trapped in a sinking ship, with no way out and no way to communicate with his team or the *Oregon*.

He groped blindly through the darkness with his hands held in front of him, using his sense of touch to locate his position within the cavernous engine room. Without his artificial leg, movement was clumsy and difficult, but he finally found another workbench he'd seen earlier. He opened drawers and felt around, identifying tools by feel, until he found what he had hoped would be there.

The flashlight wasn't as powerful as the one he'd lost, but its beam gave him a mental lift. At least now he wasn't blind. He hopped across the engine room, hampered by the rising floodwater that reached his knees. He passed the twin diesels and reached the far watertight door. This one was down securely. He searched for a manual release that would allow him to open it, but there was no such mechanism.

He felt the first tentacles of panic tickling the back of his mind and crushed them down savagely. Not knowing the extent of damage done to the ship by the scuttling charges, he didn't know how long the *Golden Dawn* would stay afloat. If she remained stable, like she was now, it would take a couple of hours for the engine room to fill, more than enough time to think up an alternative escape route or for Eddie and the others to find a way to rescue him.

No sooner had that thought occurred to him than a prolonged moan reverberated through the hull, a rending of metal pushed past its stress point. He physically felt the ship lurch toward the bow. The water in the engine room sloshed in a titanic wave that crashed against the far door. It rushed back, and Juan had to leap onto a table to keep from being crushed against a bulkhead. He shone his light across the room and could tell that the rate of water bubbling up from the forward part of the ship had doubled. Seawater fountained from under the door in angry geysers, as if the ocean were eager to claim its latest victim.

Cabrillo's hours had just turned into minutes.

He flashed the light around, looking for any way out of the sealed room. The seed of a crazy idea struck him, and he turned the beam to one of the massive engines and the ducts rising from it. The light slowly drifted upward, his eyes following. "Aha!"

JULIA TURNED TO JANNIKE DAHL, keeping her voice as soothing as she could. "Janni, sweetheart, we have to get you out of here, but, in order to do that, you need to put on a protective suit like the ones Eddie and I are wearing."

"The boat is sinking?" she asked.

"Yes, it is. We have to go."

Julia turned on the suit's battery-powered fans and scrubbers and unzipped the back. She didn't tell Janni that the garment wasn't for her protection but rather for the crew of the *Oregon*, in case she was already infected. Making sure to keep the air flowing through the tubes in her nose, Janni slid her coltish legs into the hazmat suit and shrugged it over her narrow shoulders. Julia helped tuck her long hair into the helmet. Hux could tell it hadn't been washed in several days. Jannike's asthma attack had kept her in the infirmary for a while.

"Take a deep breath through your nose and hold it for as long as you can," she ordered.

Janni's chest expanded as she drew the pure oxygen into her lungs. Julia unhooked the cannula from around Janni's ears and tossed the tubing aside. She pulled the two halves of the suit closed and zipped it up. It took her another minute to secure the seams with duct tape.

Hux had to give Eddie Seng credit. Despite the urgency, he showed not the slightest sign of impatience. He understood that the young woman was bordering on catatonic shock and needed to be treated as though she were a child. Considering what Janni had been through, Julia thought she was doing fine.

When Eddie had returned from his brief exploration, he'd taken a moment to drape sheets over the two bodies outside Janni's cubicle. The girl still stared at the shrouded figures as Julia led her past. The three reached the hallway where nothing could have been done about the multitude of corpses. Julia felt Janni's hand stiffen in hers, but, to Janni's credit, she stayed with them. In Hux's other hand, she carried her sample case.

"That way is blocked," Eddie said, jerking a thumb in the direction they had come. "Janni, is there another way to reach the main deck from here?"

"This hallway just stops." She made sure to look him in the face so as not to stare at the dead. "But there is a metal door at the end I have heard the crew use to work on something down below. Maybe there is a way out."

"Perfect," Eddie said. "Must be an auxiliary access hatch."

Following the beam of his flashlight, they threaded their way down the corridor and, as Janni had said, there was a large oval hatch embedded in the bare steel wall. Eddie undogged the lock and peered inside. He was confronted with a tangle of pipework that took him a moment to decipher. "This is the pump room for the main swimming pool. The water is dropped down here for filtering, then sent back up."

The ship suddenly creaked, as though her hull were splitting, and the *Golden Dawn* lurched, nearly knocking Jannike to the floor. Julia steadied her as she and Eddie exchanged a glance. Time was running out.

Eddie went through the open hatch and looked for another way out. There was a second hatch on the floor, surrounded by a metal railing. He dropped to a knee to free the locks and heaved the door open against its protesting hinges. A ladder dropped into the darkness. He descended as best he could, the hazmat suit making the narrow space difficult to negotiate. He was in another mechanical room ringed with electronics cabinets. It was a distribution node for the ship's electric supply and, normally, would have been buzzing with current. Now the room was silent. An open door gave way to another darkened hallway.

"Come on down," he shouted, and waited at the base of the ladder to guide Janni the last couple of rungs. Though Eddie was of below-average height, he felt he could encircle the girl's waist with his hands, even with her suit bulking her up like a snowman.

Julia descended a second later, and Eddie led them out of the room. He asked Jannike, "Do you recognize where we are?"

"I'm not sure," she replied after peering into the gloom. "Many parts of the ship are off-limits to the hotel staff, and I have not been on board for that long."

"It's okay," Eddie said reassuringly, sensing her frustration at not being more helpful.

With the *Dawn* settling bow first, Eddie turned aft. He could feel a slight strain in his thighs that was telling him he was climbing uphill. The angle was mild, but he knew it would grow steeper as more compartments flooded.

Because of his suit, he never felt the breeze that suddenly came from behind him. It was the tremor in the deck plates below his feet that told him to turn. A wall of water barreled down the hallway at the level of his thighs, a solid green mass that struck them before he could shout a warning. Caught in the maelstrom, the trio was borne along the crest of the wave, tumbling helplessly, until the swell's momentum slowly petered out. They were dropped to the deck, a tangle of limbs, as the sea continued to flow around them.

Eddie was the first on his feet, and he helped Janni stand. "Are you all right?"

"I think so."

"Doc, you okay?" he asked.

"Just a little rattled. What happened?"

"A bulkhead must have failed close to the bow and let the wave through. We still have some time."

They continued on, sloshing through the ankle-deep water. Eddie checked the stencils on each of the doors they passed, hoping to find one marked stairwell, but luck wasn't with them. Down here were rooms for dry storage and storage for spare parts. An I-beam track along the ceiling allowed the crew to use winches to move heavy equipment from there to the nearest elevator. He thought that could make an alternate plan if they didn't find stairs. He had no doubt he could climb up an elevator shaft, Hux most likely, too, but he didn't think Jannike had the strength. If not for the suit, maybe he could have her cling to his back while he made the ascent. It was something to consider.

He almost missed a door to his right and had to stop to play the light across the stencil: WATERCRAFT STORAGE.

"Bingo!"

"What is it?"

"Our ticket out of here," Eddie said, and pushed open the door.

By the light of his torch, he could see a line of gleaming Jet Skis and two-person runabout boats. They were resting on specially designed cradles. There was a large hole in the ceiling the boats could be lifted through and a set of circular stairs leading up to the next level. He climbed, with the others in tow.

This was where passengers could rent one of the personal watercraft when the cruise ship was in port. There was a registration counter along one wall, and posters everywhere with safety reminders. The floor was covered in a nonskid indoor/outdoor carpet, and on the outside bulkhead was a door sized like that of a suburban garage. A hydraulically controlled ramp was folded along the door's length. When the door was open and the ramp deployed, it would act as a small dock.

Eddie tapped the steel door with the butt of his flashlight.

Rather than return a sharp echo, it rang with a dull thud. He tried higher up and finally got the results he wanted. "The ship's sunk to within two feet of the top of the door," he reported. "When I open it, this room is going to flood."

"Will we be able to get out," Janni asked breathlessly.

"No problem." Eddie smiled to reassure her. "Once the inside and outside pressure equalize, we'll be able to swim away. And the beauty of it is, our suits will keep us afloat."

"I'll go downstairs and close off the door we came through," Julia said, understanding that, in order for Eddie's plan to work, the boat garage had to be isolated from the rest of the ship or water would just keep pouring in.

"Thanks," Eddie said. He positioned Jannike away from the door and up against a railing so she could hold on as the room flooded.

The door was operated by a small electric winch but had a mechanical handle to crank it up or down in case power was ever lost. When Hux returned and was standing next to Janni to help hold her in place, Eddie bent and grabbed the handle. As soon as he put pressure on it, the door crept up a quarter inch and water started to enter the chamber in a flat rush. He was off to the side of the door but could still feel water sweeping by his lower legs as he cranked it higher.

The sea cascaded through the opening in the floor in a thundering waterfall.

Eddie had the door a quarter of the way open when the handle jammed. He pulled on it harder but couldn't get it to budge. He looked at the door and saw what had happened. The force of water pressing against it had buckled the metal near the bottom and popped the guide wheels off their tracks. Even as he watched, the door distorted further, bending in the middle, as though it were being shoved by a giant hand.

He shouted a warning to Janni and Julia that was lost in the roar of water as the door failed completely. It tore free from its mounts and was tossed across the room as though it were a piece of paper. Free of the constraint, the ocean exploded through the opening in a green wall.

Julia and Janni were far enough to the side to be spared the brunt of the onslaught, but, as the room instantly filled, they were pummeled by the back surge of water. Had it not been for Hux's presence, Jannike Dahl would have been lost in the tumult.

Shock waves continued to reverberate through the water, sending debris, including a Jet Ski, floating dangerously by. It was only when the water settled that Eddie was able to let go of the stanchion he'd been clutching. He immediately started floating for the ceiling. Like a cat in reverse, he flipped himself around as he sailed upward, to land on the roof on his hands and knees, his flashlight still gripped in his hand. He adjusted the airflow into the hazmat suit to reduce the pressure, and, thus, his buoyancy. Otherwise, he'd remain stuck to the ceiling and immobilized.

He worked the light to spot Julia and their young charge, hanging on to a railing with their feet pointing up, the air in the suits ballooning the fabric around their legs. He crawled over to them and gently touched Hux's leg, urging her to let go and float free. She did and rose up to join him. He did the same for Janni, and turned down the airflow from the tanks. He started crawling across to the open door but felt Julia resisting his help. She tapped him on the shoulder and pressed her visor to his.

"I lost the sample case," she shouted, the vibration of her voice transferring through the plastic so he could hear the words. "We have to find it."

Eddie looked at the mass of clutter swirling inside the garage: towels, life jackets, notebooks, bottles of sunscreen and water, coolers. It could take hours to find the case, and if it had been sucked back out the door it was already falling to the seafloor, some ten thousand feet below the ship.

"No time," he said back to her.

"Eddie, we need those tissue samples."

His answer was to take her hand and start toward the beckoning door.

The sudden influx of water that swamped the boat garage had shifted the *Golden Dawn*'s center of gravity, and the vessel began to list more heavily. The stresses on her hull were pushing to the breaking point, and, deep along her keel, the steel began to tear. The sound of her death knell echoed over the ocean, as haunting as a whale song or funeral dirge.

Julia and Eddie towed Jannike through the opening. As

soon as they were free of the ship, Eddie added air to his suit and shot for the surface.

Nearby, the *Oregon* was ablaze with lights. Searchlights pierced the darkness and roamed across the *Dawn*'s deck and along her waterline. The Zodiac inflatable that had been tied off near the garage bobbed nearby, its painter pulled taut and its bow submerged by the draw of the sinking cruise liner. As Eddie untied the line from an eyebolt welded to the ship's hull, one of the searchlights stabbing out from the *Oregon* swept past them and then returned, bathing them in a pool of incandescence. Julia and Jannike waved furiously. The light blinked in acknowledgment.

The Robinson helicopter swooped over from the far side of the cruise ship. George Adams held it steady over them long enough to see they were all right before moving off again to spare them the hurricane force of the rotor's downwash.

Eddie rolled over the Zodiac's side and hoisted Julia and Janni aboard. In seconds, he had the motor running and the little boat skipping across the waves toward the *Oregon*. The door over the tramp freighter's amidships boat garage was open and a team in protective gear was standing by with spray bottles of concentrated bleach solution to decontaminate their suits.

Eddie idled the Zodiac just off the ship. With the radios shorted by prolonged immersion in the water, he couldn't communicate with the orderlies, but everyone knew his duty. They threw over a couple of scrub brushes to the Zodiac and turned on the powerful jets of bleach. Eddie and Julia first scrubbed Jannike and then each other, making certain every square inch of their hazmat suits had been decontaminated thoroughly. Six inches of bleach sloshed across the Zodiac's floorboards before they were done.

When Julia was satisfied they had killed any infection that might be clinging to the suits, she ripped away the duct tape over the zipper and freed herself of the claustrophobic garment. The warm, humid air was the freshest she'd ever tasted. "God, that feels good."

"Amen to that," Eddie said, peeling off his suit and leaving it in the boat.

He guided a still-suited Jannike onto the Teflon-coated

ramp they used to launch the SEAL assault boat. Julia took charge of her. She would take her down to the medical bay and run a battery of tests in the isolation ward to determine if the young woman was infected. Only then would Janni be allowed to interact with the crew.

Max Hanley arrived just as Eddie was preparing to sink the Zodiac. His face told Eddie that everything hadn't gone as well for the others as it had for him and Julia. "What happened?"

"Mark is safe aboard the Robinson, but we lost contact with the Chairman."

"Damnit. I'm going back. He's someplace in the engineering section."

"Look for yourself." Max pointed to the sinking cruise ship. When her keel had split, the volume of water flooding her hull had quadrupled. "There isn't time."

"Max, it's the Chairman, for God's sake!"

"Don't you think I know that?" Hanley had a tenuous grip on his emotions.

Across the gulf of water, the *Golden Dawn* was in her final moments. The rows of portholes that ran along her length below her main deck were all submerged, and, with her back broken, she was settling deeper in the middle than at her bow or stern. The two men watched silently as the ship continued to disappear.

Air trapped within the hull started to vent explosively. Windows shattered and doors were torn from their hinges by the tremendous pressure. The sea washed over her railing and began to climb her upper decks amid erupting geysers of froth. From where they stood, it looked as though the *Golden Dawn* were surrounded by boiling water.

When the ocean reached the level of the *Dawn*'s bridge, it shattered the tempered glass. Debris started floating free of the hulk—deck chairs, mostly, but one of her lifeboats had also broken free of its davits and drifted away upside down.

Max wiped at his eyes when the top of the bridge vanished and all that remained above the water were the ship's communications masts and her funnel. Gushes of air roiled the surface as the sea consumed more and more of the vessel.

Eric Stone was in the Op Center, controlling the searchlights from the weapons station. He left the ship's most powerful light focused on the *Dawn*'s smokestack, outlining the gold coins painted on it. The sea bubbled like a thermal hot spring while the Robinson hovered overhead.

Max whispered Juan's name and crossed himself when the top of the funnel was a foot from disappearing completely. A blast of air suddenly belched from the stack, ejecting a yellow object as if from a cannon. It rose twenty feet, flapping in the air like a bird trying to take flight.

"Holy sh—" He couldn't believe what he was seeing.

The yellow object was one of their biohazard suits and the flapping was Cabrillo's arms windmilling and his legs bicycling. Juan's trajectory carried him from the smokestack and over the railing before he crashed back into the sea. The impact must have stunned him, because he lay still for a couple of seconds before starting to swim away from the sinking vessel. Eric tracked him with the searchlight as Juan swam to the overturned lifeboat. He heaved himself onto its back, faced the *Oregon* on his knees, and made a deep, theatrical bow.

Eric saluted him with a blast from the ship's horn.

CHAPTER 9

DR. HUXLEY WAS CONCENTRATING SO HARD THAT she didn't hear Mark Murphy and Eric Stone rush into the lab adjacent to the medical bay. Her mind was immersed in the minute realm revealed by her powerful microscope, and it wasn't until Murph cleared his throat that she looked up from her computer screen. There was a frown on her face from being disturbed, but seeing the two men's grins she thrust aside her irritation.

Behind them, her patient lay in isolation, shut off from the rest of the ship by a sterile glass enclosure whose air was pumped through sophisticated purifiers and into a thousand-degree furnace before being allowed to leave the ship. Juan slouched in a chair by Janni's bed, still wearing his yellow biohazard suit. Until Julia knew if his brief exposure to the water in the engine room had infected him with whatever pathogen had killed the men and women aboard the *Golden Dawn*, she had to treat him as though he were a carrier. Her microscope, with its potentially infectious samples, was also in the isolation ward, and she could view them only by either wearing a bulky suit or through a dedicated computer feed.

"What is it?" she asked.

"We ran the numbers," Murph said breathlessly. Like Julia, he had gone straight to work and wore the same sweaty clothes he'd had on underneath his discarded biohazard suit. His longish hair lay limp and oily against his scalp. "There's no way the Chairman or the girl are infected."

This time Julia didn't suppress her annoyance. "What are you talking about?"

He and Eric noticed Jannike Dahl for the first time.

"Whoa!" Stone said as he eyed the young woman asleep in the isolation ward, her black hair fanned out around her pale oval face. "What a babe!"

"Forget it, Stoney," Murphy said quickly. "I was in on her rescue, so I get to ask her out first."

"You didn't even leave the bridge," Stone protested. "I have as much right as you."

"Gentlemen," Julia said sharply. "Please check your under-exercised libidos at the door and tell me why exactly you are here."

"Oh, sorry, Doc," Murph said sheepishly, but not without a last glance at Janni. "Eric and I gamed the scenario, and we know that neither of them could have possibly been infected. We knew about twenty minutes ago about the Chairman's results, but the girl's numbers just came back."

"Do I need to remind you that this is about science—biology, in particular—and not some computer program spitting out mathematical gibberish?"

Both men looked hurt.

Eric said, "But you, most of all, should know all science is mathematics. Biology is nothing more than the application of organic chemistry, while chemistry is nothing more than ap-plied physics, using the strong and weak nuclear forces to cre-ate atoms. And physics is mathematics writ in the real world."

He spoke so earnestly that Julia knew her young patient had nothing to fear from him. Eric wasn't bad looking, but he was such a geek she couldn't imagine him screwing up enough courage to even talk to her. And behind Mark Murphy's skater-punk façade and scraggly beard beat the heart of the consummate computer nerd.

"Have you found any trace of a virus or toxin anywhere in the samples you've taken?" Murph asked.

"No," Hux admitted.

"And you won't, because neither was infected. The only way to kill an entire shipload of people without causing a mass panic, as some succumb quicker than others, is food poisoning." He held up his hand and ticked off his fingers as he made his case. "An airborne pathogen wouldn't hit people who were out on the decks when it was released. Poisoning the water supply is even less likely, because not everyone is going to drink at the same time, unless you hit first thing in the morning when people are brushing their teeth."

Eric interrupted. "People with weaker immune systems would have died throughout the day, and, as we saw, everyone was dressed to party."

"Same thing if a poison was applied to surfaces around the ship like handrails and doorknobs," Murph concluded. "The killer couldn't guarantee that they would get to everyone."

"So you think it was the food?" Julia asked, unable to find fault in their logic.

"Has to be. Juan didn't eat anything while he was on board, and I bet she didn't eat tonight either." Murphy jerked his head at the glass partition separating the lab from isolation.

"To be on the safe side," Eric said, "we also ran some numbers in case there was an airborne toxin trapped in the engine room. Even if the air was saturated, the volume of water pouring in when Juan cut his suit would have cut the viral load or toxicity levels down from parts per million to parts per hundreds of billions."

Murph crossed his arms. "Besides, it's been five hours since the Chairman's exposure. From what Eddie related about your brief interrogation of your patient aboard the ship, her friends visited her just an hour or two before they were hit. Juan and the hottie are fine."

Julia had already come to the same conclusion concerning Juan, but she wasn't convinced these two were right about Jannike. Diagnosis was about dogged research, checking and double-checking lab results, until you knew what you were faced with. Just because she hadn't found a virus in Janni's blood, spinal fluid, saliva, or urine didn't mean it wasn't lurking in her kidney or liver or some other tissue Julia hadn't tested yet, waiting silently to explode out and overwhelm Janni's immune system and then move on to its next potential victims, the *Oregon*'s crew.

She shook her head, "Sorry, boys, but that's not good enough for me. I think you're right about Juan, but Jannike stays in isolation until I am one hundred percent certain she isn't infected."

"You're the doctor, Doc, but it's a waste of time. She isn't."

"It's my time to waste, Mark." She pushed back on her wheeled lab stool and rolled across the tiled floor to an intercom mounted on the wall. She hit the button. "Juan, can you hear me?"

Inside the ward, Cabrillo jerked upright in the chair. Rather then dwell on the fact his body could be harboring a deadly infection, he'd fallen asleep. He stood and threw Julia a thumbs-up and then waved at Murph and Stone. He gathered up the spare batteries used to keep his hazmat suit functioning for so long.

"You're cleared," Julia said. "You can head into the air lock for a decontamination shower. Go ahead and leave the suit inside. I'll dispose of it later."

It took fifteen minutes to cycle the air lock to the isolation ward and for Juan to stand under a thundering shower of bleach and antiviral agents before it was safe for him to hop into the lab.

"Wow, you're a mite gamey," Julia said, wrinkling her nose.

"You spend that much time sweating in one of those damned suits and see how you smell."

Julia had already taken the precaution of having one of Cabrillo's artificial limbs sent down from his cabin. She handed it over, and he settled it onto the stump below his right knee. He gave it a few experimental flexes, then lowered his trouser cuff. "There," he said, standing. "Nothing a long shower and a good bottle of Scotch won't cure." He turned to Eric and Mark, who still crowded near the lab's entrance. "How'd you make out, Murph?" With his suit's radio damaged during the engine-room flood, the Chairman had been out of the loop since being brought aboard.

"I salvaged about thirty percent of the ship's computer archives, including everything about her last voyage." He held up a hand to forestall Cabrillo's next question. "I haven't gone through anything yet. Eric and I were helping figure out if you and that piece of eye candy in there had been infected."

Juan nodded, although he didn't think he and their guest should have been their top priority. "Going through those logs is now job one for you two. I want to know everything that took place aboard that ship since this voyage began. I don't care how trivial."

"I saw you talking to our patient earlier," Julia interrupted. "How is she doing?"

"Tired and scared," Juan replied. "She has no idea what happened to everyone, and I didn't really want to press the issue. Her emotional state is pretty fragile. She did tell me something that might be pertinent. The ship was on a charter for a group called the Responsivists."

"What's this about Responsivists?" This came from Max Hanley. He strode into the lab like a bull in a china shop. Before anyone could answer, he crossed to Juan and shook his hand. "Scuttlebutt around the ship says you were out of isolation. How are you doing?"

It never ceased to amaze Cabrillo how quickly information passed through the crew, even at—he glanced at his watch—four-thirty in the morning. "Glad to be alive," he said warmly.

"That was a hell of a thing." Max grinned. "Never seen anything like it in my life. You came out of that funnel like a cork out of a bottle of cheap champagne."

"I managed to climb almost to the top," Juan said. "But then I got jammed up. I couldn't budge, and the water was rising faster and faster. Rather than deflate my suit, I inflated it as far is it would go, to completely block the exhaust stack. Air forced up the funnel by the flooding in the engine room did the rest."

"Looked like one wild ride."

"How high did I go anyway?"

"At least twenty feet, and you cleared the rail by fifteen." Max then seemed to remember his original question. "You said something about Responsivists?"

"Yeah, Miss Dahl mentioned the ship was on a charter for them. From the Philippines to Athens."

"Piraeus, actually," Eric corrected automatically. "Athens is inland. Its port is the city of Piraeus."

Murph smacked him on the shoulder. "Do you honestly think we all don't know that?"

Julia couldn't suppress a smile, more certain than ever that neither of these paramour wannabes would get very far with Janni.

"I talked to my ex again," Max said. "This really wasn't a kidnapping at all. She said that to light a fire under my tail. Kyle has always been a follower—you know, someone easily swayed by peer pressure. He fell in with the wrong crowd in high school, and that's how he ended up busted for drugs. His rehab counselor told me Kyle doesn't have an addiction problem; he has a self-esteem problem. Anyway, he met up with this group at some demonstration and within a few days he declared himself a Responsivist. He even went so far as to see a urologist about a little snip-snip and is now in Greece. Apparently, they have some sort of compound on the Peloponnesian Peninsula."

"He had a vasectomy?" Julia asked. "He's only twenty-one or twenty-two. There aren't many doctors who will perform one on a man much before thirty unless he already has a family."

"Kyle's twenty-three, and the Responsivists have their own doctors that do nothing but vasectomies and tubal ligations all day long."

"I hadn't heard of Responsivists before Jannike mentioned them," Juan said.

"I don't know much myself," Max admitted. "Just what Lisa told me."

"You guys need to read more Hollywood gossip," Julia said. "Ever heard of Donna Sky?"

"The actress?" Mark asked.

"The highest-paid actress in history, as a matter of fact. She's a Responsivist. So are a lot of people in the film world. It's the newest thing in Hollywood."

"Is it a church or a cult or something?"

"No one is exactly sure. At least, no one on the outside," she replied. "It was started back in the seventies by a geneticist named Lydell Cooper. Cooper had been instrumental in developing cheaper drugs to fight malaria and smallpox. Some credit his work for saving hundreds of millions of lives.

"He didn't see it that way, at least not after a while, as he watched population explosions all over the globe. By eradicating diseases, he had helped remove one of the natural checks and balances in human population control. People weren't having more children, but more of the ones they had were living, and then more of *their* children were surviving, too. Without disease, he started to argue, humanity was doomed to extinction because of our swelling numbers.

"He wrote a book on the subject, and began to crusade for family planning on a global scale. He founded a group of like-minded people, the Responsivists, which comes from 'those who are responsible.' Soon, the movement was known as Responsivism, and it began to attract some big-name people from all walks of life, politicians, sports stars, actors and actresses. Cooper died about ten years ago, but the movement's flourished under a husband-and-wife team. I don't know their names, off the top of my head."

"What does this group do now?" Juan asked.

"They operate family-planning centers all over the world, providing free condoms, abortions, and reproductive surgeries to men and women. They've been in a long-running battle with the Catholic Church, as you can well imagine, and with everyone on the right side of the political spectrum."

Juan looked around the room. "Next question is, what have the Responsivists done to make someone wipe out a cruise ship full of its members?"

No one had an answer to that.

CHAPTER 10

THE CIRCLING PAPARAZZI HELICOPTERS WERE FOIL-ed by the snowy white tent erected over the manicured lawns of the Beverly Hills estate. The tent was easily twice the size of the nearby azure Olympic-sized swimming pool. When a Los Angeles County sheriff's Bell JetRanger appeared, as per their instructions, the two hired choppers took off before their tail numbers could be identified for later prosecution for encroaching on the no-fly zone. The pilots weren't going to risk arrest, no matter how much the photographers tried to bribe and then harangue them.

The pampered guests under the marquee were accustomed to such intrusions of their privacy and paid scant attention to the drama. The sound of the aircraft faded, and the buzz of conversation returned to its normal level. The band, on a raised wooden platform at one end of the tent, resumed play-ing, while toned starlets in skimpy bikinis, de rigueur for any Hollywood party, ventured back to cavort around the swim-ming pool.

The house looming over the expansive backyard was a faux Mediterranean villa encompassing nearly forty thousand square feet of living space, with a separate guesthouse twice the size of the average American home. The underground garage could accommodate twenty cars. Two multimillion-dollar properties had been bought and leveled to give the new owners what they wanted, and crews had worked nearly around the clock for three years to complete the walled com-pound. In a town accustomed to garish displays of wealth, the estate had sent chins wagging since it was first proposed.

The owners were Thomas and Heidi Severance. They

weren't actors, nor were they moguls in the film industry, although Thom Severance had worked as an executive at a studio for a couple of years. They were the benefactors and guardians of the estate of the late Dr. Lydell Cooper, the founder of Responsivism, and they now headed the growing institution. The money to build the house, which doubled as the group's California headquarters, had come from donors from all over the world, although the bulk had been raised among the Hollywood elite who flocked to Responsivism in ever-increasing numbers.

Thom Severance had been among the first to recognize the brilliance of Dr. Cooper's breakout book, *We're Breeding Ourselves to Death*, and had sought the author out to help spread the word. It was natural that Thom would find a kindred spirit in Cooper's daughter, Heidi. They were married after a two-month courtship, and it was their boundless energy that had grown Responsivism into the worldwide phenomena it was today. They had taken over, as Cooper had wanted, upon his death, and continued his work. Their charisma had especially attracted followers in the entertainment industry, and when Oscar-winning actress Donna Sky had admitted to the world she had been practicing Responsivism for many years, the group's popularity exploded.

Thom Severance stood at a solid six feet, with surgically enhanced features that gave him a commanding aura. He was fifty-three, yet his sandy hair had yet to thin and his eyes had lost none of their compelling appeal. The cream linen jacket he wore was cut too large for his frame, but rather than detract from his exercise-hewed body the effect made him look even more well muscled. When he laughed, which was often, his white teeth contrasted with the permanent tan he sported.

Heidi stood at his side. She was only a couple of years younger than Thom but looked to be in her late thirties. She was the quintessential California girl, with perfectly tinted blond hair, radiant blue eyes, and the figure of a professional athlete. Her neck was her greatest asset, long and graceful, and she took full advantage of it by wearing low-cut tops and necklaces laced with flawless diamonds.

Individually, Thom and Heidi were attractive people. Together, they made such a striking couple that it was little wonder they were always the center of attention. And no more so than here, at a Responsivist function, to celebrate the grand opening of their new headquarters.

"Congratulations, Thom," a famed director said, sidling up and kissing Heidi's burnished cheek with easy familiarity. "You, too, Heids. You should both be very proud of yourselves. I know Dr. Cooper would be." He spoke the name reverently. "Future generations will look back at this center as the place where the dark tides of overpopulation were finally pushed back."

"It will be a beacon of hope for the world," Heidi Severance replied. "As my father told us, the beginning of the struggle will be the most difficult. But as word spreads and people begin to understand what is at stake, ours will be seen as the responsible lifestyle."

"I read in *Generations* about the declining birthrates in the villages around our new clinic in Sierra Leone," the director went on. *Generations* was the group's biannual magazine.

Severance nodded. "Sited far from where Christian and Muslim missionaries have plied their trade and corrupted the people with their lies, we've done better than we hoped. We're getting the villagers to understand that preventing unwanted children raises their standard of living more than handouts and platitudes from churches."

"The article didn't say if we're explaining how our lives are influenced through intra-brane interference and how we can fight back against it."

This time, Thom shook his head. "The fact that an alien presence exists in a dimension of the universe parallel to our own isn't something we feel they can handle just yet. Our guiding philosophy will come a bit later. For now, we're just content to lower the regional birthrate."

The director accepted this, and saluted the couple with his highball glass, before drifting off into the crowd so the others in the throng hovering around the Severances could add their congratulations.

"He's a good man," Heidi whispered to her husband.

"His last film grossed over two hundred million, but his contributions over the past twelve months are down five percent."

"I'll talk to Tamara." Tamara was the director's new trophy wife and one of Heidi's protégées.

Thom didn't seem to hear as he was reaching into his jacket pocket for a vibrating cell phone. He folded it open, said his name, and listened for a minute without changing his facial expression. "Thank you," he said at last, and refolded the phone. He looked at Heidi. Her shining eyes and smile were brighter than the eleven-carat diamond at her throat. "That was Kovac," Thom said quietly, so no one else could hear. "A freighter just reported spotting wreckage floating in the Indian Ocean."

"Oh my God!"

"It was positively identified from a life raft as the *Golden Dawn*."

Heidi Severance's hand went to her neck as her skin grew flush.

"There were no survivors."

Her smile blossomed, and she gushed, "That is wonderful, simply wonderful."

Thom looked as though a great burden had been lifted from his shoulders. "A few weeks, darling, and everything we and your father have worked for will come to pass. The world will be reborn, and this time we won't screw it up."

"It will be reborn in our image," Heidi added, taking his hand. She gave no thought to the seven hundred and eighty-three men, women, and children who had perished on the cruise ship, many of them members of her organization. It was only a tiny fraction of the deaths to come.

CHAPTER 11

LESS THAN TWELVE HOURS AFTER REPORTING THE sinking of the *Golden Dawn*, admitting nothing about their foray aboard, Cabrillo and his team hadn't yet formed a cohesive plan, but they had a direction. That they were going to get to the bottom of this mystery was never in doubt.

The Corporation ran strictly as a for-profit enterprise, but they were guided by Juan Cabrillo's moral compass. There were jobs they wouldn't take, no matter how much money was offered. And then there were opportunities to do the right thing, regardless of profit. As he had done in the past when there was no chance of a payday, Juan had offered his crew the chance to leave the *Oregon* until the current mission was complete. He had no qualms putting himself in harm's way for the sake of what was right, but he would never demand it of his crew.

Like the few times before, not a single man or woman aboard ship had accepted the offer. They would follow Cabrillo to the gates of hell. As proud as he was of the technological marvel that was the *Oregon*, that feeling paled next to what he felt for his crew.

They might have been mercenaries, but they were also the finest people he had ever worked with. And while they had amassed a fortune over the years, it was the unspoken truth among all of them that they put themselves in harm's way again and again for the same reasons they had during their years of government service. They did it because the world grew more dangerous every day, and if no one else stood up to face it, they would.

The ship was charging hard northward, having cut through the choke point of Bab el Mandeb, or the Gate of Tears, that separated Yemen from the African nation of Djibouti. They were in the Red Sea, and Cabrillo had already called in enough favors with Atlas Marine Services, the Egyptian company that ran the Suez Canal, to see that his ship would be part of the next morning's only northbound convoy.

It would take eleven hours to transit the one hundred and one miles from Suez to Port Said, but once they were clear their final destination was only a day away.

With the number of vessels heading into and out of the Suez Canal, the shipping lanes in the Red Sea were heavily congested. So as not to arouse undue suspicion from passing ships, Juan had posted a watch on the bridge, even though the *Oregon* was being piloted from the Op Center belowdecks.

He was on the bridge now, overseeing preparations for taking on a canal pilot in the morning. Sandstorms raged in the western sky over Africa. The sun setting through burnt sienna clouds cast the bridge in an otherworldly glow. The temperature remained near eighty degrees, and wouldn't get much cooler when the sun did finally settle over the horizon.

"What a view," Dr. Huxley commented as she emerged from a secret doorway in the chart room at the back of the pilothouse. As she stared at the distant storm, the ruddy sky made her face glow like a Plains Indian's. The kind light helped hide her deep exhaustion.

"How's our patient doing?" Cabrillo asked, unfurling a dog-eared chart across an old, scarred table.

"She should be fine," Julia replied. "If she's still asymptomatic by morning, I'll let her out of isolation. How are you?"

"There was nothing wrong with me that a hot shower and some rack time couldn't cure." Juan used carpenters' C-clamps to secure the wrinkled map, as the clips built into the chart table had been intentionally snapped off to make the *Oregon* look as dilapidated as possible. When it came to camouflaging his ship's true nature, there were no details too small for Cabrillo's discerning eye. "Have you learned anything more about her experience?"

"Linda's compiling a report right now of everything we've gotten so far, not just my notes but the stuff Mark and Eric have been able to piece together, too. When I spoke with her, she said she should be ready in a half hour."

Juan glanced at his watch without really looking at the time. "I didn't expect anything definitive for a few more hours."

"Murph and Stone are more motivated than usual."

"Let me guess: they want to impress Miss Dahl with their sleuthing abilities?"

Julia nodded. "I've taken to calling them the Hardly Boys."

It took a moment for the joke to register, and Juan chuckled. "That works on so many levels."

When Julia smiled, her nose crinkled like a little girl's. "Thought you'd like that."

An ancient intercom mounted on a bulkhead squawked like an asthmatic parrot. "Chairman, it's Linda."

Juan mashed the TALK button with the heel of his hand. "Go ahead, Linda."

"I'm set up in the boardroom. Eric and Murph are here already. We're just waiting for you, Max, and Julia."

"Hux is with me," Cabrillo said. "Last I saw Max, he was in his cabin, arguing with his ex-wife again."

"I'll send Eric to go get him. I'm ready anytime."

"Be there in a minute." Juan turned to Julia Huxley. "Go ahead. I'll be right behind you."

She thrust her small hands into the pockets of her lab coat and stepped onto the elevator that would take her down to the Op Center, the most direct route to the boardroom.

Juan walked onto the bridge wing, the wind ruffling his light cotton shirt. He could taste the distant desert in the back of his throat as he drew a deep breath. Though drawn to the sea since he was a boy, the desert also held a similar fascination. Like the ocean, it was an element that was both inhospitable and indifferent, and yet, since time immemorial, men have ventured across it both for profit and exploration.

Had he been born in a different time and a different place, Cabrillo could see himself leading camel caravans across the trackless Sahara or through Saudi Arabia's Rub' al-Khali, the Great Empty Quarter. It was the mystery of what lay beyond the next wave, or the next dune, that drew him.

He didn't yet know where delving into the deaths on the *Golden Dawn* would lead. But the mass murder of hundreds of people was an injustice he couldn't let go unpunished. His crew had been working tirelessly on gathering background material, and, in a few minutes, they would have their plan. Once their strategy was set, it would be executed with military precision. It was what they did best. Standing at the rail, his hands gripping the hot iron, Juan could allow himself the last moments of unrestrained emotion. When the briefing began, he would direct his feelings, use them to drive himself onward, but for now he let them boil inside his skull—the rage, the rampaging anger at the senseless deaths.

The injustice of what had happened to those innocent people was like a cancer eating away at his guts, with the only cure being the utter annihilation of the killers. He had no sense of who they were, their image was lost in the fires of his fury, but the Corporation's investigation would quell those flames as they drew closer to their quarry, and bring the monsters into focus.

The knuckles of Juan's index fingers popped, and he relaxed his grip on the railing. The metal had scored lines across his palms. He shook blood back into his hands and took another deep breath. "Showtime."

The conference room was filled with the aroma of spicy food. With Africa such a short distance away, Maurice had laid out an Ethiopian meal. There was a stack of *injera*—unleavened sourdough bread—and dozens of sauces, some cold and others steaming hot. There were chicken, beef, and mutton stews, lentils and chickpeas, and spiced yogurt dishes. A diner eats the meal by tearing off a section of bread, ladling on some stew, and rolling it up like a cigar, to be chewed in a couple of quick bites. The affair could get messy, and Juan suspected Maurice had served these dishes intentionally for the comic relief of watching Linda Ross, a notorious chowhound, stuffing her face.

As a veteran of the Royal Navy, Maurice strongly believed in the English tradition of grog aboard ships, or, in this case, amber bottles of an Ethiopian honey wine called *tej*, whose sweet flavor could cut the strongest spices.

Cabrillo's brain trust—Max Hanley, Linda Ross, Eddie Seng, and Dr. Huxley, as well as Stoney and Murph—sat around the table. Juan knew that, down in the armory, Franklin Lincoln was holding a meeting of his own with the Ops team. Juan didn't have much of an appetite, so he charged his glass with the wine and took an appreciative sip. He let his people fill their plates, before calling the meeting to order by leaning forward in his seat.

"As you know, we are facing two different but possibly related problems. The first is rescuing Max's son from the Responsivist compound in Greece. Using satellite images and other information that Mark and Eric put together, Linc is working with his gundogs on a tactical assault plan. When they're finished, we'll go over it separately. What do we need to do on our end, once we've gotten Kyle?"

"Will he need to be deprogrammed?" Hux asked, wondering if Kyle would require specialized psychiatric help to break the mental grip Responsivism had on him.

"By all indications, yes," Mark replied.

"So they are a cult?" There was heaviness in Max's tone, sorrow that his directionless son had fallen in with such a group.

"They fit all classic parameters," Eric said. "They have charismatic leaders. Members are encouraged to sever relationships with friends and relatives who do not belong. They are expected to live by a certain code laid out in their founder's teachings, and when someone drifts away from the group other members will try to stop him."

"Stop them how?" Juan asked. "Physically?"

Eric nodded. "There are reports of lapsed members being abducted from their homes and transported to facilities run by the group for, uh, reeducation."

"We know about the compound in Greece," Juan said, looking around the burnished table. "And they replaced their old headquarters in California with that estate Murph showed me pictures of this afternoon. What else do they have?"

"More than fifty health clinics in some of the poorest third world countries in the world—Sierra Leone, Togo, Albania, Haiti, Bangladesh, Cambodia, Indonesia, the Philippines, and several in China—where they receive a lot of government support, as you can well imagine."

"That's an interesting case," Mark Murphy interjected, with his mouth half full of food. "The Chinese hate cults with a passion. They crack down on practitioners of Falun Gong all the time, seeing it as a threat to the central party rule, but they allow the Responsivists because of their whole population-control thing." Under a ragged denim shirt, Murph wore a T-shirt that had an arrow pointing up with I'M WITH STUPID below it.

"Beijing knows they could be a threat but are willing to risk it because the Responsivist presence gives a little Western legitimacy to their draconian one-family, one-child policy," Eddie said. Given his experience inside China, no one doubted his assessment.

"Back to helping Kyle," Juan said, to move the meeting along. "Have we been in touch with a deprogrammer?"

"We have," Linda Ross replied. "Technically, we are kidnapping Kyle, so we need to get him out of Greece as quickly as possible to avoid any problems with local police. The counselor will meet us in Rome. Tiny's repositioning the Gulfstream from the Riviera to the Athens airport to fly him to Italy. We have rooms reserved at a hotel near the Colosseum. The shrink's name is Adam Jenner. He specializes in helping former Responsivists return to a normal life, and, from everything we've been able to gather, he's the best in the world."

"Was he a member himself?" Juan asked, knowing it was common for deprogrammers to have once been held sway by the group they fight against, much like recovering alcoholics helping others overcome their addiction.

"No, but he's made it his life's mission to bring the group down. He's helped more than two hundred people escape Responsivism in the past ten years."

"And before that?"

"A private-practice therapist in L.A. Not that it matters, but his fee is fifty thousand dollars, plus expenses. He guarantees, however, that, when he's finished, Kyle will be back to normal."

"He damned well better be," Max grumbled.

"For someone to make their living deprogramming, the group must be pretty big," Eddie said. "How many members are there?"

"On their official website, they claim there are more than a hundred thousand worldwide," Linda replied. "Jenner's site said that that estimate is overblown by half. Either way, it's still a significant number. And with some high-profile Hollywood types jumping on the bandwagon, recruitment is up as people copy the stars."

"Just so I know in case I meet him, what cover story did we use in our approach of Jenner?" Juan asked.

"I have it all here in my report." Linda held up a binder. "Max is a real-estate developer from L.A. who wants to get his son back. We are the private security company he's hired to coordinate his return. Jenner's assistant was pretty nonplussed when I laid out our story, so I have a feeling this is something they've seen before."

"Okay, so once we grab Kyle we get him to the airport, where Tiny Gunderson flies to Rome, and we hand him over to Jenner." Cabrillo had a sudden thought. "They'll have control of his passport, so we need to make a new one."

"Chairman, please," Linda said, as if she'd been insulted. "Max's ex has e-mailed a picture of Kyle. We'll doctor it so it looks like an official passport shot and print a new one from our store of blanks."

Juan indicated Linda should wipe some grease from her chin. "That takes care of problem number one. Now, on to problem number two. What happened to the *Golden Dawn* and why? What do we know so far?"

Linda tapped at the keys of her laptop to bring up the information. "The *Golden Dawn* and her sister ships, the *Golden Sky* and *Golden Sun*, are owned by Golden Cruise Lines. They're out of Denmark, and have been in business since the mid-eighties. They do the typical Caribbean, Mediterranean, and South Seas cruises that everyone else does, as well as charter ships for specific groups or events.

"The company was approached four months ago to ferry four hundred and twenty-seven Responsivists from the Philippines to Greece. The *Dawn* was the only ship available."

"That seems like a lot of people to staff a reproductive-education clinic," Juan said.

"I thought so, too," Linda agreed. "I'm looking into it. There is nothing on the Responsivist website about the trip or what such a large group was doing in the Philippines."

"Okay, keep going."

"They left Manila on the seventeenth, and, as far as what

Murph could get from the logs, there were no incidents reported. It was smooth sailing all the way."

"Right up to the point where everyone died," Max said caustically.

Eric glanced down the table at the Corporation's number two. "Not everyone died. I went back over the computer discs of the UAV flyby. One of the *Golden Dawn*'s lifeboats was missing." He glanced at Cabrillo. "Sorry, I didn't notice it last night."

Juan let it pass.

"The ship's computer log confirms that a lifeboat was lowered about eight hours before we showed up," Mark confirmed.

"So the killer or killers were on the *Dawn* the whole cruise?"

"That's what it looks like to us. Stoney and I hacked the cruise line's computer for a passenger manifest and list of the crew, but without having the bodies to verify who was aboard when she went down there's no way to narrow our list of suspects." Mark forestalled Juan's next question. "We already checked. There were no unscheduled crew substitutions after the charter was first proposed, and there were no last-minute changes to the passenger manifest. The people who were supposed to be on that ship were on it."

"Then who the hell killed them all?" Max asked.

"If I were to guess, I'd say the Responsivists either did it to themselves, but they aren't a suicide cult, like Jim Jones's Peoples Temple or Japan's Aum Shinrikyo. Some people claim Lydell Cooper took his own life in the ultimate act of Responsivism, but the group doesn't support suicide. They say that since you're already born, it is your moral responsibility to spread their beliefs, not kill yourself. The other option is that someone infiltrated the group."

"Any suspects?"

Linda said, "Because of their stance on birth control and abortion, they've been engaged in a running battle with the Vatican for years. The same goes with a number of conservative Christian organizations."

Cabrillo shook his head. "I can see one nut job with a rifle killing an abortion doctor. But to kill a shipload of people takes a highly organized and well-funded team. I don't buy a handful of priests and nuns infiltrating the cult in order to kill a few hundred of their members."

"My money's on a group of zealots," Mark said. "A countercult to the Responsivists, maybe made up of former members or something. You know, apart from the whole not-having-kids thing, this group's into some pretty weird stuff."

Juan ignored him. "Let's explore why they would kill some of their own. Ideas?"

"No, seriously," Mark continued. "Once you've been involved for a while, do your charity work in some third world toilet, they start letting you in on some of the bigger secrets to Responsivism, and how the knowledge will save you."

"Go on," Juan said to indulge him. Murph might be flakey, but he had a topflight mind.

"Ever heard of 'brane theory?" He'd already talked with Eric about it so only Stone didn't return a blank stare. "It's right up there with string theory as a way of unifying all four forces in the universe, something Einstein couldn't do. In a nutshell, it says our four-dimensional universe is a single membrane, and that there are others existing in higher orders of space. These are so close to ours that zero-point matter and energy can pass between them and that gravitational forces in our universe can leak out. It's all cutting-edge stuff."

"I'll take your word for it," Cabrillo said.

"Anyway, 'brane theory started to get traction among theoretical physicists in the mid-nineties, and Lydell Cooper glommed on to it, too. He took it a step further, though. It wasn't just quantum particles passing in and out of our universe. He believed that an intelligence from another 'brane was affecting people here in our dimension. This intelligence, he said, shaped our day-to-day lives in ways we couldn't sense. It was the cause of all our suffering. Just before his death, Cooper started to teach techniques to limit this influence, ways to protect ourselves from the alien power."

"And people bought this crap?" Max asked, sinking deeper into depression over his son.

"Oh yeah. Think about it from their side for a second. It's not a believer's fault that he is unlucky or depressed or just plain stupid. His life is being messed with across dimensional membranes in space. It's an alien influence that cost you that promotion or prevented you from dating the girl of your dreams. It's a cosmic force holding you back, not your own ineptitude. If you believe that, then you don't have to take responsibility for your life. And we all know nobody takes responsibility for himself anymore. Responsivism gives you a ready-made excuse for your poor life choices."

"With people suing fast-food companies because they're overweight, I can see the attraction," Juan said. "But what's this have to do with someone killing a ship filled with Responsivists?"

Mark looked a little sheepish, "I haven't thought it all the way through, but what if it's true, you know"—his voice took on a feverish edge—"and some alien from another 'brane is fighting one trapped in ours and we're caught in the middle? Like pawns or something?"

Cabrillo closed his eyes and groaned. Mark's flakiness was overwhelming his first-class mind again. "I'll take that under advisement, but, for now, let's stick to terrestrial enemies."

Mark whispered to Eric, "That sounded better when we were talking last night, didn't it?"

"That's because we hadn't slept in twenty hours and had downed about thirty Red Bulls each."

Eddie Seng popped a piece of bread into his mouth. "Could this particular group have been selected because they were trying to leave the cult and the leaders made an example out of them? Eric mentioned earlier that kidnapping isn't beyond them. What if they've taken the next step to murder?"

Max Hanley shot him a startled look, his face etched with concern over Kyle's safety.

"That's a possibility," Linda said, before seeing Hanley's obvious pain. "Sorry, Max, but we have to consider it. Besides, your son's a new convert. He doesn't want to leave them at all."

"You sure you want to be here for this?" Juan asked his closest friend.

"Yes, damnit," Max snapped. "It's just, I don't know, painful and embarrassing all at the same time. This is my son we're talking about, and I can't help but feel I've let him down. If I'd been a better father, he wouldn't have drifted into something so dangerous."

No one knew what to say for a second. Uncharacteristically, it was Eric Stone who broke the silence. So versed in technical matters, it was easy to overlook his human side. "Max, I grew up in an abusive home. My father was a drunk who beat my mother and me every night he had enough money for a bottle of vodka. It was about the worst situation you could imagine and yet I turned out okay. Your home life is only a part of who you become. You being a larger part of your son's life might have changed things or it might not have. There's no way of knowing, and if you can't know for certain there's no need for useless speculation. Kyle is who he is because he chose to be that way. You weren't around for your daughter either, and she's a successful accountant."

"Lawyer," Max said absently. "And she did it all on her own."

"If you don't feel you can take responsibility for her success, then you have no right to take responsibility for Kyle's failings."

Max let the statement hang, before finally asking, "How old are you?"

Stone seemed embarrassed by the question. "Twenty-seven."

"Son, you are wise beyond your years. Thank you."

Eric grinned.

Juan mouthed the words *Well done* to Stone and resumed the meeting. "Is there any way to check Eddie's theory?"

"We can hack into the Responsivists' computer system," Mark offered. "Something might turn up, but I doubt they're going to break down their membership into lists of who's been naughty and who's been nice."

"Try it anyway," Juan ordered. "Cross-reference the passenger manifest with everything they have going on. Some factor singled these particular people out. If they weren't about to leave the cult, it has to be something else." He turned to Linda. "I want to know why so many of them were in the Philippines at the same time. The answer to that question might be our only solid clue."

Juan stood to indicate the meeting was adjourned. "We hit the Suez Canal at oh-five-hundred tomorrow morning. Remind your staffs that we'll have a pilot on board until we clear Port Said, so we're running on full-disguise mode. Max, make sure the tanks to the smudge engine that sends smoke out our funnel are topped off, and that the decks are double-checked for anything that can give us away. Once we're in the Med, we have twenty-four hours to finalize our plans with Linc, another twelve to put everything in place, and then we extract Kyle Hanley. Forty-eight hours from now, he'll be in Rome with the deprogrammer and we'll be on our way to the Riviera on that eavesdropping job."

There was no way for Cabrillo to know how far from simple things were going to be.

CHAPTER 12

JUAN SETTLED THE EARBUD OF HIS RADIO A LITTLE deeper and tapped the throat mike to let the others know he was in position. Below him lay the Responsivist compound, a collection of rambling buildings surrounded by a white-washed cement-block wall. Behind the compound was a rocky beach with a single wooden jetty running a hundred feet into the Gulf of Corinth. With the tide just coming back in, he could smell the water on the soft breeze.

The buildings were low-slung, as if clinging to the ground, reminding Cabrillo of the work of Frank Lloyd Wright. The shallow roofs were covered in barrel tile that looked black through his third-generation night vision goggles, but he knew from their prelaunch briefing the titles were red clay. The lawns within the compound were burned brown from a drought, and the leaves on the few gnarled olive trees were dried husks. It was three-thirty in the morning, and the only lights showing were affixed to strategically placed poles.

He turned his attention to the wall. It stood ten feet high and was a double layer of thick cement blocks, running for nearly eight hundred feet on a side. As was the custom in this part of the world, upright glass shards had been embedded in the top of the wall to deter intruders. Earlier in the day, he and Linda had gone to the only security company in the nearby town of Corinth, posing as an American couple who'd just purchased an ocean-side house and wanted to install an alarm system. The store's owner boasted he'd done extensive work for the Responsivists, pointing to an autographed eight-by-ten glossy of Donna Sky as if it were proof.

The trip wire running atop the wall was one of the first things Juan observed when he got into position. Next came the cameras, and, by the time his team had finished counting, they had spotted thirteen on the exterior of the buildings alone. They could only assume there were more inside.

There was a single rolling gate bisecting the stone driveway, and another, smaller gate at the back of the facility in line with the jetty. A pair of chain-link fences jutted from the compound walls and out into the sea to prevent people walking along the shore from trespassing on Responsivist property.

Although the security measures weren't particularly overt, it did give the complex a forbidding aura—but not from the outside, Juan reflected. It didn't look as though the place was designed to keep people out but rather to keep them in.

He scoped the grounds between the buildings once again. Three jeeps were parked in front of the main building. A thermal scan showed their engines were cold. There were no guards patrolling the paths crisscrossing the compound, no roving dogs, and the cameras mounted under eaves and on the light poles remained stationary. It was likely that there was a manned security station inside one of the buildings with a guard staring at a bank of monitors, which was why Cabrillo had the advance team keep watch from the moment they could be choppered from the *Oregon* to Athens.

Linc and Eddie had needed only two hours, sitting across the coast road in an olive grove overlooking the facility, to map out the cameras' blind spots and transmit that information back to the ship. They had estimated that there were currently about forty-five Responsivists inside, although there were enough buildings to house twice that number in relative comfort.

With their strategy worked out ahead of time and final tactics honed, the crew had spent the day putting everything into place, securing rental cars, scouting escape routes, and finding a suitable place nearby for George Adams to land the Robinson and transfer Kyle to the general aviation apron at Athens's Eleftherios Venizelos International Airport. Chuck Gunderson already had the Corporation's Gulfstream executive jet prepped for the quick flight to Rome. All the paperwork had been filed, and a limousine was waiting for them at the other end.

And if things didn't go as smoothly as planned, they had alternatives ready to go at an instant's notice. The details were so meticulous that Eric Stone, aboard the *Oregon*, who'd been studying the tidal charts, had determined the precise moment they should commence their covert assault.

Although Cabrillo was taking a role in the snatch and grab, Eddie Seng, as chief of shore operations, would lead the four-person attack, and it was his responsibility to make sure everyone involved was ready.

"One minute from my mark," Juan heard him whisper over the radio. "Mark."

Juan tapped his TRANSMIT button in acknowledgment. He tested the pair of quick-draw holsters hanging from his hips, making certain the pair of compact Glock 19s came out easily. Though he favored the new Fabrique Nationale Five-seveN automatic as his personal sidearm, because the small 5.7mm bullets could defeat nearly any flak jackets, this mission wasn't about killing. The crew in the ship's armory had soft-loaded the Glocks' 9mm rounds with half their normal charge and had topped them not with lead bullets but ballistic plastic. At close range, the bullets could be deadly, but at anything beyond fifteen feet the nonlethal shells would take the fight out of the average person with a single hit.

The seconds trickled by, and, as if a sign from above, clouds slid over the quarter moon, turning the night inky. Faintly, Juan could hear the throb of the Robinson R44 as Gomez Adams got into position.

"You ready?" he asked Mark Murphy, who was hunkered down next to him in the same roadside ditch.

"Two missions in three days," Mark breathed. His face was streaked with camo paint, and his long hair was tucked into a black bandanna. "I think you've got it in for me."

"Consider yourself our resident combat hacker."

Cabrillo glanced at his sleeve. Embedded in the fabric was a tiny flexible computer screen. The e-paper's resolution was crystal clear, and the image it showed was the Responsivist's compound from an altitude of a thousand feet. Linda Ross was in a van down the road at the controls of their UAV. With the camera zoomed in, Juan had an unobstructed view of the facility, but, more important, he would know the location of anyone walking the grounds. The experimental view screen was giving off too much light, so he turned down the gain until it was a muted glow. The rig's batteries and computer were sewn into the back of his combat vest.

"Let's go," Juan heard Eddie say. He tapped Murph on the shoulder, and they ran across the road together, their soft-soled boots making no sound on the macadam.

When they reached the cement-block wall, Cabrillo turned so that his back was toward it and cupped his hands. Mark stepped up onto Juan's palms, and then, with a boost, onto his shoulders.

Mark almost made the mistake of grasping the top of the wall to steady himself but stopped just before he shredded his hands on the glass. He paused for a moment, to let the Chairman find his center of balance. Had Mark not known it was there, the monofilament security trip wire was nearly impossible to see. It ran along the perimeter of the wall, less than half an inch from the edge, supported by dozens of tiny insulators. If he were to guess, he'd say that less than ten pounds of pressure would cut the wire and trigger the alarm. He pulled a voltmeter from a pouch at his hip to test the current flowing through the delicate wire. He selected an appropriate pair of alligator clamps and attached them to the wire, letting three feet of line dangle over the far side of the wall. With his bypass in place, he snipped the wire, wincing unconsciously in case he'd gotten it wrong. There were no raised cries, no Klaxons, and no lights snapped on in any of the buildings.

From another pouch, he unfurled a role of carbon-fiber cloth and settled it over the top of the wall. Mark heaved himself atop the wall, and, even with his full weight bearing down on the razor-sharp glass, it couldn't cut through the high-tech material. He dropped down to the ground and moved slightly to his left. A moment later, he heard Juan scramble up and over the wall. He fell lightly at Mark's side.

"When we're back on the ship, you're going on a diet," Juan said, but showed no ill effects of holding Murph aloft. He keyed his throat mike. "We're in."

On the opposite side of the compound, where there was another gap in the video camera coverage, Eddie and Franklin Lincoln were making their covert entrance. Though Linc was the best the Corporation had at security bypasses, it had been Eddie who cut the wire for the simple reason that all the martial arts training in the world couldn't give him the strength to hold Linc's two-hundred-and-fifty-pound frame.

"So are we. Standing by."

Keeping flat, Cabrillo led Murph away from the wall, snaking across the grounds in a seemingly random pattern, but the route had been carefully mapped out so they avoided the numerous cameras. At one end of the main building, the roof sported several satellite dishes and a spindly radio transmission tower. This was their destination, and it took seven minutes of crawling to reach it.

Juan removed his goggles, and, cupping his hands around his eyes, pressed his face to a window. There was a dim smear of light near the back wall, the glow of a computer on standby mode. The preraid reconnaissance had confirmed that this was the camp director's office.

He noted an alarm pod attached to the window sash that would trip if the window was opened. He pulled a device from his combat vest, and, when he aimed it at the alarm, an indicator glowed red. Next, he swept the device along the glass to determine if wires had been embedded between the two panes, but the device remained dark. If this was the level of security provided by Corinth's finest company, he considered making a career change, to Greek cat burglar.

He attached two small suction cups to the glass and then scored the window with a cutter, moving slowly so the sound of the pane being sliced never rose above a rough hiss. He heard an audible sigh when the vacuum between the two pieces of insulated glass were released. He handed the cutter to Mark and carefully pulled the pane free of the frame with the suction cups. He repeated the process with the inner piece of glass and set it on the floor inside the office when he was finished.

Juan legged over the sill and ducked into the building. When Mark had scrambled through the window, Cabrillo drew down the shade. "We're in the office."

"Roger," Eddie replied.

Juan gestured to the computer. "It's up to you."

Murph cracked his knuckles and took a seat behind the

desk, turning down the screen before waking the system. From a fanny pack, he removed a battered piece of electronics covered in decals and wads of dried gum. He jacked it into the computer's USB port. A moment later, a laughing skull appeared on the monitor. When it disappeared, Mark began to pound the keyboard with one ambidextrous hand while the other rolled the mouse like a child would a toy truck.

Juan left him to his work, and examined the office using a tiny penlight, making certain he stayed away from the window in case there was a gap around the shade. They had learned from the Responsivists' website that the facility's director was another Californian named Gil Martell. A little digging showed that Martell had sold luxury automobiles in Beverly Hills prior to his joining the group, and that his name had come up several times in an investigation of a car-theft ring. Although he was charged, several key witnesses vanished back to Mexico before the trial, and the indictment was dropped.

The room's furniture was what Cabrillo expected—desk, credenza, a couple of chairs, a sofa along one wall with a coffee table. He recognized it was all expensive. The Oriental rug under the coffee table was a flat-weave antique kilim that would fetch a considerable price at auction. Framed photographs adorned the walls, Martell's shrine to himself. Juan didn't know some of the people smiling into the camera with Martell, while others were easily recognizable. He spotted several with Donna Sky. Even in these candid shots, the movie star's beauty was undeniable. With her dark hair, almond eyes, and the sharpest cheekbones in the business, she was the epitome of Hollywood royalty.

Cabrillo wondered idly what part of her life was so miserable that she would allow a cult to take it over.

Another picture caught his attention. It was an older photograph of Martell and another man on the deck of a sailboat. It was signed "Keep the faith. Lydell Cooper." The snapshot must have been taken shortly before Cooper vanished at sea on his ketch. He'd read the Coast Guard report, and it appeared that the boat simply capsized in a storm that had come out of nowhere. Five other small craft had also been caught unaware, and an additional three people drowned.

If Juan could use a single word to describe the scientist-turned-prophet, it would be *bland*. There was nothing distinguishing about Cooper. He was in his mid to late sixties, paunchy, with an egg-shaped head, glasses, and a hairline in full retreat. His eyes were a plain brown, and the gray beard and mustache neither added to nor took away from his appearance. It was as if the facial hair was expected on a retired researcher, and he'd grown it out of obligation. Juan saw nothing that could inspire thousands to join his crusade—no charisma, no charm, none of the things that would attract followers at all. Had he not known what Cooper looked like, he could have guessed Martell kept a picture of his accountant on his wall.

"Got it!" Murph cried, then looked around guiltily for speaking so loudly. "Sorry. I'm into their system. Piece of cake."

Juan strode across the room. "Can you find which room is Kyle's?"

"They have everything cross-referenced. He's in building C, which is the newest one right near where Eddie and Linc climbed the wall. Kyle Hanley's room is number one-seventeen, but he's not alone. He's got a roommate named, let's see, Jeff Ponsetto."

"Well done," Cabrillo said, and relayed the information to Eddie and Linc. "Start to download what you can off their computer."

Linda Ross came over the tactical net: "Chairman, check your view screen. You've got company coming."

Juan glanced at his sleeve. Two men dressed in maintenance workers' overalls were crossing the compound. They carried toolboxes, and appeared to be heading toward the main building, where he and Murph were. Had there been some sort of emergency call to the engineering staff, surely they would have heard voices. Whatever was going on, Cabrillo didn't like it.

"Murph, forget the download. Let's go!"

As Juan went toward the door, he tucked an electronic bug under the desk lamp. He knew it would be found quickly, once the break-in was detected, but it would transmit the first critical moments of whatever took place in Gil Martell's office.

He paused at the window and checked the view screen once again. The maintenance workers were approaching the building's front door, which gave him and Mark the time they needed to get clear.

He slowly opened the shade and eased himself over the window sash. His Glock was in his hand, though he had no conscious memory of drawing it.

Keeping low and following their carefully laid map to avoid the cameras, they moved toward building C. The grass was dry under their shoes and crackled with each step. Like the others in the Responsivist compound, building C was one-storied, with whitewashed walls and a barrel-tile roof.

Linc and Eddie were pressed to the wall next to a door, out of view of the camera mounted above it. A security keypad was to the right, and its faceplate had been removed and left dangling by a bunch of wires. Linc had already installed his bypass. Despite having such large hands, the former Navy SEAL was the best lockpick the Corporation had, and he worked his tools with the delicate touch of a brain surgeon. With a pick and torsion rod in place, he gave the lock a jerk to the left, and the door snicked open.

"Fourteen seconds," Eddie whispered.

"The maestro strikes again," Linc smirked, and stepped into a long hallway running the length of the building.

The hall was lined with dozens of identical doors and was illuminated by shaded fluorescent fixtures hanging from the ceiling. The carpeting was an institutional gray, not much softer than the concrete slab on which the building was constructed. The four men started down, peering into a large kitchen to their left and a room lined with a dozen commercial washing machines to their right. Juan didn't see any clothes dryers, and assumed they had drying lines behind the building. Part of Responsivism was to reduce one's impact on the natural world, so not having dryers fit their beliefs, as did the solar panels they'd spied on the roof of one of the buildings.

They quickly found room one-seventeen. Linc reached up to remove the cover over the closest light fixture and pulled the fluorescent tubes from their brackets. The four donned night vision goggles, and Juan turned the doorknob. The room beyond looked like a typical dorm room, with two metal-framed beds, a pair of desks, and matching bureaus. The adjoining bathroom was a small tiled enclosure, with a drain on the floor for the shower. In the eerie green cast of the goggles, shapes were indeterminate, and colors washed out to shades of black, but the silhouettes of people sleeping on the beds were unmistakable. So was the snoring.

Eddie pulled a small plastic case from the thigh pocket of his fatigue pants. Inside were four hypodermic needles. The narcotic cocktail inside the barrels would incapacitate a grown man in under twenty seconds. Because Kyle had willingly joined the cult, he would surely resist their efforts to get him out. The deprogrammer, Adam Jenner, had recommended drugging the youth to Linda, when they'd spoken, although Juan had planned to do it even without the advice.

Eddie gave a needle to Cabrillo and approached one of the beds. The man was sleeping on his stomach, his face turned to the wall. In a fluid movement, Seng clamped his hand around the man's mouth and slid the needle into his neck, his thumb coming down on the plunger with even pressure. Across the room, Juan did the same thing. His victim came instantly awake and bucked against Juan's arm, his eyes wide with panic. Juan held him down easily, even when the man's legs began to thrash.

Juan counted down from twenty in his head. When he reached ten, the man's gyrations were slowing, and when he hit three the guy was totally still. Juan flashed his penlight into the man's face. Although Kyle Hanley took after his mother, Juan saw enough of Max in the boy to know it was him.

"Got him."

As a precaution, Linc whipped FlexiCuffs around Kyle's ankles and wrists before tossing him over his shoulder.

"All set, big man?" Juan asked.

Linc grinned in the darkness. "I carried your sorry butt for eight miles in Cambodia three years ago, so this boy's nothing. Can't weigh but a buck-twenty."

Cabrillo checked the e-paper screen on his sleeve. Everything looked quiet, but he radioed Linda for confirmation.

"The janitors are still in the main building. A light came

on across the compound from where you are but went out again a minute eight seconds later."

"Pit stop."

"My guess, too. You're clear for extraction."

"Roger." He turned to his team. "We're good to go."

A bell began shrieking just as they started back down the corridor. It sounded like a fire alarm, a shrill, piercing sound that pounded on their eardrums like daggers. There was no way to communicate over the din, but the men were seasoned professionals and knew what was expected of them.

Eddie was in the lead, followed closely by Linc and Mark. All three men accelerated down the hallway, any attempt at stealth forgotten. This was no longer a snatch and grab but a race to the perimeter wall, where, if Linc and Eddie had done as ordered, a limpet mine was in place to blast through the blocks. Linda Ross was near enough to hear the Klaxon and would be on the radio instructing George Adams to bring the Robinson in for a fast extraction. He'd land directly on the road and would have the team aboard before any guards knew what had happened.

A door to one side of Juan flew open, and a sleepy-eyed man wearing pajama bottoms stepped into the corridor. Cabrillo slammed his elbow into the man's jaw, spiraling him to the carpet in a rubbery heap. Ahead, another man poked his head out of his dormitory room. Even with the deadweight of Kyle Hanley on his shoulder, Linc juked sideways and stiff-armed the Responsivist. The man's head hit the metal doorframe, and, as Juan raced past, the man's eyes rolled into his head until only the whites shone. He collapsed backward like a felled tree.

Eddie instinctively paused when they reached the exterior door. Juan checked the video feed on his sleeve, but Linda must have been occupied with Adams because the circling drone's camera showed nothing but the ocean just north of them. He could hear her girlish voice in his radio's earbud, but the alarm was too loud to make out her words. All he caught was her strident tone.

He shrugged at the lack of intel and opened the door, leading with his Glock. With the exception of alarms sounding across the compound, everything looked as tranquil as before.

There were no rushing guards, or any movement at all. It didn't even appear that additional lights had come on.

Clear of the sonic avalanche of the bell inside the dormitory, Juan pressed his hands to his ears to try to hear what Linda was shouting.

"—t of there. Guards on the far side. Gomez is coming in. Hurry."

He was fumbling for his night vision goggles when a trio of men in gray uniforms appeared around the corner of a nearby building. Juan took a fraction of a second too long to see if they were armed. One of them opened up with a compact submachine gun, spraying an arc of bullets that blew plaster dust into the air as the rounds dug into the dormitory. Cabrillo dropped flat and fired. His aim was perfect, hitting the guard center mass, but rather than going down the man simply staggered back a bit.

"Inside!" he shouted to his team, and crawled into the corridor once again, closing the door with his foot. He screamed, to be heard over the alarm: "They've got automatics and Kevlar vests. Our plastic bullets don't even slow them down."

"Talk about bringing a knife to a gunfight," Eddie yelled.

A fresh barrage of autofire tore at the building's façade, seemingly shaking the entire structure.

Linc jammed a chair under the door handle so it couldn't be opened from outside, then reached up the wall and tore the horn off its mount, silencing it. "More like a blowgun to an artillery duel, my friend."

CHAPTER 13

CABRILLO NEEDED ONLY A SECOND TO DEVISE A plan. "There's a window in Kyle's bedroom. The back of this building is closer to the perimeter wall."

He led them down the hallway again, flashing his pistol at anyone peering out of his room. The sight of the weapon was more than enough to encourage them to stay inside. Kyle's roommate continued his drug-induced sleep despite the commotion. Juan charged across the room, firing several shots at the large picture window on the far wall. The plastic bullets carried more than enough kick to loosen the glass before he hurtled himself bodily through it. Shards cascaded around him, as he rolled onto the dried-out lawn, and he felt a few rip small cuts in his hands and at the back of his neck.

With multiple lights shining from the dorm rooms, he had a clear picture of the cement-block wall fifteen yards away. The guards continued to concentrate their fire at the entrance and had yet to encircle the building. Glass crunched behind him, as Murph, Linc, and Eddie stepped through the ruined window.

Juan's actions had bought them a few seconds at best.

The explosives Eddie had planted were midway down the wall's length, the location chosen because of the cameras rather than it being the best tactical location. To reach it, they would have to cross a hundred yards of open ground, a perfect killing field for the Responsivist guards.

"Linda, give me a sit-rep." Cabrillo needed a clearer overview than the tiny e-paper screen on his wrist.

"Is that you who just went through a window?"

"Yes. What's the situation?"

"There are three guards near the dorm's entrance and another dozen or so fanning out across the compound. All are heavily armed, and two of them are on four-wheelers. George is on his way. You should be able to hear the chopper."

Juan could hear the drumming of the Robinson's rotor through the evening air. "Tell Max to get moving, too. We might have to use plan C."

"Juan, I'm on the net," Max Hanley said over the radio. "We're under way right now. Do you have Kyle?"

"We do. He's fine for the moment, but we need to get the hell out of here."

"Don't worry, the cavalry's coming."

"That's what they said at Little Bighorn when Custer showed up, and you know how that turned out."

The sound of the approaching helicopter reached a fever pitch, and just before the copter thundered over the wall Juan nodded to Eddie. There was no need to talk to each other. With plan A in ruins, they seamlessly switched to plan B. Eddie had the explosive's detonator in his hands. He waited a beat, as a guard in a four-wheel all-terrain vehicle approached the bomb, and then casually triggered it.

A section of wall erupted in a roiling cloud of white dust and flame. The guard was blown off the four-wheeler and thrown twenty feet, before tumbling to the ground in a loose-limbed roll. His ATV had been flipped onto its side, its balloon tires spinning uselessly. Bits of concrete fell like hail across the compound, as the mushroom of dust and fire climbed into the sky.

The team took off in a dead sprint, Linc easily keeping pace despite the deadweight of Kyle Hanley over his shoulder. When they reached the corner of the building, Juan peered around it. One of the guards who'd first opened fire was down, his face a sheet of blood from a scalp laceration caused by a chunk of cement. He was being tended to by another guard while the third was trying to get the door unstuck.

Taking careful aim, Juan cycled through the remaining four rounds in his Glock. Knowing their torsos were impervious to the plastic bullets and reluctant to kill the guards outright, he fired two low-aimed rounds at each man. The pairs of bullets wouldn't emasculate them, but their groins were going to be swollen for weeks. They went down screaming, clutching themselves in utter agony.

"Sorry, boys. Literally," Juan said, and relieved them of their weapons. They carried mini-Uzis, which were terrific close-work guns but useless at any meaningful range. He tossed one to Eddie and the other to Linc, who was a better shot carrying a man on his shoulder than Murph was at a firing bench with his gun bolted to the table.

The black Robinson R44 suddenly roared overhead, flying so low that the skids nearly knocked tiles off the roofs. George Adams pirouetted the chopper above the compound, using the rotor's downwash to kick up a sandstorm. The maelstrom of grit served to cover Juan and the others, as well as keep the guards pinned.

Amid the deafening throb of the blades beating the air and the chaos all around them, no one knew where a fresh burst of gunfire originated. A flurry of white spiderwebs suddenly appeared in the chopper's windshield and the copilot's window. Embers of hot metal peeled away from the aircraft's skin as bullets tore through its hull. George ducked and weaved the helo like a prizefighter in the ring, but the stream of tracers continued to pour in until a gush of smoke erupted from the engine cowling.

Juan frantically changed frequencies on his radio, shouting, "Get out of there, George. Go! Go! Go! That's an order."

"I'm outta here, sorry," Adams drawled. With that, the chopper turned like a dragonfly and veered back over the wall, trailing smoke that was blacker than the night.

"Now what?" Murph asked the Chairman.

Seventy-five yards of open ground yawned before them, and already the Responsivists were up and getting organized. The Corporation team had cover in a shallow drainage ditch, but it wouldn't last long. Already, guards were forming search parties, their flashlights lancing out into the darkness.

"Where are you, Linda?" Cabrillo asked.

"Just outside the wall, not far from where you guys blew it open. Can you reach me?"

"Negative. Too many guards and not enough cover. I swear, this place is more like a military barracks than a wacko retreat."

"Then I guess it's time for a diversion."

"Make it good."

Over the radio, he could hear the sound of an engine accelerating, but Linda didn't respond.

Thirty seconds later, the compound's main gate was torn off its hinges and the back end of the van they had rented burst through, its bumper hanging askew. The dozen or more guards covering the facility turned at once. Some began running toward this latest threat, not noticing the shadows rising out of a culvert and racing for the breach in the wall.

Guns opened up on Linda's van, forty holes appearing in its sheet-metal hide before she could wrestle the transmission back into drive. The tires kicked up feathers of gravel before regaining traction, and she drove out of the withering barrage.

As they ran for the wall, Juan called to Linc and Eddie. "Switch to plan C, and I'll see you in a bit."

"Where are you going?" Mark was panting.

Cabrillo thought idly that they really did need to get Murph to the ship's exercise room. "They got one of Linda's tires. There are jeeps in front of the main building. They'll catch us before we make it a half mile. I'm going to delay them so you can get to the bridge."

"That should be my job," Eddie said.

"Negative. Your responsibility is with Max's son. Good luck."

Juan angled away from the smoking pile of rubble that had once been the wall. The ATV was still on its side, exhaust curling from its tailpipe. He turned to see his men climb through the gap before grabbing the handlebars. He goosed the throttle and worked the wheel, using the four-wheeler's power rather than his strength to right the six-hundred-pound vehicle. It bounced onto its rubbery tires, and he threw his leg over the seat, gunning the motor before he was settled in.

The machine's 750cc engine growled as he took off across the lawn. A detachment of guards ran for the open-topped jeeps, while those closest to the wall turned to resume their hunt of Juan's team.

Cabrillo maintained the advantage of his night vision goggles, but more lights were being turned on all around the compound. The pole-mounted spots cast blinding pools of incandescence. He had a minute or less before they recognized it wasn't one of their own driving the ATV. He tore around as if searching for the intruders while trying to find a guard farthest from any illumination. He spotted a man taking cover behind one of the desiccated trees near where two of the perimeter walls met. He raced over, pulling off his goggles but pausing in a shadow so his face remained hidden. Not knowing what language the guard spoke, Cabrillo waved him over, indicating he should hop on the back of the big four-wheeler.

The guard didn't hesitate. He ran to Juan and jumped onto the seat behind him, bracing himself with one hand on Cabrillo's shoulder while clutching a machine pistol with the other.

"Not your lucky day, pal," Juan muttered, and torqued back on the throttle.

"I've got everybody," Linda Ross called. "We're on the main road now."

Glancing at the jeeps, Juan saw that the first one was ready to head out in pursuit. Apart from the driver and the guard in the passenger seat, there were two other armed men in the back, clinging to the metal roll bar. He knew his people would make a good show of themselves, but they were virtually unarmed, in a van with a flat tire that couldn't do more than fifty miles per hour. The outcome was inevitable, especially when the other jeep took off after his team, too.

It was time to level the playing field.

The guard riding the back of Cabrillo's ATV tapped him on the shoulder, pointing, that they should head toward the back of the dormitory. Juan seemed to comply, accelerating evenly across the smooth terrain. He could feel the eyes of the other guards watching him, so he waited until the last possible second to crank the handlebars hard to the right. The balloon tires tore furrows out of the ground, and had Juan not thrown his weight in the opposite direction the four-wheeler would have flipped. Coming back down on four wheels and pointing straight at the breach in the wall, Juan put on the power. He wrenched the guard's mini-Uzi from his hands and jammed it into his own belt. The guard was confused for a second but quickly recovered. He threw his arm around Juan's neck, his ropy bicep crushing Cabrillo's larynx and windpipe with unholy strength.

Juan gasped and choked, working his powerful lungs to

draw in little sips of air while keeping the ATV accelerating toward the gap. The hole had a ragged six-foot diameter, and, beneath it, was a jumbled pile of shattered cement blocks and loose mortar. They were barreling in at forty miles per hour, with less than fifteen yards to go, when bullets began to strike the wall. The Responsivist guards had seen the fleeing vehicle and assumed the two men sitting astride it were the ones who'd infiltrated their lair. Cement chips and dust erupted from the wall as rounds were sprayed at the ATV in a punishing fusillade.

Juan could feel the heat of the bullets whizzing all around them. He even felt one graze his artificial leg but ignored the distraction, keeping his diminishing focus on the hole. His lungs convulsed from lack of oxygen, as the guard redoubled his hold, bearing down with every ounce of his strength, trying to choke the life out of his prey.

Come on, you bastards! Shoot straight for once! Juan thought as his peripheral vision vanished into a rapidly expanding darkness, as though he were looking down an ever-lengthening tunnel.

Do it! Cabrillo knew it could be his last thought on earth.

Then he felt a powerful jolt, as if he'd been sledgehammered in the spine. The guard's tenacious grip came free. He made a gurgling sound as he slumped over the Chairman, blood from his ruptured lung spilling from his mouth. The burst of autofire from the Responsivists had struck their own man. He fell off the back of the quad when Juan hit the base of the pile of debris. The fat tires found easy purchase on the loose rubble. He shot up the incline and through the gap, ducking so as not to tear his head off. He soared out the other side, instinctively rising from the seat just before landing, to absorb the shock.

The big Kawasaki bounced on its suspension, bucking Cabrillo so he almost flew over the handlebars. His radio earbud popped free and dangled across his chest on its wire. He held on grimly, struggling to refill his lungs through his damaged windpipe. As soon as the ATV settled firmly again, he twisted the handlebars hard over, turning so he could get on the coast road leading to Corinth, twelve miles away.

He hit the pavement just as the first jeep burst through the ruined gate and tore down the road. Linda and the others had maybe a half-mile head start. Not nearly enough. A switch on the handlebars disengaged the ATV's front wheels, giving Juan a burst of speed. He accelerated down the road along the outside of the wall.

The gate was twenty yards away when the second jeep careened through, its tires kicking up dirt before they hit the blacktop. There were only three guards in this one, a driver, passenger, and a man standing in the rear clutching an AK-47.

Juan had the advantage of momentum and raced up behind the jeep before they knew he was there. He kicked himself up so he was standing on the saddle seat, the wind stinging his eyes. Slowing only slightly so that he was going just a few miles per hour faster than the jeep, he crashed the front of the ATV into the jeep's rear bumper.

The impact launched Cabrillo off the Kawasaki, his shoulder slamming the guard standing in the rear. The man's face smashed into the roll bar with teeth-splintering force, and he was bent backward until it seemed his heels would touch his head. If the collision hadn't killed the guard, Juan was still certain the man was out of the fight. Juan untangled himself enough to kick out with his artificial leg, a sweeping arc that caught the guard in the passenger seat on the side of the head. With the jeep's doors removed, there was nothing to keep the man from tumbling out of the vehicle and cartwheeling down the road.

Cabrillo had the barrel of the mini-Uzi pressed to the driver's head before he was fully conscious of what had happened.

"Jump or die. The choice is yours."

The driver did neither. He crushed the brake pedal to the floor. The tires lit up as the rear of the jeep nearly lifted free of the road. Juan hit the windshield, folding it flat, and he tumbled across the hood, falling over the front so quickly he didn't have time to grab the grille.

As soon as Cabrillo had vanished from sight, the driver released the brake and mashed the accelerator again, knowing the man who'd attacked them was lying helplessly on the road.

CHAPTER 14

THE OREGON'S BOW CUT THROUGH THE DARK-
ened waters of the Ionian Sea with ease. Her revolutionary
magnetohydrodynamic engines could have pushed her through
four feet of pack ice just as effortlessly. They were just west
of Corinth, having rounded the Peloponnesian Peninsula, and
were driving due east to get into position. There was little
maritime traffic around the ship. What showed on the radar-
scope were a couple of coastal fishing boats, probably trawl-
ing for squid feeding near the surface at night.

For the moment, Eric Stone was pulling double duty.
Seated in his navigator's station, he had control of the ship,
but he had turned one of Mark Murphy's computer monitors
toward him so he could take over flying the UAV still circling
over the Responsivist complex. When they got closer to shore
and steering the ship would demand his full concentration, he
would turn the drone over to Gomez Adams, who was on final approach in the damaged Robinson.

"*Oregon*, this is Gomez." Hali had put the helicopter's
comm channel on the overhead speakers. "I have you in
sight."

"Roger, Gomez. Commencing deceleration," Max said from
the captain's chair. "Five knots, if you please, Mr. Stone."

Eric made a few keystrokes to slow the volume of water
gushing through the *Oregon*'s drive tubes until he could reverse the pumps and drop the ship down to the required
speed. They had to maintain some headway in order to keep
the ship from rolling with the swells and complicating Adams's landing.

Max spun his seat so he could see the damage-control

officer standing at his station at the back of the room. "Fire teams ready?"

"In full gear, sir," he said immediately, "and I've got my fingers on the triggers for the water cannons."

"Very good. Hali, tell George we're ready when he is." Max keyed the intercom to the hangar where Dr. Huxley was standing by. "Julia, George is only a couple of minutes out."

A bullet had only grazed the pilot's calf, but Max Hanley felt as guilty as if the entire team had been wiped out. No matter how anyone tried to rationalize it, Juan and the others had put themselves in danger because of him. And now the mission, which should have been simple, had thoroughly fallen apart. So far, George's flesh wound was the only injury, but Juan had dropped off the tactical net and Hali couldn't raise him. Linda had Linc, Eddie, and Kyle with her in the van, and they reported a heavily armed jeep in close pursuit.

For the hundredth time since the Chairman was first ambushed, Max cursed their decision to use only nonlethal weapons. No one had expected an army of armed guards. Hanley still hadn't yet considered the implications of so many weapons at a cult's compound, but it didn't bode well. From everything he'd heard and read since his ex had called him, the Responsivists weren't violent. In fact, they eschewed violence in all its forms.

How this connected to the mass murder aboard the *Golden Dawn*, he didn't know. Were the Responsivists at war with some other group? And, if so, who were they? Another cult no one had heard of, a group willing to kill hundreds of people just because the Responsivists believed in population control?

To Max, none of it made sense. Nor did it make sense that his only son would get mixed up with a group like this. He so wanted to believe that none of it was his fault. A lesser person would have been able to convince himself of just that. But Max knew where his responsibilities lay, and he had never shied away from them.

For now, he compartmentalized his guilt and focused on the big screen, where a window had opened with a camera view of the helipad over the *Oregon*'s aft-most cargo hatch.

Lit only by the moon, the damage to their R44 looked extensive, as George flared the chopper over the stern railing. Smoke poured from the engine cowling in dense waves that were twisted into a wreath by the whirling blades.

This was another example of why no one ever questioned Adams's courage. He'd flown the crippled chopper over twenty miles of empty sea rather than do the safe thing and land it in some farmer's field. Of course, that would have raised all sorts of questions with the Greek authorities. And the Chairman's plan C called for everyone to be on the boat and in international waters as quickly as possible.

George hovered the helicopter a few feet off the deck and slowly lowered it. An instant before the skids kissed, a massive gush of smoke erupted from the chopper's exhaust. The engine had seized, and the Robinson smacked into the landing pad hard enough to crack a strut. Max could see George calmly shutting down the helo's systems, one by one, before unstrapping himself. As the hangar elevator began to descend, George looked straight at the camera and threw a cocky, one-sided grin.

One safely home, Max thought. Six more to go.

WITH A FLAT REAR TIRE, the rental van drove like a pig. Linda had to wrestle it through the corners, as she maneuvered them toward the New National Road, the main artery back off the Peloponnese. Her rearview mirrors were thankfully clear, but she knew that wouldn't last. While Linc prepared the ropes, Eddie scrounged the inside of the van for anything they could use to slow their eventual pursuers. Linda had used a laptop to control the UAV, so that was useless, but she had installed a rolling chair and a small desk Eddie could toss out the back doors. He'd also pooled all their weapons and ammunition. He had three pistols and six extra magazines of plastic bullets. The rounds would probably blast through a windshield but bounce off tires like spitballs.

They flashed through tiny villages that clung to the sides of the road, a clutch of stucco buildings, homes, a taverna with seating under grape trellises, an occasional staked goat.

Although foreigners were building vacation houses along the coast, just a mile or two inland it looked as if life hadn't changed in this part of the world for a hundred years.

Something caught Linda's eye, a flash in the mirror. There had been no other traffic this late at night, so she knew it had to be the headlights of one of the jeeps she'd spied back at the compound.

"We're about to have company," she said, and pressed the accelerator a bit harder, balancing speed against the burst tire's shredding.

"Let them get right up to us," Eddie called from the rear of the van, his voice jumping in time with the flattened wheel. He had one hand on the door handle and the other on a pistol.

The jeep had to be doing eighty miles an hour and ate the distance in seconds. Peering out the back window, Eddie watched them come and realized they weren't going to tuck in behind the van but come alongside it.

"Eddie!" Linda cried.

"I see it."

He threw open the door when the jeep was ten yards back, firing as fast as he could pull the trigger. His first rounds bounced off the jeep's hood and grille, but the next few found the windshield. They punched neat holes through the glass, forcing the driver to swerve and slow. For a moment, it looked like he was going to roll the four-by-four, but at the last second he cranked the wheel in the opposite direction of the jeep's slide, and its left wheels crashed back to the pavement.

Almost immediately, he started after the fleeing van.

"Linc, down! Linda, hold on," Eddie shouted when the guard in the jeep's passenger's seat raised himself over the windscreen. He cradled an assault rifle.

The gun's chattering and the metallic whine of bullets chewing through sheet steel came at the same time. The windows in the van's back doors exploded, showering Eddie Seng in a cascade of diamond chips. Metal crackled with heat where rounds punched through, and one bullet ricocheted inside the van before embedding itself in the back of Linda's chair.

Eddie raised his second pistol over a window frame and

fired blindly, while Linc used his body to shield Kyle Hanley's unconscious form.

"I don't know how you did it," Linda called from the driver's seat. She was hunched over the wheel and looking at the side rearview mirror. "You hit the shooter in the chest."

"Did I kill him?" Eddie was slamming home fresh magazines.

"Can't tell. A guy in the back is taking his gun. Hold on!"

Linda hit the brakes and swerved into the jeep's lane. The two vehicles came together with a sickening crash, the van riding up onto the jeep's bumper for a moment before coming back down with a hard bounce. The limp passenger was thrown from the jeep, while the men in back crashed into the roll bar.

Hitting the gas again, Linda bought them a hundred-yard head start before the guards could regain the hunt.

"*Oregon*, how far are we?"

Eric Stone answered immediately. "I have you in sight from the UAV. You've got another six miles."

Linda cursed.

"To make matters worse," Stone continued, "there are two more jeeps coming up behind the first. One's maybe a quarter mile back and the other a little farther."

The jeep came up on them again, but rather than get too close, it hung back, and the armed guard started firing at the van's tires. Linda worked the wheel to foul his aim, but she knew it was only a matter of time. "Any bright ideas back there?"

"I'm afraid I'm out," Eddie admitted, but then his face brightened. He tapped his radio mike. "Eric, crash the UAV into the jeep."

"What?"

"The drone. Use it like a cruise missile. Hit the passenger compartment. It should still have enough fuel on board to blow up on impact."

"Without it, we won't be able to pick up the Chairman," Stone protested.

"Have you heard from him in the past five minutes?" The question hung in the air. "Do it!"

"Yes, sir."

. . .

NO SOONER HAD CABRILLO hit the pavement in front of the jeep, its driver hit the gas. Juan had a fraction of a second to flatten himself and reach up, as the bumper loomed over him. He grasped its underside, with the jeep picking up speed, dragging him down the road. He reached up higher to get his backside off the rough pavement, while rubber was chewed off his boots.

He hung on like that for a couple of seconds to catch his breath. He'd lost the mini-Uzi but still had a Glock in a holster at his hip. He doubled his grip with his left hand and used his right to grab his earbud and set it in place in time to hear the last exchange between Eddie and Eric.

"Negative on that," he said, his throat mike easily negating the engine roar inches from his face.

"Juan," Max shouted in jubilation, "how are you?"

"Oh, I'm hanging on." He tilted his head back so he could look up the road. Even with everything upside down, he saw two sets of car taillights and the unmistakable flicker of rifle fire from one of them. "Give me thirty seconds and the van'll be in the clear."

"That's about all the time we have left," Linda cautioned.

"Trust me." With that, Cabrillo tensed his shoulders and pulled himself higher, so that he was lying across the bumper just out of the driver's view. Clutching the grille as tightly as he could, he cross-drew the Glock from its holster with his left hand. He pushed off with his right to vault over the hood.

He drew down as he came up, double-tapping the driver in the chest. At this range, the plastic bullets would have been fatal, had the driver not worn a Kevlar vest. As it was, the two slugs hit with the kinetic energy of a mule, blowing every molecule of air out of the driver's lungs.

Cabrillo scrambled across the hood, clutching the wheel as the driver released it, his face already a deathly white as his mouth worked soundlessly to draw air. Cabrillo kept to the middle of the road by looking back at where they'd been rather than forward where they were heading. It didn't help that the driver kept his foot pressed to the gas pedal.

Juan had no choice but to reach over the dash with his pistol and shoot the man in the leg. Blood splattered the dash, the driver, and Cabrillo, but the shot had the desired effect. The driver's foot came off the gas and the jeep began to slow. When they were down to twenty miles per hour, Cabrillo leveled the pistol between the driver's pain-seared eyes. "Out."

The driver jumped clumsily, falling to the macadam, clutching his bleeding thigh and coming to a stop in a heap of abraded skin and broken limbs.

Juan swung over the lowered windscreen, settled into the driver's seat, and started after the first jeep. In his mirror, he could see a set of headlights barreling down the road and rightly assumed it was another contingent of Responsivist guards. The tenacity of their pursuit set off all sorts of alarm bells in his mind, but that was something to think about when they were well away from here.

The men firing at the van had no reason to suspect Juan's jeep as he came up behind them, even as the third jeep narrowed the gap. They flashed under a sign announcing in both Greek and English that they were fast approaching the entrance ramp for the New National Road and its vital bridge over the Corinth Canal, so it was the timing, not the execution, that worried him. It would have to be perfect. The ramp was coming up on their right. The third jeep was fifty yards back, and bullets continued to ping off the side of the van ahead.

"Linda," Juan said, eyeing the jeep in front and the one coming up behind him, "speed up as fast as you can go. Don't worry about losing the tires. Just floor it."

The van started to open a gap between it and the jeep, but the jeep's driver fed it a bit more gas and closed the gap again. Cabrillo came up to the jeep's bumper and hit it with what police refer to as PIT, or Precision Immobilization Technique. The impact wasn't very hard and didn't need to be. The trick was to hit in such a way that the back end of the target vehicle gets spun around.

Feeling like a stock-car driver gunning for the lead, Juan hit the jeep a second time, just as the driver corrected from the first impact. This time, there was no saving it, and Juan had to crank his wheel hard to the left as the Responsivists' four-by-four careened out of control, swinging in a wide arc across the road, before its two left tires hooked and the jeep began to flip over and over, shedding bits of sheet metal and the bodies of its occupants as it rolled.

The jeep came to rest on its roof, lying across the single-lane entrance to the thruway, effectively blocking it. Linda's back was covered, and she was clear to make her run for the bridge. Juan kept watching his rearview mirror. The party in the third jeep slowed as they approached the on-ramp but must have soon realized their quarry had escaped, because they accelerated again after Cabrillo, who continued to drive toward the heart of Corinth.

NO ONE IN THE OP CENTER could believe what they saw from the flying drone until Eric radioed Cabrillo. "Is that you in the second jeep, Chairman?"

"Affirmative."

"Nice piece of driving."

"Thanks. How's everything look?"

"Linda and her team are in the clear. There are no other vehicles coming out of the Responsivists' stronghold, and, so far, your fireworks display hasn't caught the attention of the local authorities. We're about two minutes from entering the canal. George just came in from the hangar and will be taking over the UAV."

"What about my route through town?"

"Last sweep looked clear. As soon as Linda reaches the bridge, you'll have primary aerial coverage."

"Okay. See you soon."

Wearing his flight suit with the pant leg cut off and a large bandage taped to his thigh, George Adams settled himself at a computer, keeping the injured leg extended stiffly.

"How you doing?" Max asked, trying to sound more gruff than normal to hide his guilt.

"One more scar to impress the ladies. Hux only needed eight stitches. I'm more worried about the Robinson. Talk about giving something the Swiss cheese treatment. There were eleven holes in the canopy alone. Okay, Stoney, I'm ready."

Eric flipped UAV control to Adams so he could concentrate on getting the big freighter through the Corinth Canal.

First proposed during Roman times, a canal across the narrow isthmus was beyond their capabilities. Being master engineers, the Romans built a road, which the Greeks called the *diolkos*, instead. Cargo was removed from ships at one end, and both freight and vessel were loaded onto wheeled sleds that were dragged by slaves to the other terminus, where the ships were refloated and reloaded. It wasn't until the end of the nineteenth century that the technology had evolved to excavate a proper canal and save modern cargo vessels the one-hundred-and-sixty-mile journey around the Peloponnese. After a failed French effort, a Greek company took over and completed the canal in 1893.

At a little less than four miles long and only eighty-two feet wide at sea level, there wasn't much to note about the canal except for one special feature. It was carved through solid rock that soared more than two hundred and fifty feet above the ships transiting through it. It was as though an ax had cleaved the living rock to create the narrow passage. A favorite tourist activity was to stand on one of the bridges that span the canal and peer down at the oceangoing ships far below.

Had it not been for the lights of the tiny town of Poseidonia, the view on the *Oregon*'s main screen would have looked as though the ship were racing toward a cliff. The canal was so narrow it was difficult to spot. It was just a fractionally lighter slash on the dark stone. An occasional headlight swept along the main bridge a mile inland.

"You sure about this, Mr. Stone?" Max asked.

"With the high tide, we'll have four feet clearance on each side of our wing bridges. I can't promise I won't scrape some paint, but I'll get us through."

"Okay, then. I'm not going to watch this on TV if I can get the live show. I'll be up on the bridge."

"Just don't go outside," Eric cautioned, a little uncertainty in his voice. "You know. Just in case."

"You'll do fine, lad."

Max took the elevator topside and emerged on the dim pilothouse. He glanced aft, to check where crewmen were making preparations under the direction of Mike Trono and Jerry Pulaski, two of Linc's best gundogs. Crewmen were also stationed at the bow.

The ship was steaming at nearly twenty knots as it made its approach. Though the canal is used today primarily by pleasure boats and sightseeing craft, any large vessel was towed through by tugs because of its tight confines and speed was limited to just a few knots. Max had supreme confidence in Eric Stone's ship-handling abilities, but he couldn't ignore the tension knotting his shoulders. He loved the *Oregon* as much as the Chairman and hated to see even a scratch mar her intentionally scabrous hide.

They passed a long breakwater to starboard, and the collision alarm sounded through every compartment on the ship. The crew knew what was coming and had taken the proper precautions.

Small bridges running along the coast roads spanned each end of the canal. Unlike the high truss bridges that towered over the water, these two-lane structures were just above sea level. To accommodate ships transiting the waterway, the bridges could be mechanically lowered until they rested on the seafloor so that vessels could pass over them. Once the ship was clear, the bridges were cranked back into place and cars could cross once again.

With her bow configured and reinforced to crash through sea ice, the *Oregon* slammed into the bridge, riding up on it in an earsplitting squeal of steel. Rather than crush the bridge, the tremendous weight of the hull snapped the locks that held it in place and it sank under the hull. The *Oregon* came back down with a tremendous splash that sloshed back and forth against the canal sides and dangerously slewed the ship.

Max looked up. It was as if the canal's featureless rock walls reached the heavens. They dwarfed the ship, and, up ahead, the automobile and railroad bridges looked as light and delicate as girders from his boyhood Erector set.

The tramp freighter continued to charge through the canal, and, to Eric's credit, he kept it dead center, using the *Oregon*'s athwartship thrusters with such delicacy that the flying bridges never once touched the side. Max chanced stepping out on one and walking all the way to the end. It was foolish and dangerous. If Eric made a mistake, a collision at this speed would tear the platform off the superstructure. But

Max wanted to reach out and touch the stone. It was cool and rough. At this depth, the canal remained in shadow for most of the day, so the sun never had the chance to warm it.

Satisfied, he hurried to the bridge just as the *Oregon* heaved slightly and the railing smacked the canal wall. Eric shifted their heading infinitesimally, so as not to overcorrect, and centered them once again.

"Linda's van is just about at the New National Road bridge," Gomez called over the intercom. "I can see the Chairman, too. He's still got a good lead on the jeep chasing him."

"On my way down," Max said, and moved for the elevator.

The damaged tire finally shredded a quarter mile from the bridge, and they covered the distance riding on the rim, sparks shooting from the back of the van like a Catherine wheel. The sound was like fingernails across a chalkboard, something Linda hated more than any other noise in the world. She wasn't sure what made her happier when they reached the center of the span: that they were almost home free or that the unholy shriek had ended.

Franklin Lincoln threw open the side door as soon as they stopped. He could see the *Oregon* fast approaching and heaved three thick nylon climbing ropes off the bridge. The ropes were secured around the van's seats and through a frame member that was exposed in the cargo area. They uncoiled as they fell through space and came up just ten feet shy of the sea.

Linda quickly jumped out of her seat and donned her rappelling gear—harness, helmet, and gloves—while, two hundred feet below them, water frothed at the *Oregon*'s stern as reverse thrust was applied to slow her. With the power of her massive engines, she lost headway almost immediately.

Linc had already strapped himself into a harness used by tandem parachute jumpers, and, with Eddie's help, they had clipped an unconscious Kyle Hanley to him. The three of them then secured themselves to the lines and waited for word from down below.

On the *Oregon*, crewmen at the bow grabbed the dangling ropes and guided them aft as the vessel crept forward, making sure they didn't become entangled with the superstructure, communications antenna, or any of the hundreds of things that could snag them. As soon as the men reached the aft deck, Max ordered his people to go.

Never one to be bothered by heights, Linda stepped onto the guardrail and started lowering herself from the bridge. Eddie was on one side of her, and Linc, carrying Kyle, made his way down the other. They lowered themselves down the bridge's underpinning girders, and then, suddenly, they were dangling two hundred feet over their ship, nothing holding them in place but the three-quarter-inch lines.

With a whoop, Linda shot down her rope like a runaway elevator. Eddie and Linc quickly followed, almost free-falling through space before using their rappelling harnesses to slow their descent. They touched down at almost the same time, and stood still so that their crewmates could unhook them from the ropes. The lines' trailing ends were quickly knotted around cast-iron bollards bolted to the ship's deck.

Breathless from the adrenaline rush, Linda said, "Now for the fun part."

Watching the action on deck from the closed-circuit television system, Eric Stone didn't wait for orders. He eased the T-handle throttle forward slightly to edge the ship farther up the canal. The slack in the ropes vanished in an instant, and then they quivered for a second before the ship's thrust rolled the rental van over the guardrail. It plummeted like a stone, smashing into the water just behind the *Oregon*'s fantail. The impact flattened its roof and blew out all its windows. The weight of its engine caused the van to upend, like a duck diving for food, and it bobbed in the ship's wake for a moment before filling with water and sinking out of sight. They would tow the ruined vehicle well into the Aegean before cutting the ropes and allowing the van to sink to the bottom.

The van was rented by a disguised crew member using false identification, and there would be no link back to the Corporation. And only one more person needed to rejoin the ship for the mission to be considered a success, even if they had to go so deep into their playbook that they had to use plan C.

. . .

CABRILLO RACED TOWARD the Corinth Canal, flashing by villages and small farms in a blur. In the moonlight, stands of conical cypress trees looked like army sentries guarding the fields.

No matter how recklessly he took corners or how brutally he punished the jeep's transmission, he couldn't shake his tail. Denied returning their kidnapped member, the men chasing him wanted blood. They drove just as hard, using both lanes of the road and often skidding into the gravel verge in their pursuit. They had managed a few potshots at Cabrillo, but at the speeds they were traveling there was no chance to fire accurately, and they'd stopped, presumably to conserve ammunition.

Juan regretted not raising the windscreen as he squinted against eighty-mile-an-hour wind. It didn't help that a breeze had picked up, and grit as nebulous as smoke drifted across the road and scoured his eyes. He flashed past the site of ancient Isthmia. Unlike other ruins dotting Greece, there was nothing to see on the low hillock, no temples or columns, just a sign and a tiny museum. What he noticed most, however, was a sign stating the modern town of Isthmia was two kilometers ahead. If the *Oregon* didn't get into position soon, he was going to be in trouble. The jeep's gas gauge was staying above EMPTY on the sheer force of his will.

He heard his name in his earbud and had to adjust the volume on his radio. "Juan here."

"Chairman, it's Gomez. Linda and the others are safely aboard. I've got you on the drone, and Eric's making his calculations now, but you might want to slow down a touch."

"You do see that other jeep behind me, right?"

"I do," the chopper pilot drawled. "But if we don't get this just right, you're going to end up like a fly on the wrong side of a swatter, if you know what I mean."

The simile was more than apt. "Thanks for the mental picture."

The road started to descend down to the coast. In order to save fuel, Juan mashed the clutch and let momentum and gravity take over for a few seconds. He drove with one eye on the side mirror, and a few seconds after spotting the Responsivists' headlights he eased off the clutch to let the engine engage again.

The motor sputtered. It caught instantly, but gave another weak cough. Cabrillo used an old stock-car driver's trick, weaving the jeep to slosh the gasoline in the tank. It seemed to work because the engine purred.

"Juan, Eric's finished with his number crunching," Adams said. "You're eight hundred and seventy meters from the bridge, meaning you're too close. You need to slow down to fifty miles an hour if we're to make this happen."

The pursuing jeep was eighty yards back and closing. The road was too straight for Juan to do much maneuvering, and, when he tried to swerve again so they would waste a shot, the motor wheezed. He cursed.

"I'm coming in hot. Tell Eric to goose the old girl and meet me."

He entered the town of Isthmia, a typical Greek seaside village. He could smell the sea and the iodine taint of drying fishing nets. The buildings were mostly whitewashed, with the ubiquitous red-tiled roofs. Satellite dishes grew from many of them like high-tech mushrooms. The main drag opened on a small village square, and Cabrillo could see the stanchions that raised and lowered the narrow bridge to cross the canal beyond.

"Okay, Chairman." This time, it was Eric in the earbud. "You need to slow down now. Exactly fifty-two kilometers per hour or you're going to hit us."

"You're sure?"

"It's simple vectors. High school physics," Eric replied as if he'd been insulted. "Trust me."

The crack of a rifle sounded behind Cabrillo. He had no idea where the bullet went but had no choice but to ignore it and comply with Eric's directions. As he slowed, the AK-47 chattered on automatic. He could hear the bullets striking the jeep. One passed over his shoulder close enough to ruffle the cloth of his uniform shirt.

The bridge was fifty yards away and the Responsivists maybe fifty yards behind him. Traveling at the required speed took every ounce of self-control Cabrillo possessed. The primitive part of his brain was screaming for him to floor it, to get out of there as fast as he could.

Appearing like a colossus, the bow of the *Oregon* suddenly emerged from behind a four-story building that was blocking Juan's view of the canal. She never looked so beautiful.

And, suddenly, she was rearing up, her plates scraping against the bridge, as she had done when she'd first entered the canal. She rose higher and higher, climbing up the bridge as if she were cutting an ice pack. With a shearing clang, the mechanical systems that operated the bridge gave out under her titanic weight, and the ship crashed back into the canal with barely a check in her speed.

Juan kept driving at her, seemingly bent on crashing into her armored flank. The men chasing him must have thought he was bent on suicide.

Fifteen yards to go and panic began to hit him. They'd timed it wrong. He was going to slam into the ship as she glided out of the canal. He could feel it. More gunfire erupted from behind him. It was answered by someone firing from the *Oregon*'s railing. He saw the muzzle flash against the darkened hull.

Seconds now. Speed, vectors, timing. He'd gambled and lost and was about to crank the wheel over when he spotted the yawning opening of the boat garage bathed in red battle lights. The *Oregon* was ballasted perfectly to the bottom lip of the ramp they used to launch Zodiacs and their assault boat was just slightly lower than the roadway.

Keeping it at exactly fifty-two kilometers per hour, he hit the end of the road, jumping the one-foot gap separating the damaged bridge from the *Oregon* and landing inside his ship. He hit the brakes and caromed into reinforced netting set up to stop boats during high-speed maneuvers. The jeep's air bag deployed, further cushioning Juan from the brutal deceleration.

From outside, he heard the squeal of brakes. Tires dug in hard but not hard enough. Spinning sideways, the pursuing jeep slammed into the hull with a dull ring and teetered against the plates as the ship passed by. Metal tore against metal, as the *Oregon* ground the jeep against the side of the canal, flattening the vehicle and its occupants, until Eric Stone gave a little lateral thrust and the jeep fell into the water.

Max materialized at Cabrillo's side and helped him dig out from under the deflated air bag. "Plan C, huh?"

"It worked, didn't it?" They exited the boat garage, Juan moving a little stiffly. "How's Kyle?"

"He's sedated down in medical with Hux."

"We'll get him straightened out."

"I know." Max stopped and looked into Juan's eyes. "Thank you."

"No thanks necessary." They started walking toward the infirmary.

"If plan C was this nuts, you've got to tell me about plan D."

"Oh sure." Juan grinned. "Only problem with that one was, we couldn't find enough Spartans to re-create the battle of Thermopylae."

CHAPTER 15

A PATROL CRAFT FROM THE HELLENIC COAST Guard approached the *Oregon* just as the dawn sun crested the horizon. After a mad sixty-mile dash from the Corinth Canal, they were cruising at a steady fourteen knots, an appropriate speed for such a dilapidated ship. The sooty smoke pouring from her funnel made it appear as though the engine was burning as much oil as bunker fuel. Over the radio, the captain of the forty-foot patrol boat didn't sound too concerned about a rust-bucket freighter, so far from the scene of the crime, being the culprit.

"No, Captain," Juan bluffed smoothly. "We've been nowhere near Corinth. We were on our way to Piraeus when our agent radioed that our contract to haul olive oil to Egypt had been cancelled. We are continuing on to Istanbul. Besides, I don't even think this old girl could fit in the canal. Too wide in the hips." Cabrillo gave a lewd chuckle. "And if we had hit a bridge, our bows would have been crushed. As you can see, that is not the case. You are welcome to board and inspect them, if you wish."

"That won't be necessary," the Coast Guard captain replied. "The incident occurred a hundred kilometers from here. By the looks of your vessel, it would take you eight hours to travel that far."

"And only with the wind at our backs," Juan quipped.

"If you see any ships acting erratically or have damage to their bows, please contact the authorities immediately."

"Roger that, and good hunting. *Atlantis* out." Juan waved at the small cutter from the wing bridge and ambled back inside, blowing out a long breath. He hung the radio hand mike back on its hook. The coiled cord trailed onto the floor.

"Did you have to invite them over for an inspection?" Eddie Seng asked from where he stood at the ship's wheel, pretending to steer.

"They never would have taken me up on it. The Greeks want to nail someone's hide to the outhouse door for what happened back in Corinth. They're not going to bother with a ship that couldn't possibly be involved."

"What happens when they correlate all of their eyewitness accounts of what happened and come to the conclusion that we are the only vessel that fits the description?"

Juan slapped him on the shoulder. "We'll be deep into international waters and they'll be looking for a ship called the *Atlantis*. As soon as there's no other boat traffic around, I want the name plates on the fantail and fairleads changed back to *Oregon*." He paused for a moment before adding, "Just in case someone has an eye for detail and a long memory, we'll be avoiding Greece for a while."

"Prudent precaution."

"First watch should be up any second. Why don't you head below and get some well-earned rest. I'll want your after-action report on my desk by four this afternoon."

"Should make for some interesting reading," Eddie remarked. "In my worst nightmares, I never expected that hornet's nest we walked in on."

"Me neither," Juan admitted. "There's a lot more to these people than what we saw on their website and what the deprogrammer told Linda. That level of paranoia means they're hiding something."

"The obvious question is, what?"

"Maybe we'll get lucky and no one will notice the bug I planted."

Eddie shot him a dubious look. "The first thing their head of security's going to do is sweep every square inch of that place looking for listening devices."

"You're right. I know. So if an electronic spy doesn't work, we send in a human one."

"I'll go."

"You don't exactly have the look of a lost soul searching for meaning in life who's willing to blindly follow some wacko's rants."

"Mark Murphy?" Eddie suggested.

"He fits the bill to a tee, but he doesn't have the skill sets to pull off an undercover job like this. Eric Stone would be another candidate, but the same problem crops up. No. I was thinking of Linda. As a woman, she would draw less suspicion automatically. She's got a background in intelligence work, and, as we have both seen a dozen times over, she knows how to keep her head."

"How would you make it work?"

Juan smiled tiredly. "Give me a break, will ya? I'm making this up as I go along. The three of us will meet before dinner and brainstorm a strategy."

"Just so long as it doesn't turn into a plan C," Eddie teased.

Cabrillo threw up his hands in mock exasperation. "Why is everyone giving me a hard time about that? The plan worked."

"So do most Rube Goldberg contraptions."

"Bah!" Juan dismissed him with a wave.

Before heading for his cabin for what he hoped to be about ten hours of uninterrupted sleep, Juan took the elevator down to the Op Center. Hali Kasim was bent over his workstation, papers strewn about his desk as though a hurricane had just passed through. A pair of headphones flattened his otherwise-curly hair. Unlike others whose faces turn to stone when deep in thought, Hali's Semitic features were serene, a sure sign his brain was churning.

He startled when he felt Cabrillo standing over him. He stripped off his headphones and massaged his ears.

"How's it coming?" Juan asked. Moments after checking in on Dr. Huxley and Kyle Hanley when he'd returned to the *Oregon*, Juan had asked Hali to monitor the bug he'd placed in Gil Martell's office.

"Reminds me of that urban legend about hearing voices in the white noise of a television tuned to a station that's off the air." He handed the headphones to Juan.

They were warm and a little damp when he slipped them on. Kasim hit a button on his computer. Static filled Juan's ears, but in it he could hear something. To call them words would be an overstatement. They were more like low tones underlying the crackle of electronics.

He pulled off the headphones. "Have you tried scrubbing the tape?"

"This is scrubbed. Twice."

"Put it on speaker and play it from the beginning," Juan told him.

A few keystrokes later, the recording began. Because the bug was sound activated, it had remained dormant until someone entered the office.

"Oh no, oh no, oh no. This can't be happening." The voice, Gil Martell's, was panicked, but managed to retain its California charm. Then came the sound of drawers opening and closing, presumably Martell checking to see if he'd been robbed. A chair creaked as he sat. "Okay, Gil, get ahold of yourself. What time is it in California? What does it matter?" A telephone handset rattled, and, after a long pause, Martell began to speak. "Thom, it's Gil Martell."

Juan knew that Thom would be Thomas Severance, who headed the Responsivist movement with his wife, Heidi.

"Someone broke into the compound about fifteen minutes ago. It looks like a rescue operation. One of our members was abducted from his room . . . What? Ah, Kyle Hanley . . . No, no, not yet. He'd only been here a short time . . . My security guys tell me there were a dozen of them. They were all armed. They're chasing them now in jeeps so there's a chance we'll get the kid back, but I wanted you to know." There was a long pause while Martell listened to his superior. "That'll be my next call. We've thrown enough money around to the local authorities so they won't dig too deep. They can claim the local cops stopped arms traffickers or al-Qaeda or something . . . Could you repeat that? The connection's terrible . . . Oh yeah. They first broke into my office and then went . . . Hold it!" Martell's voice rose defensively. "You don't need to send Zelimir Kovac. We can take care of this ourselves . . . Bugs? This whole country's crawling with them. Oh, electronic bugs. Damnit! Sorry."

Cabrillo heard the sound of drawers opening and closing again as Martell looked for something, and then came the blast of static. Martell had turned on an electronic jammer to defeat any listening devices that might have been left behind.

Hali killed the recording. "I can keep working at it, but I don't know how much good it will do."

"Whatever you can find in all that static will be worth the effort." Cabrillo rubbed his tired eyes.

"You ought to get some sleep," Hali suggested needlessly. Juan was dead on his feet.

"Do you have someone looking into this Zelimir Kovac?"

"I Googled him, but there wasn't anything there. When Eric comes back on duty, he's going to try to find out about him."

"Where's Eric now?"

"Wooing our young charge down in medical. He's bringing her breakfast, and taking advantage of Mark being asleep in his cabin."

Juan had forgotten all about Jannike Dahl. He knew she had no immediate family, but there had to be some people back home, believing she had been lost with all the others aboard the *Golden Dawn*. Unfortunately, they would have to suffer awhile longer. He wasn't sure why he wanted to delay announcing her rescue, but the sixth sense that had served him so well over the years was telling him to keep her survival a secret.

The people responsible for the attack on the cruise ship believed they had succeeded in killing everyone. There was an advantage in knowing something they did not, even if Juan didn't yet recognize what it could be. For the time being, Janni was safe with them aboard the *Oregon*.

He turned away from Kasim. "Helm, what's our ETA in Iraklion?"

"We'll be there around five o'clock this afternoon."

They were diverting to the capital of Crete, where Chuck Gunderson would be waiting with their Gulfstream to take Max, Eddie, and Kyle to their rendezvous in Rome. Juan had until then to reconsider keeping the young woman aboard. He went to his workstation and typed out some instructions to Kevin Nixon down in the Magic Shop to prepare a passport for her, just in case. He also made a mental note to consult with Julia Huxley before making his final decision. By keeping Janni on the ship, there was a chance Hux could discover something about her physiognomy that had helped the young woman survive the toxin, if Mark and Eric were wrong about acute food poisoning.

Ten minutes later, Cabrillo was sprawled across his bed, sleeping so soundly that, for the first time in a long time, he didn't need the mouth guard to keep him from grinding his teeth.

CHAPTER 16

ZELIMIR KOVAC ENJOYED KILLING.

He hadn't discovered this particular interest until civil war erupted in his native Yugoslavia and he had been drafted into the military. Prior to going into the army, Kovac had been a construction worker and amateur heavyweight boxer. But it was in the military that he found his true vocation. For five glorious years, he and his unit of like-minded men had torn a swath through the country, killing Croats, Bosnians, and Kosovars by the hundreds.

By the time of NATO's intervention in 1999, Kovac, who had been born with a different name, heard rumblings about trials for people who had committed crimes against humanity. He was certain he would head the list of those sought by the authorities, so he deserted, fleeing first to Bulgaria, eventually to Greece.

Standing at six feet eight inches, with the build of a wrestler, it hadn't taken him long to find a niche in the Athens underworld as an enforcer. His street cunning and ruthlessness were rewarded with promotions within the organized-crime world, and he cemented his reputation by killing an entire gang of Albanian drug dealers trying to horn in on the heroin trade.

During his first few years in Athens, he began reading books in English to learn the language. The material itself was unimportant to him, and he read biographies of people he'd never heard of, histories of places he had no interest in, and novels whose plots he didn't care about. The fact that the books were in English was all that was important.

That is, until he found a dog-eared book in a secondhand shop. The title intrigued him: *We're Breeding Ourselves to*

Death, by Dr. Lydell Cooper. He mistakenly thought it was a book about sex and bought it.

Between the covers was a rational explanation for everything he had believed since the war. There were too many people on the planet, and, unless something was done about it, our world was doomed. Of course, Dr. Cooper didn't single out any ethnic groups in his treatise, but Kovac read the book with his own racist perspective and was certain Cooper meant the inferior races, like the ones Kovac had slaughtered for so long.

> With no natural predators, there are no limits to our burgeoning population, and the hardwiring in our DNA to procreate means we will not stop ourselves. Only the lowly virus stands in our way, and each day we draw closer to eradicating this threat as well.

He took this to mean that mankind needed predators to cull the weak so that the healthy could thrive. This wasn't Cooper's point at all. He wasn't espousing violence of any kind, but that didn't matter to Kovac. He had found a cause he could truly believe in. Man needed predators again, and Kovac wanted to be part of that.

When he discovered that the Responsivist movement had opened a facility outside of Corinth, he knew finding that book was providential.

Thomas Severance himself was at the compound the day Kovac had shown up to offer his services, and the two men talked for hours, discussing fine points of Dr. Cooper's work and the organization it had spawned. Severance subtly made Kovac understand the true philosophy behind Responsivism but never once tried to blunt the Serb's rough edges.

"We ourselves aren't violent, Zelimir," Severance had told him, "but there are others who don't understand us, who want to ensure that our great founder's message isn't spread. No one has tried to hurt us yet—physically, I mean—but I know it's coming, because people don't want to be told they are part of the problem. They are going to lash out at us, and we will need you to protect us. That will be your function."

So Zelimir Kovac would continue his role as an enforcer, only this time he did it for the Responsivists and himself rather than for drug lords and dictators.

Gil Martell looked sleek behind his desk, his bronze hair slicked back and his capped and bleached teeth shining when Kovac strode in. Martell could only hold the pose for a second before his smile faded.

Hooking up with Thom Severance had been good for him. It got him out of L.A. before the police closed in on his auto-theft business again. He had a huge house facing the ocean just down the road from the compound and any number of willing women for his bed from the transient population of Responsivists who came to Greece on retreat. Part of him even believed that there were too damned many people on the planet. He didn't believe any of that garbage about alien membranes, but he was a consummate salesman and could feign belief better than the most devout.

As for Thom and Heidi's master plan, what did he care about a bunch of rich people on cruise ships?

It was only around Kovac that his façade cracked. The big Serb was a psychopath, plain and simple. Gil didn't know the man's background but could only assume he'd been involved in the ethnic cleansing he'd read about in Yugoslavia back in the late nineties. The rescue of Kyle Hanley had been a disaster, but Martell felt he could handle the fallout. He didn't need Kovac watching over his shoulder and reporting every little detail back to Thom and Heidi. He admitted he should have anticipated his office had been bugged, but he'd said nothing substantive before turning on the jamming device. It was a minor lapse that didn't warrant Thom calling in his creepy lapdog.

Kovac held a finger to his fleshy lips in a shushing gesture before Martell could speak. When Kovac reached the desk, he shut off the jammer, then took a small piece of electronics from the inside pocket of his black leather jacket. He systematically swept the room, his small eyes never leaving the electronic readout as he moved the device over bookshelves, furniture, and the carpet. Satisfied, he slipped it back into his pocket.

"So there weren't any—"

The weight of Kovac's stare pressed Gil Martell farther into his chair.

Kovac upended the desk lamp and peeled the tiny eavesdropper from the base. He wasn't familiar with the particular brand, but he recognized its sophistication. Because the bug was so small, he knew that somewhere within a mile or so of the compound a booster transceiver retransmitted whatever the bug heard to a circling satellite. Searching for it would be futile.

"End transmission," he said into the microphone, doing his best to mask his accent. He then crushed the bug between his thick fingernails, grinding it until it was as fine as particles of sand. He finally looked to Martell. "Now you may speak."

"Was that the only one?"

Kovac didn't bother answering such an inane question. "I will need to sweep everywhere the intruders penetrated." It would be tedious but necessary. "Have the guards draw up a map of the possibly infected areas."

"Of course. But I can tell you that they only entered my office and the dorm."

Feeling his head throb at Martell's utter stupidity, Kovac had to physically calm himself. When he spoke, his English was heavily accented but clear. "They had to breach the perimeter wall and cross the compound to this building and then make their way to the dormitory. They could have dropped bugs along the paths, thrown them into bushes, stuck them to trees, and even left some on top of the walls."

"Oh. I didn't understand."

Kovac gave him a look that said: *You are right. You don't understand.* "Was there anything on your computer pertaining to the upcoming mission?"

"No. Absolutely not. All that stuff is in my safe. It's the first thing I checked after getting off the phone with Thom."

"Give me that material," Kovac ordered.

Martell considered defying the Serb and calling Severance, but he knew that Thom trusted Kovac on all matters concerning security and that his protests would fall on deaf ears. The less he had to do with their scheme the better. In fact, maybe it was time to move on from here. The break-in might be a sign telling him to cash in while he could. He'd skimmed almost a million dollars from the Greek retreat. It wasn't enough to live on for the rest of his life, but it would certainly establish him well enough until he found something else.

He got up from behind his desk and strode across to his office sitting area. Kovac did nothing to help him move the furniture off the Oriental rug or fold it back to reveal a trapdoor and, below, a midsize safe embedded in the floor.

"The chairs and tables were in their exact position when I came in, so I know nothing was moved," he explained as he worked. "And look, the wax seal over the keyhole is intact."

Kovac didn't bother telling Martell that a professional team, like the one who'd entered the retreat, would know to replace the furniture in its correct position, and, while a wax seal was a good touch, it could be duplicated if they'd had enough time. But he wasn't all that worried that the safe had been their objective. He'd glanced at the file they had on Kyle Hanley, and he suspected the young Californian's family had hired a hostage-rescue team to return their son. No doubt they would have hired a deprogrammer as well. Most likely Adam Jenner.

The very thought of the man's name balled Kovac's hands into fists.

"Here we go," Martell said, and pulled a strongbox out of the safe. There was an electronic keypad on its lid. The facility's director tapped a numerical sequence and smirked at Kovac. "According to the box's memory, it hasn't been opened in four days, which is when I got the latest updates from Thom."

A child could have reprogrammed the strongbox with a UBS cord and a laptop, but, again, Kovac held his tongue. "Open it."

Martell entered his pass-code numbers. The box beeped and the lid lifted slightly. Inside was a three-inch-thick manila folder. Kovac stretched out his hand for Martell to hand him the file. He glanced through the pages quickly. It was lists of names, ships, ports of call, schedules, as well as short biographies of crew members. Completely innocuous to anyone who didn't know their significance. The dates mentioned weren't too far in the future.

"Close the safe," Kovac said absently as he thumbed the file.

Martell complied, settling the lockbox back into its niche and securing the door. "I'll put on the wax seal later."

Kovac glared.

"Or I'll do it now." Martell's tone was flippant. He kept the wax in his desk, and the seal was the prep school ring he wore but had never earned. A few minutes later, the kilim rug was back down and the couch, chairs, and coffee table in their places.

"Did Kyle Hanley know anything about this?" Kovac held up the file like a zealot proffering a holy book.

"No. I explained it to Thom. Hanley had only been here a short time. He'd seen the machines but knew nothing of the plan."

Martell's casual response triggered a look of suspicion on Kovac's face. The room seemed to chill a few degrees. Gil made his decision. As soon as Kovac left, he'd head to his house, pack up a few things, and hop the next plane to Zurich, where he kept his numbered account.

"It's possible he might have heard rumors," he amended.

"What sort of rumors, Martell?"

Gil didn't like how Kovac said his surname and swallowed. "Ah, a few of the kids here are talking about a Sea Retreat, like those that went on the *Golden Dawn*. They make it sound like a big party."

For the first time, Kovac's cool veneer seemed to slip. "Do you have any idea what happened to that ship?"

"No. I don't let anyone here watch the news or use the Internet. I haven't either. Why, did something go wrong?"

Kovac recalled Mr. Severance's words when he'd phoned from California this morning: *Do what you think is right.* Now he understood what the Responsivist leader had meant. "Mr. Severance doesn't trust you much."

"How dare you. He put me in charge of this retreat and the training of our people," Martell blustered. "He trusts me as much as he does you."

"No, Mr. Martell. That is not the case. You see, two days ago I was on the *Golden Dawn* and participated in an experiment. It was glorious. Everyone on that vessel died in ways I haven't imagined in my worst nightmares."

"They what?" Martell shouted, sickened by the news and the reverent way Kovac said it, as though he were talking about a favorite piece of art or the peacefulness of a sleeping child.

"They are dead. All of them. And the ship scuttled. I had to secure the bridge before releasing the virus, so nobody could report what was happening. It swept through the ship like wildfire. It couldn't have taken more than an hour. Young and old, it didn't matter. Their bodies couldn't fight it."

Gil Martell backed around his desk, as if it could act as a barrier to the horror he was hearing. He reached for the phone. "I have to call Thom. This can't be right."

"By all means. Call him."

Martell's hand hovered over the handset. He knew that if he made the call Thom would verify everything the twisted thug had said. Two things flashed through his mind. The first was that he was in far over his head. And the second was that Kovac wasn't going to let him out of his office alive.

"Just what did Mr. Severance tell you about the operation?" Kovac asked.

Keep him talking, Martell thought frantically. There was a button under his desk that buzzed his secretary in the outer office. Surely Kovac wouldn't attempt anything with witnesses.

"He, ah, he told me that our team of researchers in the Philippines had engineered a virus that causes severe inflammation of the reproductive ducts in both men and women. He told me that three out of every ten people exposed who are infected will become sterile and will never be able to add to the earth's population, even if they tried in vitro techniques. The plan is to release it on a bunch of cruise ships, where everyone is basically trapped, so they all become infected."

"That's only part of the story," Kovac said.

"So what is the truth?" *Where is that damned woman?*

"Everything you said about the effects of the virus is true, only there is something you don't know." Kovac gave a triumphant smile. "You see, the virus is highly contagious for about four months after infecting a host, even though it shows no symptoms. And, from a handful of cruise ships, it will spread around the globe, infecting millions upon millions, until every man, woman, and child on the planet has been exposed. That three-out-of-ten sterility number is closer to five in ten unable to breed, once the infection has run its course. This isn't about preventing a few thousand passengers and crew from having children. It's about stopping half the world."

Gil collapsed into his chair. His mouth worked to form words but no sound came out. The past three minutes had been too much. The *Golden Dawn*. He knew a hundred of the people on that ship, probably two hundred. Now this. This monster telling him that he'd been working for two years on a plan to intentionally sterilize three billion people.

He wasn't going to lose any sleep over the sterilization of a couple thousand cruise ship passengers. They'd be depressed, but life would go on, and, as a bonus, he bet a few orphanages would be emptied.

He should have seen it was going to go far beyond that. What was it Dr. Cooper had written in *We're Breeding Ourselves to Death*:

> *Arguably the greatest transfer of wealth in human history occurred when the Plague swept Europe and wiped out a third of its population. Lands were consolidated, allowing for a greater standard of living, not only for the owners but for those who worked for them. This event single-handedly paved the way for the Renaissance and gave rise to European domination of the world.*

"We have taken Dr. Cooper's words and turned them into action," Kovac said, giving voice to the horror echoing in the empty chasm that had once been Martell's soul.

Martell thought he was safe behind his desk for the moment, but he hadn't counted on the big man's strength. As if the desk were no more than a cardboard box, Kovac shoved it into Gil, pinning him in his seat against the back wall. He opened his mouth to shout out to his secretary. Kovac wasn't especially quick, and the Responsivist director managed a hoarse croak before his throat was closed with a jab to his

Adam's apple. His eyes bulged from their sockets as he fought for a breath he could not draw.

Kovac looked around the office. There was nothing he could see that would make this look like a suicide until he spied the pictures hanging on the wall. He scanned the faces quickly and knew which one he would use. Leaving Martell struggling to fill his lungs, Kovac crossed to a photograph of Donna Sky.

The actress was too skinny for his tastes, but it wasn't much of a stretch to believe Martell would be in love with her. He snatched the picture off the wall and carefully slid the glossy from the frame. He smashed the glass on the edge of the desk.

Kovac pressed Martell into his seat with one massive hand, while, with the other, he selected the largest glass shard, a dagger at least five inches long. He released Martell's head and grabbed one of his arms, making sure to keep his grip loose enough so he didn't bruise the tanned skin.

The glass cut into his flesh with spongy resistance and dark blood welled up from the wound, pooling on the desk before drizzling to the floor. Gil Martell struggled, thrashing in his seat, but he was no match for the Serb. He could only manage a rough cawing sound that wouldn't be heard beyond the office walls. His movements became slower and more uncoordinated as his strength ebbed through the gash until he finally went limp.

Careful not to leave bloody footprints, Kovac slid the desk back to its proper position. He hefted Martell's body from his seat and reversed the chair so he could set the corpse astride it. He lowered Gil's head until the bruise on his throat was hard up against the chair's wooden seat back. The coroner would attribute the bruising to his head tipping forward when he passed out from blood loss. The final detail was to arrange the photograph of Donna Sky so it seemed to be the last thing Gil Martell saw before his death.

As Kovac closed the office door behind him, Martell's secretary entered the building through the main door. She was carrying a ceramic coffee cup and a large purse. She was in her late fifties with a bad dye job, and an extra fifty pounds hanging from her frame.

"Well, hello there, Mr. Kovac," she said brightly.

He didn't recall her name, so he said, "Mr. Martell is at his desk already. As you can guess, he's very upset about what happened last night."

"Terrible thing."

"Yes, it was," Kovac agreed with a somber nod. He felt his cell phone vibrate in his pocket. "He asked that he not be disturbed for any reason today."

"Are you going to find out who attacked us and get that poor boy back into the fold?"

"That's why Mr. Severance called me down here." Patricia, he thought. Her name was Patricia Ogdenburg. He checked the screen on his phone. It was Thom Severance, requesting a secure phone call. Considering they had spoken earlier that morning, something critical must have happened. Kovac repocketed the cell.

Patricia looked him in the eye, tilting her head back to do so. "Pardon me for being blunt, but you must know that a lot of folks here are intimidated by you." When he didn't reply, she plowed on. "I think you are as tough as you look, but I also think you are a very caring and thoughtful person, too. You understand social responsibility, and I find your presence a comfort. There are so many ignorant people out there that don't understand all the good we do. I'm glad that you're here to protect us. Bless you, Zelimir Kovac." She laughed. "You're blushing. I think I embarrassed you."

"You are very kind," Kovac said, imagining the loneliness that had driven her, like him, to Responsivism.

"Well, if a compliment can make you blush then I know I'm right."

Oh, how wrong you are, Kovac thought as he left the building without a backward glance.

CHAPTER 17

THE HOTEL WAS IN A HISTORIC SIX-STORY BUILDING not far from the Colosseum. The suite they had rented encompassed nearly a quarter of the top floor and had a wrought-iron balcony that wrapped around the outside walls.

Kyle was still in a chemically induced stupor when Max pushed his wheelchair into the sumptuous entrance, but he could tell by how his son muttered that he was no more than an hour or two of coming awake.

"Hello," someone called from deeper in the suite.

"Hello," Max replied. "Dr. Jenner?"

"Yes, that's right."

Jenner stepped into the foyer from the living room. He wore a dark charcoal suit with a faint stripe and white silk pullover. Max noticed that he also wore thin leather gloves and that his hands were curled unnaturally.

Max couldn't pin down the psychiatrist's age. He had a full head of hair with only a few streaks of gray and a tanned face that looked like it could have had some cosmetic work. There were traces of wrinkles around the eyes and mouth, but they seemed to have been smoothed out surgically. For what Jenner charged for his deprogramming services, he could afford the best plastic surgeons in the world, but his face had that startled, deer-caught-in-the-headlights expression so common with inferior cosmetic work.

It was an incongruity of little importance, but Max was still surprised by it. He held out his hand. "Max Hanley."

Jenner held up his own gloved hands. "You will forgive me if I don't shake. My hands were burned in a car accident when I was younger."

"Oh, certainly. No problem. This is Eddie Seng, from the company that rescued my son, and this is Kyle."

"Pleased to meet you, Doctor," Eddie said. "Sorry we couldn't tell you the name of the hotel until you arrived in Rome. Operational security."

"I quite understand." Jenner led them into one of the suite's three bedrooms. They settled Kyle, wearing a hospital johnny, into the king-sized four-poster and closed the heavy drapes. Max ran the back of his hand along his son's jaw. His eyes were a sea of love, pain, hopelessness, and self-incrimination.

"We'll bring him back," Adam Jenner said, doubtlessly having seen Max's expression on countless parents over the course of his career. Back in the living room, the French doors leading to the balcony were opened, so the sound of Rome's notorious evening traffic was a background hum. Over the roof of the apartment building across the street, they could see the towering travertine walls and arches of the city's most famous landmark. With seating for nearly fifty thousand, the Colosseum was as large as any modern sports arena.

"I trust things went smoothly," Jenner said. He had a trace of an accent Max couldn't place, almost as if he were raised by parents who didn't speak English.

"Actually, they didn't," Max told him.

"Really? What happened?"

The eyes, too, Max thought. There was something about them. Behind Jenner's stylish glasses, his hazel eyes seemed strange. Max could usually read people's eyes in an instant and tell what kind of person they were, but with Jenner he got nothing.

"The Responsivists now employ armed guards," Eddie said when Max didn't respond.

Jenner settled into a plush sofa with a sigh. "I've been afraid this day would come. Thom and Heidi Severance have been increasingly paranoid in the past few years. I guess it was inevitable that they would start keeping weapons. I am truly sorry. I should have warned you of my growing suspicions."

Eddie dismissed Jenner's concern with a wave. "None of my people were hurt, so it isn't a big deal."

"You are being too modest, Mr. Seng. I've been in combat, so I understand what you've been through."

Vietnam, Max thought, putting Jenner near his own age. Mystery solved, and he felt better for it. "So how does this work?" he asked.

"Normally, we would hold an intervention with Kyle's friends and family to let him know he has the support he needs to break away from the Responsivists. However, in this type of situation I will need to speak with Kyle alone for the first few sessions. It's going to be quite a shock when he wakes up and realizes what's happened to him." Jenner gave a wan smile. "And it's my experience that shock turns to anger very quickly."

"Kyle's not violent, if you're concerned," Max assured him. "Unlike his old man, the boy doesn't have a temper."

"I usually prescribe something to keep subjects calm anyway, until the shock wears off." He waved one of his gloves at a side table where an old-fashioned black doctor's bag was perched next to an arrangement of fresh flowers.

"How many people have you helped, Doctor."

"Please, call me Adam. Well over two hundred."

"All successful?"

"I wish I could say yes, but that's not the case. I've had a handful commit suicide, and even more return to the cult. It's sad, really. People get sucked in by what they perceive to be the good works of the Responsivists, but it's only when they have been there for a while that the group begins to exert more and more control, especially by making its members lose contact with their loved ones. Once that happens, it is sometimes difficult to get them to return to their real lives."

"Why do people let it happen?" Eddie asked, but he already knew the answer. It was the same in Chinatown when he was a kid. The pressure to join a gang was intense, and, once you did, they never let you go.

"Loneliness, a sense of disconnect from the world. The Responsivists make them feel they are part of something much larger than themselves, something important that can give them meaning. It's pretty much the same symptoms that lead others to drugs or alcohol, and the rehabilitation is similar. So you have successes as well as failures."

"According to his mother, Kyle's been involved with Responsivism for only a few months, so I think he should be okay."

"Duration has nothing to do with it," Jenner countered.

"It's how deeply he has allowed them to poison his mind. I had a case once where a woman had been going to Responsivist meetings for only two weeks when her husband became concerned and hired me. She ended up leaving him and is now the secretary to the director of their Greek retreat where you rescued your son. Pattie Ogdenburg. Funny how you remember the names of your failures but never those of your successes."

Max and Eddie nodded in unison. They had shared many of each together.

"I'm curious," Eddie said into the gathering silence, "how does someone as successful as Donna Sky get mixed up in something like this?"

"Same as everyone else. Just because she has awards and accolades and an entourage doesn't mean she's any less lonely than anyone else. Oftentimes, celebrities are more estranged from reality than most and are easily swayed. Out in the real world, she's mobbed by fans, but within the organization she's just Donna. And yet, her fame helps recruit new members all the time."

"I will never understand any of this," Max groaned.

"Which is why you hired me." Jenner spoke in a bright voice to lighten the somber mood. "You don't need to understand it. All you have to do is be ready to show your son how much you love him."

"Do you know anything about a Responsivist center in the Philippines?" Eddie asked to change the subject.

Jenner paused to think about the question. "Not specifically. I wouldn't be surprised if they had family-planning clinics there, but . . . No, wait, that's right. There was talk about them opening another retreat. I believe they have bought land someplace, but nothing's been built. Or very little anyway."

"What about leasing a cruise ship?"

"You're talking about the *Golden Dawn*? What a horrible tragedy. I suspect that is what they call a Sea Retreat. They have done that a number of times over the past couple of years. They often lease out an entire ship, or book at least half the cabins, and hold meetings and discuss the movement. I went on one just to see what it was all about. It seemed to me that it was a recruiting tool to get at lonely widows still flush with their late husbands' pensions."

Jenner stood. "I should go check on Kyle."

When he was out of the room, Max crossed to the sideboard where bottles of liquor were lined up like soldiers on parade. He splashed some whiskey into a cut-glass tumbler and indicated to Eddie if he wanted one, too. The former spook declined.

"This isn't a mission," Max said, taking a sip. "You don't need to teetotal."

"Just the same. So what do you think?"

"I think we hit the jackpot with him. He certainly knows what he's dealing with. You?"

"I agree. Linda did a great job finding him, and I'm sure that Kyle will be fine."

"Thanks for babysitting us," Max said, but there was much more behind the words.

"You'd do the same for any of us."

Max's cell phone purred. He reached into his pocket for it. The caller ID read CHAIRMAN.

"We're here, safe and sound," he said by way of greeting.

"Glad to hear it," Cabrillo replied. "Was Jenner there?"

"Yes. Eddie and I were just talking about how lucky we feel to have found him."

"Good."

"How's everything on the *Oregon*?"

"I just got off the phone with Langston. I think I need Julia to install a colostomy bag, because he ripped me a new one for driving the ship through the Corinth Canal."

"Little angry, was he?"

"Oh, my friend, angry was not the word. Through back channels, he's trying to convince the Greeks it wasn't some terrorist plot to destroy the canal. They want to call out NATO, for heaven's sake."

Max winced. "What did I tell you about you and your damned plan Cs."

Juan chuckled. "If any future operation requires a plan C, you can have my resignation."

"I heard that, and Eddie's my witness."

Cabrillo turned serious. "How's Kyle doing?"

"He'll be coming out of the drugs pretty soon. We'll know then."

"You've got a whole boatload of people pulling for the both of you."

"This has been tough," Max admitted. "A lot tougher than I had realized."

"He's your son. Even if you two aren't close, you still love him. Nothing changes that."

"It's just that I'm so angry."

"No, Max, you're guilty. Two separate things, and you've got to get over it or you won't be able to help him. Life happens the way it happens. Some things we can change and some things we can't. You just have to be smart enough to know the difference and act accordingly."

"I feel like I let him down, you know?"

"And there isn't a parent in the world who doesn't feel that way about their kids at some point in time. That's all part of the process."

Max digested what Cabrillo said and nodded. Realizing Juan couldn't see the gesture, he grudgingly said, "You have a point. It's just . . ."

"Tough. I know. Max, when we're on an op, we plan out every detail, every possible contingency, so we're never surprised. And, even then, we get thrown curves. Think about trying to do that in the other parts of our lives. It's impossible. You're doing what any good parent does. You're there for Kyle now. You can't say that this would or wouldn't have happened if you'd been around when he was growing up. Just deal with the here and now. Okay?"

"You're going to make a hell of a father someday."

"Are you kidding me?" Juan laughed. "I know how rotten the world is. I wouldn't let a kid out of his bedroom until he was at least thirty, and even then I'd only let him go as far as the fenced-in yard."

"Where are you guys now?"

"Almost due south of you. We'll hit the Riviera late tomorrow night and have full surveillance of the arms dealer in place by the following morning."

"I should be with you."

"You should be with Kyle. Don't worry about anything. Take all the time you need. Okay?"

"Okay." Eddie gestured for the phone. "Hold on, Eddie wants to talk to you."

"Juan, I was talking with Jenner, and he mentioned the Responsivists have hired cruise ships in the past."

"And?"

"Could be a wild-goose chase, but it wouldn't hurt to have Eric and Mark cross-reference those voyages to see if anything weird went down."

"Not a bad idea. Anything else?"

"He said there are rumors they are building a new retreat in the Philippines. If there was something like four hundred Responsivists on the *Dawn* when she sank, I think they're further along in construction than Dr. Jenner knows. Might be worth checking out."

"Two for two," Cabrillo remarked.

Jenner stepped out of the bedroom, closing the door behind him. In a stage whisper, he said, "Kyle's coming awake. I think it's best if you two leave us for a while." He went to his medical bag and withdrew a cylindrical object about the size of a soup can. "This is a locking device that goes over the suite's doorknob so it can't be opened from the inside."

"Juan, we have to go," Eddie said into the phone and cut the connection.

Max was on his feet. "For how long?"

"Give me your cell phone number and I will call you. Probably an hour or two. Kyle and I will talk some, and then I will administer a sedative."

Max looked at the closed bedroom door and at Jenner, conflicted about what was right.

"Trust me, Mr. Hanley. I know what I'm doing."

"Okay." Max jotted down his number on a piece of hotel stationery. He let Eddie lead him out of the suite and into the richly paneled elevator vestibule. Eddie could see the concern in Hanley's face even in the distorted reflection of the polished brass doors. Behind them, they heard Jenner slipping the clamshell lock over the doorknob.

"Come on, I'll buy you dinner."

"I think I'm in the mood for Italian," Max quipped, to show he wasn't totally out of it.

"Sorry, mate. Chinese food or nothing."

CHAPTER 18

As the *Oregon* drove through the dark waters of the Mediterranean at a little over twenty knots, far below her true capabilities because there were dozens of other vessels plying the shipping routes, there was almost no sensation of movement in her tastefully appointed dining room. If not for the background hum of her magnetohydrodynamic engines and her pump jets, Cabrillo felt like he could be sitting at a five-star restaurant on some fashionable boulevard in Paris.

Juan wore a summer-weight sports jacket over a custom dress shirt open at the collar. His cuff links were tiny compasses and his shoes were Italian leather. Across from him, Linda Ross wore cargo pants and a black T-shirt, and, even without makeup, her skin glowed by the candlelight, highlighting the dusting of freckles across her cheeks and nose.

Juan twirled the stem of his wineglass and took an appreciative sip. "If Maurice is going to have his staff prepare a special dinner, the least you could do is dress for the occasion."

Linda slathered a piece of still-warm bread with unsalted butter. "I had brothers growing up. I learned to eat fast and as often as there was food around. Otherwise, I'd go hungry."

"That bad, huh?"

"Ever watch one of those nature shows when sharks are in a feeding frenzy or a pack of wolves have taken down a deer? My oldest brother, Tony, would sometimes even growl at us." She smiled at the memory.

"My parents insisted on table manners at all times," Juan said. "I'd get grounded for putting my elbows on the table."

"Our only rule was, utensils had to be used on the food and not each other."

"Are you sure about tomorrow?" Juan asked, turning the conversation back to work. Even in these sumptuous surroundings, the specter of their chosen profession was never far off.

"I've been cramming all day. I might not be ready to lead a Responsivist revival, but I can more than hold my own in a conversation with one of them. I have to admit that the more I learn about them, the weirder it gets. How anyone can believe that an alien intelligence from a parallel universe can control your life is beyond me."

"It takes all kinds, I suppose," Juan said. He'd always believed that as long as it didn't hurt others, people's belief systems were their own individual choice, and he wasn't one to judge. "You know that after what we did to them, their security is going to be on heightened alert."

She nodded. "I know. They may not even let me in, but it's worth the risk."

Juan was about to respond when four people appeared at the dining room's double-door entrance. Julia Huxley wore her lab coat, as always, while, flanking her, Mark Murphy and Eric Stone had cleaned themselves up. Both sported jackets and ties, although the tails of Mark's shirt were sticking out. Eric's naval background had given him a sense of deportment, but he was clearly uncomfortable in his clothes. Or perhaps it was the fourth in their party that made him uneasy.

Julia untied the scarf from around Jannike Dahl's eyes that had kept her from seeing any part of the ship, other than medical, and now the mess. Juan had relented, giving her a temporary reprieve from the infirmary, but had insisted on the blindfold. Janni wore a borrowed dress from Kevin Nixon's Magic Shop, and, despite her weakened condition, Juan could understand how young Masters Stone and Murphy could be so vexed. She was a lovely, delicate woman who could leave even the most cynical player tongue-tied. Now that she had lost her pallor from being ill for so long, her normally dusky complexion had returned. Her hair was an obsidian wave that swept off her head and across one bare shoulder.

He instinctively got to his feet as they approached. "Miss Dahl, you look beautiful."

"Thank you, Captain Cabrillo," she replied, still trying to get her bearings in the room.

"I apologize for having you blindfolded, but there are sensitive parts of this ship I couldn't have you seeing." He smiled to himself, while Eric and Mark were in a pushing match to be the one to pull out Jannike's chair.

"You and your crew saved my life, Captain. I would never question your wishes." Her voice and accent had a charming lilt that captivated all three men. "I am just grateful to be out of bed for a little while."

"How are you feeling?" Linda asked.

"Much better. Thank you. Dr. Huxley is able to control my asthma, so I have not had any more attacks."

Eric won the honor, so he got to sit to her left. Mark glared as he circled the table to take a chair next to Linda.

"Unfortunately, there was a mix-up in communications with the cooking staff." As the words left Cabrillo's mouth, waiters, led by Maurice, marched out from the kitchen bearing trays. The *Oregon*'s chief steward blamed Juan for the gaffe. "Somehow," Juan continued, pointedly eyeing Maurice, "they were under the impression you were from Denmark rather than Norway. They had wanted to make some of your native dishes, but we have a traditional Danish meal instead."

"That is very thoughtful of you all," Janni said, smiling. "And the two are so close that I won't even notice."

"Hear that, Maurice?"

"I did not."

"I believe we're having herring," Juan said, "which is the traditional start to any meal, followed by *fiskeboller*, which I understand to be fish dumplings. Then there is roast pork loin with red cabbage and browned potatoes, followed by your choice of *pandekager* pancakes with ice cream and chocolate or *ris à la mande*."

At this, Janni's smile widened. "That is a rice dessert," she explained to the others, "With cherry sauce. It is my favorite in the world. We have it, too."

"Are you from Oslo?" Linda asked as the first dishes were laid on the linen tablecloth.

"I moved there when my parents died, but I was born in the far north, in a small fishing village called Honningsvad."

That explained her darker complexion, Juan thought. The native Lapps, like the Inuit of Alaska or the indigenous people of Greenland, had evolved darker skin as protection from the relentless glare of sunlight off the ice and snow. She must have some native blood.

Before he could ask a question, he spotted Hali Kasim framed in the dining-room entrance. His hair stuck up in tufts at the side of his head, and even at a distance Juan could see the plum-colored circles under his eyes and the fatigue that made his flesh look like it was slipping off the bone. Juan stood. "Would you all please excuse me?"

He strode across to his communications specialist. "You've looked better."

"I've felt better, too," Hali agreed. "You said you wanted the results of my work cutting through the static jamming our bug as soon as I finished. Well, here it is." He handed a single sheet of paper to the Chairman. "I even used the sound-mixing board Mark has in his cabin. This is the best I could do. Sorry. The numbers in parentheses are the elapsed time between words."

I DON'T . . . (1:23) YES . . . (3:57) 'BOUT DONNA SKY . . . (1:17) (ACT)IVATE THE EEL LEF . . . (:24) KEY . . . (1:12)   TOMORR(OW) . . . (3:38)   THAT WON'T BE . . . (:43) A MIN(UTE) . . . (6:50) BYE.(1:12)

"That's it, huh?" Juan struggled to not show his disappointment.

"That's it. There are a few unidentifiable sounds that the computer wouldn't give more than a ten percent certainty of their meaning. Heck, it gave Donna Sky's name only a forty percent chance of being right, but I'm pretty sure it is."

"How long was Martell's conversation with Severance from the time he turned on the scrambler to when he said good-bye?"

"Twenty-two minutes six seconds."

Cabrillo read through it again. "The four things that stick out are *Donna Sky*, a key of some kind, and the word fragments *eel* and *lef*. What's the computer probability on the accuracy of those last ones?"

Having spent countless hours poring over the data, Hali didn't need to refer to his notes. "Sixty-one percent. Key was ninety-two."

"Eel, lef, and the key came within twenty-five seconds of one another, so it's a fair bet they're related. And coming a minute seventeen seconds after mentioning Donna Sky, it wouldn't be a stretch to think she's somehow connected, too."

Hali gaped at him. "I stared at this piece of paper for hours before noticing that."

"That's because you were trying to deduce meaning from the words rather than the pauses."

"I do have one more thing." Kasim slipped a microcassette recorder from his pant pocket and hit PLAY. Juan heard the same static as before, and then it suddenly stopped. "End transmission," a voice said clearly.

"Who the hell was that?"

"I ran it through the computer. English isn't that guy's native language. Best it could come up with is Middle European, and it put his age between thirty and fifty."

"Ah," Juan said, remembering the snippets of conversation they had managed to record before the jammer was activated. "I bet this is Zelimir Kovac. Come on."

They returned to the table, where Mark Murphy was stammering his way through a joke that wasn't going well. He seemed relieved when Juan interrupted. "Eric, did you manage to find anything on Zelimir Kovac this afternoon?"

"Nada, zip, and zilch."

"I think I know this man," Jannike said. "He was on the *Golden Dawn*. He is an important person with the Responsivists."

"He never showed up on any of their websites, payroll, or anyplace else," Eric responded, as if she'd insulted his research abilities.

"But he was there, I tell you," Janni said defiantly. "People never talked to him but always about him. I think he is close to the group's leader."

Cabrillo wasn't concerned that Kovac hadn't come up on their radar. He was thinking about how he had been aboard the ill-fated cruise liner and now shows up in Athens. Then he remembered that one of the *Dawn*'s lifeboats had been missing from its davits when the *Oregon* found the ghostship. "He killed them."

"What did you say?" Julia asked with her fork poised halfway to her mouth.

"Kovac was on the *Golden Dawn* and now he's at the Responsivist retreat in Greece. He escaped the ship on one of her lifeboats, and the only reason he would have done that is if he knew all those people were going to die. Ergo, he killed them." He turned to Janni. "Could you describe him?"

"He was very tall. Almost two meters." That put him at six foot five. Big dude, Juan thought. "He looked very strong and serious. I only saw him a few times, and he never smiled. In truth, I was a little frightened of him."

"Would you sit down with Eric and Mark and try to create a picture of him?"

"I can't draw."

"We have a computer that will do that for you. All you have to do is describe him and they will do the rest."

"I will do anything you ask if it means he gets punished for what he did." She started sobbing as the memories of that horrible night welled up. Eric put his arm around her shoulder, and she leaned into him. Juan gave him credit for not beaming at Mark Murphy.

Julia Huxley dropped her fork and tossed her napkin on the table as she stood. She was at Janni's side in an instant. "That's enough excitement for one night. Let's get you back down to medical." She helped the stricken young woman to her feet.

Mark and Eric looked like they were going to help.

"Gentlemen," Juan said in a warning tone, and they both sank back into their seats, dejected. "There is a time and place. This is neither."

"Yes, sir," they said in unison, like contrite children. Had Juan not been occupied by all the information he'd gotten in the last couple of minutes, he might have smiled at their display.

He sat, turning his attention to Linda Ross. "Your mission's scrubbed."

"What? Why?"

"I won't let you go into that compound unarmed knowing Kovac is there."

She flared. "I can handle myself."

"This isn't open for discussion," Juan said, his voice flinty sharp. "If I'm right, then Kovac is a mass murderer on an unimaginable scale. You aren't going in there. Period. Hali scrubbed our recording further, and Donna Sky's name featured prominently in Martell's conversation with Thomas Severance. We know she's a notable Responsivist and may have information on what's going on. That'll be our conduit into their plans."

"If she's a hard-core believer, then she won't talk to us," Linda said.

"She's an actress, not a trained agent. Five minutes with her and she'll tell you everything you want to know. We just have to find her and get to her."

"She's arrived in Germany to film a movie recently."

Cabrillo was surprised Linda had that kind of information at her fingertips. He arched an eyebrow.

His vice president of operations blushed under her freckles. "What can I say—I'm addicted to Hollywood gossip."

Eric Stone leaned forward in his seat. "As for getting to her, I have an idea. Kevin Nixon worked in Hollywood for years before coming to us. I'm sure he knows someone who knows someone."

Nixon had been an award-winning effects and makeup artist for one of the big studios. He'd turned his back on that part of his life when his sister was killed during the 9/11 attacks. He had offered his unique talents to the CIA when Cabrillo poached him from the Agency.

"Good thinking. If he can get access to her on the set, maybe we can finally get a handle on what the hell's going on."

"Just playing devil's advocate here, but what if she doesn't know anything?"

"Pray that she does, Linda, because I'm not sending anyone into their retreat."

"Speaking of sending people places, did you want me to go with you to the Philippines?"

"No, Mark. Thanks for the offer, but I'm taking Linc."

"Spreading us kind of thin, aren't you, boss?" Eric remarked.

Cabrillo didn't disagree. "Of course Max is tied up for as long as he needs, but Eddie will be back from Rome the day after we reach Monaco. That will give us four of the senior staff including Julia. Linda, you won't be gone for more than a day or two, and Linc and I will be back within three. Besides, the surveillance job is straightforward and passive for the most part, so I'm not concerned. Now, let's enjoy our traditional *Danish* meal."

Juan said this loud enough for Maurice, hovering by the kitchen door, to hear.

The steward scowled.

CHAPTER 19

Eddie was leaning against the elevator's rear wall when the car reached the lobby. Max was to his right. When the doors opened, he pushed himself off the wall as two strangers in suits charged inside.

Eddie thought nothing of this lapse in elevator etiquette as the men brushed against him. Then he felt one of them reach a hand into his coat pocket and start to lift the Beretta hanging in his shoulder holster. He turned to react, and a gun fitted with a silencer was pressed between his eyes. Max was just as quickly disarmed. It took all of two seconds.

"Either of you move and you're dead," the larger of the two men said. His English was accented.

The close quarters negated most of Seng's power martial arts moves, but that didn't mean he wasn't going to put up a fight. He tensed fractionally, and the gunman somehow sensed it. The pistol was rammed into Max's gut, expelling his breath in an explosive whoosh.

"That is your last warning."

The doors whispered closed and the elevator began to rise.

As Max struggled to reinflate his lungs, thoughts swirled through Eddie's mind. He wondered how they had been tracked so easily and quickly, and if he should reveal that he suspected this was Zelimir Kovac, the man mentioned on the bug Juan had planted at the retreat. He also wondered why Kyle Hanley was so important to the Responsivists that they would take a chance like this to get him back. It didn't make sense.

"You're going to have to kill me," Max was finally able to say. "You're not getting your hands on my son again, Kovac."

The Serb appeared surprised that Max knew his name, but

the look quickly faded. He must have deduced they had heard the tape from the bug. Despite Kovac's thuggish appearance, Eddie realized he wasn't a stupid man.

"That is the most likely outcome," Kovac agreed.

Not until you know who we are, Eddie said to himself, *and how much we've already learned*.

As bargaining chips went, it wasn't much, but it was better than nothing. If he were in Kovac's shoes, he would need to know how deeply the Responsivists' security had been penetrated. How much time that would buy them depended on how they were interrogated. And what they could do with that time was a whole separate issue. He and Max were on their own. There would be no rescue, and the hotel staff had already been informed that their guests in the top-floor suite weren't to be disturbed for any reason.

By the time the elevator reached the sixth floor, Eddie had come to the depressing realization that Kovac had them boxed in.

That meant he and Max had to split up if they wanted to get out of this alive. Max had been a hell of a war fighter in his day, and Eddie put him up there with the Chairman when it came to cunning, but he wasn't physically up for an escape, and, with his son hanging in the balance, he wasn't there emotionally either.

The elevator doors opened. Kovac and his silent partner stepped back, motioning with their weapons for Eddie and Max to precede them. The two Corporation operatives exchanged a glance that conveyed their thinking had been on a parallel course and had come to the same conclusion. Just the tightening of Max's eyes and the barest of nods told Eddie that Max knew they had to make a break for it on their own but that he wouldn't leave his son behind. Eddie saw Max's permission to go, as well as his acceptance of the consequences.

They walked down the hallway to their suite. They paused at the door. Eddie considered attacking again. Kovac's lieutenant was close enough to kill with one blow, but the Serb was several paces away. It was clear he understood the dynamics of moving prisoners.

"Using your left hand, remove your key card," Kovac ordered.

Again, Eddie understood that most right-handed people would put the key in their right pocket. It would be awkward reaching for it with the off hand.

Eddie turned to partially face Kovac and said, "There is a special lock on the door. We can't get in."

"I am familiar with such a device. You can still enter. Talk again and I shoot your left kneecap."

Eddie jammed his left hand in his right pant pocket and fished out the electronic key card and used it. The insert light on the lock flicked from red to green, and he could turn the handle.

"Step back," Kovac ordered.

Eddie and Max did as ordered. Kovac's partner entered the suite. In just seconds, they heard Dr. Jenner cry out, "What is the meaning of this?" The gunman ignored him as he made the demand again. Twenty seconds later, the partner shouted out to Kovac, in clear American English, "Suite's secure. Only the deprogrammer and the kid."

Kovac flicked the gun barrel, and Max and Eddie entered the room. The Serb inspected the lock Jenner had placed around the door knob and smartly didn't let the door swing closed.

"Dad?" Kyle Hanley stood from the sofa, looking none the worse for the drugs that had been coursing through his veins for the past twenty-four hours.

"Kyle."

"How dare you do this to me?" Kyle shouted.

"I did it because I love you," Max said helplessly, conflicting emotions wrenching his words.

"Silence!" Kovac roared.

He strode up to Jenner, towering over him. Jenner seemed to shrink into his skin, and his latest protest died on his lips.

When the Serb assassin spoke, his rage was barely contained.

"Mr. Severance gave me express orders not to kill you, but he didn't say anything about this." He slammed the butt of his pistol into the psychiatrist's head.

Two things happened at that instant. Jenner started to collapse to the floor, the wound pumping blood, and Eddie Seng took off running, using the momentary distraction to its fullest.

The French doors leading to the balcony were ten paces away, and he'd covered three-quarters of that distance before anyone knew he was moving. Max instinctively shifted a foot to the right to block the second gunman's aim while Kovac continued to gloat over the collapsing shrink.

Eddie hit the doors at a full run, hunching his shoulders at the last second as he burst through the delicate wood mullions and antique panes of bevel-cut glass. Shards ripped at his skin as a bullet whizzed by, striking the building opposite in a puff of brick dust.

He barely slowed as he reached the railing. Using just his legs, he vaulted over it and twisted around in midair so that he was facing the building as he started to fall. He grabbed two of the countless wrought-iron spindles, his hands slick enough with sweat to allow him to slide down smoothly, while seventy feet of nothingness separated him from the traffic crawling below.

His hands smashed into the concrete deck just as the tips of his toes touched the fifth-floor balcony railing. Without a moment's hesitation, he let go and stepped back, falling all over again in a headlong plunge toward the sidewalk. As the fifth-floor balcony whipped by his face, he reached out and clutched two of the wrought-iron bars again, slowing himself just enough so that he was in constant control of his descent. It was an awesome display of strength, balance, and a total lack of fear.

He was teetering on the fourth-floor railing, centering himself for the next plummet, by the time Kovac reached the suite's balcony. At first, expecting to see Eddie's corpse sprawled on the asphalt, Kovac didn't spot Seng until he stepped back from the baluster below. The Serb opened fire, raining down a storm of bullets.

Eddie felt the shots ripple the air around him as he slid down the spindles. His hands slammed into the concrete. No matter how he stretched his body, he couldn't quite reach the next balcony down. His wrists were screaming with the strain, so he let go, falling just an inch before he found purchase. He windmilled his arms for a second before dropping again. If his hands weren't broken by the time he reached street level, he'd consider it a miracle.

Kovac couldn't get an angle, and rather than risk being spotted by passersby who were starting to gawk at Eddie's insane stunt Kovac holstered his pistol and stepped back into the suite.

For a moment, Eddie considered leaping onto the balcony and entering the third-floor room, but he had no idea how many men Kovac had covering the building. His best chance was to get away as quickly and cleanly as he could and regroup later.

He stepped back again, smearing skin off his now-dry palms as he slid down the spindles. The second-floor balcony was a story and a half above the pavement, to allow for a high ceiling in the hotel's lobby. The drop was nearly twenty feet. Just off to Eddie's left was a bright yellow canopy arching out over the sidewalk to protect the entrance from the elements. Like a tightrope walker, he padded across the top of the railing and dove for the canopy, torquing his body so his back slammed into the stiffened fabric.

Sliding down its curved face, he was able to reach between his legs and grab onto the underlying metal frame. He somersaulted over the edge, holding on as tightly as his damaged hands would allow, and dangled for a second before nimbly dropping to the ground. A few in the gathered crowd cheered, not understanding what was happening.

Eddie started running down the sidewalk, dodging through the throngs as best he could. The noise of a powerful engine roared over the din of regular commuter traffic. He whirled to see a black motorcycle jump the curb and start after him, panicked people scattering out of its path as the rider hit the throttle hard. Less than fifteen feet separated him from the bike, and the big Ducati was accelerating.

Making like he was running for the entrance of the bookstore next to the hotel, Eddie leapt to his left instead, flying onto the hood of a parked car. His momentum slid him across the vehicle and dumped him in the road just ahead of a Volvo truck that had found a little room in the congestion to speed up. The driver never saw Eddie fly over the car, so he kept on the gas. Eddie had a second, at most, to twist out of the way of the heavy-duty tires. He covered his head in a vain attempt to protect it as the ten-wheeler rolled over him.

Heat from the engine was like the open door of a blast furnace on his back.

The truck suddenly braked, wheels skidding on the asphalt. Eddie heard the bike again. It must have returned to the road between two parked cars right in front of the Volvo.

He scrambled from underneath the vehicle. An open-topped double-decker tourist bus was in the opposite lane. It had paused to let people off. Eddie was near the rear of the vehicle, far enough away from the driver that he most likely wouldn't be noticed. He jumped hard at the side of the bus, thrusting upward to get himself off of the roadway. He kicked out with his other foot, connecting with the truck, still idling three feet away, gaining himself another foot. He did this again and again, kicking each vehicle in turn, ignoring the startled faces of passengers in the bus, as he used his strength and dexterity to shimmy up the gap between the two trucks until he reached the top of the Volvo. He rolled onto its roof, panting, and would have paused to catch his breath except a sizzling hole appeared inches from his face.

He looked up. Kovac was on the balcony again, taking deliberate aim. With little chance of alerting pedestrians with the shots, he could take his time. Eddie jumped to his feet, running along the top of the truck, and leapt for the bus as it started to pull away. He sailed over a bench seat of Japanese tourists and tumbled into the aisle. He ran to the back of the bus to see the Ducati pull out from in front of the Volvo truck and start after him.

Eddie might have made it clear of the hotel, but he hadn't escaped yet.

The motorcyclist in black leathers stayed right behind the bus, making no attempt to hide the fact he was following it. Eddie didn't know if the man had a radio tucked into his helmet. If *he* was running the operation, he'd make sure all team members stayed in constant communication, which meant the guy on the bike would have reinforcements soon. And since Kovac must have a detailed report on the hostage-rescue team that had snatched Kyle Hanley, he would most likely bring a large force to get Hanley back.

The bus pulled out onto a four-lane road, picking up speed

as it approached the Colosseum. Cars zipped by, horns blared, and the occasional rude gesture was thrown out the window by their drivers. The Ducati rode in its wake like a manta ray following a whale.

Eddie flexed his fingers to work some blood back into them as he thought of a way out of this mess. He'd left his cell phone in the suite because Max had been carrying his. A crazy idea popped into his head and, if he hadn't felt he was running out of time, he would have dismissed it entirely, but he was getting desperate.

A set of spiral stairs at the rear of the bus led Eddie down to the first level. He was relieved that there weren't many tourists taking this part of the trip. There had been only fifteen people upstairs and just a handful were downstairs. No one paid him any attention as he strode down the aisle. Eddie kept in a crouch as he approached the driver. There was a translator sitting in the front seat, working on her nails with an emery board between her canned speeches from the tour script. Seeing Eddie approach, she set aside her file and smiled brightly. Judging by his appearance, she assumed he was part of her group and asked him something in Japanese.

He ignored her entirely. The driver wore a white shirt, black tie, and a cap more befitting an airline pilot. Eddie was just thankful he had a slender build. In one motion, Eddie grabbed the driver's right arm and heaved him out of his seat. Seng ducked, as the man rolled across his shoulder, and then straightened quickly, hurling the driver down the couple of steps near the bus's main door. He hit the door upside down and collapsed in an untidy heap.

The big diesel barely slowed before Eddie was in the driver's seat, his foot on the gas pedal. The tour guide was screaming, and passengers farther back began to look frightened. Watching the big wing mirrors, Eddie hit the brakes.

Horns immediately erupted all around, and the Ducati shot from around the back of the bus, narrowly avoiding the car that rear-ended the double-decker. The guide wailed at the impact. The bike was hugging the center line, riding the gap between traffic, and Eddie let him travel halfway down the bus's length before hitting the gas again and swerving left. The bike had nowhere to go. The other lane was bumper-to-bumper. Had he hung back near the rear of the bus, he might have been able to tuck back behind it again, but he had committed himself to the gap. He dropped a gear and wrenched the throttle. The front wheel leapt off the tarmac, as the 1000cc engine shrieked, the rider bending low over the handlebars to reduce air friction and give him a fraction more speed.

He never stood a chance. The bus clipped him ten feet shy of where Eddie was sitting. The Ducati careened into a car in the left lane. The rider was launched over the front of his bike. Limbs flailing, he smashed headfirst into the rear window of the next car in the line of traffic. The safety glass turned into a glittering explosion of diamond chips. Eddie could only hope the helmet saved his life. The collision started a chain reaction of minor accidents behind him that quickly engulfed all four lanes.

Eddie stopped the bus and hit the controls that opened the door. It swung only partially inward, blocked by the unconscious form of the driver. As the adrenaline surge that had sustained Eddie over the past frightening minutes began to ebb, he thought of the Chairman and how he always made some sort of joke at a time like this. It wasn't Seng's style.

"Sorry," he said to the tour guide, and pushed his way out the door.

He looked back at the accident. The road was blocked from curb to curb with damaged cars. Drivers were out of their vehicles now, shouting and gesturing as only Italians can. He was about to turn on to a side street when a sedan smashed through the wreckage like a charging battle tank. Two men dove out of the way as their cars were crushed up against other vehicles. The sedan barely slowed, its front end mangled and its driver and passenger invisible for a moment behind their inflated air bags.

Eddie knew they were coming for him.

He ran back onto the bus, clipping the slowly rising driver behind the ear to keep him down. The pretty tour guide screamed when she saw him jump into the driver's seat again, jabbering at him in Italian so fast that the words blended into one long, continuous sound.

He slammed the automatic transmission into gear. The bus

took off with a lurch that sent the few passengers who'd gotten out of their seats sprawling.

Cranking the wheel one-handed, to keep the bus on the road ringing the Colosseum, Eddie grabbed the PA system microphone dangling over his right shoulder. He shouted, "Everybody! Upstairs! Now!"

The handful of terrified tourists rushed to the rear of the bus, jamming the stairs in their effort to follow his order. Eddie kept his eye on the rearview mirror as the red sedan, a Fiat Bravo, he thought, bulled its way through the congestion in pursuit. It roared up alongside the bus. Eddie could see three men inside. The front passenger's hands were below the doorsill, but he spotted a weapon cradled in the arms of the man in the rear seat.

The man in back thrust the barrel of an assault rifle through the window and sprayed the side of the bus. Glass exploded as the rounds found their mark, and seat stuffing was blown into the air like confetti. Eddie swerved into the car, forcing it back once again, while the shrieks of the passengers upstairs grew to a fevered pitch.

Turning even tighter to avoid a stalled lane of traffic, Eddie felt the bus go light on its inside wheels as centrifugal force made the vehicle want to roll over. He edged the steering wheel slightly, and the heavy bus mashed back down on its suspension, rocking precariously. The road straightened out as they completed their sweep around the Colosseum and headed northeast. On either side of the road, the new blended with the ancient, as they raced past office blocks, churches, and ruined temples. The Fiat tried to pass the bus again, and Eddie swerved, feeling the satisfying crunch of metal.

Accelerating past fifty miles per hour, Eddie thought that he had damaged the sedan more than he'd thought, because they didn't try to pass him again. That's when he heard the hammering crack of an automatic rifle. Despite the bus's size, he could feel the weight of shots through the chassis. They were firing at the engine in the rear, hoping to disable the vehicle and gun Eddie down at their leisure.

Ahead, Eddie could see what he could only describe as a giant wedding cake. The building was massive, constructed entirely of marble, and seemed to loom over the area. He dimly recalled from somewhere that this was the monument to Victor Emmanuel II, the ruler who united all the Italian states into the modern nation it was today. The pomposity of the architecture was made worse by the sheer size of the building, its columns and steps making it look more like an enormous set of dentures than a memorial to a great leader.

The road swept around to the left, revealing a huge bronze statue of Victor on horseback. With the sun beginning to set, tourists and backpackers still lounged on the marble steps, sipping drinks sold by vendors from carts.

Another barrage pummeled the back of the bus, and the tourists outside started to scatter like startled birds.

Eddie knew it was only a matter of time before they hit something critical or that he'd run into a police roadblock. The distant sound of sirens blaring was drawing closer by the second. A sign said he was on the VIA DEI FORI IMPERIALI, not that it meant anything to him. The road was broad, by Roman standards, and too open for Eddie's tastes. It divided ahead, next to an open parking area filled with buses much like the one he'd commandeered.

He veered left down a street hemmed in by four- and five-story brick buildings. The storefronts offered everything from leather goods to electronics to exotic pets. But it was still too wide for what Eddie had in mind. Brake lights suddenly flared in front of the bus as traffic came to a crawl. Eddie pounded on the horn, and he steered the bus onto the curb. The sidewalk wasn't nearly wide enough for the large vehicle. As he made his way down the cobbled walkway, the bus mowed down parking meters like wheat before a combine and shouldered aside automobiles amid a cacophony of car alarms and shouts.

The bus plowed through the outside displays of a tourist shop, sending up a blizzard of brightly colored postcards and what Eddie thought, for one terrifying moment, was the body of a woman, but it turned out to be a mannequin displaying a T-shirt. The right-side mirror was ripped off when the bus scraped against a building.

He burst out onto an intersection. Cars screeched all

around him, as Eddie guided the bus toward a narrow lane that was more of a trench cut between buildings than a road. There were cars going into the alley but not emerging from it.

Kovac's men fired at the bus again, having replaced spent magazines. The gas pedal suddenly felt mushy under Eddie's foot, and in the undamaged left-side mirror he could see smoke erupting from the back of the bus.

"Come on, baby, fifty more yards."

The engine coughed and caught again and again, sputtering and surging in its death throes. Eddie reached for the microphone, as the gap between the buildings grew closer but not larger.

"Everybody, brace yourselves."

Eddie sensed the engine about to let go, so he slipped the transmission into neutral and coasted the last thirty feet. Behind him, he heard the motor seize, in a tearing of metal that would have lanced Max's engineer heart.

The bus entered the dim alley with barely five inches of clearance on either side. The remaining left mirror was sheared off. Eddie saw that the road constricted even further just ahead, because one apartment building was slightly larger than its neighbors. He hit the brakes an instant before the bus struck the building, bounced back, and smeared against the opposite apartments, before becoming completely jammed. The impact caused a fresh wave of frightened screams from above, but Eddie could tell by how quickly the sound faded that no one had been hurt.

A large red fire extinguisher was clipped just below his legs. He popped it free and smashed it into the windshield. The glass starred but didn't break. He hit the windshield again and again until he'd opened a man-size hole. He jumped though it, setting a hand on the warm asphalt when he landed to steady himself before taking off at a run. When he looked back, he could see dense smoke boiling from behind the bus. Kovac's men couldn't climb over the vehicle, so they would have to backtrack around the apartment block, provided they weren't boxed in by other cars who'd followed them into the alley.

He rounded the corner and slowed to a normal pedestrian gait, blending in with the flow of people headed home from their offices or out to dinner with their families. A minute later, he heard car tires screeching as he ducked into a taxi. The cab pulled away as the Fiat Bravo braked in front of the alley. He'd lost them.

A few minutes later, he threw some Euros at the driver and jumped out of the vehicle while it was stalled in traffic. He bought a prepaid disposable cell phone from a tobacco stand. Eddie walked into a crowded bar, ordered a beer from the girl behind the counter, and dialed the hotel. The staff was still buzzing about the man who'd climbed down the balconies, so it took him a few minutes to explain that gunmen had broken into his room. The reception-desk staffer promised to call the *polizia*. Eddie gave him his cell number.

Fifteen minutes later, Eddie's beer gone, his phone chirped.

"Mr. Kwan?" That was the alias they'd used to book the suite.

"Yes."

"Our desk manager entered your room with the police. There was a man in your suite named Jenner with a cut to the head," the clerk said apologetically. "They would like you to return here to get your information, a statement, I think you call it. They have many questions about what took place and about an incident that happened nearby."

"Of course, I'll be happy to cooperate with the authorities. I'll be there in twenty minutes."

"Thank you, Mr. Kwan."

"Thank you." Eddie dialed another number. When it was answered, he said, without preamble, "Tiny, file a flight plan out of the country. I'll be there as quickly as I can."

He didn't wait for the pilot's reply before cutting the connection and dialing again. As he listened to the ringing over the line, he knew that there was no way Kovac would remain in the city—or in Italy, for that matter—so there was no reason for him to wait around for the police to pick him up.

"Hello."

"Chairman, it's Eddie. Kovac has kidnapped Max."

A heartbeat passed before Juan responded. "What about his son, Kyle?"

"I think the little punk was in on it."

CHAPTER 20

"HOLD ON ONE SECOND," CABRILLO SAID, GETTING his mind around the situation.

He was alone in his cabin. His desk was strewn with paperwork that had gone ignored too long. He hit the intercom button for the communications station in the Op Center.

"Yes, Chairman," the night-duty supervisor answered at once.

"What's the status of Max Hanley's radio ID chip?"

Each member of the Corporation had a locator microchip surgically embedded in the leg that beamed a faint signal to the constellation of communications satellites circling the globe. Powered by the nervous system, with an occasional transdermal boost of electricity like with a pacemaker, the devices allowed Juan to know where any member of his team was at all times.

"I'm not getting a signal. Hold on. Here we go. The computer says his transponder stopped working eleven minutes ago, about two miles from the hotel where he was staying with his son. Eddie's is working fine. I show him in central Rome, about a quarter mile from the Colosseum."

"Thank you." Juan released the intercom and spoke into his desk telephone, a modern instrument disguised to look like a Bakelite phone from the 1930s. "Max's transponder's out."

"I already figured it would be," Eddie replied.

"That's how they tracked you to Rome, isn't it? Kyle Hanley was chipped when he was in Greece. And they took the precaution of sweeping Max in case we did the same thing."

"They probably carved it out of his thigh, in whatever vehicle they used to make their getaway."

"But even the best chips can only give you a rough approximation, they aren't as powerful as GPS," Juan said.

"That's why I think Kyle helped them. When they ambushed us in the hotel's elevator they brought Max and me back to the suite. Kyle didn't look all that drugged to me. I think he came to during our flight from Crete and was faking it for the last part of our trip. He was left alone for a few minutes in one of the bedrooms while we spoke with Dr. Jenner. Supposedly, he was unconscious, but if he was awake he could have called Kovac, or someone else in the movement, and given them the name of the hotel and the room number."

"So Kovac tracked him to Rome using a radio tag and Kyle guided him to the exact location."

"That's the only way it makes any sense."

"Just spitballing here, but what about Jenner? He could have blown our location to the Responsivists."

"He could have," Eddie agreed, "but I could tell he hates them the way a drug counselor hates crack. Also, you didn't see the way Kovac pistol-whipped him. No, Jenner's definitely on our side on this."

"Like I said, just throwing it out there."

"You know, Juan, they took a hell of a risk to get the kid back. Doesn't make any sense if Kyle's just some low-level believer."

"Then he's somehow involved in whatever they're planning."

"Or at least exposed to the information at the retreat," Eddie said.

"They snatched him back to keep operational security absolutely airtight."

"If they're at this level of paranoia, there's no way they will let Linda into that compound."

"I already scrubbed her mission. We learned that Kovac was aboard the *Golden Dawn* and was most likely responsible for those murders. She's going to babysit Kevin Nixon until he can make contact with Donna Sky."

Eddie thought about this for a moment before saying, "I was with Kovac for only a minute before I escaped, but I could see that. The guy looks like Boris Karloff, with crazier eyes. I just thought of something. Kovac said that Severance gave him explicit orders not to kill Jenner. I don't understand the reasoning behind that, but why would they leave Jenner behind and snatch Max?"

"They don't know if Kyle talked to him during the time he was with us."

"No. What I mean is, why not simply kill them both? They had the opportunity, and it would have been a lot easier."

"Same reason. They need to know if Kyle talked."

"Max is in for a rough time, isn't he?"

"Yeah," Juan said softly. "Yeah, he is."

"What do you want me to do?" Eddie said after a lengthy pause, as both men thought about the implications of Cabrillo's answer.

"Meet the *Oregon* in Monaco. I'm putting you in charge of the eavesdropping job."

"You're still going to the Philippines?" Eddie was surprised.

"I have to," Juan replied, resignation in his voice. "We need some sort of leverage over Severance if we're going to get Max back."

"It's going to take the better part of a day just to get you there. God knows how long to find something, even if it exists. Do you really think Max can hold out that long?"

Juan's next words were as much for his benefit as they were Eddie's. "You don't know this because Max never talks about it, but he spent six months as a POW during his second tour in Vietnam. The stuff they did to him during his confinement defies belief. He'll hold out. Of that, I am certain."

"Juan, that was forty years ago. Max isn't a young man anymore."

"Surviving torture isn't about your physical strength. It's about how tough you are mentally. Do you think Max has lost any of that? If anything, he's tougher now than he was then. And he knows that we will do whatever it takes to get him back."

"How did he get out of it? Was he rescued?"

"No. During a forced march to a new location, he and two buddies jumped their guards. They killed four VC with their bare hands and vanished into the jungle. Only Max found his way to an American firebase. The other two are still considered MIA."

JUAN WAS ON THE WING BRIDGE of the pilothouse just after dawn the next morning to watch the sun reveal the principality of Monaco and the city of Monte Carlo perched on rocky cliffs over the warm Mediterranean. One of the last functioning monarchies in the world, the tiny state had been ruled by the Grimaldi family for more than seven centuries. Only Japan's Chrysanthemum Throne was longer lived.

Monaco was long a playground for the world's elite and its harbor was carpeted with gleaming luxury yachts, many over a hundred feet in length, several approaching three hundred. Juan spotted the *Matryoshka*, the target of the eavesdropping job on Russian arms merchant Ivan Kerikov. High-rise apartment blocks rose all around the harbor, and luxury villas clung to the hillsides. He knew that real estate here was some of the most expensive in the world. From his vantage, he couldn't see the fabled Monte Carlo casino, but he had a few fond memories of the place.

From within the inner harbor, he saw a sleek speedboat rocketing toward the ship, where it lay at anchor a mile from the coast. Harbor authorities had already been informed that the ship's engine was disabled and the crew were awaiting parts from Germany. Although the vessel was inside Monaco's three-mile territorial limit, the harbormaster had declined to come aboard, after observing the *Oregon* through binoculars fifteen minutes earlier.

The speedboat ate the distance to the ship at nearly sixty knots, cutting across the light chop like an offshore racer. Juan descended to the main deck near the ship's boarding ladder. Linc was waiting for him with their overnight bags, his eyes hidden behind stylish sunglasses.

"I don't like leaving right now," the big former SEAL said, and not for the first time.

"This is the best way we're going to get Max back. I've called Thom Severance's office in California a dozen times, all but telling them who I am and what I know, and the bastard won't call back. We've got to force his hand and to do that we need leverage."

"Langston Overholt won't help?"

"Not without evidence. I talked to him for an hour last night. The bottom line is, the Responsivists have a lot of money, which means they have a lot of clout in Washington. Lang won't act on anything other than solid proof that Severance is up to something."

"This sucks."

"Tell me about it."

"Why don't we bypass the Philippines, go straight to the source, and take on Severance for ourselves?"

"Don't think I haven't thought of that. Lang warned me specifically about not going after Severance. And you and I both know if we get caught operating in the United States, we will never see the outside of a prison again."

"So we don't get caught."

Juan looked at his friend. Linc was dead serious. "If it comes down to that, I'll put it to the crew." He knew every member of the Corporation would risk everything to get Hanley back, even if they knew they would never get another contract from Overholt again, which the cagey CIA veteran had threatened if Thomas Severance or his wife so much as suggested they were under surveillance.

The executive water taxi pulled up alongside the ship. As sleek and beautiful as the boat was, it was nothing compared to its driver, a young blonde wearing a blouse that couldn't be cut any lower and a skirt that couldn't be raised any higher. With their chopper still in pieces down in the hangar, the harbor taxi was the fastest way to shore without calling undue attention to the *Oregon*.

"*Capitaine Cabrillo, je suis Donatella,*" she called over the burble of the boat's idling engine. Her accent sent a wolfish grin flashing across Linc's face.

"Only in Monaco," Juan whispered to Linc.

"You think some rich guy wants an ugly driver taking him out to his yacht after a night at the casino?"

The young woman kept her craft steady by holding the boarding ladder as the two men made their way down with leather duffels over their shoulders. At the end of the twenty-foot climb, Juan tossed his bag onto the rear bench seat and stepped over the gunwale.

"Thank you," he said.

When Linc jumped into the boat, it bobbed as if it had been hit by a wave. Donatella gave them both a big smile, her eyes lingering on Linc much longer than Cabrillo, as she reached for the chrome throttle controls.

"Chairman! Hold up!" Eric Stone leaned far over the railing overhead to get his attention.

"What is it?"

"I found something."

"Can it wait? They're holding a chopper for us to take us to the airport in Nice."

"Hold on a sec." Eric climbed over the rail and awkwardly descended the ladder while clutching a laptop computer. He noticed Donatella for the first time when he reached the boat but barely gave her a first, let alone a second, glance. Obviously, he was distracted by whatever news he had.

Juan nodded to her and she eased forward on the throttles. He went aft to let Linc chat her up while he pushed aside their luggage so he and Eric could sit. They had to raise their voices over the rush of the wind and the throb of the powerful motor.

"What do you have?" Juan asked.

Eric opened his computer. "I've been checking for any unusual incidents that may have occurred on ships where the Responsivists were holding their Sea Retreats."

"Did you find anything?"

"Did I? Oh yeah. Do you remember recently how there have been reports of viral outbreaks on cruise ships, usually a gastrointestinal norovirus?"

"Seems there have been a lot more in the past couple of years," Juan remarked.

"It's not a coincidence. At first, I was checking passenger manifests from the cruise companies." Juan didn't need to ask how Eric obtained such confidential information. "I cross-referenced those to Responsivist membership lists. When I started seeing a pattern, I switched my focus to cruise liners struck by unusual illnesses. That's when I hit pay dirt. Of the seventeen outbreaks I've looked into in the past two years, sixteen of them occurred when Responsivists were on board. The seventeenth wasn't a norovirus and was traced back to *E. coli* found on lettuce grown on one specific farm in California. That strain also hit people in Florida, Georgia, and Alabama."

"I'll be damned."

"It gets worse. Mind you, there's no pattern to cruise lines or ports of call. But there is one definite pattern we could see. During the first incident, only a handful of passengers were sickened, and most of them were elderly. The second one saw forty people showing symptoms. But by the time we get to the seventeenth, which happened two months ago aboard a ship called *Destiny*, nearly every passenger and crewman was infected. The cruise line had to chopper in a medical team and a healthy group of officers to get the ship back to port."

Juan leaned back in the soft leather seat, feeling the engine's vibration trying to loosen the knotted muscles in his back. In the cockpit, Linc towered over their driver, and he could tell she was delighting in his company. Her laughter carried through the air. He suddenly leaned forward again. "They're perfecting dispersal methods."

"That's what Mark and I think, too. They got better every time until they achieved a near one hundred percent infection rate."

"How does the *Golden Dawn* fit into the pattern?"

"Once they worked out how to infect an entire shipful of people, they needed to test the lethality of their toxin."

"On their own people?" Cabrillo was shocked.

"They could be the ones who developed the agent in the first place. Why take the risk of one of them having a change of heart?"

"Good God! Why?" The pieces of the puzzle were there before him, he just didn't know how they fit together. What could the Responsivists possibly gain by killing people aboard cruise ships? And the answer that kept coming back to him was, absolutely nothing.

He could see other terrorist organizations jumping at such a chance, and he considered one of them had paid for such a weapon-and-delivery system, but the Responsivists were flush with money from their Hollywood believers.

They espoused population control. Did they think killing fifteen or twenty thousand retirees who were blowing the children's inheritance on Caribbean cruises would make a difference to the world's overcrowding? If they were that insane, they would go for something much bigger.

The puzzle hung tantalizingly close in the front of Juan's mind, but he knew it was incomplete. "We're missing something."

The speedboat slowed as it entered the inner harbor and made its way to a pier next to an elegant restaurant. A waiter was hosing off the wooden jetty in anticipation of a breakfast crowd looking to lessen the effects of their hangovers.

"What are we missing?" Eric asked. "These whack jobs plan to infect people on cruise ships with a toxin that shows to be one hundred percent fatal."

"It's not one hundred percent. If they released it on the *Dawn*, Jannike shouldn't be alive."

"She was breathing supplemental oxygen," Eric reminded him.

"Even with cannulas in her nostrils, she was still inhaling air pumped through the ship's ventilation system."

"Wouldn't matter if it wasn't airborne. It could have been in the water or food. Maybe she didn't eat or drink."

"Come on, Eric, you're smarter than that. They had to hit everyone at the same time or someone would have radioed for help. You can't control when someone takes a sip of water or eats, for that matter, which negates your earlier idea about food poisoning."

Stone looked chagrined. "Sorry. You're right. Too much Red Bull and not enough sleep."

"What if the attack on the *Golden Dawn* was an aberration and not part of their pattern of escalation?"

"What do you mean?"

"I don't know. It's just a thought. They had achieved nearly one hundred percent on that ship two months ago."

"The *Destiny*."

"Right. The *Destiny*. There wasn't any reason to hit another ship. They knew they had their system."

"So the people on the *Dawn* were wiped out to keep them quiet?"

Juan stood up as Donatella finished tying off the lines. "I don't know," Juan repeated. "Listen, we've got a charter jet waiting to take us to Manila. I'll call Langston and pass this along. If he won't go after Severance, at least he can get a warning out to the cruise lines about a potential terrorist threat."

Overholt would pass on Cabrillo's information, he was certain, but he doubted much would be done. In the years since 9/11, nonspecific threats came in all the time, and, like the boy who cried wolf, they were mostly ignored.

"Donatella?"

"Oui, Capitaine."

"Would you mind returning my young friend here back to my ship. Charge it to the account I set up with your boss."

"Of course, sir. It would be my pleasure."

"His, too, I'm sure." Juan turned back to Eric. "Keep on it and call me with anything new."

"You got it, boss man."

Linc and Cabrillo stepped off the boat and onto the dock, lugging their bags. "What was that she gave you?" Juan asked.

Linc pulled a business card from the pocket of his light-weight leather jacket. "What, this? Her home and cell number."

"With everything going on, you can think about sex?"

"Chairman, I've learned that life is all about reproduction and evolution, and pretty soon she's going to be missing Linc."

"Reproduction and evolution, huh?" Juan just shook his head. "You're as bad as Murph and Stoney."

"Big difference, Juan, is I get dates, while those homeboys only fantasize about 'em."

CHAPTER 21

MAX HANLEY AWOKE IN A SEA OF AGONY.

Pain radiated from his thigh and from his head. It came in alternating currents that crashed against the top of his skull like a hurricane storm surge. His first instinct was to rub his temples and determine why his leg was throbbing, but even in his barely conscious state he knew he had to remain motionless until more of his faculties returned. He wasn't sure why, only that it was important. Time passed. It might have been five minutes, it could have been ten. He had no way to judge other than the rhythmic pounding in his head and the ache in his leg that grew and subsided in time with his heartbeat.

As he became more aware, he realized he was lying on a bed. There were no sheets or pillows, and the mattress was rough under his shoulders. Pretending he was still asleep, he shifted slightly. At least they had left him the dignity of his boxer shorts, although he could feel the cold caress of steel around his ankles and wrists.

It came back to him in a rush. Zelimir Kovac, Eddie's escape, and the sickly sweet smell of the rag being clamped over his nose and mouth. The headache was a result of being drugged. And then the other horror hit him like a slap to the face, and he involuntarily gasped.

He was back in a van, driving away from their hotel. Kovac had given him only enough narcotic to make him compliant, like a drunk who needs to be led away from a party. In the van Max was laid out in the back. He was dimly aware of other figures. Kyle? Adam Jenner? He couldn't tell.

Kovac had run a wand over his body, like an airport metal detector, and when it chimed over Max's leg Kovac sliced open his pants with a boot knife. It took him only a second to find the scar, and he unceremoniously rammed the blade into Max's flesh. Even under mild anesthesia, the pain had been a molten wire driven into his body. He screamed into the gag tied around his mouth, and tried to thrash away from the agony, but someone had pressed his shoulders to the van's floor.

Kovac twisted the knife, opening the wound so when he withdrew the blade he could stick his fingers into Max's flesh. Blood gushed from the cut. Max strained against the pain, fighting it as though he stood a chance. Kovac continued to probe the wound, uncaring that he wasn't wearing gloves and that blood had soaked his shirtsleeve.

"Ah," he said at last, and withdrew his hand.

The transdermal transponder was roughly the size and shape of a digital watch. Kovac held it up so that Max, staring goggle-eyed, could see it. The Serb then dropped it to the floor and smashed it repeatedly with the butt of his pistol until nothing remained but bits of plastic and ruined electronics.

He then slid a hypodermic needle into Max's arm, whispering, "I could have waited for this drug to take effect, but where is the fun in that?"

It was the last thing Max remembered until just now, coming awake.

He had no idea where he was or how long he'd been held captive. He wanted to move, to massage his temples and check his leg, but he was sure he was being watched, and he doubted there would be that much play in his manacles. There wasn't anyone in the room. He'd been awake long enough to hear or sense them, even with his eyes closed. That didn't mean cameras weren't mounted on walls and microphones planted nearby. He wanted to wait for as long as possible before alerting his captors to his consciousness and use that time to let more of the narcotics work their way out of his system. If he was going to withstand what he knew was coming, he needed to be as fresh as possible.

An hour passed—or it might have been ten minutes—Max wasn't sure. He had lost all concept of time. He knew that time deprivation, the inability to set the body's internal clock, was an essential tool in the interrogator's arsenal, so he purposefully forced himself to lose all conscious awareness of its passage. A prisoner could be driven over the edge trying to determine if it was night or day, noon or midnight, and by willing away that natural need Max took away his captor's ability to torture him with it.

That had never been a problem in Vietnam. The cages and boxes they kept him and his fellow prisoners in were rickety enough to always allow at least a sliver of light to enter. But Max kept apprised of interrogation techniques as part of his job, and he knew time deprivation was effective only if the captors let it remain a factor in their thinking.

As for whatever else they had in store, he would just have to wait and see.

A heavy lock was opened nearby. Max hadn't heard anyone approach, so he knew the door had to be thick. The room, then, was most likely designed as a jail cell and not something temporary that had been converted to hold him. That the Responsivists had such a cell, ready and waiting, did not bode well.

The door creaked open with a screech of rusted metal. Either the hinges weren't often used or the cell was located in a humid climate or possibly underground. He didn't move a muscle, as he listened to the sound of two separate and distinct pairs of feet approaching the bed. One had a heavier tread than the other, but the latter was definitely male. Kovac and an accomplice?

"He should have come around by now," Zelimir Kovac said.

"He's a big man, so he should have," another man agreed. He had an American accent. "But everyone is different."

Kovac lightly slapped Max's cheek. Max made a mewling sound, as if he were dimly aware of the contact but was too far under to care.

"It has been twenty-four hours," the Serbian killer said. "If he doesn't wake in an hour, I will inject him with a stimulant."

"And risk cardiac arrest?"

Max had slightly elevated blood pressure. He would make damned sure he'd be awake the next time they entered the room.

"Mr. Severance will be here soon. We need to know what conversations took place between this man and his son. They kept him sedated the entire time they had him. Who knows what he could have told them under the influence of drugs?"

They needed information quickly, Max thought. Contrary to popular belief, proper interrogation takes weeks and oftentimes months. The only remotely effective way to extract information quickly was the application of pain, tremendous amounts of pain. A victim in that circumstance will tell the interrogator anything he wants to hear. It was the interrogator's job to not reveal his intentions so the prisoner had no choice but to tell the absolute truth.

Max had one hour to figure out what Kovac wanted to hear, because there was no way in hell he would ever tell the bastard the truth.

KEVIN NIXON FELT SICK to his stomach as he stepped past the barricade and onto the movie set. Being there, he was breaking a vow to his dead sister. He could only hope, given the circumstances, that she would forgive him. This part of Donna Sky's new movie was being filmed in an old warehouse left to decay after German reunification. The building reminded Kevin a little of the *Oregon*, only here the rust was real. A half-dozen semitrailers, catering trucks, scaffolding, dolly cranes for cameras, and narrow-gauge railroad tracks for what were called tracking shots were spread across the acres of parking lot. Men and women buzzed around the set, moving at double time, because, in the movie business, time quite literally is money. Nixon judged by what he saw that the film's producers were spending about a hundred and fifty thousand dollars a day here.

To him, the organized chaos of a big-budget motion picture was familiar but now, at the same time, utterly alien.

A guard, wearing a uniform but without a weapon, was about to approach when a voice called out from across the lot, "I can't believe it's really you."

Gwen Russell breezed past the security officer and hugged Nixon tightly, burying her face in his thick beard after kissing both cheeks. Always a bundle of energy, she quickly broke the embrace and regarded him.

"You look fantastic," she said at last.

"I finally admitted that no diet on earth was helping, so I had the stomach bypass surgery two years ago." In his life-long battle with his weight, it had been a desperation play that had paid off. Before the operation, Kevin hadn't seen the underside of two hundred and twenty since college. Now he weighed a respectable one eighty-five, which he carried on a solid frame.

The chefs aboard the *Oregon* prepared him special meals, in keeping with his postoperative diet, and, while he would never be a fan of exercise, he kept to his daily regimen religiously.

"It worked awesome, buddy boy."

She spun him around and slipped her arm through his, so he could lead her back to a row of trailers parked along one side of the lot.

Gwen's hair was hot pink, and she wore brightly colored bicycle pants and a man's oxford shirt. At least fifteen gold necklaces were hung around her throat, and each of her tiny ears had a half-dozen piercings. She had been Nixon's assistant when he had been nominated for an Academy Award and was now a highly sought-after makeup artist in her own right.

"You dropped off everyone's radar some years ago. No one knew where you were or what you were doing," she said in a rush of words. "So dish, and tell me everything you've got going on."

"Not much to tell, really."

She blew a raspberry. "Oh pooh. You vanish for, like, eight years and you say there's nothing to tell? You didn't find God or anything? Wait a minute, you said you wanted to talk to Donna. Did you join that group of hers, the Reactionaries?"

"Responsivists," Kevin corrected.

"Whatever," Gwen shot back, using her best Valley Girl accent. "Are you part of that?"

"No, but I need to talk to her about it."

They reached the makeup trailer. Gwen swung open the door and glided up the retractable stairs. The waxy smell of cosmetics and potpourri was overwhelming. There were six chairs lined up under a long mirror in front of a counter littered with bottles and jars of every size and shape, as well as eye-liner pencils and enough makeup brushes to sweep a football stadium. Gwen pulled two bottled waters from a small fridge, tossed one to Kevin, and dropped into one of the chairs. The intense lights made her hair glow like cotton candy.

"So, come on, it was just after the Oscars—which you should have won, by the way—and, poof, you're gone. What gives?"

"I had to get away from Hollywood. I couldn't stand it anymore." Obviously, Kevin wasn't going to tell her what he'd been doing since turning his back on the movie business, but she had been a good friend and deserved to know the truth.

"You knew me," he started. "I was a lefty, like everyone else. I voted Democrat across the board, hated everything to do with the Republican Party, donated to environmental groups, and drove a hybrid car. I was as much of the Hollywood establishment as anyone."

"Don't tell me you've become a conservative," Gwen said in mock horror. She'd never shown the slightest interest in politics.

"No. It's not like that," he said. "I'm just putting what happened into context. Everything changed on 9/11." Just the mention of the date caused Gwen to blanch, as if she knew where the story was headed. "My sister was coming to see me from Boston."

"Don't tell me."

"Hers was the plane that struck the North Tower of the World Trade Center."

She reached across to where he was sitting to grab his hand "Oh, I am so sorry. I had no idea."

"I couldn't bring myself to tell anyone."

"So that's why you left. Because of your sister's death."

"Not directly," Kevin said. "Well, maybe. I don't know. I went back to work three weeks after her memorial service, trying to get my life back to normal, you know? I was doing makeup for this period drama. I won't tell you who the star was because she's even bigger today than she was then. She was sitting in the chair, talking to her agent about the attacks. She said something like, 'You know, I think what happened to those people was terrible, but this country deserves it. I mean, look at the way we treat the rest of the world. It's no wonder they hate us.'

"That wasn't an uncommon thought," Nixon added, "then or now. But then she said the people who died—my sister—were as much at fault for the attacks as the hijackers.

"I couldn't believe what I was hearing. My little sister was twenty-six years old and about to start her medical residency, and this overpaid bimbo says the attacks were my sister's fault. It was the disconnect, Gwen. People in Hollywood are so disengaged from reality that I just couldn't take it. This actress made millions parading around on screen in her underwear in an offense to Muslim sensibilities and she lays the blame for hatred on my sister.

"I listened to what people in the industry were saying for another couple of months and knew everyone felt pretty much the same. I could take the 'it's America's fault' stuff. What I couldn't stomach is that no one there believed they were also part of that America."

Kevin didn't add that he had gone straight to the CIA to offer his unique abilities or that he'd been presented a much more challenging and lucrative job with the Corporation, most likely because Langston Overholt had passed his name on to Juan before the CIA even knew he was interested.

Adjusting to the gung ho paramilitary nature of Cabrillo's band of pirates had been remarkably easy, and, for the first time, Nixon had come to understand the lure of the military. It wasn't the action and adventure, because most days were filled with tedium. It was the camaraderie, the sense of loyalty that the men and women shared for each other. They gave each other the ultimate responsibility, of keeping the other person from harm, which formed bonds far deeper than Kevin thought were possible.

But his time with the *Oregon* hadn't really changed him much. He still gave money to liberal causes, he voted the Democratic ticket whenever he remembered to get an absentee ballot, and the hybrid car was garaged in a storage unit in L.A. He just valued the freedom to do those things all the more.

"Wow, I am so sorry," Gwen said into the lengthening silence. "I don't really pay attention to that stuff much."

"I didn't use to either, but now . . ." His voice trailed off, and he shrugged. He could sense that he made her uncomfortable. Maybe he had changed more than he'd thought.

The trailer door was suddenly thrown open. On the interview circuit of morning talk shows or on the red carpet of a movie premiere, Donna Sky was a luminous presence that could fill any room. She was the epitome of style, poise, and elegance. Storming into the makeup trailer with her hair hidden by a baseball cap and no cosmetics to hide the fact she had acne, she looked like any harried twenty-something with a chip on her shoulder and a sense of entitlement. Her eyes were bloodshot and ringed by dark circles, and, from across the room, Kevin could smell last night's alcohol binge.

"Who the hell are you and what are you doing here?" she demanded harshly of Nixon. Her trademark voice was frayed because of an apparent hangover. Then she paused, studied him, and finally recognized him. "You're Kevin Nixon, aren't you? You did my makeup on *Family Jewels*."

"That was your big break, as I recall," Kevin said, standing.

"It would have come eventually," Donna said, filled with self-importance. She took the chair Kevin had vacated and looked over her shoulder at Gwen, "Get rid of these bags under my eyes, will you? I don't shoot for a couple of hours, but I can't stand looking this way."

Kevin felt like saying that she shouldn't have gone club hopping the night before but held his tongue.

Gwen shot Kevin a knowing look and said, "Sure thing, honey. Anything for you."

"Are you working on this movie now?" Donna asked Nixon as Gwen got to work with her brushes and eyeliner.

"Actually, no. I'm here to speak with you, if you don't mind."

She let out a bored sigh, and then said, "What the hell. What do you want to talk to me about?"

Kevin glanced at Gwen. She got the hint. "Donna, honey, why don't you let Kevin do your makeup so you can chat in private?"

"Fine."

Nixon mouthed the words *Thank you* to Gwen as she stepped away, handing him a brush. He waited until she'd left the trailer before getting to work. "I'd like to talk about Thom Severance and the Responsivist movement."

Donna Sky instantly tensed. "Sorry, but that subject is closed."

"It's important. Lives may be at stake."

"I don't want to talk about it, all right? You want to talk about my career or my social life, fine. But I don't discuss Responsivism with anyone anymore."

"Why?"

"I just don't!"

Kevin tried to recall everything Linda had taught him about interrogation over the past twenty-four hours. "About a week ago, a ship chartered by the Responsivists sank in the Indian Ocean."

"I know. I saw it on the news. They say it was hit by a wave. They had a special name for it."

"Rogue wave," Kevin offered. "They're called rogue waves."

"That's right. The ship was hit by a rogue wave."

Kevin pulled a sleek laptop out of the backpack he'd brought with him and set it on the counter, pushing aside Gwen's clutter of junk. It took him a few seconds to find the file he wanted.

The quality of the video was poor because there was so little light for the camera Mark Murphy had used aboard the *Golden Dawn*, but it was still clear enough to see the horrified expressions of the dead bridge crew and the gallons of blood that was splashed across the deck. He let it play for about five minutes.

"What was that? A movie you're working on?"

"That was taken aboard the *Golden Dawn*. Every passenger and crewman on board had been murdered, poisoned with something so toxic that no one even had time to use the radio." He found another piece of stored video. This was taken from the *Oregon*'s mast-mounted camera and showed the ship sinking. Her name was clearly visible when the searchlight swept the bows.

Donna Sky was clearly confused. "Who took those pictures and why wasn't this reported to the media?"

"I can't tell you who shot the footage, but it's not being reported yet because this was a terrorist attack and the authorities don't want the terrorists to know what we know."

He gave her credit. She caught his use of the possessive. "Are you, like . . . I mean, do you work for . . . ?"

"I can't answer that question directly, but my having possession of this video should tell you enough."

"Why are you showing this to me? I don't know anything about terrorism."

"Your name came up prominently during the investigation, and evidence points to this attack being carried out by elements within the Responsivist movement." He said it as gently as he could, and either she would believe him or she would call security and have him thrown off the lot.

Her reflection in the mirror stared at him fixedly. Kevin had built his career covering faces, not reading them. He had no idea what she was thinking. He wondered how he would react if someone told him his minister was a terrorist.

"I don't believe you," she said at length. "I think you created that footage to discredit Thom and Heidi."

At least she hasn't tossed me out on my ear, Kevin thought. He asked, "Why would I do that? What possible motive would I have to fabricate those videos and travel halfway around the world to show them to you?"

"How should I know what you think?" Donna snapped.

"Please, think this through very logically. If my goal was to discredit Responsivism, wouldn't I take this to CNN or FOX?" When she didn't say anything, Kevin asked for her honest answer.

"Yeah, probably."

"Since I haven't, then my goal must be something else, right?"

"Maybe," she conceded.

"Then why can't I be telling the truth?"

"Responsivists don't believe in violence. There is no way members of our group did this. It was probably a bunch of radical antiabortionists or something."

"Miss Sky, believe me when I tell you that we have checked every known group in the world looking for those responsible. It keeps coming back to Responsivists. And I'm not talking about the rank and file." Kevin was on a roll now and the lies kept coming. "We believe there is a splinter group that perpetrated this atrocity, and may have other such attacks in the works.

"You and I both know that some people take their faith to the extreme. That's what we think we're dealing with here: extremists within your organization. If you truly want to help your friends, you have to tell me everything you know."

"Okay," she said meekly.

They spoke for almost an hour before Gwen returned. She had several of the movie's extras with her that needed makeup for upcoming scenes. In the end, Kevin was convinced that Donna Sky knew absolutely nothing about what the Corporation had stumbled upon. He also felt that she was a sad, lonely young woman who had become imprisoned by her own success, and that the leadership of the Responsivist movement had singled her out for recruitment for that very fact. He could only hope that someday she would find an inner source of strength that would allow her to stand on her own. He doubted it would happen, but he could hope.

"Thank you very much for talking to me," Kevin said as he packed up his laptop.

"I don't think I was that helpful."

"No. You were great. Thanks."

She was regarding her face in the mirror. She again had the allure that so captivated movie audiences. Gone were the ravages of last night's excess. Kevin had restored her face's artful mix of innocence and sex appeal. The sadness in her eyes was hers alone.

CHAPTER 22

FLYING TO THE PHILIPPINES HAD TAKEN Cabrillo and Franklin Lincoln a little over fourteen hours. Getting from the capital, Manila, to Tubigon, on Bohol Island, in the center of the seven-thousand-plus-island archipelago, had taken almost as long, although the distance was a little more than three hundred miles as the crow flies. Juan knew from experience that the proverbial crow rarely flew in third world nations.

Because ground transportation couldn't be guaranteed on Bohol, they had been forced to first fly to nearby Cebu Island and rent a sturdy, if aged, jeep and wait for the ferry to take them across the Bohol Strait. Linc had remarked that the ferry was so old, the tires slung over her rusted sides should have been whitewalls. The boat had a pronounced list to starboard, despite being loaded intentionally heavy on the port side. Any thought of sleep during the crossing was nixed by the tractor trailer lashed next to their jeep loaded with pigs that suffered *mal de mer* even in these sheltered waters. The smell and their squeals were enough to wake the dead.

Twice during the crossing, the engines inexplicably went silent. The first time was for only a few minutes. The second lasted nearly an hour, as crewmen under the eye of a snarling engineer tinkered with the machinery.

Worrying about surviving the trip was a welcome distraction for Cabrillo. It allowed him to stop dwelling on Max's fate for a while. But when the engines belched to life again, his thoughts immediately returned to his friend. The irony wasn't lost on him that Hanley's own father had died in the Philippines defending Corregidor Island in the opening months of the Second World War.

Juan knew that Max would do whatever it took to protect both his son and the Corporation. The man had a sense of loyalty that would make a Saint Bernard proud. He could only hope that they would find the leverage needed to ensure Max's freedom. He had no illusions about the methods Zelimir Kovac would use to extract information. And if Max couldn't hold out, once he started talking his life was forfeit.

That thought ran like a loop of tape through Cabrillo's mind.

As the lights of Tubigon finally resolved themselves, Juan's satellite phone chimed. "Cabrillo."

"Hi, Juan, it's Linda."

"Any word yet?"

"Nothing from Severance, if that's what you're asking."

"Damn. Yes, it was."

Ten calls to the director of the Responsivists and still nothing. Juan had posed as the head of the security company supposedly hired by Max to rescue his son. He'd spoken to the receptionist enough to know she read romance novels during her lunch break. She had apologized each time he'd called, stating that Severance wasn't available, and patched him through to voice mail. Juan had offered <u>any</u> reward Severance wanted for Max's return, and when that didn't garner a response he'd started threatening. His last call had warned Severance that if Max wasn't released unharmed, he was going to come after his family.

It was an empty threat, thanks to Langston Overholt, but Severance didn't know that. Nor, it seemed, did he care.

"What's up?" Cabrillo asked.

"Kevin just finished up with Donna Sky. She doesn't know anything."

"Is he sure?"

"They talked for an hour," Linda said in her pixielike voice. "She's just an actress who belongs to a loony cult. She's too high-profile to be directly involved with anything untoward. And, according to the celebrity scandal rags, she's tied up shooting her new movie for at least the next four months, apparently to the chagrin of her latest paramour who's in Australia touring with his band, which, by the way, Mark Murphy says sucks."

"Then I'd probably like them," Juan said, digesting this latest piece of information. "If Gil Martell didn't say her name when he was talking to Severance after we broke into his office, then it has to be something else. Can you ask Hali to go over that tape one more time?"

"He cursed up a storm when I told him he might be wrong and then volunteered to listen to it all again."

"Tell him he gets an extra ration of grog. Anything else?"

"Eddie's back from Rome, and we're getting good audio on the arms dealer's yacht but nothing pertinent so far."

Cabrillo had completely forgotten about that mission. "Okay. Good. Keep me posted. Linc and I are about three hours from where the Responsivists have their Philippine retreat. We'll keep you posted."

"Roger that, Chairman, and good hunting. *Oregon* out."

Juan clicked off the phone.

"The whole Donna Sky thing's a bust?" Linc asked in the darkened confines of the jeep. Wearing all black, Linc was just a large shadow sitting next to Cabrillo.

"Yeah. She doesn't know anything."

"It was a long shot anyway. Woman like that can't take her dog for a walk without the paparazzi following her."

"Linda said about the same thing," Juan said moodily. "I should have realized that."

"Chairman, we've been grasping at straws since the beginning. No need to get all morose on me now. We go with the intel we have and see where it takes us. Dead end or not, we have to check it all."

"I know," Juan agreed. "It's just—"

"—that Max's butt is on the line this time," Linc finished for him "And you're concerned."

Cabrillo forced a tired smile. "That's putting it mildly."

"Listen, man, this is our best lead yet. There were four hundred Responsivists here for God knows how long and now they're all dead, most likely so they'll never talk about what they were doing. We'll find what we need and get Max and his son back."

Juan appreciated the pep talk, but it did little to make him feel better. That would come only when Max was back aboard the *Oregon*, and Thom Severance and Zelimir Kovac were nailed to the most convenient outhouse door.

The ferry staggered into the harbor, slamming into the wooded pilings in one of the worst displays of seamanship Cabrillo had ever seen. Ten minutes later, with the boat secured to the dock and the ramp lowered, Linc fired the jeep's engines, and they eased onto the quay. They immediately opened the windows to dissipate the pig smell that had permeated the vehicle.

"Good a time as any," Juan said, and put his foot up on the dashboard.

He rolled up his pant leg. The prosthesis he wore was a bulbous, ugly limb of flesh-toned plastic. He pulled the leg free, and unlaced his boot, pulling it and his sock free. There was a tiny hole in the bottom of the prosthetic foot. He plucked a small Allen wrench from his pocket, inserted it in the hole, and turned it counterclockwise. This released a mechanism built into the leg that allowed him to split open the calf like an old-fashioned lunch box. Cached inside what he called his smuggler's leg were two Kel-Tek pistols.

Despite its small size, the Kel-Tek fired P-rated .380 caliber bullets. For this particular mission, the armorer aboard the *Oregon* had hollowed out the seven rounds each pistol held and filled the voids with mercury. When the bullet struck flesh and slowed, the momentum would cause the mercury to explode out of the round and shred tissue the way a shaped explosive cuts through a tank's armor. A hit anywhere center mass was fatal, and even a glancing shot to the shoulder or hip would sever a limb. Cabrillo handed one of the diminutive pistols to Linc and slipped the other into the small of his back.

A small block of plastic explosives and two detonator pencils, set at five minutes, were also in the smuggler's leg. Juan had found over the years that when his prosthesis set off airport metal detectors and he pulled up his cuff to show the limb, he was waved through with an apologetic smile every time. Although they hadn't encountered any bomb-sniffing dogs on this run, he was ready for that contingency with a small bottle of nitroglycerin pills and an explanation of having a bad heart.

The road out of town and into the hills hadn't seen new asphalt in decades. The Responsivists had worked on the opposite side of the island, and it took an hour to reach the area. The sun had crested the horizon during the drive, revealing primal rain forest and jungle that hemmed in the road like a continuous emerald tunnel. The few villages they passed were composed of a couple of crude thatched huts and the odd corrugated-metal lean-to. With the exception of the Japanese occupation during the war, the pace of life in this part of the islands hadn't changed in millennia.

When they were five miles from their destination, Linc pulled off the road, easing the jeep into a thicket of underbrush deep enough to hide the vehicle. They had no idea if the Responsivists had left guards at their facility and weren't going to take unnecessary chances. He and Cabrillo spent a few minutes putting finishing touches on the camouflage and erasing the tracks the jeep had sunk into the soft soil. Even knowing where it was hidden, neither man could see it from the road. Juan built a small cairn of pebbles on the verge to mark the location.

Shouldering packs stuffed with gear, they stepped into the jungle and started the long walk in. The sun seemed to vanish, replaced by a green-filtered glow that barely penetrated the high canopy of trees. The color reminded Cabrillo of the *Oregon*'s moon pool at night when the underhull lights were turned on.

Despite his size, Lincoln moved through the jungle with the easy grace of a predatory cat, finding the tiniest openings between the dense vegetation so as not to disturb anything. His feet seemed to barely brush the loamy ground. He was so stealthy that the background symphony of insects and bird cries never dropped in volume or rose in alarm.

Cabrillo walked in his wake, constantly scanning behind them for any sign they were being followed. The air was so humid, it seemed that his lungs were filling with fluid with each breath. Sweat ran freely down his back, and soaked the band of his baseball cap. He could feel it cold and slick where his stump met his artificial leg.

After two hours of stalking silently through the rain forest, Linc held up a fist, then lowered himself to the ground. Cabrillo followed suit, crawling up next to the big SEAL. They were at the edge of the jungle. Ahead of them was open grassland that stretched for a quarter mile before dropping to the sea in a line of near-vertical slopes and eroded cliffs.

With the sun behind them, Cabrillo didn't worry about reflections off his binoculars as he scanned his surroundings. The Responsivists had built a single metal building a short distance from the cliffs. It was as large as a warehouse, with a gently sloped roof to deal with the thirteen and a half feet of annual rainfall. Opaque panels in the roof would let in diffused sunlight, as there were no windows. The sides were bare metal painted with a red oxide anticorrosion paint, and there was just a single door facing a parking lot big enough for fifty or so vehicles.

About thirty yards from the warehouse were four rows of rectangular concrete pads. Cabrillo counted forty of the empty pads per row.

Linc tapped him on the shoulder. He drew a rectangle in the dirt and pointed at the warehouse. Then he made a second rectangle and pointed at the field of concrete. Cabrillo was with him so far. Then Linc drew a much larger square around the whole compound and pointed across the open field.

Juan studied the area through the binoculars and noticed a slight variation in the grass, which ran in a straight line before abruptly turning ninety degrees. He looked at Linc. The Navy vet placed the edge of his hand on the line he'd drawn, indicating he thought there had once been a fence running the perimeter of the field. He then used his fingers to rather crassly raise the corners of his eyes.

Cabrillo nodded his agreement. This had once been a Japanese compound of some kind, most likely a prison camp. The fence had been removed years ago, and all that remained of the cell blocks were the concrete pads. He wondered if the Responsivists chose this location because there was already an existing foundation for their building.

The duo watched the structure for another two hours, passing the binoculars back and forth when their eyes began to tire. Nothing moved in the clearing except when a breeze blew in off the ocean and made waves ripple through the knee-high grass.

Juan suddenly cursed and stood. "That's it. Nobody's home." His voice seemed unnaturally loud after so many hours of silence.

"How can you be so sure?" Linc asked in a hoarse whisper.

"Listen." His tone made it clear he was angry with himself.

Linc cocked his head. "Nothing but the ocean hitting the base of the cliffs."

"Exactly. See the empty brackets on the roof? It's got to be ninety degrees out here, which means it's at least a hundred and twenty in that building. Those brackets once held some pretty big air-conditioning units. They took them when they bugged out. Unless that building is packed to the rafters with water, a guard detail wouldn't last an hour in there, let alone the weeks it's been since they abandoned this place."

Cabrillo held out a hand to haul Lincoln to his feet. It was a testament to Juan's time working out aboard the *Oregon* that the effort didn't tear the muscles in his back.

Although he was reasonably certain of his deduction, they approached the structure carefully, keeping well away from the door until they were tight up to the metal side. The building's skin was hot enough to singe Juan's fingertips when he touched it.

With their pistols drawn, they approached the door. Juan set his pack on the ground and fished out a length of rubber tubing. He wrapped it around the knob and handed one end to Linc while he kept the other. They stood on opposite sides of the door, and Juan pulled at the tubing. The friction of the rubber against the metal knob caused it to turn, and the door clicked open. Had it been set with explosives, Cabrillo's trick would have kept them well out of the blast radius.

"Not even locked," Linc commented.

Juan peeked inside. "No reason it would be. Take a look."

With pearly light shining through the skylights, the warehouse remained murky, but there was enough illumination to see the vast interior was completely empty. There weren't even support columns for the roof trusses to break up the monotony of the expanse of concrete. If not for the small door, Juan would have thought this had been an aircraft hangar. The floor had been painted a uniform gray and was spotlessly clean. When Juan stepped inside, he caught a trace scent of bleach.

"Looks like the Merry Maids beat us here, eh?" Linc joked as he stood at Juan's shoulder.

Cabrillo remained silent. He knew in his heart that they would find nothing to incriminate Severance, so there would be no leverage to get Max back. The Responsivists had removed any hint of what had gone on inside the building. The air-conditioning ducts were gone, all traces of wiring and plumbing—everything.

"Waste of damned time," he finally said in disgust.

Linc was hunched down, examining the floor. He straightened, saying, "This concrete is pretty weathered. My guess is that it was laid by the Japanese when they built the rest of the prison."

"Why the hell would they need such a large building?" Juan wondered aloud. "The ground's too hilly for an airstrip, so it's not a hangar."

"I don't know. Storage of some kind?"

"A factory," Juan said. "I bet they used prisoners of war as slave labor here. God knows, they used them everywhere else they occupied."

Linc touched the tip of his broad nose with his finger. "Bet you're right."

Juan grabbed his satellite phone and dialed the *Oregon*. With Hali working on the audio from the bug, Juan asked the on-duty communications staffer to plug him through to Eric Stone.

"What's up, boss man?" Eric asked when he answered the phone in his cabin.

"Do me a favor and check into the Japanese occupation of Bohol Island in the Philippines. I'm interested if they had any prisons or factories set up here."

"What, now?"

"You can plan your assault on Janni Dahl's honor later."

"Okay. Hold on a second." The connection was so clear he could hear Eric's fingers tapping furiously at his computer terminal. "I've got something. There was a prison for indigenous criminals opened on the island in March of 1943. It was closed the day MacArthur made his return, on October twentieth, 1944. It was overseen by something called Unit 731. Want me to run a check on that?"

"No," Juan said. It was a hundred and eighteen degrees in the building, and Juan shivered, the blood in his veins suddenly turning to ice. "I know what that is."

He killed the connection. "This place was a death factory," he told Linc, "operated by an outfit called Unit 731."

"Never heard of them."

"Not surprised. Unlike the Germans who apologized for the Holocaust, the Japanese government hasn't really acknowledged their own war crimes, especially Unit 731's."

"What did they do?"

"They had factories and laboratories set up all over China during the occupation and were responsible for Japan's biological-warfare efforts. There are some estimates that claim Unit 731, and others like it, killed more people than Hitler did in his extermination camps. They experimented on prisoners by subjecting them to every virus known to mankind. They engineered bubonic plague, typhus, and anthrax outbreaks in several Chinese cities. Sometimes they used aircraft that sprayed the landscape with disease-ridden fleas or packed them into bombs. Another favorite trick was to take over local waterworks and intentionally contaminate a city's drinking supply."

"They got away with it?"

"For years. Another part of their job was to determine the effect of explosives and other weapons on the human body. They would gun down, blow up, or incinerate hundreds of prisoners at a time. You think of any torture imaginable, and I guarantee Unit 731 tested it thoroughly. I recall one experiment where they hung prisoners by their feet just to see how long it would take them to die."

Linc had gone a little pale under his ebony skin. "And this place was one of their laboratories?" he asked, looking around.

Juan nodded. "And the local Philippine prisoners were the lab rats."

"You thinking what I'm thinking?"

"That Severance chose this place for a very specific reason?"

"Using a toxin on the *Golden Dawn* after its people were

working at an old germ-warfare factory can't be a coincidence. Just throwing something out there, but is it possible they all contracted something left over by the Japanese?"

"It wouldn't have killed the crew all at the same time," Cabrillo replied. "I thought of that as soon as Eric mentioned Unit 731. No, it has to be something they created here."

"Do you think it's a bright idea to be walking around without a biohazard suit?"

"We'll be fine," Juan said confidently.

"Man, I'd settle for a surgical mask and some rubber gloves," Linc groused.

"Try one of Linda's yoga techniques and breathe through your eyes."

Using flashlights and starting at opposite corners, the men examined every square inch of the building. There wasn't so much as a gum wrapper on the floor.

"There's nothing here," Juan admitted.

"Not so fast," Linc said. He was studying the warehouse's back wall. He tapped one of the exposed steel support columns. It sounded tinny. Then he placed his hand against the metal siding. It was hot to the touch but not scalding. That, in itself, didn't prove anything, since the sun might not shine directly on it, but it was an encouraging sign.

"What have you got?" Juan asked.

"A harebrained thought. Come on." He turned and started for the door, counting his paces as he went. "Ninety-eight, ninety-nine, one hundred," he said as he reached the opposite wall. "Three feet per step so we've got us a three-hundred-foot-long building."

"Great," Juan replied with little enthusiasm.

"Ye of little faith."

Linc led Cabrillo outside and paced off the exterior wall, again counting each step. "Ninety-eight, ninety-nine, one hundred, one hundred and one."

"You unintentionally shortened your stride." Juan said flatly.

"Touch the back of the building," Linc said, knowing what the Chairman would discover.

Juan yanked his fingers away. The metal was scorching hot. He cocked an inquiring eyebrow.

"The columns we saw on the other side of this wall aren't load-bearing. The metal is too thin-gauged."

"Are you sure?"

"SEAL training, my friend. They teach us how a building is put together so we better understand how to blow it up. That's a false wall in there, and behind it is a three-foot void."

"What the hell for?"

"Let's find out."

They returned inside the sweltering warehouse. Linc pulled a matte-finish folding knife from his pack. He flipped open the blade and rammed it into the metal siding, cutting the thin steel as if it were paper. He wrenched down on the blade, slicing a long gash nearly to the floor. Then he cut across the tear, sawing the blade back and forth with a sound that sent Cabrillo's teeth on edge.

"Emerson CQC-7a," Linc said, holding the knife proudly. There wasn't a mark on the blade. "Read about them a few years ago and didn't believe the hype. I do now."

He kicked at the torn metal, peeling back the siding like the petals of a flower, until he could step into the secret room. The beam of his flashlight revealed . . .

"Nothing. It's empty. Just like the rest of this place," Linc said with obvious disappointment.

"Damn."

Together, they walked the width of the building in the tight space, sweeping their lights over every surface just to be sure. The heat was horrendous, like standing beside a crucible in a steel mill.

Linc had his light pointed at the floor when something caught his attention. He stooped, brushing his fingers lightly across the painted concrete. There was a grin on his face when he looked up at the Chairman.

"What have you got?"

"This concrete is new. Not the whole floor, just this section."

Juan noticed it, too. An area about ten feet long and the full width of the secret chamber was much smoother than the rest and showed no signs of weathering.

"What do you think?" Juan asked.

"Perfect place for a stairwell to a basement level. The size is right."

"Let's find out."

Juan rummaged through his pack for the block of C-4 plastic explosives. He molded it to direct its detonative force downward and inserted the timer pencil. A quick glance at Linc to make sure he was ready and Cabrillo activated the detonator.

They dashed out of the hidden room and sprinted across the warehouse floor, their lungs sucking in the overheated air and their footfalls echoing. Linc flew through the door with Cabrillo at his heels, and they ran for another fifty yards before they slowed and turned.

The explosion was a muted crump that blew the skylight panels off the roof and filled the warehouse with a roiling fog of concrete dust. Dust coiled through the damaged roof, making the building look like it was burning.

Waiting for the cloud to settle, Juan felt a vague apprehension creeping up his spine, so he carefully scanned the jungle. The glint of sunlight off a reflective surface was all the warning he needed. He shoved Linc aside and dove to the ground as a pair of bullets from two separate rifles split the air where they had been standing a microsecond earlier. The well-hidden gunmen switched their weapons to automatic and sent a devastating wall of fire into the parking lot where they believed Cabrillo and Linc were pinned.

The two men were hopelessly outgunned, and, if they didn't find cover, they would be dead in the next few seconds. Without needing to communicate, they sprinted back into the warehouse, their legs peppered by bits of gravel thrown up by the bullets that stitched the ground in their wake.

Juan was the first to reach the blast site. The concrete had been shattered by the plastique, leaving a large crater in the floor that reeked of the explosive. But it hadn't been enough. The plug was too thick for the amount of plastique they'd brought. Casting his flashlight over the bottom of the crater, he couldn't see a single spot where they had breached all the way through.

Defeat was a bitter taste on the tip of his tongue.

A constellation of bullet holes appeared in the metal wall of the building. He whirled, not realizing he'd already drawn his Kel-Tek. Two gunmen stood on either side of the door. He fired three covering shots, the range far beyond the gun's capabilities. Neither man flinched.

Linc jumped past him, landing in the bottom of the crater they'd created. When his feet hit the stressed cement, a hole opened up beneath him and he vanished into the earth. His weight had been enough to cause the plug to give way.

As more and more concrete splintered and tumbled down a flight of stairs, Juan tossed himself into the darkened hole, noting that the breeze blowing up from the depths carried the cold stench of death.

CHAPTER 23

THE PUNCH SANK DEEP INTO MAX'S STOMACH, doubling him over as much as the ropes holding him to the chair would allow. Zelimir Kovac hadn't used half of his tremendous strength, and Hanley felt as though his guts had been turned to jelly. He grunted at the pain, spraying saliva and blood from his ruined mouth.

It was the fourth consecutive body blow, and he hadn't expected it. Blindfolded, he could only rely on his torturer's natural rhythm to anticipate the blow, and so far Kovac hadn't established one. His punches were as random as they were brutal. He'd been at it for ten minutes and hadn't yet asked a single question.

The duct tape covering Max's eyes was suddenly ripped away, taking with it some of his heavy brows. The sensation was like having acid splashed on his face, and he couldn't contain the yowl that burst from his lips.

He looked around, blinking through the gush of tears. The room was bare and antiseptic, with white cinder-block walls and a concrete floor. Ominously, there was a drain in the floor at Max's feet and a water spigot with a length of hose coiled on a peg next to the metal door. The door was open, and beyond, Max could see the hallway had the same block walls and shabby white paint.

Kovac stood over Max, wearing suit trousers and a sleeveless undershirt. The Serb's sweat and Max's blood stained the shirt's cotton. A pair of guards in matching jumpsuits leaned against the wall, their faces stony. Kovac thrust a hand toward one of the guards, and the man handed him a sheaf of papers.

"According to your son," Kovac began, "your name is Max

Hanley, and you are part of the merchant marine, a ship's engineer. Is this correct?"

"Go to hell," Max said, in a low, menacing tone.

Kovac squeezed a nerve bundle at the base of Max's neck, sending torrents of pain lancing to every part of his body. He kept up the pressure, squeezing even harder, until Max was literally panting. "Is that information correct?"

"Yes, damnit," Max said through clenched teeth.

Kovac released his grip and slammed his fist into Max's jaw hard enough to twist his head. "That's for lying. You had a transdermal transponder embedded in your leg. That isn't common for the merchant marines."

"The company I hired to get Kyle back," Max mumbled, wishing more than anything to be able to massage some feeling into his face where it had gone numb. "They implanted it as part of their security."

Kovac punched Max in the face again, loosening a tooth. "Nice try, but the scar was at least six months old."

It was a good guess. Hux had implanted his new one seven months ago.

"It's not—I swear it," Max lied. "That's how I heal, fast and ugly. Look at my hands."

Kovac glanced down. Hanley's hands were a patchwork of old crisscrossed scars. It meant nothing to him. He leaned in so his face was inches from Max's. "I have inflicted more scars in my life than a surgeon and know how people heal. That implant is six or more months old. Tell me who you are and why have you such a device?"

Max's response was to slam the crown of his balding head into Kovac's nose. The restraints binding him to the chair prevented him from breaking the bone, but he was satisfied with the jet of blood that flew from one nostril until the Serb staunched it with his fingers.

The look Kovac shot Hanley was one of pure animal rage. Max had known the strike was going to earn him the beating of his life, but, as Kovac glared, smears of blood like war paint on his face, Max felt certain he had gone too far.

The blows came in a flurry. There was no pattern, no aim. It was an explosive reaction, the instinct of the primeval hindbrain toward a perceived threat. Max took shots to the face, chest, stomach, shoulders, and groin in a rain of punches and kicks that seemed inexhaustible. The strikes came so fast, he felt certain more than one person was hitting him, but, as his eyes rolled back so that only the whites showed, he could tell the punishment was being meted out by Kovac alone.

Two full minutes passed after Max had slumped over in his chair, his face a pulped mass, until one of the guards finally stepped in to restrain the Serb butcher. Kovac turned his murderous gaze at the interruption and the guard hastily backed away, but the distraction was enough to cool his rage.

He looked contemptuously at Hanley's unconscious form, his chest heaving with exertion and adrenaline. Kovac snapped his wrists, making the taxed joints pop audibly and sending droplets of their mingled blood to the floor. Reaching over, he pushed up Max's right eyelid. All that showed was a veined white orb.

Kovac turned to the guards. "Come back and check on him in a couple of hours. If he doesn't break next time, we will have his son flown here from Corinth and see how much of a beating he can watch the kid take before he tells us what we want to know."

He strode out the open door. The two guards waited a moment and then followed, closing the heavy door behind them. They never looked back or felt movement in the room, because it was the last thing they would have expected.

Watching them leave through nearly closed eyes, Max was in motion the instant their backs turned. All throughout the terrible pounding, he had worked his body back and forth in the chair to loosen the ropes. Kovac's fury had blinded him to this, and the guards had assumed Hanley's jerky movements were in response to the blows. But Max's actions had been cold and deliberate.

He bent over and grabbed one of the pieces of paper Kovac had tossed aside when Max had hit his nose. Shuffling with the metal chair strapped to his back, he lunged toward the door. He had one shot at this, because, even if he survived another beating, he would tell them whatever they needed to know to protect Kyle no matter the consequences.

His aim was perfect. The piece of paper slipped between the door and the jamb the instant before the lock engaged, preventing the bolt from sliding home.

Max sagged back into the chair. It had been the worst pounding he had ever taken. Even more savage than when he was in a Vietcong prison, and there they had taken turns so that the blows went on for an hour or more. He felt around his mouth, moving two teeth freely with his tongue. It had been a minor miracle that his nose hadn't broken or one of the body blows hadn't caused his heart to fibrillate and stop.

The spot where they had cut out the bioelectric transponder was a dull ache compared to the rest of his body. His chest was a mottled sea of bruised flesh, and he could only imagine the damage done to his face.

Well, I wasn't all that pretty to begin with, he thought grimly, and the wry smile that followed brought fresh blood from the cuts on his lips.

Max promised himself ten minutes to recover. Any longer and he would have cramped up to the point of immobility. There was a glimmer of hope amid his pain—at least they hadn't brought Kyle to this hellhole. He was back in Greece. Even in the Responsivists' grasp, he was relatively safe. Max clutched that thought to his heart and let it buoy his spirits.

By his estimation, six minutes had passed when he started working on the loosened ropes. He had created enough slack to work his wrists free of them so he could use his hands to pull away the ropes wound around his chest. Finally, he was able to untie his legs and stand. He groped for the back of the chair to keep from toppling over.

"I don't feel so good," he muttered aloud, and waited for his blurred vision to clear.

He eased open the heavy door as quietly as he could. The hallway was empty. The industrial fluorescent fixtures bolted to the concrete ceiling cast stark pools of light interspersed with deep shadows, giving the cinder-block walls a dingy look despite their apparent newness.

Max balled the piece of paper into the lock so the door wouldn't close, and, keeping in a low crouch because his muscles wouldn't let him stand upright, he padded down the hallway, making certain he wasn't leaving a telltale trail of blood.

At the first intersection, he heard faint muffled voices to his left, so he turned right, casting an eye backward every few seconds. He passed an occasional unlabeled door. Pressing an ear to the cool metal, he heard nothing beyond and moved on.

It was the dankness of the air and the fact he'd seen no windows that made him think he was underground. He had no direct proof but didn't doubt his assessment.

Turning two more times in the monochromatic maze, he came to another door and could hear the whine of machinery inside. He tried the handle and it turned easily. He opened it a crack, and the level of noise rose in timbre and volume. He could see no light escaping from the room, so he assumed it was deserted. He ducked in quickly and closed the door behind him. Groping blindly, he found a light switch.

Arc lights snapped on, revealing a cavernous space sunk below the level of the floor he was standing on. He was in the control room overlooking the facility's powerhouse. Behind thick insulated glass were four huge jet engines bolted to the floor, fed by a tangle of fuel lines and exhaust ducts. Mated to each was an electrical generator. The assemblies were slightly larger than a locomotive, and although only one of the turbines was in operation the room buzzed and crackled with undisguised power.

Either this place is massive, Max thought, casting an expert eye over the room again, because they can produce enough juice for a couple thousand people, or they have some other, unknown use for this much electricity.

He mentally filed away the incongruity and retreated back into the hallway.

With no visible cameras and no guards patrolling the corridors, Max had a sense that Kovac must feel pretty secure here. It was another fact that he tucked away as he sought an exit from the labyrinth.

He finally came to a door marked STAIRWELL, but, when he opened it, he discovered the stairs led only downward.

"In for a penny, in for a pound," he muttered, and headed deeper into the facility.

The scissor-style stairs zigzagged four stories before coming to an end on a dimly lit landing. The only door led into an even-darker tunnel that ran perpendicular to the stairwell.

Unlike the other areas Max had seen, the perfectly circular tunnel was of rough-hewn native rock and was just large enough for him to stand. He could see where some sort of machine, like a continuous miner or a tunnel borer, had left ragged toolmarks on the dark stone. There were no lights, so he had no way of knowing how long the tunnel was or what it was for. The only clues were thick copper wires strung along the ceiling from ceramic insulators. There had to have been a hundred of them, each carefully spaced from its neighbor. His engineering background told him they could easily take the electrical load of the generators he'd seen on the upper level.

"What are you supposed to do, my beauty?" he mused aloud. But, of course, there was no answer.

He considered following the wire, blindly hoping it led to an exit, but the stillness of the air made him think that the tunnel had no outlet. He also hadn't forgotten he was at least fifty feet underground, possibly more.

Max set himself the arduous task of climbing the stairs. His body protested every step, and, as the exertion deepened his breathing, it felt like a vise was clamped around his chest. Even if his ribs weren't fully broken, he laid a silent wager that a couple of them sported hairline cracks.

He was panting when he reached the upper landing and had to clamp his elbows to the sides of his chest to ease away some of the pain.

Pressing his ear to the door, he heard muffled voices, and, as they faded, he thought he heard one person say to another, ". . . sky two days from now, so we'll need . . ." He waited another few moments before opening the door. The hallway was deserted. He couldn't even hear the echo of their foot-falls.

Padding silently, he renewed his search for a way out. He was halfway down one long hallway when he heard people approaching. Their movements were swift and sure, making him think it might be Kovac and his goons heading back to his cell for another go at him, although only a half hour had passed since they had left him. Knowing he couldn't run even if he wanted to, Max had no choice but to duck through one of the metal doors lining the corridor.

He held the knob open as he closed the door so the lock

couldn't engage and stood pressed against it as the footfalls drew nearer. It was only after they strode past that Max glanced over his shoulder at the darkened room. By the glow of a small light plugged into an outlet, he saw six cots laid out in rows and the obvious outline of six people asleep on top of them. One person must have been the lightest sleeper in the world because he suddenly grunted and shot bolt upright, peering myopically into the gloom.

"Steve?" he called out.

"Yes," Max answered at once. "Go back to sleep."

The youngish man fell back onto his cot and rolled away from Max, his breathing relaxing in an instant.

Max couldn't say the same about his own breathing. He felt certain his heart was going to hammer through his ribs at any moment, although he was grateful for the anesthetic effects of the adrenaline jolt his near discovery had sent into his veins. He gave it a few more moments before sliding back out of the dormitory room.

In all, Max skulked around for nearly an hour before finding a stairwell that led upward, confirming his suspicions that this was a subterranean base of some kind. Depending on the sizes of the rooms he hadn't explored, he estimated the facility was at least a hundred thousand square feet. As to its purpose, he could only guess.

He climbed two stories before coming to yet another door. He waited with his ear pressed to the metal. He heard sounds from the other side but was unable to identify anything. He eased the door open a crack, pressing his eye to the narrow slit. He saw a wedge of what looked like a garage. The metal trestle roof lofted twenty feet or more, and there was a ramp that led to a pair of industrial-sized garage doors. Embedded in the rock walls next to them were thick steel blast doors that could be swung closed. They looked impregnable to nothing less than a nuclear bomb. Max heard a radio playing some music that, to him, sounded like cats fighting in a burlap bag but was doubtlessly something Mark Murphy had on his iPod.

He saw nobody, so he quickly dashed through the door and found shelter under a wooden workbench littered with greasy tools. Just as the door snicked closed, he realized with horror that it had a sophisticated electronic lock mechanism activated by a palm reader as well as a numeric keypad. There was no returning to his cell and hoping he could talk his way out of another beating.

Although the garage was dimly lit, there was a pool of light on the far side where two mechanics were working on a four-wheel-drive pickup. From the looks of it, they were replacing the radiator and doing some welding near the front of the vehicle. He could see the blue glow of an oxyacetylene torch and smelled the tang of seared metal. There were other vehicles parked in the garage. He spotted two larger trucks and several four-wheelers, like the one Juan had used to escape the Responsivists in Greece.

Max felt time slipping by and wished Cabrillo was with him now. Juan had an innate ability to form and execute a plan with the barest glance at the situation. Max, on the other hand, was more of a plodder, attacking a problem with brute force and dogged determination.

Kovac would be returning to the interrogation chamber shortly, and Hanley needed to get as far away from this place as he possibly could.

Moving cautiously, he realized the garage doors were the only exit and was certain the radio wouldn't mask the sound of one of them rattling open. There was really only one avenue open to him.

Brute force it is, he thought.

The wrench he grabbed was at least eighteen inches long and weighed ten pounds. He hefted it like a surgeon taking up a scalpel, fully knowing his capabilities with the instrument. He had gotten into his first real fight as a teenager when a strung-out junkie brandishing a knife had tried to rob his uncle's gas station. Max had knocked out eight of the would-be thief's teeth with a wrench identical to the one he carried now.

He moved cautiously across the garage, finding cover where he could and stalking slowly because the human eye's peripheral vision is adept at picking up movement. Any sound he made was drowned out by the radio.

One of the mechanics had his face covered by a darkened welder's shield to protect his eyes, so Max concentrated on the second, a tall, lanky man in his thirties with a bushy beard and greasy hair tied in a ponytail. He was bent over the engine compartment, running his hands over a bundle of hoses, so he never felt Max's presence behind him until Max brought the wrench down with a measured swing.

The blow dropped the mechanic as if he'd been poleaxed, and the egg it left on his skull would last him weeks.

Max turned. The welder had sensed motion and was just straightening, reaching to pull off his mask, when Hanley stepped forward and, like a batter in the all-star game, swung the wrench. At the perfect moment in his swing, Max let the wrench fly. The case-hardened tool smashed the plastic visor, which saved the welder from having his face torn off, while the power of the throw tossed the man bodily into a nearby rolling toolbox. The blowtorch, on its long rubber lines, dropped at Max's feet, the blue jet flame making him step back when he felt the heat on his bare feet.

A third mechanic who had been hidden on the far side of the truck suddenly appeared around the front bumper, drawn by the commotion. He stared at the unconscious welder sprawled against the toolbox before turning toward Max.

Max watched as confusion became understanding and then anger, but before the man could give in to his flight-or-fight reflex Max scooped up the still-burning torch and tossed it in an easy underarm throw. Another instinct took over, and the mechanic automatically grabbed for it as it came at him.

At over six thousand degrees Fahrenheit, the tongue of burning oxygen and acetylene needed the briefest contact to char flesh. The mechanic caught the torch with the nozzle pointed directly at his chest. A smoldering hole opened in his overalls instantly, and skin and muscle sizzled away to reveal the white of his rib cage. The bones blackened before the massive load of shock made him drop the brass torch.

His expression didn't change in the seconds it took his brain to realize his heart had stopped beating. He collapsed slowly to the concrete floor. The smell made Max want to retch. He hadn't intended to kill the hapless mechanic, but he steeled himself. He had to save his son, and, unfortunately, this man stood in his way.

The welder was the closest to his size, so he took a moment

to strip him out of his coveralls. He had to take the third mechanic's boots because the others were hopelessly small. He did so without looking up from the man's feet.

With a pair of wire cutters, he moved to the two trucks and opened the hoods, cutting the wires that sprouted from the distributor caps like black tentacles. As he started for the quad bikes, he saw a coffee machine set up on a workbench. Apart from filters, mugs, and a plastic container of creamer powder, there was a box of sugar. Max grabbed it, and, rather than waste time messing with the Kawasakis' electronics, he unscrewed their fuel caps and dumped sugar into their tanks. The bikes wouldn't run for more than a quarter mile, and it would take hours to clean out their fuel lines and cylinders.

A minute later, he was astride the one idling four-wheeler he hadn't tampered with and pressed the button that opened the garage door. It was night, and wind-ripped rain lashed through the opening. Max couldn't have asked for better conditions. There was no point closing the door. Kovac would know he was gone and how he was making his escape.

Slitting his eyes against the rain, he twisted the throttle and shot out into the unknown.

CHAPTER 24

Kovac's orders had been specific to the five men he'd dispatched to watch over the dismantled Responsivist facility in the Philippines. They weren't to interfere with people investigating the building unless it became apparent that they were going to breach the underground sections. In the weeks they had observed the site, the only interest shown had been a couple of Filipinos on a well-used motorcycle. They had remained only a few minutes, looking over the building to see if there was anything worth looting. When they realized everything had been stripped, they had roared off down the road in a cloud of blue exhaust.

The way the two approached today had put the guards on immediate alert, and when the blast echoed across the open field they knew their caution had been well founded.

Amid the tumult of crashing cement, Juan fell through the hole Linc had created, landing solidly on his feet on a flight of steep stairs. The air was an impenetrable wall of dust, forcing Cabrillo to run blindly down the steps, trusting that Linc had cleared out of the way. A piece of cement the size of his head hit his shoulder with a glancing blow, but it was enough to throw him off his feet. He tumbled the last few steps and lay dazed on the landing, as more debris rained down all around him.

A powerful hand groped for the back of his bush shirt and drew him into an antechamber and out of what was becoming an avalanche.

"Thanks," Juan panted as Linc helped him to his feet.

Both men's faces and clothes were a uniform shade of pale gray from the dust.

The timber scaffolding that supported the weight of the concrete plug gave way entirely, and tons of cement and broken wood crashed onto the staircase, completely filling the entrance to the antechamber with rubble. The darkness inside the chamber was absolute.

Linc pulled a flashlight from his haversack. The beam was as bright as a car's xenon headlamp, but all it revealed were clouds of concrete dust.

"Remind you of anything?" Linc asked with a dry chuckle.

"Little like Zurich when we sprang that banker a while back," Juan answered with a cough.

"What do you think of our reception committee?"

"I feel like an idiot for thinking it was going to be that easy."

"Amen, brother." Linc flashed the beam across the choked-off doorway. Some of the concrete slabs had to weigh half a ton or more. "It's going to take a couple of hours to dig our way out of here."

"As soon as we open even a small hole, they're going to gun us down like fish in a barrel." Juan purposefully engaged his pistol's safety and slid it into his waistband at the small of his back. "Outgunned and most likely outnumbered. I don't fancy clawing our way into an ambush."

"Wait them out?"

"Won't work. We've got one canteen and a couple of protein bars. They could sit out there from now until doomsday." As he spoke, Juan was fiddling with his satellite phone.

"Then we can call in the cavalry. Eddie can have an assault force here inside of forty-eight hours."

"I'm not getting a signal." Cabrillo turned the phone off to conserve its battery.

"All right, you've shot down all of my suggestions, what's up your sleeve?"

Juan took the light from Linc's hand and played it along the downward-sloping tunnel that had been bored into the earth decades ago. "We see where this leads."

"What happens if they come in after us?"

"Hope we have enough warning so we can lay an ambush."

"Why not wait for them right here?"

"If I was leading that team, I would lob in a bunch of grenades before committing my men. We'd be mincemeat before they needed to fire a single shot. If we hung back out of grenade range, we'd be too exposed in this tunnel. Better to find a more defensible position. On the bright side, if they do bother to come after us it most likely means there's another way out of here."

Linc considered their options, and with a broad sweep of his arm indicated they should proceed down the subterranean passageway.

One wall of the tunnel was a long, continuous slab of stone, while the other showed signs that it had been worked by tools. The two men could walk comfortably side by side, and there was at least ten feet of headroom.

"This is a natural fissure the Japanese expanded during their occupation," Cabrillo said as he studied the rock.

"Most likely split open by an earthquake," Linc agreed. "They built their factory, or whatever the hell it was, where the hole reached the surface."

Juan pointed out dark splatters on the stone floor. The spray pattern indicated it was blood—copious amounts of blood. "Gunshot."

"More than one victim, too."

Juan jerked the light away from the grisly tableau. His mouth was a thin, grim line.

The air temperature dropped and the humidity built as they descended deeper into the earth. It was thinking about the misery that had occurred here rather than the plummeting temperature that made Cabrillo shiver.

The tunnel wasn't straight, but rather corkscrewed and twisted as it fell away at a gentle angle. After twenty-five minutes and more than two miles, the cave floor leveled out, and they discovered the first side chamber. The entrance was partially blocked by a minor cave-in, and the tunnel's ceiling was a fractured mess of stone ready to collapse at any moment. This cavern, too, had been a natural geologic feature that the Japanese had expanded. The room was roughly circular, fifty feet across, with a ceiling that was at least fifteen feet high. There was nothing in the cavern except some bolts along the walls that had once carried electrical wiring.

"Administration area?" Linc wondered aloud.

"Makes sense, being the closest room to the surface."

They found two smaller side caves before discovering a fourth in which the Japanese had left artifacts behind. This chamber had a dozen iron bunks bolted to the floor and several flimsy pressed-metal cabinets along one wall. As Juan checked the drawers, Linc examined the bedsteads.

"You wouldn't think they would have bothered giving their prisoners beds," Linc said.

"There's nothing in any of these drawers." Juan looked at Lincoln. "They needed the beds because they had to restrain their victims. Someone intentionally infected with typhus, cholera, or some type of poison gas is going to thrash around."

Franklin snapped his hands away from the metal bunk as though he'd been burned.

They found four more side chambers like this one, some large enough to hold forty beds. They also found a small, waist-high cave entrance in the main tunnel. Juan wriggled his head and shoulders into the aperture and saw that the cave beyond dropped precipitously. At the extreme end of his light's range, he could see the floor of the cavern littered with all sorts of unidentifiable junk. This had been a communal dump, and amid the rubbish were human bones. They had become disjointed over the decades, so Cabrillo couldn't tell how many there were. Five hundred would be a conservative estimate.

"This place is like a slaughterhouse," he said when he pulled himself free. "A death factory."

"And they kept it running for eighteen months."

"I think the surface facility was used solely to maintain the secret laboratories down here, where they experimented with the really nasty stuff. Using a cave system meant they could isolate it in a hurry if they ever had a viral outbreak."

"Ruthless and efficient." There was no admiration in Linc's voice. "The Japanese could have taught the Nazis a thing or two."

"I'm sure they did," Juan said, still a little unsettled by

what he'd just seen. "Unit 731 has its roots going back to 1931, two years before Hitler came to power. Just before war's end, information and technology transfers went the other way. Germany supplied Imperial Japan with jet and rocket engines for suicide aircraft, as well as nuclear materials."

Linc's next comment died on his lips.

Deadened by distance and the surrounding rock, they couldn't hear the explosion at the cave's entrance. Rather, both men felt a jolt of air pressure against their bodies, like the windblast of a passing truck. The Responsivists had breached the pile of debris and were now in the tunnel system hunting them.

"They probably know the tunnels and will be coming on fast," Cabrillo said grimly. "We have maybe a half hour to either find a way out of here or someplace we can defend with a pair of pistols and eleven rounds of ammunition."

The next medical chamber hadn't been stripped as much as the others. There were thin mattresses on the beds, and the cabinets were stocked with jars of chemicals. The labels were in German. Juan pointed this out to Linc, as it proved his earlier point.

Linc studied the labels, then read aloud in English: "Chlorine. Distilled alcohol. Hydrogen peroxide. Sulfur dioxide. Hydrochloric acid."

Cabrillo had forgotten Linc spoke German. "I've got an idea. Find me some sodium bicarbonate."

"I don't think this is the time to worry about a bellyache," Linc remarked blandly as he scanned the bottles and jars.

"High school chemistry lessons. I don't remember too much about the safe stuff, but my teacher delighted in showing us how to make chemical weapons."

"Lovely."

"He was this aging hippie who thought we needed to defend ourselves when the government eventually came to seize all private property," Juan explained. Linc threw him an odd look and passed over the appropriate glass container. "What can I say?" Cabrillo shrugged. "I grew up in California."

Juan asked Linc to find one other jar of chemicals.

"So what do you want to do with this stuff?" Linc handed over a jar containing an amber liquid.

"Chemical warfare."

They agreed on a spot to lay their ambush in one of the smaller medical wards. Linc bundled up some blankets and mattresses, in the shape of two men huddled under the farthest bedstead. Juan rigged a booby trap using a roll of electrical tape from Linc's bag, the chemicals, and his canteen. In the uncertain glow of a flashlight, the mannequins were more than sufficient to lure the Responsivists. He placed Linc's cell phone on walkie-talkie mode between the two inert figures.

Linc and Juan backed off into a room opposite and a little farther down the tunnel to wait.

If Juan had any difficulty with what they were about to do, he only had to think about the victims aboard the *Golden Dawn* to harden his resolve. The minutes trickled by, the luminous second hand of Cabrillo's watch moving as if the battery were nearly spent. But he and Linc had lain in countless ambushes, and they remained perfectly still, their eyes open, although they could see nothing in the stygian tunnel. Each leaned against the stone wall with his head cocked, his ears straining to pick up the slightest sound.

After only twenty minutes, they heard them. Juan picked out two, then three distinct footfalls, as the Responsivist gunmen rushed headlong down the tunnel. There were no lights, so he reasoned they carried an infrared lamp and night vision goggles capable of seeing in that spectrum.

The gunmen slowed well before they came to the side cave, as if expecting an ambush. Although Juan couldn't see the guards, he could tell by the sounds what they were doing. They had gone almost silent as they approached the entrance, advancing only when they knew they were covered by their teammates.

Metal clattered against stone, and almost immediately a voice called out.

"I see you there. Give yourselves up and you won't be harmed."

The sound had been one of the guards leaning his weapon against the cave entrance to steady his aim as he pointed his assault rifle at the bundles of mattresses at the far end of the chamber.

Standing behind Linc so the big man's bulk shielded his voice, Juan triggered his cell phone and said, "Go to hell."

With the volume of the phone left inside the medical ward set to maximum, it must have sounded like a defiant shout. Two guns opened fire at once, and, in the burst of the muzzle flashes, Juan could see all three figures. These men were no rank amateurs. Two were right outside the cave while the third held back, watching the tunnel for a flanking attack.

In such an enclosed space, the sound was an assault on all Cabrillo's senses.

When the firing stopped, he waited to see what they would do. They had poured enough rounds into the chamber to kill a pair of men a dozen times over. The cover man snapped on a flashlight, as all three stripped off their goggles, their optics temporarily overwhelmed by the barrage. The two who had fired moved cautiously across the threshold while the third remained vigilant for a trap.

And Cabrillo didn't let them down.

The trip wire he'd rigged was near the bedstead where he and Linc had supposedly made their last stand, and the lead guard was so intent on his victims he never saw it.

The electrical tape was tied to the bottles of chlorine and sodium bicarbonate, and when the gunman brushed against it they fell. The glass shattered in a pool of water from the canteen and one other chemical that Juan had poured on the floor.

At the sound of the bottle breaking, Juan and Linc fired. The third guard had reacted to the sound of the smashing glass, but he didn't stand a chance. One bullet caught him under the arm and tore apart his internal organs while the second hit him squarely in the windpipe. His corpse spun to the ground, never relinquishing its grip on the flashlight or assault rifle. The beam came to rest on the cave entrance, where tendrils of a sickly greenish cloud were just beginning to emerge.

Inside the chamber, the chemical reaction had produced a small lake of hydrochloric and hypochlorous acids. In the seconds it took for the two men to realize something was wrong, their throats and lungs were burning. The fumes attacked the delicate tissues lining their airways, making even the shallowest breath a torture beyond pain.

Forced to cough from the irritant, they drew more of the toxin into their bodies, so that by the time they staggered out of the room they had gone into convulsions. They hacked blood mixed with sputum from deep inside their lungs.

The exposure had been brief, but without immediate medical attention the two gunmen were living corpses, and their deaths would be slow and agonizing. One of them must have realized it, and before Cabrillo could stop him he had pulled the pin on a hand grenade.

There was a split second to make a decision, but with the roof already so unstable there was only one thing to do. Cabrillo grabbed at Linc's arm and took off running, not wasting a moment even to turn on his flashlight. He ran with his fingers brushing the tunnel wall. He could feel Linc's towering presence behind him. They had both been counting the seconds and, at the same moment, threw themselves flat just as the grenade exploded.

Shrapnel peppered the tunnel all around them, and the overpressure wave hit in a wall of light and sound that felt like a sledgehammer blow. They scrambled to their feet as a new sound grew, seeming to fill the tunnel. The roar became deafening, as slabs of rock dislodged by the blast crashed to the tunnel floor in a cascading avalanche that threatened to engulf them. Dust and bits of rock fell on their heads and shoulders as more of the ceiling gave way. Juan flicked on the flashlight just as a chunk of stone the size of a truck engine slammed into the ground in front of him. He leapt over it like a hurdler and kept running. Overhead, cracks appeared in the roof, jagged lines that branched and forked like black lightning, while behind them the din of collapsing rock rose to a crescendo.

And then it began to subside. The roar petered out until only a few stones plinked and clattered. Juan finally slowed, his chest sucking in draughts of dust-laden air. He aimed the light toward the tunnel behind them. It was choked floor to ceiling with rubble.

"You okay?" he gasped.

Linc touched the back of his leg where a shard of stone had hit him. There was no blood when he looked at his fingers.

"Yeah. You?"

"I'll be better when we get out of all this dust. Come on."

"Look on the bright side," Linc said as they started walking again. "We don't have to worry about them coming up behind us anymore."

"I always had you pegged for a Pollyanna."

They spent another two hours exploring the underground facility. They found bunks for one hundred and eighty prisoners, rooms that had once been laboratories, and a piece of equipment Linc recognized as an atmospheric chamber.

"Probably to test the effects of explosive decompression," he'd remarked.

At last, they came to the end of the long tunnel. It didn't peter out or pinch off. Rather, a section of the roof had collapsed, and both men recognized that it had been blasted free. Juan inhaled next to the mound of rubble, noting that a faint trace of explosive lingered.

"This was brought down recently."

"When the Responsivists pulled out?"

Juan nodded, not giving in to his disappointment just yet. He scrambled up the sloping pile of loose rocks, his feet dislodging debris as he neared the top. He pressed himself flat, and ran the light along the seam where the shattered stone met the ceiling. He called down for Linc to join him.

"There was nothing in this catacomb that the Responsivists would care that we see. It's all just old junk left by the Japanese Army."

"So whatever they're hiding is beyond this."

"Stands to reason," Juan said. "And since they risked coming down here after us, I bet that our exit is on the other side, too."

"So what are we waiting for?"

With the water used up to improvise the gas attack, an hour of backbreaking work left Juan's tongue a sticky swollen mass, as if some scaly reptile had curled up and gone to sleep in his mouth. His fingers were raw and bleeding from shifting the jagged stones, and his muscles ached from the cramped position. At his side, Linc worked with the efficiency of an indefatigable machine. It looked as if nothing fazed him, but Juan knew even Lincoln's vast reserves of strength weren't inexhaustible.

Bit by bit, they burrowed their way into the rubble, moving carefully, testing the ceiling to ensure their actions didn't bring down more of the shattered stone. They changed positions every thirty minutes. First Juan attacked the debris and passed stones back to Linc's waiting hands, and then Linc would take point, loosening boulders and handing them back to the Chairman. Because Linc was so broad in the shoulders and chest, the passageway had to be expanded to almost twice Juan's size.

Juan was back at the rock face and reached for a handhold on a particularly large stone, but, no matter how he tried, he couldn't loosen it from the rest. It seemed to have been locked into place. He shifted some smaller, fist-sized stones, hoping to get leverage, and pulled with everything he had. The rock didn't so much as wiggle.

Above the lump of stone, the ceiling was rife with cracks and fissures, as unstable as the area the Responsivists brought down with their grenade. Miners called such a ceiling a bunch of hanging grapes, and Juan knew that a chunk could dislodge without warning. He'd never felt the chilling effects of claustrophobia before, but he could feel the icy fingers of panic trying to worm their way into his mind.

"What's the problem?" Linc panted behind him.

Juan had to work his tongue around his mouth to loosen his jaw enough to speak. "There's a stone here I can't move."

"Let me at it."

They laboriously swapped places, with Linc moving feet first into the tight space. He braced his boots against the rock and his back against Cabrillo's outstretched legs and brought his strength to bear. In the gym, he was able to leg-press a thousand pounds. The boulder weighed half that, but it was wedged tightly, and Linc was in the beginning stages of dehydration. Cabrillo could feel the intense strain in every fiber and tendon of Linc's body as he pushed. Linc let out a growl, and the rock slid up and out of its socket of loose stones and packed dirt like a rotten tooth.

"Now, that's what I'm talking about," he whooped.

"Nicely done, big man."

Linc was able to wriggle forward, and as Juan followed him he realized he was gaining headroom. They had crossed the highest point of the debris pile and were making their way down the back side. Soon, he and Linc could crawl over the remaining stones on their hands and knees and then they could stand upright, so they walked down the last of the rubble and onto the cave floor. When Juan pointed the light back at the pile, the gap near the top seemed impossibly small.

He and Linc rested for a few minutes, with the flashlight off to conserve its batteries.

"Smell that?" Juan asked.

"If you're talking about a mug of ice-cold beer, you and I are having the same hallucination."

"No. I smell seawater." Juan got to his feet and turned on the light again.

They proceeded down the tunnel for another hundred yards, until it opened into a natural sea cave. The grotto was at least fifty feet high and four times as broad. The Japanese had constructed a concrete pier on one side of the subterranean lagoon. There was a set of narrow-gauge iron train tracks embedded in the cement for a mobile crane that had once been on the dock for unloading supplies.

"They brought ships in here?" Linc said incredulously.

"I don't think so," Juan replied. "I noticed when the ferry docked that the tide had just crested. That was seven hours ago, which puts us near low tide." He played the light along the side of the quay where a thick carpet of mussels clinging to the cement indicated that high tide almost swamped the dock. "I think they supplied the base using submarines."

He killed the light, and, together, they peered into the dark waters for any indication of sunlight penetrating this far into the cavern. There was a spot opposite the pier that glowed so faintly that it looked as if the waters weren't exactly blue, only less black.

"What do you think?" Juan asked when he turned on the light.

"Sun's at its zenith. For it to be so dark in here, the tunnel has to be a quarter mile long or more."

He didn't add that it was too far to swim on a single breath. Both men knew it.

"All right, let's look around and see if there's anything left down here we can use."

There was only a single side chamber off the main cavern. Inside, they discovered a trickle of freshwater that seeped from a tiny crevasse high up the wall. The water had eroded a small bowl in the floor before meandering to the ocean.

"It's not cold beer," Linc said, cupping his hands in the bowl, "but nothing's ever looked so refreshing."

Juan, aiming the flashlight around the room, indicated that Linc should drink his fill. Propped against one wall was a row of strange stone tablets. All thoughts of thirst vanished as Juan studied the artifacts. They were roughly four feet tall and two wide, made of baked clay that was less than an inch thick. It wasn't the stones themselves that held him rapt. It was the writing. An awl or stick had been used to etch the clay before it had been fired, and despite the tablets' obvious antiquity there was absolutely no sign of weathering. It was as if they had spent their entire existence in a temperature-controlled museum.

Then he spotted the wires. Thin lines arced from the back of one tablet to the next. Juan shone the light in the gap between the tablets and the cave wall. Blocks of plastic explosives had been stuck to the backs of all four ancient texts and rigged to one another. He followed the wire and realized it went out toward the main tunnel. He figured it had been set to blow when they took down the ceiling, but the wire must have been cut before the signal reached this chamber. Judging by the amount of plastique, the Responsivists wanted to leave nothing of the tablets but dust.

"What have you got?" Linc asked. He had washed the grime from his face, and water had cut runnels through the dust on his neck.

"Cuneiform tablets rigged with enough SEMTEX to send them into orbit."

Linc studied the explosives and shrugged. They knew well enough not to touch it. If it had decided not to go off when it was supposed to, they weren't going to give it any reason to do so now.

"It's cuniflower?"

"Cuneiform. Perhaps the oldest written language on earth. It was used by the Sumerians, dating back five thousand years."

"What the heck are they doing down here?" Linc asked.

"I haven't the foggiest idea," Cabrillo replied, reaching for his camera phone so he could take pictures of the tablets. "I know later cuneiform script had a more abstract look to it, like a bunch of triangles and spikes. This looks more like pictographs."

"Meaning?"

"Meaning these date to the very earliest uses of the language." He checked the images captured by his camera and reshot a few of them so they were clearer. "These could very well go back fifty-five hundred years or more, and they're in pristine condition. Most examples of cuneiform have to be pieced together from fragments as small as stamps."

"Listen, man, this is all well and good, but it isn't exactly helping our situation. Get some water, and I'll finish looking around."

Cabrillo had drunk from thousand-dollar bottles of wine, but nothing could compare to that first sip of water from the spring. He drank palmful after palmful, and could almost feel fluid coursing through his body, recharging his muscles and clearing the fog of exhaustion that had been clouding his mind. His stomach was sloshing by the time Linc finished his reconnoiter.

"Looks like we stumbled into the Responsivists' love shack," Linc said. He held up a box of condoms with only two remaining, a wool blanket, and a trash bag with a half-dozen empty wine bottles."

"I was hoping you'd find a scuba tank and a couple of dive masks."

"No such luck. I think we're just going to have to swim for it and hope like hell one of us makes it."

"Let's head back into the main chamber. I don't do my best thinking around explosive charges."

Cabrillo considered inflating the trash bag with air and towing it behind them so they could each take a breath halfway down the tunnel, but its buoyancy would make it scrape along the roof of the submerged tunnel. The plastic would tear before they'd gone two feet. If they counterweighted it so it maintained neutral buoyancy, the drag would make their progress impossibly slow. There had to be a better way.

Linc handed him a protein bar, and for the next few minutes the men chewed silently, racking their brains to come up with a solution. Juan had shut off the light again. The faint glow coming from the far end of the cavern beckoned with both freedom and frustration. They were tantalizingly close, but the last obstacle seemed insurmountable. And then an idea hit him out of the blue that was so outlandishly simple, he couldn't believe he hadn't thought of it first.

"Any chance you recall the German words for sodium chlorate? It's a toxic salt used as a pesticide."

"*Natrium Chlor.* I remember seeing a jar or two of it back in the dispensary."

"And you still have that second detonator pencil?"

"Yes."

"We're going to make an oxygen candle. While I'm gone, I want you to scrape up iron filings from the railroad track. When you mix the two and ignite them, the reaction produces iron oxide, sodium chloride, and pure oxygen. I'll swim halfway down the tunnel and find someplace to fire it off. The oxygen will displace the seawater, and we'll have a bubble where we can breathe."

"More voodoo chemistry from your high school teacher?"

"Actually, I got this from Max. We have oxygen generators aboard the *Oregon* for when we rig the ship for fire or chemical exposure. He explained how the system works."

Juan was going to need the flashlight, so he left Linc at the railroad track to scrape the shavings they would need with his knife. It took Cabrillo forty minutes to navigate his way back through the partially collapsed section of the tunnel, reach the dispensary, and return to the sea cave. In that time, Linc had managed to produce more than enough iron filings from the old rail.

Working under the beam of the now-dying light, Cabrillo mixed the chemicals in one of the empty wine bottles and wound the rest of the electrician's tape around the glass while Linc took apart the detonator to reduce its explosive charge. When they were finished, Juan inserted the detonator into the top of the bottle and wrapped the makeshift oxygen generator in the plastic bag.

"Rube Goldberg would be proud," Linc joked.

Juan kicked off his boots and pants at the edge of the quay and tossed his bush shirt aside. "Back in five," he said, and lowered himself in the bath-warm water. The sea around him clouded with the dust that washed off his skin. Using an easy sidestroke, holding the bag and flashlight, he swam across the grotto to where he and Linc thought there was an exit.

Juan left the bag floating on the surface as he dove down, pressing hard with his legs and arms, the waterproof light turning the water turquoise. The salty water made his eyes sting, but it was a pain he had grown accustomed to over the years so he set it aside. At first, all he saw was jagged stone covered in kelp and mussels, but when he reached a depth of fifteen feet a yawning tunnel opened up in front of him. It was easily fifty feet around, more than enough to accommodate a World War II–era submarine. When he turned off the torch, he could see the faint glow of sunlight at the very extreme periphery of his vision.

He returned to the surface and corralled the bag. He began taking deep breaths, filling his lungs to the maximum, purging as much carbon dioxide out of his system as he possibly could. When he began to feel light-headed, he thrust himself out of the water to clear his chest so he could take an even-deeper breath, filled his lungs, and dropped back into the gloom. He followed his flashlight beam downward and entered the tunnel. The tidal action that had created the cavern system kept the sides free of marine life. He counted the seconds in his head as he swam. He hit the one-minute mark and noted the sunlight was markedly brighter. He kept going, keeping his mind clear and his body relaxed as he went deeper into the tunnel. At a minute thirty seconds, he turned the flashlight to the ceiling. Ten feet farther, there was a concave space in the rock, a natural dimple, easily five feet across and a foot deep.

The bag had just enough air in it to keep it pressed to the ceiling. Juan felt through the plastic for the timing pencil and activated the detonator. He turned and started swimming away, keeping the same measured pace he'd used to enter the tunnel. He'd been under three minutes when he cleared the tunnel's mouth and angled for the surface. He broached like a dolphin, coming halfway out of the water, expelling the air from his lungs in an explosive whoosh.

"You okay?" Linc called out from the darkness.

"I might have to give up my occasional cigar, but, yeah, I'm fine."

"I'm coming over."

An instant after Linc said it, Juan heard him dive into the water. He was at Cabrillo's side moments later, with their boots laced across his shoulders and their clothes tied around his waist. "I double wrapped your cell with the condoms," Linc said. "It's in your pant pocket."

"Thanks. I forgot all about it."

"That's why you're giving me a raise when we get back aboard ship." Linc's bantering tone then vanished. "Just so we're clear, if your little Frankenstein experiment doesn't work and there's no pocket of oxygen we just keep going?"

The distance was too great for even the best swimmer, so when Juan replied he knew it was their death sentence. "That's the plan."

The detonator was too distant and small to feel through the water, so Juan let ten minutes tick by on his watch before asking Linc if he was ready. They began to hyperventilate, each knowing their bodies enough to keep from becoming euphoric from too much oxygen.

Together, they dove for the tunnel. For some reason, it looked ominous to Cabrillo. Like a massive mouth, and with the slight ebb tide sucking at him, it seemed the rock wanted to swallow him whole. The flashlight was fading fast, so he shut it off as he and Linc swam for the distant glow coming from beyond the cave. After a minute and a half, he turned the light back on and began searching for the oxygen pocket. The tunnel's ceiling was featureless rock. The underside of the bubble should flash silver, like a pool of suspended mercury, but the light revealed nothing but blank stone. Juan had slowed as he searched and had just a second to decide if they should accelerate in a desperate, but hopeless, dash for the exit or keep searching for the dimple.

He panned the light around and realized they had drifted

to the right. He cut left, followed by Linc, and still couldn't see the bubble.

The taste of defeat was as bitter as the salt water pressing his lips. His oxygen generator hadn't worked, and he and Linc were going to die. He started stroking hard toward the distant tunnel exit when he felt Linc's hand on his ankle. Linc was pointing a bit more to their left, and when Juan hit the spot with the light he saw a flash like a mirror. They swam to it, expelling the air in their lungs before surfacing carefully so as not to hit their heads.

Neither cared that the oxygen was still warm from the exothermic chemical reaction and had a foul smell. Juan was inexorably pleased with himself and was grinning like an idiot.

"Nice piece of work, Chairman."

There was only enough oxygen for a three-minute break. The men filled their lungs greedily before they committed themselves to the final leg of their journey.

"Last one to the entrance buys the beer when we get back," Juan said, taking one last breath before dropping into the tunnel.

A second later, he could feel the water churning as Linc swam in his wake. A minute into the dive, it looked as though the outlet had grown no closer. Even with the tide working in their favor, their progress was much too slow. When he was in his twenties, Juan could free-dive for almost four minutes, but there had been a lot of hard living in the years since. Three minutes fifteen seconds was the best he could manage now, and he knew Linc's big body burned oxygen even faster.

They continued onward anyway, stroking through the crystal water as efficiently as they could. At two minutes thirty seconds, the mouth of the cave had finally brightened but remained impossibly out of reach. Juan felt the first flutter at the base of his throat telling him he needed to breathe. Fifteen seconds later, his lungs spasmed without warning, and a little air escaped his lips. There were twenty yards to go, sixty tantalizing feet. By force of will, he clamped his throat to fight his body's urge to inhale.

His thoughts started to drift as his brain burned up the last of his air. He was growing desperate, his motions uncoordinated. It was as if he no longer remembered how to swim, or even how to control his limbs. He'd been close to drowning before, and he recognized the symptoms, but there was nothing he could do about it. The broad ocean beckoned. He just couldn't reach it.

Juan stopped swimming and felt water sear his lungs.

And as soon as he did, he started accelerating. Linc had recognized the trouble Cabrillo was in and had grabbed the back of his T-shirt. The ex-SEAL had to be as desperate to breathe as the Chairman, but his legs kicked like pistons, and each great arc of his right arm propelled them closer and closer. Juan had never seen a more determined display. Linc was simply ignoring the fact he was drowning and kept swimming anyway.

The water suddenly grew lighter, as they emerged from the cavern. On guts alone, Linc dragged them to the surface. Gasping, Juan spewed a mouthful of water and coughed up what felt like lungfuls more. They clung to rocks like victims of a shipwreck, as the sea surged gently around them. Neither man could speak for several minutes, and, when they could, there was nothing to say.

It would take an hour of hard climbing and another two and a half to circle far around the former Japanese installation before they reached their hidden jeep. Cabrillo had put the ordeal behind them even before they reached the top of the cliff. His mind was focused solely on the images stored on his cell phone. He didn't know how or why, but he was certain it was the evidence he needed to blow the case wide open.

CHAPTER 25

HALI KASIM FOUND EDDIE SENG IN THE *ORE-gon*'s gym. Seng was wearing the baggy pants of a martial arts *gi* but no shirt. Sweat coursed down his lean flanks as he went through a series of karate moves, grunting with each punch and chop. Eddie noticed the look on Hali's face and ended the routine with a roundhouse kick that would have taken off the head of an NBA center.

He grabbed a white towel from a bin next to a Universal weight machine and wiped his neck and torso.

"I screwed up," Hali said without preamble. "After Kevin interviewed Donna Sky, I went to that damned tape again, programming new parameters into the computer. Gil Martell didn't say 'Donna Sky.' He said 'Dawn' and 'Sky.' I checked, and the *Golden Dawn* has a sister ship named *Golden Sky*. Eric and Murph did some digging. The Responsivists are holding one of their Sea Retreats aboard her as we speak."

"Where is she now?" Eddie asked.

"Eastern Mediterranean. She's scheduled to dock in Istanbul this afternoon. Afterward, she heads to Crete." Hali then added, before Eddie could ask, "I've already tried to call Juan. He doesn't answer."

With the Chairman incommunicado and Max still in the hands of Zelimir Kovac, Eddie was in command of the ship, and any decision would fall on his shoulders.

"Have there been any reports of illness on the ship?"

"Nothing in the news and nothing on the cruise line's internal communications logs." Hali recognized the hesitation in Eddie's dark eyes. "If it helps, Linda, Eric, and Mark have all volunteered. They're already packing."

"If the ship is hit with a chemical or biological attack, they'll be at risk as much as anyone else," Eddie reminded.

"This is too much of an opportunity to pass up. If we can get our hands on some of their people, the intelligence will be invaluable." Hali had put into words the other half of a dangerous equation.

Balancing risk versus reward was the most difficult of all military decisions because lives invariably hung in the balance.

"They can get to shore on the Rigid Inflatable Boat. The jet's waiting at Nice. Tiny can file an emergency flight plan, and our people can be in Turkey as the *Golden Sky* arrives. It isn't likely the Responsivists will attack while they're in port, so we can at least sneak aboard and have a look-see."

"Okay," Eddie agreed, and then stopped Hali as Hali turned to go. "But under no circumstances are they to remain on that ship when she sets sail."

"I'll make sure they understand. Who do you want to send?"

"Linda and Mark. Eric is a first-rate navigator and researcher, but Mark's weapons background will give him an edge finding a chemical- or biological-dispersal system."

"You got it."

"By the way," Eddie said, to stop Hali from rushing off a second time, "what's the status on our little eavesdropping gig?"

An hour before sunset, the *Matryoshka*, Ivan Kerikov's luxury yacht, had eased out of Monte Carlo's harbor with Ibn al-Asim and his entourage on board. Al-Asim was an up-and-coming Saudi financier who had begun funneling money into radical Islamic schools and some fringe terror groups, with an eye toward linking up with al-Qaeda. The CIA was particularly interested in him and his meeting with the Russian arms dealer because there was a chance he could be turned, and thus give access to the upper echelons of the terrorist world.

Nothing of any great importance had been discussed while the yacht was in port. Most of the men's afternoon had been taken up by the women Kerikov had provided. But when the *Matryoshka* slipped out of the harbor and headed into the waters of the Mediterranean, everyone on the *Oregon* knew the real negotiations were going to take place far from prying eyes.

With her running lights doused, the *Oregon* had followed the *Matryoshka*, staying low over the horizon so that just the tip of her tallest mast peeked above the earth's curvature. The Russians went out twenty miles before idling the megayacht's engines. Feeling comfortable that they had the seas to themselves, Kerikov and al-Asim had started talking in earnest over an al fresco dinner on the boat's back deck.

Using the Global Positioning System and the ship's thrusters, Eric had programmed the computer to keep the *Oregon* dead even in relation to the drifting *Matryoshka*, while, high atop the tramp freighter's mast, sophisticated electronics monitored the yacht. Utilizing state-of-the-art parabolic receivers, high-resolution cameras to read lips, and a focused-beam laser that could sense the faint vibration of a conversation taking place on the other side of a window, they were able to eavesdrop on everything.

"Last I heard, al-Asim and the Russian were talking about SA-7 Grail missiles."

"The Grail's a piece of junk," Eddie said. "They'd never be able to hit any of our jets with those. Ah, but a civilian aircraft would be vulnerable."

"Kerikov made it clear early on he didn't want to know what al-Asim planned to do with the arms, but the Saudi alluded to hitting airliners."

Born in New York's Chinatown, Eddie was especially enraged by the idea of terrorists targeting commercial aviation. Although he didn't know anyone killed on 9/11 personally, he knew dozens of people who did.

"Anything else?" Seng asked.

"Al-Asim has already asked about nuclear weapons. Kerikov said he didn't have access but would sell them if he could."

"Lovely," Eddie spat with a grimace.

"The Russian went on to say he would be willing to deliver something he called Stalin's Fist, but said there were too many technical challenges to make it practical. When al-Asim tried to pursue it, Kerikov told him to forget he'd mentioned it. That's when they started talking about the Grails."

"Ever heard of anything called Stalin's Fist?"

"No. Neither has Mark."

"Langston Overholt might know something about it. I'll ask when we turn over the raw-data intercepts. That's his problem anyway. Let me know the minute you hear from Juan, or if Thom Severance ever calls us back."

"Do you think Max is okay?" Hali asked.

"For Severance's sake, he had better hope so."

ZELIMIR KOVAC WATCHED the chopper emerge from the leaden sky. It was a bright yellow dot amid the pewter clouds. He showed no outward sign of his anger. He had been unable to find the escaped American, and that failure rankled. He was not a man prone to make excuses, but that was exactly what he was rehearsing in his head as the helicopter flared over the pad, whipping up storm water that had pooled nearby.

Apart from the pilot, another man was with Thomas Severance. Kovac paid him no heed, focusing his entire attention on his superior, a term he meant quite literally. Thom Severance was superior in every way Kovac thought important, and Kovac's loyalty to him and his cause knew no bounds. From that devotion sprang Kovac's self-recrimination, and he hated himself for letting Severance down.

Severance threw open the chopper's door, his windbreaker and hair whipping in the maelstrom. He somehow managed to make his movements elegant as he ducked from under the whirling blades. Kovac could not manage to reply to Severance's dazzling smile, a smile he didn't deserve. He glanced away, recognizing the second passenger.

Confusion replaced his anger.

"Great to see you, Zelimir," Thom bellowed over the whine of the helicopter's turbine. He recognized the startled look on his security chief's face and chuckled. "I bet he's the last person in the world you ever expected to see with me, eh?"

Kovac found his voice without moving his eyes away from Dr. Adam Jenner. "Yes, sir."

Severance dropped his voice an octave, making his next words a gesture of intimacy and trust. "It's time you understand everything. Past time."

Jenner approached and touched a gloved hand to the bandage where Kovac had pistol-whipped him back in the Rome hotel. "No hard feelings, Mr. Kovac."

Ten minutes later, they were in the underground base's most luxurious suite. It was here that Thom and his wife would wait out the coming chaos. In total, there were facilities here for two hundred of the top members of the Responsivist organization.

The last time Severance had been here, the four rooms had been nothing but bare concrete walls. He admired the work that had gone into the suite, and, apart from the fact the windows were actually flat-panel televisions, could find no evidence he was fifty feet belowground.

"This is almost as nice as our new house in Beverly Hills," he remarked, brushing his fingers against a silk damask wall. "Heidi's going to love it."

He asked a waiting attendant, who was beaming just to be in the presence of their group's leader, for coffee service and sat in one of the wingback chairs in his office. The flat-panel monitor behind him showed the sea crashing against a rocky coast. The live feed was from a camera mounted not too far from the base's entrance.

Jenner lowered himself onto a plush sofa, while Kovac stood at almost rigid attention in front of Severance.

"Zelimir, sit, please."

The Serb took a chair but in no way relaxed.

"You know the old expression 'keep your friends close but your enemies closer'?" Severance asked once the valet had poured coffee. He didn't wait for Kovac to answer. "Our greatest enemies aren't only those who ridicule our beliefs without fully understanding them. They are those that once believed but have lost their faith. They do us the greatest harm because they are privy to secrets we would never share with outsiders. Lydell Cooper and I talked about this at great length."

At the mention of the Responsivist founder, Kovac nodded and shot a glance at Jenner, as if to say Jenner didn't deserve to be in the same room when that name was uttered. The psychiatrist looked back at him with a fond, almost paternal smile.

"We decided to create an expert on Responsivism, a man

who families would turn to if they felt they had lost control of their loved ones. He could also approach those who left on their own, in order to determine their intentions. He could then report back to us so, ah, appropriate actions could be taken."

There was a trace of respect on Kovac's face when he looked at Dr. Jenner. "I had no idea."

"You don't know the best part," Severance went on. "There was really only one person we believed could do a credible job."

"Who?" Kovac asked.

"Why, me, my dear boy," Jenner said. "Only, with the plastic surgery to my face, the contact lenses, and the passage of almost twenty years, you don't recognize me."

Kovac stared hard at Jenner, as if the intensity of his gaze could see through the disguise. "I don't . . ." His voice trailed off.

"I am Lydell Cooper, Mr. Kovac."

"But you're dead," Kovac blurted without thinking.

"Surely a man of your background knows that no one is truly dead until their body is found. I have sailed for most of my life. The storm that supposedly killed me was nothing compared to some of the weather I've been through."

"I don't understand."

Severance spoke up. "Lydell had laid the foundation of Responsivism with his writings, giving us our basic tenets, the core of what we all believe."

"But I am no organizer," Cooper said. "That is where Thom and my daughter, Heidi, outshone me. I detest public speaking, holding meetings, or any of the mundane day-to-day details. So as they grew the movement, I took on a different role, that of protector. By acting like our biggest detractor, I was able to keep watch over everyone trying to harm us."

Kovac finally found his voice. "All those people you turned against us, you reprogrammed?"

"Would have left anyway," Dr. Cooper replied airily. "What I did was minimize their criticism of us. They had left the fold, so to speak, but for the most part none of them revealed much about us."

"What about what happened in Rome?"

"That was a close thing," Cooper admitted. "We had no

idea Kyle Hanley's father had the resources to hire a rescue team. I called Thom as soon as I knew they were taking him for the initial deprogramming in Rome, so you could be in position, and then later called in with the name of the hotel and number of the room so you could snatch him back. We weren't sure how much the boy knew or what he told his father."

"By the way, how are you coming on that front?" Thom Severance asked.

Kovac dropped his eyes. As bad as it was to admit his failure to Severance, he couldn't speak of it in front of the great Dr. Lydell Cooper, the man whose philosophy gave purpose to his life.

"Zelimir?"

"He escaped, Mr. Severance. I don't know how, but he got out of his cell and made his way to the surface. He killed one mechanic and injured two others."

"Is he still on the island?"

"He stole an ATV last night. The storm was severe, and visibility was only a couple of meters. He must not have seen the cliff. A search party found the machine when the tide went out this morning. There was no sign of the body."

"No one is dead until you see their remains," Lydell Cooper intoned.

"Sir, you have my greatest respect and admiration," Kovac said, "but it's much more likely that this man Hanley had an accident during a storm. He was in very poor condition when he escaped, and I seriously doubt that he could have survived a night out in the elements."

He said nothing about the bioelectric implant he'd found and the implications behind it, because he didn't want to sow seeds of doubt. The search teams were still combing the Responsivists' private Aegean island, and if they found the fugitive they knew to report it directly to him. Kovac would get the information they needed and dispose of Hanley before any more damage could be done to his reputation. He did add, "Of course, we will keep up the search."

"Of course," Cooper said.

Kovac turned his full attention to Cooper. "Sir, may I tell you what a privilege it has been to work for you for the past few years? Your teachings have fundamentally changed my life in ways I never knew existed. It would be my greatest honor if I could shake your hand."

"Thank you, Zelimir, but, alas, I cannot. Despite my youthful appearance, I am almost eighty-three years old. When I was still doing genetic research, I developed an antirejection drug tailor-made to my DNA so I have been able to receive a new heart, lungs, kidneys, and eyes from enterprising sources, and cosmetic surgery keeps me looking younger than I should. I have artificial hips, knees, and discs in my back. I eat a balanced diet, drink only occasionally, and have never smoked. I expect I should be able to enjoy a full and vigorous life well past one hundred and twenty years old." He held up his gloved hands. The fingers were bent and twisted like the limbs of an ancient tree. "However, arthritis runs in my family, and I have been unable to arrest its crippling effects. Nothing would give me more pleasure than to shake your hand in recognition of your kind words and excellent service, but I am simply unable."

"I understand." Kovac saw no irony in a man espousing a smaller world population while artificially lengthening his own life span.

"And, don't worry," Cooper added, "there isn't much that Kyle Hanley could have deduced during his brief stay on Greece. And even if his father gets that information to the proper authorities, there isn't time for them to react. Interrogating the father is just a minor detail, the mere tying of a loose thread, as it were. Don't trouble yourself about it."

"Yes, sir," Kovac said automatically.

"On to other business," Severance said. "We are pushing up our timetable."

"Because of Kyle Hanley's rescue?"

"Partially. And Gil Martell's, er, suicide. We had no trouble from the local Greek authorities, but the government in Athens has started showing an interest in our affairs. Lydell and I thought it best if we sent out the trainees now. There is nothing more that they need to know, so there really isn't any reason to delay. Naturally, we paid a premium for the tickets on such short notice." Severance gave a wry chuckle, "Of course, we can afford it."

"You're sending out all fifty teams?"

"Yes. Well, forty-nine. There's already a team on the *Golden Sky* for the final test of the transmitter. So fifty teams and fifty cruise ships. It will take three or four days to get everyone in position. Some of the ships are at sea while others are on the other side of the globe. Our people will carry the virus that Lydell perfected and we manufactured in the Philippines. How long will it take to initialize a test?"

Kovac thought for a moment. "Perhaps by this afternoon. We need to run up the other engines to fully charge the batteries, as well as stabilize power distribution in order to protect the antenna."

"The test virus we gave the people on the *Golden Sky* is a simple, fast-acting rhinovirus, so we will know within twelve hours if the receiver got the signal. As long as we send it no later than tonight, we should be fine. Of course, there's a second team aboard her that is planting our principal virus."

"This is a great moment, gentlemen," Lydell Cooper said. "The culmination of everything I have worked for. Soon, there will be a new beginning, a fresh dawn, where humanity will shine like it was meant to. Gone will be the burdensome multitudes that tax our natural resources and return nothing but more mouths to feed. In one generation, with half of the world unable to bear children the population will return to a sustainable level. There will be no more want or need. We will abolish poverty, hunger, even the threat of global warming.

"Politicians all over the world give lip service to these problems by offering short-term plans that make their constituents think something is being done. We know it is all lies. One just has to read a newspaper or watch the news to see that nothing is going to change. In fact, it is getting worse. Struggles for land and water rights are already sparking conflicts. And how many have already died to protect dwindling oil supplies?

"They tell us we can fix everything if humans changed their habits—drove less, bought smaller houses, used different lightbulbs. What a joke. No one is willing to take a step back from their luxuries. It goes against our deepest instincts. No, the solution isn't to call for minor sacrifices that in reality don't address the crux of the problem. The answer is to change the playing field. Rather than have more and more vying for less and less, just reduce the population.

"They all know this is the only way, only they don't have the courage to say it, so the world spins closer and closer to chaos. As I have written, we are breeding ourselves to death. The desire for offspring is perhaps the strongest force in the universe. It cannot be denied. But nature has natural mechanisms to regulate it. There are predators to cull the population of prey animals, forest fires to renew the soil, and cycles of flood and drought. But man, with his large brain, has continuously found ways to sidestep nature's efforts to contain him. We killed off any animal that sees us as prey so that there are only a handful left in nature and the rest are caged in zoos. That left the lowly microbe to thin our ranks with disease, so we created vaccines and immunizations, all the while breeding as if we still expected to lose two out of every three children before their first birthday.

"Only one country has had the courage to admit their numbers were growing too fast, but even they failed to slow population growth. China tried to legislate population with its one-child policy, and there are two hundred million more of them now than there were twenty-five years ago. If one of the most dictatorial countries in the world can't stop it, no one can.

"People simply can't change, not in any fundamental way. That's why it is up to us. Of course, we are not madmen. I could have engineered our virus to kill indiscriminately, but I would never consider the outright murder of billions of people. So what was the solution? The original hemorrhagic influenza virus I started with had the side effect of leaving its victims barren but also had a mortality rate near fifty percent. After I gave up medical research, I worked with the virus over tens of thousands of generations and mutations, coaxing out its lethality while maintaining the one trait I desired. When we release it on those fifty ships, it will infect nearly one hundred thousand people. It sounds like a large number, but it is just a drop in the bucket. The passengers and crews aboard the ships come from every part of the world and from every socioeconomic background. On a cruise ship, one finds a microcosm of society, from the titan of industry to the lowly deckhand. I wanted to be entirely democratic. No one will be spared. When they return to their suburban homes in Michigan, their villages in Eastern Europe, or their slums in Bangladesh, they will carry the virus with them.

"It will remain symptomless within its host for months, as it is spread from person to person. And then the first sign of infection will come. It will seem like every person in the world has come down with mild influenza and a high fever. The mortality rate should be less than one percent, a tragic but unavoidable cost to those with weakened immune systems. Only later, when people seek out answers to why they aren't having children, will they learn that one half of the world's population has become barren.

"When that harsh reality strikes, there will be rioting, as frightened people seek answers to the questions their leaders had been afraid to ask. But it should be brief—weeks or months at most. And the world economy will stutter as we adjust, but adjust we will, because that is humanity's other great driving force: its ability to adapt. And then, oh my friends, then we will have solved all those problems, cured all those ills, and ushered in a period of prosperity the likes of which the world has never known."

A tear ran unabashedly down Zelimir Kovac's cheek, and he made no move to wipe it away. Thom Severance, who had known Cooper for all of his adult life and had heard him speak a thousand times, was equally moved.

CHAPTER 26

"THOSE TWO THERE," LINDA ROSS SAID AND pointed.

Mark Murphy followed the line of her arm and spotted the couple immediately. While many of the passengers streaming off the *Golden Sky* were elderly, or at least middle-aged, she had spotted a man and woman in their thirties. Each held a hand of a little girl, about eight years old, wearing a pink dress and Mary Janes.

"Candy from a baby," Mark said when he saw the woman hand her credit card–sized ship ID to her husband. He slipped it into his wallet and returned his wallet to his front pocket.

Behind the army of disembarking passengers, eager to tour Hagia Sophia, the Blue Mosque, Topkapi Palace, and get fleeced at the bazaar, the *Golden Sky* looked eerily like her sister ship. Chilling memories rushed in on Mark every time he glanced up at her. He hadn't thought through his emotions very carefully when he'd volunteered for the mission and wasn't thrilled with the prospect of boarding her.

"They're heading for the buses." Linda nodded to where the young family was veering toward the curb, where a dozen chartered buses idled. Passengers were showing attendants their day passes to board.

"Do it now or follow them downtown?"

"No time like the present. Let's do it."

They waited for the three to get ahead of them before easing into the crowd. They moved effortlessly through the mostly slow-walking people until their target was just ahead of them, and had no idea they were being tracked.

"Hurry!" Linda suddenly called out. "I think our bus is going to leave."

Mark quickened his pace and brushed against the man as he passed. The man immediately felt for his wallet. Keeping it in his front pocket and feeling for it when someone accidentally brushed into him showed the hallmark of a seasoned traveler. In most instances, this security practice would have been sufficient. But as they had planned, when Linda breezed by him the passenger felt secure that the Americans rushing by weren't a threat and he didn't check his pocket a second time.

He hadn't felt Linda's small hand reach into his khakis and pull his wallet free.

An amateur would have veered away from the mark as soon as the pocket had been picked, but Linda and Murph continued their ruse of being hurried passengers and strode for the buses. They loitered near one of them until the young family had showed their passes to an attendant on another bus and climbed aboard. Only then did Linda and Murph break from the crowd and head back to where they had parked their rental car.

With Linda standing next to the open back door to shield the interior from curious passersby, Mark worked on one of the laminated identification cards with a kit especially packed back on the *Oregon*. He used a scalpel to remove the transparent plastic and cut away the photograph. He then inserted an appropriate-sized picture of Linda from the stash he'd brought and ran the card through a battery-powered laminator. He spent a moment smoothing it out and trimming away excess plastic.

"There you go, Mrs. Susan Dudley," he said, showing Linda the still-warm card.

"You seem to know what you're doing," Linda remarked.

"I was fifteen when I arrived at MIT, so you can best believe I know all about making fake IDs."

There was a hint of something wan in his voice that Linda noticed. She said, "It must have been rough."

Mark paused from his work and looked up at her. "You can imagine that place was loaded with *uber*-geeks, but I was a standout. Briefcase, tie, pocket protector, the whole enchilada. The school administration assured my parents they had counselors for accelerated students to make the transition easier. What a crock. I was on my own in the most competitive environment in the world. It only got worse when I went into the private sector. That's why I joined Juan and the Corporation."

"Not for the money, huh?" Linda teased.

"I'm not bragging or anything, but I took a serious pay cut when I joined up. It was worth it, you know. You guys treat me like an equal. When I was designing weapons systems, these macho generals would strut around, looking at us like we were insects or something they had to scrape off the bottom of their shoe. Sure, they liked the toys we gave them, but they detested us for being able to deliver. It was like high school all over again, in the cafeteria, with the military guys sitting by themselves like a bunch of jocks and the rest of us hanging around the fringe, hoping to get noticed. Kinda pathetic, really.

"That doesn't happen on the *Oregon*. We're all on the same team. You and Linc and Juan don't make Eric and me feel like outsiders even though we push it a little with the whole nerd thing. And for the first time in my life, I don't feel I have to search for an empty table when I go into the mess hall." He seemed to look as though he'd said too much, so he threw her a grin and said, "I hope you don't charge for geekotherapy."

"You can buy me a drink tonight on board."

Mark looked startled, and then a knowing smirk raised his lip. "We're not getting off the *Golden Sky* until we find something, are we?"

She pressed a hand to her breast in a shocked gesture. "Are you actually accusing me of disobeying Eddie's direct order?"

"Yup."

"Surprised?"

"Nope."

"Still game?"

"I'm fixing the second ID, aren't I?"

"Good man."

Mark fed the two cards into an electronic device attached to a laptop computer and recoded the embedded magnetic strips. Ten minutes later, he and Linda stood at the bottom of the *Golden Sky*'s gangplank. Nearby, a forklift was loading pallets onto the ship through a large hatch while gulls wheeled and squawked above the vessel like warplanes in a dogfight.

"Is everything all right, Mr. Dudley?" the assistant purser manning the gangplank asked when they said they wanted to return to their cabin.

"Just my knee," Mark said. "I blew my ACL playing college football, and it flares up every once in a while."

"As you know, we have a doctor aboard who can look at it for you." The purser swiped the two cards through an electronic monitor. "That's odd."

"Problem?"

"No, well, yes. When I swiped your cards, my computer crashed."

As part of any major cruise line's security, the electronic ID card brought up a file on the computer that had a picture of the bearer as well as information about his or her itinerary. Mark had recoded the stolen cards so that nothing would show on the screen. The purser would either have to trust that the two people standing before him were who they said they were or delay them while someone fixed the computer. With customer service being so important, it was unlikely he would inconvenience passengers over a simple glitch.

The purser ran his own employee identification through the scanner, and when his picture popped up on his screen he handed the two IDs back to Murph. "Your cards don't work anymore. When you get back to your cabin, ring the purser's office and they will arrange replacements."

"Will do. Thanks." Mark took the IDs and shoved them in his pocket. Arm in arm, he and Linda climbed the ramp, with Murph playing up a limp.

"College football?" she questioned when they were out of earshot.

Mark patted his less-than-taut belly. "So I've let myself go to seed."

They entered the ship on the main atrium level. The ceiling lofted four stories and was crowned with a stained-glass dome. A pair of glass elevators gave access to the upper levels, and each deck was fringed by safety-glass panels capped by gleaming brass rails. A rose marble wall with water sheeting down its face and collecting in a discreet fountain was opposite the elevators. From their vantage, they could see signs for small luxury stores one deck up and a neon fixture lighting the way to the casino. The overall effect was opulence bordering on tacky.

They had discussed their plan while still on the *Oregon*,

and both had studied the layout of the ship from the cruise line's website, so there was no need to talk now. They went straight for the public restrooms behind the fountain. Linda handed Mark a bundle of clothing from her utilitarian shoulder bag. Moments later, they reemerged dressed in workers' overalls with the cruise line's logo stitched in gold thread over their hearts, thanks to Kevin Nixon's Magic Shop. Linda had scrubbed off most of her makeup, and Mark had tamed his unruly hair with a cruise-line baseball cap. The maintenance-crew uniforms gave them the virtual run of the ship.

"Where do we meet if we get separated?" Linda asked as they started walking.

"The craps table?"

"Don't be cute."

"Library."

"Library," she parroted. "All right, let's go play Nancy Drew."

"Hardy Boys."

"It's my operation, so it's my call. You can be my sidekick, George Fayne."

To Linda's surprise, Mark asked, "Not Ned Nickerson?" It was the name of Nancy's boyfriend.

"Not in your wildest dreams, and someday we need to talk about your adolescent reading habits. Or maybe we shouldn't."

The easiest way to leave the ship's public accommodations was through the galley, so they climbed a flight of nearby stairs and found the main dining room. Large enough to seat three hundred people, the room was empty except for a house-cleaning crew vacuuming the carpet.

They weaved purposefully through the tables toward the back and entered the kitchen. A chef looked up from his cooking but said nothing as the duo strode in. Linda glanced away. Unlike the dining room, the galley was loaded with staff preparing the next meal. Aromatic steam rose from bubbling pots as assistant chefs cleaned, chopped, and sliced away in a twenty-four-hour-a-day operation.

There was a door at the rear of the kitchen that led to a brightly lit hallway. They found a staircase and descended, passing a bevy of waitresses heading up for their shift. They encountered several more people, but no one paid them the slightest attention. As janitors, they were practically invisible.

Mark spotted a folding ladder leaning against a bulkhead and grabbed it to further their disguise.

With the *Golden Sky* tied to the dock and most passengers ashore, she was drawing minimal power, and, as a result, her engineering spaces were deserted. Linda and Mark spent the next several hours crawling over every pipe, conduit, and duct, looking for anything out of the ordinary. Unlike Juan's time on the *Sky*'s ill-fated sister ship, their search was unhurried and methodical, but, in the end, the results were essentially the same.

"Nothing," Mark said, the frustration in his voice coming from his anger at himself for not figuring it out. "Not one damned thing that shouldn't be here. Nothing attached to the ventilation system or the water supply."

"Those are the most efficient ways of spreading a virus, sure." Linda used a ball of cotton waste to wipe grease off her hands. "What else is there?"

"Short of walking around and spritzing every surface on the ship with an atomizer, I can't think of anything. If we've had this much time down here by ourselves, the Responsivists probably did, too." He pointed overhead, where ducts as big as barrels were anchored to the ceiling. "In two hours, I could take apart a section of that and set up my dispersal system inside."

Linda shook her head. "The risk of being caught is too great. It has to be something much simpler and quicker."

"I know, I know, I know." Mark rubbed his temples, where the beginnings of a headache was pressing in on his brain. "I remember Juan on the *Golden Dawn* saying he wanted a look at the main intakes for the air-conditioning system. That might be something to check."

"Where would they be?"

"Topside. On the front of the funnel, most likely."

"That's pretty exposed."

"We should wait until tonight."

"Then let's head back to the public areas and change."

Meandering their way out of the labyrinthine engine room, they finally came out into a corridor filled with people.

Guest-service workers in various uniforms were gearing up for the passengers' return, and engineers were making their way to the engine room in preparation for leaving Istanbul.

A chance glimpse through a doorway near the laundry suddenly brought Linda up short. A man in his thirties, wearing a uniform much like the one she had on, was standing just outside the laundry. It wasn't the man or even his casual stance that caught her eye. It was the way he looked away when their eyes met. She recognized the same furtive glance she herself had given the first chef she'd seen in the galley. It was the look of someone who was somewhere he wasn't supposed to be.

He turned away slightly but then peeked back over his shoulder. As soon as he saw Linda still studying him, he took off running in the opposite direction.

"Hey!" Linda shouted. "Stop!"

She started after him, with Mark a pace or two behind.

"No," Linda said sharply. "Check if there are any more of them down there."

Mark turned and ran back, leaving Linda in sole pursuit.

The runner had a twenty-foot head start and six-inch-longer legs. The advantages seemed to do him no good because Linda's determination to catch him was simply greater than his body's ability to get away. She quickly cut down his lead, running around corners without a check in her pace, springing as lightly as a gazelle but with the ferocity of a hunting cheetah.

He gained some distance when they climbed a flight of stairs. He was able to take the steps three at a time to Linda's two. They raced past startled workers. Linda wished more than anything that she could call out for help, but that would leave her explaining her illegal presence on the ship.

The man flashed through a doorway, and when Linda reached it a moment later she scraped her arm cutting it so close.

She never saw the fist. He coldcocked her right on the point of her chin. Even though the man was no trained fighter, the blow was enough to snap Linda's head back and slam her into a wall. He stood over her for a second before running, leaving Linda struggling to clear her mind.

Before she was certain she was up to it, she was on her feet and after him again, swaying dizzily with each pace.

"Hit a girl, will you," she grunted.

They broke out onto Broadway, the long central corridor that ran nearly the length of the ship and was used by the crew to get from their cabins to their duty areas. Some artistic crew member had even made up theater-style marquees like those along the famed New York street the hallway took its name from.

"Coming through. Emergency."

Linda could hear the man calling out, as they dashed through the congestion of workers either heading to their posts or hanging out and socializing. He moved through the crowd like a snake, weaving around people and gaining precious ground, while Linda felt like her head was going to explode from the growing ball of cotton that had been her brain.

He twisted through another door and started climbing more stairs. Linda pounded open the door five seconds after him. She used the handrail to launch herself up each flight of steps, throwing her body around the corners because she knew that they were fast approaching the passengers' accommodations area. If the guy was smart, and if he knew the ship, they could emerge close to his cabin. If Linda didn't see which one, she'd never be able to find him again.

He burst through the door at the top of the stairs, bowling over an elderly woman and knocking her husband out of his wheelchair. He lost precious seconds disentangling himself from the couple. Linda flew through the door before the automatic mechanism could close it. She gave a savage grin. They'd emerged on the upper level near the atrium.

The man looked back to see Linda only a few paces behind. He quickened his stride, running for the elegant stairs that curled around the twin glass elevators. There was very little for passengers on the top level of the atrium. The shops were one level down, and the lower levels would certainly be more crowded. Linda had seen guards outside the ship's exclusive jewelry store earlier, and she couldn't gamble being stopped by security.

They were almost to the stairs when she leapt, her arms outstretched. Her fingers caught on the cuffs of the man's jumpsuit, which was enough to trip him up. They had been running flat out, so his momentum propelled him headfirst into the glass-panel railing. The panel was designed for just such an impact, but a weld that held a bracket in place popped and the entire panel broke free. It tumbled four stories before hitting the floor in a tremendous explosion of flying fragments. Startled screams filled the atrium.

Linda had lost her grip as soon as she made contact and sprawled on her chest, sliding on the slick floor after the Responsivist. He managed to grab on to a brass banister as he tumbled over the edge and, for a moment, he looked up at her as she tried to reach his hand. She imagined the look in his eye was that of a suicide bomber the instant before detonation—resignation, fear, pride, and, most of all, defiant rage.

He let go before she could clutch his wrist and didn't turn from her gaze as he plummeted. He dropped the forty feet, flattening himself out so he hit the tile floor on his back, his head turning to the side at the last second. The sound was a wet slap, and slivers of shattered bone burst through his clothes in a dozen bloody patches. Even from this height, Linda could tell his skull had lost half its width.

Giving herself no time to digest the horror, she sprang to her feet. The elderly couple was still struggling to get the old man back in his wheelchair and hadn't seen a thing. She moved behind an enormous potted palm and stripped off the overalls and stuffed them into her bag. There was nothing she could do about the damp stains under the arms of her blouse.

The library was well forward, near the ship's movie theater, but Linda turned aft. There was a bar that overlooked the pool near the stern, and she knew that if she didn't get a brandy in the next two minutes her breakfast was going to make an encore appearance.

She was still sitting there an hour later when a Turkish ambulance pulled away from the ship, its lights off and siren silent. Moments later, the ship's horn gave a trumpeting blast. The *Golden Sky* was finally leaving port.

CHAPTER 27

Every time Juan blinked, it felt like he was scraping his eyes with sandpaper. He'd had so much coffee it had soured in his stomach, and the painkillers he'd swallowed hadn't made a dent in his headache. Without looking in a mirror, he knew he had a deathly pallor, like his body had been drained of blood. Running a hand over his head, even his hair hurt, if such a thing were possible.

Rather than refresh him as it usually does, the wind streaming past the windscreen of the water taxi made him shiver despite the balmy temperatures. Next to him on the rear bench, Franklin Lincoln sprawled in a relaxed pose. His mouth was slack, and an occasional snore rose above the engine's rumble. The lithesome driver who'd brought them into Monte Carlo from the *Oregon* forty-eight hours earlier had the day off, and Linc had no interest in her substitute.

Anger was the only thing keeping Juan going now, anger at Linda and Mark for disobeying Eddie's order to disembark the *Golden Sky* before she left Istanbul. The pair of stowaways was continuing to search for evidence of the Responsivists' plan to hit the ship with their toxin.

Cabrillo was going to throw them in the brig when he saw them again and then give them raises for their dedication. He was fiercely proud of the team he'd assembled, and never more so than now.

His thoughts returned to Max Hanley and Cabrillo's mood became more foul. There still hadn't been any reply from Thom Severance, and every minute that ticked by made Juan think there never would be, because Max was already dead. Juan wouldn't let himself say that aloud and felt guilty even thinking it, but he couldn't shake the pessimism.

With Ivan Kerikov's megayacht *Matryoshka* returned to the inner harbor, the *Oregon* lay at anchor a mile off shore once again. When he studied his ship, Juan could sometimes glimpse what a beauty she must have been in her prime. She was well-proportioned, with just a hint of rake at bow and stern, and her forest of derricks gave her a look of commerce and prosperity. He could imagine her with fresh paint and her decks cleared of debris, facing a backing sea off the Pacific Northwest, where she'd had a career as a lumber hauler.

But as they now approached, all he saw was the rust-streaked hull, the patchwork paint, and the sagging cables draped across her cranes like disintegrating spiderwebs. She looked forlorn and haunted, and nothing shone on her, not even the propeller of the lifeboat hanging off its amidships davit.

The sleek taxi nosed under the boarding stairs, the waters so calm and the driver so deft at the controls that she didn't bother setting out rubber fenders.

Juan tapped Linc's ankle with his foot and the big man grunted awake. "You'd better hope I return to the same spot in the dream I was just having," he said, and yawned broadly. "Things were just getting interesting with Angelina Jolie and me."

Juan offered a hand to lift him to his feet. "I'm so damned tired I don't think I'll ever have a carnal thought again."

They each hefted their bags, thanked the young woman who'd piloted them out, and stepped onto the boarding ladder. By the time they reached the top, Juan felt like he'd just scaled Everest.

Dr. Huxley was there to greet them, along with Eddie Seng and Eric Stone. She was beaming at Juan with a high-wattage smile and nearly hopping from foot to foot. Eddie and Stoney were smiling, too. For an instant, he thought they had news about Max, but they would have told them when he'd called from the airport following the flight from Manila.

As soon as he was firmly on deck, she threw her arms around his shoulders. "Juan Rodriguez Cabrillo, you are a bloody genius."

"Far be it from me to disagree, just remind me what feat of brilliance I performed this time."

"Eric found an online database of cuneiform from a university in England. He was able to translate the tablets from the pictures you e-mailed with your phone."

Cabrillo had sent those as soon as they reached the Manila airport.

"The computer was able to translate," Eric corrected modestly. "I don't speak a word of ancient Sanskrit."

"It's a virus after all," Julia gushed. "From what I'm able to deduce, it's a form of influenza, but unlike anything science has ever seen. It has a hemorrhagic component almost like Ebola or Marburg. And the best part is that I think Jannike Dahl has natural immunity because the ship where it first broke out landed near where she grew up, and I believe she's a descendant of the original crew."

Juan could barely keep up with the rapid flow of words. "What are you talking about? Ship? What ship?"

"Noah's ark, of course."

Cabrillo blinked at her for a moment before reacting. He held up his hands like a boxer begging for the fight to be over. "You're going to have to start this from the top, but I need a shower, a drink, and some food, in whatever order they come. Give me twenty minutes, and meet me in the conference room. Tell Maurice I want orange juice, half a grapefruit, eggs Benedict, toast, and those potatoes he does with the tarragon." It was nearly dinnertime, but his body was telling him it wanted breakfast. He turned to go but glanced back at Julia. "Noah's ark?"

She nodded like a little girl dying to tell a secret.

"This I've gotta hear."

Thirty minutes later, his meal gone, the sourness in Juan's stomach had been replaced with a contented glow, and he felt he had just enough energy to listen to Julia's report.

He looked to Eric first, since he had done the translation. "Okay, from the top."

"I won't bore you with the details of enhancing the pictures or finding an online archive of cuneiform, but I did. The writing you found is particularly old, according to what I was able to learn."

Cabrillo recalled thinking the same thing. He motioned for Stone to continue.

"I turned the problem over to the computer. It took about five hours of tweaking the programs to start producing anything coherent. The algorithms were pretty intense, and I was bending the rules of fuzzy logic to the breaking point. Once the computer started to learn the nuances, it got a little easier, and after passing it through a few times, adjusting here and there, it spat out the entire story."

"The story of Noah's ark?"

"You may not know this, but the epic story of Gilgamesh, which was translated from cuneiform by an English amateur in the nineteenth century, chronicles a flood scenario a thousand years before it appeared in Hebrew texts. Many cultures around the globe also have flood myths as part of their ancient traditions. Anthropologists believe that because human civilization sprang up in coastal areas or along rivers, the very real threat of catastrophic flooding was used by kings and priests in cautionary tales to keep people in line." Eric adjusted his steel-framed glasses. "As for myself, I can see tsunami events being the genesis for many of these stories. Without written language, stories were passed down orally, usually with added embellishments, so, after one or two generations of retelling, it wasn't just a giant wave that wiped out your village, it was the whole world that had become inundated. In fact—"

Cabrillo cut him off. "Save the lecture for later and stick to what you've discovered."

"Oh, sure. Sorry. The story starts out with a flood, but not a sudden swell of water or a heavy rain. The people who wrote the tablets describe how the water of the sea they lived by rose. I believe it rose about a foot a day. While nearby villages simply moved to higher ground, our folks believed the rising would never stop and decided the only way to survive was to build a large boat. It was in no way as large as the boat described in the Bible. They didn't have that kind of technology."

"So we aren't really talking about Noah and his ark?"

"No, although the parallels are striking, and it is possible that the people who remained behind and described what happened laid the foundation for *Gilgamesh* and the biblical story."

"Is there a time frame for this?"

"Fifty-five hundred B.C."

"That seems pretty precise."

"That's because there is physical evidence of a flood just as it's described on the tablets. It occurred when the earthen dike at what is now the Bosporus collapsed and flooded what had been, up until that time, an inland sea that was some five hundred feet lower than the Mediterranean. We now call this area the Black Sea. Using underwater ROVs, marine archaeologists have confirmed that there were humans living along the ancient shoreline. It took more than a year for the basin to fill, and they estimate the falls at the Bosporus would make Niagara look like a babbling brook."

Cabrillo was amazed. "I had no idea."

"This has only been confirmed in the last few years. At the time, there was a lot of talk that this catastrophic event could be the origin of the biblical flood, but scientists and theologians both agreed that it wasn't."

"Seems, with what we've discovered, that the debate isn't over yet. Hold on a second," Juan said as a thought struck him. "These tablets were written in cuneiform. That comes from Mesopotamia and Samaria. Not the Black Sea region."

"Like I said, this is a very early form of the writing style, and it was most likely brought southward by people leaving the Black Sea region and taken up by those other civilizations. Trust me on this, Chairman: the tablets you found are going to fundamentally alter our understanding of ancient history."

"I believe you. Go on."

"Okay, so this one seaside village thought the rising waters would never stop. Like I said, it took a year of flooding to match the sea level, so I can imagine how they came to that conclusion. They also write that with so many refugees there was a great deal of sickness."

Dr. Huxley interrupted. "It would have been the same stuff we see today in refugee populations. Things like dysentery, typhus, and cholera."

Eric picked up the thread of his story again. "Instead of joining the mass exodus, they cannibalized the buildings in their town to build a boat that was large enough to take all four hundred of them. They don't mention the dimensions but did say the timber hull was caulked with bitumen and then sheathed in copper.

"Now, this was the very beginning of the Copper Age, so it must have been a prosperous area to have enough of the metal to cover the hull of a ship that size. They brought livestock, like cattle, pigs, sheep, and goats, as well as chickens, and enough silage to last them a month."

"I'd estimate the boat was at least three hundred feet long, for all of that."

"The computer agrees. It came up with three hundred and eighteen feet, with a beam of forty-three feet. She probably would have had three decks, with the animals on the bottom, supplies in the middle, and the villagers on top."

"What about propulsion?"

"Sails."

Cabrillo held up a hand. "Sails didn't appear until two thousand years after the period we're talking about."

Eric scrolled down on the laptop sitting in front of him on the conference-room table. "Here's a direct translation: 'From two stout poles anchored to the deck a sheet of animal skins was stretched to catch the wind.'" He looked up. "Sounds like a sail to me."

"I'll be damned. Keep going."

"The water eventually rose high enough to float the boat, and they started off. It's kind of ironic, because they must have started their journey not long before the water level stabilized. Otherwise, they never would have made it out of the Black Sea. Anyway, they stayed at sea much longer than a month. In the places where they tried to land, they either couldn't find freshwater or they were attacked by people already living there.

"After five lunar months, countless storms, and the loss of twenty people, the boat finally grounded, and no amount of work could get it free."

"Where?"

"The area is described as 'a world of rock and ice.'"

Julia leaned forward to catch Juan's eye. "This is where Eric and I started using some deductive reasoning."

"Okay. Where?"

"Northern Norway."

"Why Norway?"

Eric replied, "You found the tablets in a facility that Imperial Japan's Unit 731 used to perfect biological weapons. The Japanese were very keen on this kind of research, unlike a certain ally that preferred chemical agents to do their mass killings."

"You mean the Nazis?"

"Who else would have given the tablets to them?"

Juan rubbed his eyes. "Hold it. I'm missing something here. Why would Unit 731 want some old writings about an ancient boat?"

"The disease," Julia said. "The one that broke out on the boat after they landed. The scribe who wrote the tablets described it in detail. As best I can tell, it was an airborne hemorrhagic fever with a contagion level equal to influenza. It killed half their population before burning itself out. What's really interesting is, only a small handful of the survivors could bear children after they recovered. A few managed to breed with the indigenous people living nearby, but the virus had made most of them sterile."

"If the Japanese were looking for a way to pacify mainland China," Eric said, "they would definitely be interested in a disease like this. Julia and I think that, aside from the tablets, the Germans also gave them any mummified bodies they found when they discovered the boat."

"Ah. I get it now. If the Japanese got the tablets from the Germans, you're guessing they found them in Norway, because Germany occupied Norway, starting in 1940."

"Right. A land of rock and ice could describe Iceland, or parts of Greenland, but the Germans never took those countries. Finland fell to the Russians, and Sweden remained neutral throughout the war. We guessed Norway, most likely a fjord on the northern coast, which is sparsely populated and largely unexplored."

"Wait. Julia, out on deck you said Jannike was immune to this disease?"

"The more I thought about it, the more I couldn't come up with a definitive answer for why she wasn't affected when everyone else on the *Golden Dawn* had died. The disease mentioned on the tablets is airborne, and if it is the basis of whatever new virus the Responsivists have developed then she still would have breathed some contaminated air even if she was on supplemental oxygen.

"However, if an ancestor of hers had been exposed to the virus and survived, there's a good chance she has the antibodies coded into her DNA. The fact that she comes from a small town in northern Norway only bolsters our hypothesis."

"Can you test for it?" Juan asked.

"Sure, if I had a sample of the virus."

Cabrillo tried to stifle a yawn. "Sorry. I need sleep. I think we're still missing another piece of the puzzle. Let's assume that the Germans discovered the boat and translated the tablets. They learn about this horrible disease, and it's something they aren't interested in, but their Japanese allies are, so the Germans ship it to Japan, or, more precisely, to an island in the Philippines, where Unit 731 is conducting its experiments. We don't know if they managed to perfect it, but we can assume they didn't, since a disease like this has never been mentioned in the history books."

Julia and Eric nodded.

"How do we make the jump to the Responsivists getting their hands on it? If the Japanese failed sixty years ago, how did Severance and his gang succeed?"

"We thought about that," Eric admitted, "but couldn't come up with any sort of link, other than the fact that their founder, Lydell Cooper, was a leading disease researcher. They used the same facility that the Japanese had used during the war, so it's obvious they knew about their work on the virus. We just don't know how."

"The next question is, why?" Juan said. "They used the virus or a derivative to kill everyone aboard the *Golden Dawn*. What do they plan to do with it now?" He overrode whatever answer Eric was going to give and added, "I know they see overpopulation as the worst crisis facing the planet, but unleashing a virus that kills off humanity, or even a majority of it, would leave the world in such a state of chaos that civilization would never recover. This thing is a doomsday weapon."

"What if they don't care?" Eric said. "What I mean is, what

if they want civilization to collapse? I've read up on these people. They're not rational. Nowhere in their literature do they espouse going back to the Dark Ages, but it could be that that's exactly what they want—the end of industrialization and the return to humanity's agrarian roots."

"Why attack cruise ships?" Juan asked. "Why not just release the virus in every major city in the world and be done with it?"

Eric made to reply and then closed his mouth. He had no answer.

Juan pressed himself up from the table. "Listen, guys. I really appreciate all the work you've done, and I know this will help figure out the Responsivists' end gambit, but if I don't hit the rack I am going to fall asleep right here. Have you briefed Eddie about all of this?"

"Sure have," Julia said.

"Okay, ask him to call Overholt and tell him the entire story. At this point, I don't know what he can do, but I want the CIA in the loop. Are Mark and Linda scheduled to report in anytime soon?"

Eric said, "They didn't bring a satellite phone, so they have to use the *Golden Sky*'s ship-to-shore telephone. Linda said they would check in again"—he looked at his watch—"in another three hours."

"You tell Linda that I want the two of them off that ship even if they have to steal a lifeboat or jump off the damned rail."

"Yes, sir."

IT SEEMED THAT JUAN had just put his head on his pillow when the phone rang.

"Cabrillo." His tongue was cemented to his mouth, and the weak twilight streaming through the curtains was like the glare of an arc lamp.

"Chairman, it's Hali. I think you had better come down to the Op Center to see this."

"What is it?" He swung his legs off the bed, cradling the phone to his ear with his neck and shoulder so he could reach for his prosthesis.

"I think we're being hailed on the ELF band."

"Isn't that what our Navy uses to talk to submarines?"

"Not anymore. The two transmitters they operated were dismantled a couple of years ago. Besides, they transmitted on seventy-six hertz. This is coming in at one hundred and fifteen."

"What's the source?" Juan tugged on a pair of pants.

"We haven't received enough to pinpoint a location, and because of the nature of Extremely Low Frequency transmission we may never know."

"Okay, you've got my interest. I'll be there in a few minutes." Juan threw on the rest of his clothes, not bothering with socks, and spent a moment brushing his teeth. According to his watch, he'd been asleep for three hours. It had felt like three minutes.

Entering the Op Center always gave Cabrillo a charge. It was the sleek design, the quiet hum of the computers, and the thought of all the power that could be controlled from this room, not just the *Oregon*'s revolutionary engines but also the awesome firepower the vessel could unleash at a moment's notice.

Hali had a steaming mug of coffee ready for him.

Cabrillo grunted his thanks and took a sip. "Better," he said, setting the cup next to Kasim's monitor. "Tell me what you've got."

"As you know, the computer automatically scans every frequency in the radio spectrum. When it detected something transmitting at the ELF level, it paused to record the signal, and when it recognized the beginning of the word it alerted me. When I got here, this is what has been sent so far." He tilted his flat panel so Cabrillo could see what was on the screen: OREGON.

"That's it?" Juan didn't try to hide his disappointment.

"ELF waves are incredibly long, upward of twenty-two hundred miles. It's their length that lets them circle the globe and penetrate deep into the ocean. Basically, an ELF transmitter turns the earth into a giant antenna. The downside is, it takes a long time to send anything, and submarines can't reply because they can't carry a transmitter of their own. That's why the Navy abandoned the whole system. It was just too inefficient."

"Remind me why a sub can't carry an ELF system."

"The antenna alone is roughly thirty miles long. And even though it's only an eight-watt signal, it would use more electricity than a sub's reactor has the surplus capacity for. But the biggest reason is, a transmitter has to be located in an area with extremely low ground conductivity in order to avoid the absorption of the radio waves. There are only a handful of places in the world where you can send in the ELF band and a submarine definitely isn't one of them."

"Going back through the logs," Hali continued, "I found that there was another ELF transmission on this same frequency at ten o'clock last night. It consisted of only a random jumble of ones and zeros. I have the mainframe trying to crack it, if it is a code, but I'm not optimistic."

The letter I appeared on Hali's screen, followed sixty seconds later by the letter T.

"This is worse than pulling teeth," Juan remarked. "Besides us, who else has built ELF antennas?"

"Just the Soviets. Their only use is to contact submarines in deep water and over great distances. There's no other reason to set one up."

"So if ours were dismantled, then it has to be the Russians. I wonder if this has something to do with us spying on Kerikov."

"We'll know in a minute." Hali then amended: "Well, ten or fifteen."

And so they waited, as a letter a minute appeared on the computer. So far, they had OREGON ITSMA. When the next letter came through, Juan stared at it for a second before letting out a triumphant whoop. It was the letter X.

"What is it?" Hali asked.

"It's Max. That crafty SOB. He's found a way to contact us on the ELF band."

Hali suddenly cursed. He opened another window on his computer and retrieved the archive of the wiretap they had installed in Gil Martell's office. "Why didn't I see this right away," he mused aloud, angry at himself. On his screen popped:

I DON'T . . . (1:23) YES . . . (3:57) 'BOUT DAWN AND
SKY . . . (1:17) (ACT)IVATE THE EEL LEF . . . (:24)
KEY . . . (1:12) TOMORR(OW) . . . (3:38) THAT WON'T
BE . . . (:43) A MIN(UTE) . . . (6:50) . . . BYE.(1:12)

"What am I not seeing?" Juan asked.

"The fourth word cluster. Activate the 'eel lef.' It's not 'eel
lef,' it's ELF. Activate the ELF. The Responsivists have their
own ELF transmitter."

"What the heck for?" Juan asked before giving the answer.
"If they're releasing toxins on cruise ships, an ELF transmitter would allow you to synchronize an attack all over the
planet."

Cabrillo was burning with impatience at how slowly Max's
message was coming through, but he was still fighting a sleep
debt he could barely pay the interest on. "Hali, this is taking
forever. I'm going back to my cabin. Wake me when you have
everything, and I want you to pinpoint their transmission site.
This takes precedence over everything else. Get Eric to help
with whatever you need." He turned to the computer, as if
Max Hanley could hear him. "I don't know how you're pulling this off, but you, my friend, are a piece of work."

CHAPTER 28

IT HAD BEEN THE OLDEST TRICK IN THE BOOK AND it had worked flawlessly.

Max had discovered the cliff only moments after escaping the underground bunker. He'd hopped off the ATV and gunned the throttle, sending it over the edge. It had been too dark to see how it landed, but he knew Kovac would scour the countryside, looking for his escaped prisoner, and the little machine would be found.

He had then returned to the bunker's entrance and, amid the confusion of search teams heading out and medical staff attending to the injured mechanics, Max had brazenly walked right back in. Returning to the scene of the crime, so to speak, was the last thing Kovac would ever expect, and the facility was the last place he would think to search.

There were more than enough hiding places within the subterranean complex. He felt more confident exploring dressed as a mechanic, so he opened some of the doors he'd passed during his earlier exit. Many of the rooms he found were laid out like dormitories, with countless bunks with cloth curtains for privacy and large locker-room-style showers. Max estimated they could house several hundred people here, although only a fraction of that number were in residence at the time. One room was a massive cafeteria. Checking the stoves' burners, he could tell nothing had ever been used. The walk-in freezers were packed with food, and he found a storage area that was stacked from floor to ceiling with pallets of bottled water and canned goods.

He figured that the facility was like a Cold War–era fallout shelter. It appeared to be fully self-sufficient, with enough food, water, electricity, and space for people to ride out a disaster in comfort, if not style. The fact that it was new, and built by the Responsivists, led him to believe that they would be causing the disaster. He thought back to the horror Juan and his team had discovered aboard the *Golden Dawn* and shuddered.

He helped himself to two bottles of water and a large can of pears, eating with his hand, so that the sweet syrup dripped down his battered chin. He also wound cling wrap around his torso, even though he knew modern medical practice was to leave cracked ribs unbound. The pressure of the plastic wrap eased a great deal of the pain, and the food and water gave him a modicum of strength.

Max stuffed a couple more waters into the deep pockets of his overalls and continued his exploration. He passed a few people in the meandering corridors. They looked askance at his injuries, then nodded with sympathy when he explained he had been attacked by the escaped prisoner.

He was one level above where they had held him in the cell when he discovered that not all the Responsivists would ride out Armageddon in a concrete maze. There was a set of double doors with a security keypad. The electronics were in the process of being dismantled, and tools lay on the floor next to a small stool. It looked like the repairman had dashed off to retrieve something he'd forgotten.

Max wasted no time in entering the secured area. The floors were covered in a thick green carpet and the walls were covered in sheetrock and wainscoting. The paint gave off a slightly acrid smell that told him it had been recently applied. The lighting was still fluorescent, but the fixtures were of a better quality, and there were even occasional sconces. The framed artwork hanging on the walls was gaily colored but bland. For some reason, it reminded him of the law office of one of his divorce attorneys. It was institutional, but a higher quality of institutional. The dining facility was more like an upscale restaurant, with flat-panel monitors on the walls in place of real windows. The chairs were heavy and covered in soft leather, and the top of the bar was a plank of solid mahogany.

He found a cubicle farm for a small army of secretaries outside a suite of offices and a communications center that would have made Hali Kasim drool. He entered the center and started looking for a phone or radio, but the system was unlike anything he had ever seen. Feeling exposed in the small room, he decided he would try again later and continued his exploration.

Set away from the functional side of what Max had dubbed "the executive wing" were bedrooms appointed like a five-star hotel, right down to the minibars. There weren't any Gideon Bibles in the bedside tables but rather copies of Lydell Cooper's book, *We're Breeding Ourselves to Death*. There were enough rooms for forty people or couples, depending on the sleeping arrangements. Max guessed that this would be for the very cream of the Responsivist movement, the leaders, board of directors, and wealthiest believers. At the very farthest reaches of the executive wing was a suite of rooms that had to belong to Thom Severance and his wife. They were, by far, the most luxurious. The bathroom alone was the size of a studio apartment, and the tub looked big enough to need a lifeguard.

Max spent the night on Severance's bed, and, in the morning, brushed his teeth with what would be Severance's toothbrush, once he arrived. To Hanley's utter shock, he heard voices from the living room while he was rinsing. He recognized Zelimir Kovac's thick accent and precise diction, and heard a second, smoother voice he assumed to be that of Thom Severance and a third voice that gave his heart another jolt. It was Dr. Adam Jenner, the deprogrammer.

Max listened to their conversation in stunned horror. Each revelation seemed more shocking than the next. Jenner was really Lydell Cooper. There was a simple genius to the ruse, one that Max couldn't help but grudgingly admire. Their dedication to their cause was deeper than anyone had ever believed. This really was a religion, with prophets and martyrs, and a body of faithful willing to do anything for their beliefs.

Severance said something about Gil Martell's suicide that Max took to mean Kovac had killed him. And then Max heard the terrifying truth about their plans to release an engineered virus on the world and sterilize half of humanity.

There was no admiration this time, but Max understood the genius of this plan as well. Civilization would never survive a coordinated global bioattack that killed half its victims, but what they intended was survivable. Mankind would be set back a generation but would emerge more prosperous in the end. He had read up on Cooper's movement when his ex had told him their son had joined. Cooper had written that the Dark Ages never would have ended if not for the plague that wiped out half of Europe and ushered in a new era of prosperity.

He was pretty sure it wasn't as simple as that, but he wondered how today's world of twenty-four-hour information and high-speed travel would react. Fifty years after the pandemic, populations would have shifted to fill the gaps left by the reduced number of people, and the world very well might be a better place.

But it was no place Max wanted to be a part of. In his mind, Cooper, Severance, and Kovac had no more right to decide what was best for humanity than Larry, Moe, and Curly.

He wanted to rush from the bathroom and take them on single-handedly. He thought he might get five, maybe six, paces before Kovac gunned him down. By force of will alone, Max made his body relax. There would be another opportunity. He would just need to be patient.

After the three men had left, Max slunk out of the suite and holed up in the closet of one of the unused hotel-style rooms, reasonably confident that he was safe for the time being. As much as his brain wanted to focus on the hell Severance and his band were about to unleash, Max concentrated on how they were going to pull it off.

They had mentioned a transmitter. They were going to coordinate the release of the virus by transmitting some sort of activation code. Max saw the flaw immediately. An aerial broadcast, even on shortwave, couldn't encompass the entire world with any measure of reliability. There were too many variables, from atmospheric conditions to sunspot activity, that could cause a signal failure.

Not shortwave, he thought.

He recalled the tunnel at the subbasement level and the coils of thick copper wire, as well as the excess power-generating capacity, the Responsivists had installed.

"It's a bloody ELF antenna," he whispered, and knew exactly how he was going to warn Juan.

He waited until after Kovac had run their test before sneaking into what he had first thought was the communications room. It took him nearly twenty nerve-racking minutes to figure out how to operate the ELF transmitter. He fine-tuned the frequency and sent his message:

OREGON ITS MAX BUG ATTACK 50 CRUISE SHIPS NOT KILL WORSE ELF IS KEY NUKE IT >72 HRS

He would have loved to add the location of the transmitter, but he had no idea where he was. He would just have to trust that Hali would be able to trace back the source of the signal. He had also used the word *nuke* deliberately because he felt this was an impregnable bunker and could only hope Juan would figure out a way to destroy it.

He returned to his hidey-hole in the closet, after helping himself to a couple of protein bars and a beer from the mini-bar. He was certain that with the day of their attack fast approaching, Severance would have Kovac station guards near the exit, so Max knew he wouldn't be leaving that way. With no intention of sacrificing himself, he had less than three days to find another way out.

THOM SEVERANCE WAS in his office, chatting with Lydell Cooper, when someone knocked. He looked up from his desk and hastily whipped off the glasses he had been recently forced to use. Zelimir Kovac stood just inside his door. The normally dour Serb looked downright morose. Whatever had happened, Severance knew it couldn't be good.

"What's the matter?" he asked.

"It was just on the news, a death on a cruise ship in Istanbul. It was one of our people on the *Golden Sky*, Zach Raymond."

"He was heading the cell we put aboard her, wasn't he?"

"Yes, sir."

"Do we have any details?" Cooper asked

"Apparently, he fell from the balcony of the ship's atrium and was killed instantly."

"So it was an accident?"

"That's what the news is saying, but I don't believe it. It is too much of a coincidence that our team leader died."

"You think that whoever was behind Kyle Hanley's abduction has people on the *Golden Sky*?" Severance asked with obvious sarcasm. "Don't be ridiculous. There is no way that anyone could make that connection."

"There's more. I just received word from our team in the Philippines. They said that two men arrived at the abandoned virus factory and discovered the old Japanese catacombs. The two men were buried inside following an explosion, but the very fact that they were there is troubling."

Severance steepled his fingers under his cosmetically cleft chin. "If someone did a little digging, they would know we had a facility in the Philippines. I don't know how they knew about the abandoned Japanese tunnel system. Maybe they did more than a little digging. Either way, it doesn't matter, because they're dead, and we left nothing behind that could incriminate us."

"I don't like this, Thom," Cooper said, leaning forward. "There is too much at stake to risk exposure now, and I don't believe in coincidences. I could discount the idea of a threat to our operation if we only had the Hanley kid's abduction to consider. But now there are two separate incidents: the incursion in the Philippines and Zach Raymond's death. Someone is on to us."

"If that were the case, the FBI would have raided our California headquarters by now, and put enough pressure on Athens to do the same in Greece."

The Responsivist founder didn't have an argument for that.

"What if it's the company Hanley hired to get his son back?" Kovac suggested. "They could still be operating under their original instructions and are probing our defenses, trying to find a way to rescue both the boy and his father."

Cooper jumped at that idea. "It makes perfect sense."

"So you don't think they know about our plan?" Severance asked.

"It's probable that they don't," Kovac replied. "But if they had time to interrogate Zach Raymond, then the raid Thom mentioned could be in the planning stages as we speak."

"Do you have any suggestions?"

"Yes, sir. I need to get to the *Golden Sky* to make certain the virus isn't discovered. If it has been and is turned over to the authorities, it would give them a tremendous advantage to develop a cure before people start showing symptoms. I would also suggest that there be a complete communications blackout of the ship. No passengers should be allowed to use the Internet or make ship-to-shore calls. This way, the operatives on board won't be able to contact their superiors."

"Where is the ship heading now?"

"It's en route from Istanbul to Iraklion, Crete. I could easily meet it as it comes down through the Greek islands."

Few people outside of the organization were aware that the owner of Golden Lines, the company that operated the *Golden Sky* and her ill-fated sister ship, the *Golden Dawn*, was a Responsivist. He had come to the group because he and his wife were unable to have children, and Lydell Cooper's teachings made them come to accept that fact and even celebrate it. Although he made substantial contributions to the cause and allowed them to use his boats for their Sea Retreats at a deep discount, the shipping mogul wasn't part of the inner circle that had conceived the plan to use ocean liners to spread the genetically modified virus.

"You can call the president of the line," Kovac continued, "and explain that the same group who targeted the *Dawn* might be planning something similar for the *Golden Sky*. Let me on board, and keep the ship at sea until after the virus is released. That way, even if they discover it they can't warn anybody about it."

"If that's the case, he will want to cancel the cruise entirely."

"Tell him to do it as a favor, then. There are fifty Responsivists on that ship as part of a Sea Retreat. Most of them have no idea what's about to happen, but that gives me more than enough people to search for anyone acting suspiciously."

Severance looked over to Lydell Cooper. The former researcher may owe his youthful appearance to surgery after surgery, but the fire burning behind his eyes was his own. It was the flame of utter conviction and total dedication to a belief.

"Thom," Cooper said, "our species is teetering on the brink of disaster. There are too many mouths to feed, and natural resources are drying up at an ever-accelerating pace. We both know this is the only humane way to prevent the collapse of five thousand years of civilization. And it is from the very beginning of that civilization that we found the means of our salvation. This is just and right, and we must do whatever it takes to guarantee our success.

"I don't like deviating from our plan, but I believe Mr. Kovac is correct. Somehow, someone knows something. I know that sounds vague but we can't afford to take any chances now. We are just too close. Days rather than weeks. If they have people on the *Golden Sky* searching for our virus, they will be able to tell the maritime authorities how it is to be released and all our work will have been for nothing."

Severance nodded. "Yes, of course you are right. I think it's a bit of hubris on my part to think that we are so good as to be invulnerable. Zelimir, I'll talk to the cruise line. Make whatever arrangements you need and bring whatever personnel and equipment you feel is necessary. I will make sure the captain knows to give you his full cooperation. Remember this: under no circumstances is that virus allowed to leave the ship. Do whatever it takes. Do you understand?"

"Yes, sir. Whatever it takes."

"Can't you feel it?" Cooper asked. Both men looked at him questioningly. "We are fighting the dark influence from beyond our dimensional membrane. For thousands of years, they have shaped and molded man to become the self-destructive creature he is today. These forces have pushed humanity to the point that it is ready to consume itself. But we are now pushing back and taking control of our destinies again. I can feel it. I can feel their dismay that we are not bending to their will but starting to carve our own path.

"When we succeed, their grip on us will be over. We will flourish in a new world where they can no longer touch us. We are casting off the invisible shackles of a slavery most people haven't known they were suffering under. But suffer we have.

They made us unable to resist our baser instincts, and look where it has brought us. Wars, starvation, hunger, want. It was their subtle control, spanning countless generations, that brought us to this.

"Until I finally understood that no rational society would choose to live the way we do, I realized we were not in control at all, that there were influences from outside the universe. They have held sway over our thoughts and were leading us to Armageddon for reasons even I don't comprehend. I was the first to see them for what they are, and like-minded people such as you have also come to understand that the world just wouldn't be this way if not for something plotting against us.

"Their machinations are almost at an end. They will have no say in what comes next in our societal evolution because we will make certain that everyone understands who they were and what they did. Oh, gentlemen, I cannot tell you how excited I am. A great awakening is coming, and we will stand shoulder to shoulder to enjoy it."

Kovac had always been uncomfortable about the transdimensional mind-control aspect to Dr. Cooper's teachings. He understood the hard numbers of overpopulation and dwindling resources, and the ultimate result of the two colliding, so he said nothing. It was enough for him to be part of saving humanity from itself. And, right now, he was more interested in hunting possible enemies on the *Golden Sky* than any great awakening.

CHAPTER 29

JUAN CABRILLO SAT IN HIS CUSTOMARY SEAT IN the Op Center listening intently to Hali Kasim's presentation. Eddie Seng hung out near the back of the room with Linc and two gundogs, Mike Trono and Jerry Pulaski. With Eric Stone's assistance, Hali had performed nothing less than a miracle.

"While Max was still broadcasting, I got in touch with a few amateur radio buffs I've gotten to know over the years and had them tune in to Max's frequency. I had them jack the clocks that regulate our GPS satellites so we were one hundred percent synchronized. As each character came through, I had them write down the exact time they received it. Now the radio waves propagate at various speeds through various materials, so some extrapolations were necessary. That's where Eric came in. He computed out those discrepancies so we had a clear time versus distance calculation, and we were able to triangulate the transmitter's location."

He typed at his computer for a moment, and an overhead picture of a barren island appeared on the main monitor. It was shaped like a teardrop ringed with cliffs, except for one inhospitable-looking rocky beach at the southern tip. The ground rose and fell in craggy hillocks, and there was virtually no vegetation except a few patches of grass and a couple of gnarled trees bent into odd shapes by the constant wind. According to the scale at the bottom of the picture, the island was roughly eight miles long, and two wide at its thickest point.

"This is Eos Island. It's located four miles off the coast of Turkey, in the Gulf of Mandalay. The Greeks and Turks have fought over it for a couple of centuries, though, judging by what we've found, I can't understand why. Geologically, it's interesting because it's a chunk of Precambrian bedrock in an otherwise-active volcanic zone, but it is basically uninhabitable. This picture is dated four years ago."

Just seeing a picture of where Max was being held sent a jolt of energy firing through Juan's body. It took him all he had not to order the *Oregon* to flank speed and charge in with guns blazing.

Hali flashed another shot of the island on the screen. "This was Eos Island last year."

Clustered near the southern part of the island were a dozen large earthmovers in distinctive yellow paint. A huge pit had been excavated and a cement plant had been erected. A dock had been extended from the beach and a road graded up to the work site.

"The work was done by an Italian heavy-construction company and paid for through a numbered Swiss bank account, although there is little doubt who was behind it. The Turkish authorities were told it was going to be the largest movie set ever built."

Up came another picture. "This shows the same site a few months later. As you can see, they have built concrete structures inside their excavation."

Eric added, "Using the heavy equipment to establish scale, the facility's footprint is nearly fifty thousand square feet. And, at this point in the construction, it has three levels."

Hali picked up their story again. "Eight months into construction, the bogus movie company said they ran out of money and were pulling the plug on the project. As part of the original contract with the Turks, they were supposed to return the island to its natural state. So that is, more or less, what they did."

He brought up a third picture on the main monitor. There was no sign of the massive excavation. It looked as if nothing had ever happened. All of the material removed from the pit had been returned to it, and the surface was reconfigured to appear like natural stone. The only thing remaining was the dock and a macadam road that led seemingly nowhere.

"This picture is from the official Turkish government environmental-impact report," Hali continued. "We have to assume that some baksheesh exchanged hands and the report was doctored to indicate that Eos was back to normal."

"Where's the ELF antenna?" Juan asked.

"Buried beneath the underground bunker," Eric replied. "Max was very specific when he said in his message to nuke it. He could have easily said bomb it. Same number of letters, so it wouldn't have added to the transmission time, but he specifically used the word *nuke*.

"I would have liked to consult Mark about this, but I did a quick computer simulation, and if they were pouring concrete for five or six months and then piled the debris on top I estimate it will take probably two kilotons to crack that nut open."

"Why not one of the Air Force's bunker-buster bombs?" Juan asked smartly.

"That would work fine so long as we hit either the antenna or the power generators directly. But looking at this from a purely practical point of view, do you see us getting our hands on one of those?"

Eric had a habit of not getting sarcasm. "No more than us finding two thousand tons of TNT," Juan shot back, instantly regretting his sharp tone. "Sorry." He tried to never take his frustrations out on his people.

"Commando raid seems the only way," Eddie said, and moved up from the back of the Op Center. "We could hit the beach there, on the south tip of the island, or try to scale one of the cliffs."

"The chance of success is, statistically, zero," Eric replied. "Probability dictates that the entrance to the bunker is heavily defended and easily sealed. At the first sign of an attack, the outer defenses are closed off, and successive barricades within the bunker will be raised."

"So we find a back door," Juan suggested. "There have to be air intakes for the ventilation system, as well as vents for the exhaust from their power plant."

"Both of which I believe lie under the dock." Eric nodded to Hali, who brought the first construction picture back up on the screen. "Look carefully at where they are still working on the road."

Hali manipulated the picture to zoom in on where a paving machine was laying down a ribbon of asphalt. Just ahead of the machine, graders were smoothing the track, while a bit farther ahead excavators were laying dirt into a deep trench.

"They dug out under where the road was going to be laid in order to bury the vent pipes and then layered blacktop over it. Again, we have to assume that the intakes and vents are well guarded and that at the first sign of an intrusion the facility goes on lockdown. A team might be able to gain access to the conduits, but, once inside, they would be trapped."

Juan glanced at Eddie to get his opinion of Stone's grim assessment.

Seng said, "One misstep and we would be targets at a shooting gallery. And even if we made it in, we'd have to cut ourselves out of those pipes with torches, not knowing who or what is waiting to greet us."

"Okay, give me another option," Juan said.

"Sorry, Chairman, but Eric's right. Without knowing how that place is laid out—its security systems, guard strengths, and about a hundred other things—we can't get inside."

"Two weeks ago, we stole a pair of rocket torpedoes from the damned Iranian Navy. There has to be a way to get Max out of there."

"With all due respect"—Eric's voice was hesitant but determined—"our focus should be on silencing that transmitter rather than on Max's rescue. If the attack is coordinated using an ELF signal to cruise ships scattered all over the globe, then its destruction should be our primary concern."

The silence was long and pregnant.

"Do you have a suggestion?" Juan asked with stiff formality.

"Actually, I do, sir. It's called Stalin's Fist."

The code name rocked Juan back in his chair. "How do you know about that?"

"I read through the transcripts of our intercept between Ivan Kerikov and Ibn al-Asim."

Those transcripts were on Juan's computer, but he hadn't had the time to peruse them let alone read them in their entirety. Anyway, they were the CIA's bailiwick, as far as he was concerned. They had been hired to eavesdrop, not sift through the information.

"Kerikov mentioned he had access to something called

Stalin's Fist. When he mentioned it, I did some research. You're familiar with it?"

"Why do you think it doesn't work?" Juan asked with a smirk.

"You boys mind filling us in?" Linc called.

Eric typed at his computer and brought up an artist's rendition of a satellite, unlike anything ever orbited before. The main body was a long cylinder, and ringing it were five enclosed canisters that were more than thirty feet in length. No one needed to see the hammer-and-sickle emblem on its side to know it was Russian. The drawing itself had that distinctive Soviet style that was both pompous and amateurish at the same time.

Eric commenced, "Though its real code name was November Sky, it was known almost exclusively by the nickname Stalin's Fist. It was launched in 1989 at one of the warmest periods during the Cold War in direct violation of about a dozen treaties."

"That's all fine and dandy," Linc grumbled, "but what in the heck is it?"

"Stalin's Fist is an OBP, or Orbital Ballistic Projectile, weapon. Our military played around with the idea, calling it Rods from God. The theory is incredibly simple. Inside those tubes are tungsten rods weighing eighteen hundred pounds apiece. When fired, they fall through the atmosphere and hit whatever they are aimed at. Coming in at an orbital velocity of eighteen thousand miles per hour, multiplied by their mass, they hit with the kinetic energy of an atomic bomb, only there is no fallout, and defensive reaction time to such a weapon is cut in half because there is no ascent stage like with a conventional ballistic missile. You might see a flaming object in the sky for a moment, but that's it. No warning and no chance to escape."

"The Soviets intended it as a first-strike weapon," Juan added. "The idea was to target several major Western cities lying along the same longitudinal axis and blame a freak meteor shower. With no radioactive fallout, and the rods themselves vaporized on impact, there would be no way to say it wasn't. They even had astronomers ready to show doctored photographs of the meteors moments before they entered our atmosphere. With the Western world reeling from losing five cities, the Sovs thought they could roll across the border and Europe would be theirs."

"How do you know it didn't work?" Eric asked Juan.

"Because one of my first Black Ops for the agency was to infiltrate the Baikonur Cosmodrome, where it was being launched on an Energia rocket, and disable it. I rigged it so the satellite couldn't receive a signal from the ground because of earth's magnetic field. It will only react if the order comes from above the atmosphere."

"Why not just blow it up on the pad?"

"It was a manned mission. Two cosmonauts went up with it to manually deploy its solar panels. It was three days into the mission before they discovered the bird had been sabotaged."

Hali asked, "They couldn't just boost a ground signal?"

"It would have fried the electronics."

"Couldn't they have sent a signal from *Mir*, their space station?"

"They knew the jig was up, so they left it floating around up there in a polar orbit."

"Do you think it still works?" Eric asked.

"Unless it's been hit by space debris, it should work perfectly." Cabrillo was warming to the idea. "Okay, hotshot, you found us an alternative to a nuke. How do you propose we get a transmitter sixty miles into space so we can commandeer the satellite?"

"If you can get me the codes from Ivan Kerikov"—Stone typed again and brought up yet another picture—"I'll get it up there using this."

Juan and the others stared slack-jawed for a moment at the audacity of the plan. Cabrillo finally found his voice. "Eric, you got yourself a deal. I'll call Overholt to arrange your transport. Eddie and Linc, come up with a plan to get those codes from the Russian arms dealer tonight. Then, we leave port."

"You still want to head to Eos Island?" Eddie asked.

"I'm not abandoning Max."

CHAPTER 30

LOOKING AT HIS REFLECTION IN THE MIRROR, Juan couldn't tell where his face ended and Kevin Nixon's makeup began. He glanced at the enlarged pictures that Kevin had taped to the mirror as a guide and then at his face again. It was a perfect match. The wig he wore was the exact shade, and the style was the same as well.

"Kevin, you've outdone yourself," Juan said, and plucked away the paper collar Kevin had put around his throat to protect the tuxedo shirt he was sporting.

"Making you look like Arab terrorist Ibn al-Asim is nothing. If you'd asked me to make you look like one of their floozies, then you can call me a miracle worker."

Juan deftly tied his bow tie and shrugged his broad shoulders into a white dinner jacket. While nearly every man looks good in a tux, Cabrillo pulled it off with extra aplomb, even with the padding around his middle that filled out his physique to match al-Asim's. It didn't hurt that their surveillance showed the terrorist financier favored Armani. He had a flat holster at the base of his spine for his preferred weapon, the FN, Five-seveN, automatic pistol.

"You look like James Bond with a paunch," Mike Trono said from across Kevin's cluttered workroom.

In his best Sean Connery brogue, Juan shot back, "The janitorial staff is to be seen and not heard."

Mike and Jerry Pulaski were wearing uniforms that matched the janitorial staff of the world-renowned Casino de Monte Carlo, having gotten the designs during a brief afternoon reconnoiter. Kevin and his staff kept hundreds of uniforms, everything from a Russian general to a New Delhi traffic cop to a Parisian zookeeper, so it took them only a few minutes to modify a standard jumpsuit to the style they wanted.

Mike and Jerry carried a heavy-duty trash can on rollers, as well as a rolling mop bucket, and a plastic sign warning SLIPPERY FLOOR.

The chief steward appeared at the doorway, silent and unobtrusive as always. He wore a crisp white apron over his suit. There was a debate among the crew as to whether he changed aprons before leaving the pantry or simply never spilled anything on himself. The odds favored the latter by a huge margin. He held a sealed plastic container in one hand like it was loaded with live snakes, and his face was cleaved by a deep frown.

"For Pete's sake, Maurice," Juan teased, "it's not the real stuff."

"Captain, I made it, so it is real enough."

"Let's take a look."

Maurice set the container on Kevin's makeup counter and stepped back, steadfastly refusing to remove the lid. Juan pried it off and quickly turned his head. "Whoa! Did you have to make it so pungent?"

"You asked me to make you fake vomit. I treated this as I would any dish. So smell is as important as appearance and texture."

"Kinda smells like that fish thing you made for Jannike," Mike quipped, resealing the lid and placing the container in his mop bucket.

Maurice threw him the look of a school principal dressing down a rowdy pupil. "Mr. Trono, if you want anything other than bread and water for the foreseeable future, I would apologize."

"Hey, I liked that dish," Mike said, backpedaling as fast as he could. No one on the *Oregon* took Maurice's threats lightly. "So what's in it?"

"The base is pea soup, and the rest of the recipe is a trade secret."

Juan looked at him askance. "You've done this before?"

"A prank in my youth against Charles Wright, the captain of a destroyer I was serving on. He made Bligh look like

Mother Teresa. The prig prided himself on his iron stomach, so during an inspection we poured some of this concoction in his private head moments before a visiting admiral used it. The nickname Upchuck Chuck dogged the remainder of his career."

They all laughed harder than the story warranted, as a means of releasing tension. They always played their emotions close to the vest, especially just before an operation, so any chance to vent was seized on immediately.

"Will that be all, Captain?"

"Yes, Maurice. Thanks."

"You're welcome." He bowed out of the room, passing Dr. Huxley as she made her way to the Magic Shop.

The men gave a chorus of catcalls and whistles. Hux wore a strapless dress in magenta silk that clung to her curves like a second skin. Her hair had been teased from its regular ponytail into an elegant halo of curls and ringlets. Makeup accentuated her eyes and mouth, and gave her skin a healthy glow.

"Here you go," she said, and handed Cabrillo a slim leather case. He folded open the top to reveal three hypodermic needles in protective slots. "Inject this in a vein and it's night-night in about fifteen seconds."

"The pills?" Juan asked.

She pulled a standard plastic pill bottle from her matching clutch purse and shook the two capsules. "If al-Asim has kidney problems, he's going to end up in the hospital before he needs to use the bathroom."

"How long before they take effect?"

"Ten, maybe fifteen, minutes."

"You're sure he won't taste them?"

Hux rolled her eyes. They had already gone over this three times. "Completely undetectable." She also showed him she had her passport. Because native Monegasques aren't allowed into the casino, identification is verified at the entrance.

"Everybody have phones?" Juan asked. Rather than draw attention to themselves with earbud radios and lapel microphones, they would use the walkie-talkie mode of their cell phones for communication. When everyone nodded, he said, "All right, then, let's get ashore and do this."

. . .

DESIGNED BY CHARLES GARNIER, the architect of the fabled Paris Opera House, the Casino de Monte Carlo is nothing less than a cathedral dedicated to gambling. It was built in the sumptuous Napoleon III style that Garnier created, with beautiful fountains at its entrance, two distinctive towers, and an aged copper roof. The elegant atrium was lined with twenty-eight onyx columns, and marble and stained glass abounded in every room. When Juan arrived, there were three Ferraris and a pair of Bentleys lined up under the porte cochere. The clientele streaming inside were the crème de société. The men were uniformly dressed in tuxedos, while the women looked like jewels in their gowns and dresses.

He shot his cuff to check the time. Kerikov and al-Asim never arrived before ten, so he was a half hour early. More than enough time to find an unobtrusive place to pass the time. It wouldn't do for al-Asim to meet his doppelgänger across the roulette wheel.

His phone chirped.

"Chairman, Ski and I are in position," Mike Trono reported.

"Any problems?"

"Dressed like janitors, we're practically invisible."

"Where are you now?"

"Just off the loading dock. We're keeping ourselves busy cleaning up a few jugs of cooking oil that Ski accidentally spilled on purpose."

"Okay, hang tight, and wait for my signal."

Cabrillo flashed his passport and paid his entrance fee. The crowds were all moving to the right, toward the elegant gaming rooms, so Juan followed the throng. He ambled his way upstairs to a bar, got himself a martini he had no intention of drinking but thought appropriate considering his surroundings, and found a dark corner to wait.

Hux called in moments later to announce she had also arrived and was in the Salon de l'Europe, the casino's principal gambling hall.

While he waited, Juan put his mind to how he was going to rescue Max before they leveled Eos Island with the Orbital

Ballistic Projectile. There was no question in his mind that he would follow through with the island's destruction if they couldn't get Max. The stakes were too high, and even Max would agree.

He wished there was a way to communicate back to Hanley using the ELF equipment, but it was a transmitter, not a receiver. Juan went through a dozen ideas, worked them in his mind, and ultimately rejected every one as being ill-conceived.

"They're here," Julia said over the phone, after he'd been at the bar for twenty minutes. "They're heading for a chemin de fer table."

"Let them get settled and have a few drinks first."

Down in the casino, Julia Huxley divided her attention between the roulette wheel and their target. Her pile of chips ebbed and flowed as time wore on, while, across the room, Ibn al-Asim was on his third drink.

She thought it ironic that he was willing to finance arms for fundamentalist Muslim terror groups and yet flout one of the best-known Muslim laws by drinking alcohol. She suspected he thought of himself as a *takfir*, a true believer in Islam who ignored its tenets in order to infiltrate Western society. Of course, he accomplished this merely by eschewing traditional robes and not sporting a heavy beard. The drinking and the womanizing weren't necessary. They were simply activities he obviously enjoyed.

"I think it's time, Juan," she said into her phone, pretending to check a text message.

"Okay. Do it. Mike, get ready for Operation V."

Julia waited until the roulette ball dropped into the number six slot and the dealer raked the losing chips, hers included, from the table before tossing him a tip and collecting her remaining stack. She pulled the two pills from her purse and started across the room. A few men eyed her as she passed, but most everybody was concentrating on his or her game.

There were no empty seats at the table where Kerikov and al-Asim were playing, so Julia hung back, waiting for her opportunity. When the Russian won a particularly large hand, Julia leaned close to him and whispered "Congratulations" in his ear. He was startled at first, then smiled when he saw how Hux looked.

She did it again when another player hit it big, and, suddenly, her presence here wasn't that of a stranger but part of the gaming circle. She then placed a small wager on top of this second player's stack, so that if he won so would she.

When he didn't win, he apologized, but Julia only shrugged, as if to say it was no big deal.

She then gestured to al-Asim, wordlessly asking permission to place chips with him. He nodded, and, when she reached across the table, she set her hand next to his drink to balance herself. When she straightened, she almost knocked the glass over. She grabbed it just before it spilled, dropped the two pills in it, and set it back on its coaster.

The pills were a homeopathic compound that addicts on probation use to flush their bodies of drugs prior to testing, as a way of avoiding more jail time. Julia had studied the compounds and found they didn't really work, but they had a side effect of making a person need to urinate. Doping al-Asim with it was their way of getting him to the casino's restroom on their schedule rather than on his.

Al-Asim didn't suspect a thing. He played his hand and won, grinning wolfishly when he handed Julia her winnings.

"Merci, monsieur," she said. She played one more time with a different player, lost, and drifted away from the table. When she stepped out of the gambling hall and back into the towering atrium, she called Cabrillo to tell him it was done.

"Okay, find a place to watch him, and let us know when he's headed for the bathroom and then get yourself back to the marina," Juan ordered as he headed down to the lavatory closest to the Salon de l'Europe. "Mike, you and Ski move into position."

"On our way."

There was a doorway a short distance from the restroom that led to the building's service corridors, so the guests didn't need to be bothered with seeing things like the janitors or the waitstaff who fetched patrons' drinks. Juan loitered next to the door for just a moment before it opened slightly and Mike handed him the bottle of fake vomit. Juan let a few more minutes trickle by, to give the drug time to work, before entering the restroom.

Like everything else about the casino, the restroom was all

marble and gilt. There was a man washing his hands when Cabrillo entered, but he left before Juan could even reach the stalls. With no one to hear his performance, he didn't have to act out being ill. He just poured the noisome concoction on the floor and retreated to a stall.

It took only one patron entering the bathroom for a casino employee to be summoned. Juan didn't understand much French, but the attendant's assuring tone meant that the janitorial staff would be notified immediately. He could picture the attendant making for the nearest service entrance to notify housekeeping only to discover two janitors in the hallway already, as if they had been told of the mess.

The bathroom door opened again, and Juan heard the big trash barrel's wheel squeaking as they pushed it in.

"Howdy, boys," he said, and stepped from the stall.

"Why do we always get the glamour jobs?" Mike asked with heavy sarcasm.

"Because you know how to make a floor shine."

The door opened again. Ski was there to shoo the patron away with an apologetic nod toward the filth being mopped from the floor.

"He just got up from the table," Julia informed Cabrillo. "He's going to be the next guy coming into the bathroom."

"Roger that. See you later." Juan retreated back into the stall.

When the door opened, Ski let al-Asim enter the restroom. The Arab made a face at the smell, but his need was greater than his revulsion and he practically sprinted to a urinal.

Cabrillo waited for him to finish before stepping silently behind him. Al-Asim felt his presence at the last moment and turned. His eyes widened at seeing his identical twin, but, before he could understand what was happening, Juan jammed the hypodermic needle into his neck and depressed the plunger. Al-Asim made to cry out, so Juan clamped a hand over his mouth and held him until he slipped into unconsciousness.

Ski had to refuse entry to another patron as Juan and Trono dumped the terrorist financier into the large trash can. Juan replaced his own watch with the slim Movado al-Asim wore and slipped al-Asim's large ring on a finger.

"I should be finished with Kerikov before he comes to," Juan said, checking himself in the mirror. "Just leave him where he won't be found for a few hours and get yourselves back to the *Oregon* with Julia."

"There's a utility closet near the loading dock. At this hour, no one will be using it." Mike finished restoring the floor to its glossy shine and tossed the mop in the bucket.

"See you boys later."

Juan made his way back to the chemin de fer table where Kerikov was dealing from the shoe.

"Are you all right, my friend?" the Russian asked in English, the only language he shared with the Arab.

"A little stomach trouble, Ivan. Nothing to worry about." Cabrillo had listened to several hours of taped conversation between the two men and knew how they spoke to one another. The arms dealer hadn't given his appearance a second glance. The disguise worked perfectly.

They played for another forty-five minutes, Juan acting as though his condition were worsening, and it showed in how he played. He bet foolishly and cut al-Asim's fifty thousand dollars' worth of chips in half.

"Ivan, I'm sorry," he said, holding a hand across his stomach. "I think I need to return to the boat."

"Do you need a doctor?"

"I don't think it's that serious. I just need to lie down." Juan declined the shoe when it was his turn to deal and got unsteadily to his feet. "You keep playing, please."

It was a risk to make the offer, but it was something al-Asim definitely would have done.

Kerikov seemed to give it thought. He was up about thirty thousand dollars since they'd started gambling and he hated to walk away from a winning streak. On the other hand, the way things were going with al-Asim he might become one of his clients.

"I have taken enough of their money for one night." He pushed the six-deck shoe to the Asian man to his left. When he stood, his jacket bunched across his heavy shoulders.

They handed in their chips and left the money on account with the casino for when they returned the next evening. As they walked through the ornate atrium, Kerikov called his driver on his cell phone so the limousine would be around front when they exited the building.

The driver pulled up to the entrance but remained behind the wheel. It was Kerikov's bodyguard who jumped from the front seat and opened the rear door. He was a good four inches taller than Cabrillo, with dark, distrusting eyes. He scanned the crowd, as Kerikov maneuvered himself into the car, and pegged Juan with a hard stare.

Instinct would have been to look away, and, if Cabrillo had, the guard would have known something was amiss. But Juan had spent a lifetime training to ignore instinct. Instead of lowering his eyes, he stared back just as fiercely, and asked, "Is there something wrong?"

The bodyguard softened his expression. *"Nyet."*

Juan got into the car and the door was closed behind him. It was a short drive to the marina. Juan played up his intestinal discomfort so he wouldn't need to talk with the Russian as the limo wound its way down to the waterfront.

Kerikov had a private launch from his yacht, *Matryoshka*, waiting for them at the marina. The guard sprang out of the car as soon as it stopped to open the back door.

"Good thing we didn't waste money on any ladies this evening," Kerikov remarked as they walked to where the gleaming white launch was tied.

"I don't feel well enough even to look at a woman right now. In fact, I'm not really eager for this ride out to your boat."

Kerikov placed a beefy hand on Cabrillo's shoulder. "It's only a short hop, and the harbor is as smooth as glass. You'll do fine."

The bodyguard fired up the launch's engine while the limo driver helped with the bow and stern lines. Five minutes later, they approached the broad transom of the *Matryoshka*, where a teak dive platform had been lowered and a flight of stairs gave access to the monster boat's main deck.

"I should think you are going straight to your cabin," Kerikov remarked as they stepped aboard. A servant was waiting at the top of the steps, should the Russian require anything, and Juan saw two guards, one up on the sundeck behind the bridge and the other patrolling near the ship's pool.

His team had estimated there were at least eighteen crewmen to run the megayacht and a ten-man security detail.

"Actually," Juan replied, "I would like to talk to you in your office."

"Nothing too sensitive?" Kerikov inquired at once. He knew how easily someone could eavesdrop on his ship so close to shore.

"No, no, no," Juan said at once. "Just something that occurred to me tonight."

Kerikov led them through the luxurious vessel, passing by a dining room that could seat twenty and a movie theater with double that capacity. The former hard-line communist spy had certainly availed himself of the trappings of capitalism.

They reached the Russian's private office, and, as soon as Kerikov closed the door behind them, Juan had his pistol out and pressed to Kerikov's throat hard enough to tear skin.

"One sound and you're dead." Juan had dropped his phony Arabic accent and spoke in Russian.

To his credit, Kerikov didn't move. He had probably been on the giving end of this situation enough to know that if his attacker's motive was assassination, he would already be dead.

"Who are you?"

Juan said nothing while he fitted Kerikov's wrists with a pair of FlexiCuffs.

"Even though you speak my language, you are CIA, I think, and not FSB. I must congratulate you. When I did my research on Ibn al-Asim, his background was unimpeachable. You went a very long way in establishing his bona fides. A great many trusted people assured me he was legitimate."

"I'm not Ibn al-Asim," Juan said.

Kerikov smirked. "Obviously not."

"He's back at the casino, in a trash can near the loading dock. He should regain consciousness in another couple hours."

Kerikov's eyes narrowed as he tried to get his mind around the situation.

Juan let him dangle a moment longer. "As far as I know, you and al-Asim are old college roommates in Monte Carlo having a few laughs together. I don't care what you two are scheming. I'm here about something you stole from your former employers."

"I stole a great deal from them," Kerikov said with unabashed pride.

Juan had done enough research on the Russian arms dealer to want to put a bullet through his brain and rid the world of one less dirtbag. It took effort not to pull the trigger.

"I want the codes for Stalin's Fist."

The fact that he had mentioned the weapon only a short while ago to al-Asim wasn't lost on Kerikov. He again asked who Juan was.

"Your assassin, if you don't give me what I want."

"You've had me under surveillance, haven't you?"

"My organization has been watching you for some time," Juan told him, which wasn't exactly a lie. "We are only interested in the codes for the Orbital Ballistic Projectile satellite. Give me what I want and you and al-Asim can continue your arms deal without interference. Otherwise, you die tonight."

When Juan had cleared this operation through Langston Overholt, the CIA man had insisted that it in no way jeopardized their long-term plan to turn al-Asim.

Cabrillo cocked his pistol to punctuate the statement.

Kerikov tried to stare him down, and didn't blink when he saw Juan's finger beginning to squeeze the trigger.

"Pull that trigger and my security team will be in here in twenty seconds," he warned.

"My soul is prepared for martyrdom," Juan retorted, clouding his role by making it sound like he was on a religious quest. "Is yours?"

Kerikov blew out a heavy sigh. "God, I miss the Cold War. You're Chechen, aren't you?"

"If it appeases whatever remains of your conscience, I am not Chechen, and the weapon won't be used anywhere within the former Soviet Union." He could almost see Kerikov thinking that the weapon wouldn't be used at all.

"The codes are locked in the safe behind that painting." He nodded toward a nude hanging on one wall.

Juan used the barrel of his pistol to swing the painting back on its long hinge in case it was booby-trapped. The safe was about two feet square, with a ten-digit electronic pad. "Combination?"

"Two-five, one-zero, one-nine-one-seven."

It took Juan a second to recognize the numbers, because Europeans put days ahead of months when giving dates. "The date of Russia's October Revolution. Nice touch."

He punched in the numbers, and made Kerikov stand directly in front of the safe when he threw the handle. Juan had recognized the safe model, and knew if an incorrect code had been entered a stun grenade would detonate. The code was legitimate.

Inside were stacks of currency, a pistol, which Juan stuffed into his pocket, and countless folders and files.

"Should be near the bottom," Kerikov offered, to get this ordeal over with quicker.

Juan scanned some of the documents as he searched. The Russian was involved in some heavy deals, including arming Saddam Hussein before the U.S. invasion, and a triangle trade of Afghan opium for Russian weapons for African conflict diamonds.

Near the bottom was a file with the label November Sky in Cyrillic. Juan leafed through a couple of pages, satisfying himself that it was what he was after. Once the computer aboard the *Oregon* translated it into English, he assumed Eric and Hali could understand the technical jargon.

He slid the document into a waterproof bag and turned to Kerikov. As much as he wanted to tell Kerikov what he thought of him, Juan held his tongue. "When you find al-Asim, tell him what happened tonight is unrelated to your business together. Tell him it is a piece of your past coming back to haunt you, but the situation is now resolved. Now please turn around and drop to your knees."

For the first time since Juan had pulled the gun on him, Kerikov showed fear. It was in his eyes, though he managed to keep it out of his voice. "You got what you wanted."

"I am not going to kill you." Juan withdrew the hypodermic case and removed one of the needles. "It's the same drug I gave al-Asim. You'll be out for a few hours. Nothing more."

"I hate needles. I'd rather have you hit me over the head."

Juan smashed his FN into Kerikov's temple so hard that a

pound or two of extra force would have shattered the bone and killed him. He collapsed like an imploded building. "Suit yourself," Juan said, and jabbed the needle home anyway.

The outside wall of Kerikov's office was curved glass that bowed out from the hull in a shallow arc. Juan opened one of the windows and peered upward. There was no one hanging over the railing above him. He stripped out of his tux jacket, shirt, and the fat suit. Beneath it, he wore a skintight black T-shirt with long sleeves. After stuffing the waterproof bag under the shirt and tossing Kerikov's pistol out the window, he kicked off his shoes and eased himself into the water.

So long as he remained silent and didn't look up, so his face wouldn't show, his black wig made him blend in with the inky Mediterranean. He swam forward along the *Matryosh-ka*'s hull until he came to the anchor chain. There, he dove under the surface, crawling link by link down the chain until he came to the diving equipment Eddie and Franklin had cached earlier.

He donned the Draeger rebreather, weight belt, fins, and mask, and took a bearing off the luminous compass they had left for him. The *Oregon* was only a mile away, and, with the slack tide, his going would be even easier.

As he swam, he made a silent vow that this wouldn't be the last time he paid a visit to Ivan Kerikov, and that the Russian wouldn't fare so well in their next meeting.

CHAPTER 31

IT HADN'T BEEN TOO DIFFICULT FOR MARK AND Linda to hide the fact they didn't have an assigned cabin. They purchased clothing and toiletries from the shops, and could shower in the locker rooms adjacent to the ship's fitness facility. They slept in shifts on poolside deck chairs during the afternoon and spent their nights in the casino. With his photographic memory, Murph was an expert card counter, and had turned the four hundred dollars they brought with them into a sizable pot. He could have made a fortune, had he wanted to, but they needed to maintain their anonymity so he kept his winnings reasonable.

That all changed on the second day.

To the other passengers, the closing of the ship-to-shore communications room was mostly just an inconvenience. A few businesspeople grumbled, but most people either didn't notice or didn't care.

Mark and Linda knew otherwise. And there were other subtle signs as well. They saw more crewmen roaming the decks, ostensibly to perform maintenance. However, they spent a great deal of time watching the passengers. No one was asking to see room keys yet, but Linda and Murph knew it was only a matter of time.

It was clear that the word was out that there were stowaways on the *Golden Sky*, and the cruise line was determined to find them.

More troubling than this information were the sniffles.

On the morning of their second day aboard ship, a number of passengers and crew had runny noses and suffered occasional bouts of sneezing. By listening to people talking near the pool and around the dining room, the two pieced together that everyone had felt fine the night before but that the ones who were sick had all gone to the midnight buffet, and that the waitstaff and cooks who'd worked the buffet shift were ill as well.

"It has to be a test," Mark surmised.

"How can you be so sure?" They were just finishing breakfast in a secluded corner of the cavernous dining room.

"Two reasons. Most natural shipboard viral outbreaks are of a gastrointestinal nature. This is presenting like a rhinovirus. Second, if this was the main attack, we'd all be dead."

"What do you think we should do?" Although her appetite was legendary, Linda only picked at her food.

"Don't shake anyone's hand, don't touch any handrails, do not—and this is critical—do not touch your eyes. It's a cold's favorite way of entering the body. We wash our hands every half hour, and immediately if we break any of the other rules. And, last, we find out how the hell they are going to release the deadly virus they used to hit the *Golden Dawn*."

"Did we screw up by staying on this ship?" Linda asked, wiping her mouth and setting her napkin next to her plate.

"No, because we are going to find out how they are releasing it before the main attack."

"Be reasonable. We've checked the water system, the air intakes, the air-conditioning plant, hell, even the ice makers. If we haven't found it yet, what are the odds we will?"

"They get better every time we check off another vector source from our list," Mark replied. "Have you ever wondered why, when you lose something, you always find it in the last place you look?"

"Why?"

"Because you stop looking when you find it. Therefore, it is invariably in the last place you searched."

"What's your point?"

"We haven't checked the proverbial last place yet."

Even through the insulation of the dining room's walls, they heard the distinctive beat of a helicopter's rotor. They got up from the table and made their way aft. There was a swimming pool at the *Golden Sky*'s fantail. A hard cover had been placed over its aqua waters, and deckhands had cordoned off the area with rope to keep passengers well clear.

The chopper was a Bell JetRanger, with POSEIDON TOURS emblazoned on its flank. From several decks up, Mark and Linda could see the pilot and three passengers in the cabin.

"This can't be good," Linda said over the growing din.

"You think they're here for us?"

"People rarely die on cruise ships, so when one of his followers was killed in Istanbul Thom Severance must have acted fast. I wonder how he got the cruise line to agree to this. Gomez Adams makes it look easy, but landing a helo on a moving ship is dangerous."

"They've got deep pockets."

The chopper flared in over the jack staff, the downwash kicking up a little spray from where crewmen had washed the deck of grit. It hung poised like a hovering insect, as the pilot judged speed and windage before lowering the craft toward the pool cover. He kept the power on, so the skids barely put any pressure on the cover, and three doors opened at the same time. The men jumped from the chopper, with nylon packs over their shoulders. The pilot needed to make a quick power adjustment to account for the sudden drop in weight. As soon as the doors were closed, the chopper lifted clean and peeled away from the ship.

"Eddie said something about Zelimir Kovac looking like Boris Karloff on a bad day." Mark pointed with his chin.

"The big guy in the middle?"

"It's got to be him."

The three men were greeted by a ship's officer but made no move to shake hands. They somehow managed to make their casual clothes—khakis, polo shirts, and light windbreakers—look like military uniforms. It was the matching backpacks, Linda thought.

"What do you think is in those bags?" she asked.

"Change of underwear, fresh socks, a razor. Oh, and guns."

Before now, they had only risked being placed in whatever passed as a brig aboard the *Golden Sky* and having a lot of explaining to do when they reached shore. That had changed. Kovac and his two henchmen were coming for them, and there wasn't any doubt what would happen if they caught them. Mark and Linda's only advantage was, Kovac didn't know how many people were hunting for the virus. However, with the ship's officers and crew acting more vigilant about possible stowaways, the two of them could be flushed out at a moment's notice.

"Something just occurred to me," Mark said as they turned away from the rail.

"Yeah, what's that?"

"Would Kovac risk being aboard this ship if they are going to hit it with the virus they used to kill everyone on the *Golden Dawn*?"

"He would if he'd been vaccinated."

By noon, three-quarters of the people on the ship were suffering coldlike symptoms, and, despite precautions, Mark and Linda were included in that group.

CHAPTER 32

THE HIGH DESERT WIND SHRIEKED ACROSS THE airfield throwing up towering clouds of dust that threatened to block out the sky. The pilot of the chartered Citation jet came in on the runway fully thirty feet to the left, to account for the crosswind hammering the fuselage.

The gear came down with a mechanical whine and thump, and flaps were extended. The turbojets roared to keep the aircraft aloft for a few more seconds.

The sole passenger seated in the cabin paid no attention to the weather conditions or the dangerous landing. Since catching a commercial flight from Nice to London, and then on to Dallas, where the leased executive jet was waiting, he sat with his laptop open and his fingers dancing across the keys.

When Eric had come up with his plan to fire the Russian ballistic projectile weapon, it had been the barest outline of an idea. He hadn't considered the tremendous amount of data he needed to make it work. Orbital speeds, vectors, the rotation of the earth, the mass of the tungsten rods, and a hundred other elements—all had to be factored into his computations.

With his naval background, he was more than confident he could do the mathematics, although he would have liked Murph's help. Mark had an innate grasp of trigonometry and calculus that would have made this so much easier. But, then, he would have insisted on taking command, and the Chairman would have rightly given him the slot. Mark was simply more qualified to do this than Eric.

Because this broke down to a communications exercise between the satellite and the computer, Hali Kasim would have been the next logical choice. The only problem was that

Hali got sick on carnival rides and wouldn't have been able to do the work.

Eric got tapped to do what only a handful of people had ever done. He would allow himself to get excited about it later, but, for now, he had to work the numbers. He had told Jannike Dahl about needing to do this, embellishing the danger, while not spelling out the reason. And with Mark trapped on the *Golden Sky*, he had stepped up his pursuit of the beautiful young Norwegian. He was already up to the eighth item on his courtship checklist and almost pushed it to number nine by trying to hold her hand when he explained why he had to leave the ship. He wished he knew what it meant when she had cocked her head and parted her lips just before he left her in the infirmary.

He should have asked Dr. Huxley.

The plane touched down, swaying dangerously on two wheels for a moment before the pilot could kick in the rudder to even her out again. They taxied a long way—the airstrip was over three miles long—and finally came to a massive hangar next to another unmarked executive jet. Above the hangar door was the name of a long-defunct airline. The engines spooled to silence, and the copilot emerged from the cockpit.

"Sorry, Mr. Stone, but we can't taxi into the hangar in this sandstorm. But, don't worry. It's going to die down by tonight."

Eric had already checked a dozen weather sites on the Internet and knew to the minute when this cold front would move on. By midnight, there wouldn't even be a breeze.

He closed up his laptop and grabbed his suitcase, an old Navy duffel that had followed him from Annapolis.

The copilot opened the door and Eric fought his way down the stairs, slitting his eyes against the sand blowing across the tarmac. There was a man near a small door set into the larger hangar door waving him over. Eric jogged the forty feet to the door and ducked through. The stranger immediately closed it. There was a large aircraft in the center of the hangar covered in canvas tarps. Its shape was hard to make out, but it was unlike anything else in the world.

"Damned dust plays havoc on the planes," the man griped. "You must be Eric Stone. I'm Jack Taggart."

"It's an honor to meet you, Colonel." Eric said with a touch of hero worship. "I read about you when I was a kid."

Taggart was in his sixties, with a leathery weather-beaten face and clear blue eyes. He was ruggedly handsome, like an idealized figure of a cowboy, with a firm jaw and a day's worth of silver stubble. He wore chinos, a flight uniform shirt, and a bomber jacket despite the heat. His handshake was like iron, and his baseball cap had the logo for one of the early Space Shuttle missions. He had been its pilot.

"You ready for the ride of your life?" Taggart asked, leading him to an office in one corner of the hangar. His voice had a West Texas twang.

Eric grinned. "Yes, sir, I am."

There were two men in the office. Eric recognized one of them right away by his thick muttonchop sideburns. It was legendary aircraft designer Rick Butterfield. The other was a tall, patrician figure with a shock of white hair. He wore a banker's three-piece suit, with the chain of a Phi Beta Kappa key arcing across his waistcoat. Eric put his age on the high side of seventy.

"Mr. Stone," he said, extending a hand. "I so rarely get to meet members of Juan's team."

"Are you Langston Overholt?" Eric asked with awe.

"I am, my boy, I am. Although you have never, and most likely will never, meet me. Do you understand?"

Eric nodded.

"I really shouldn't have come at all. This is a private deal between the Corporation and Mr. Butterfield's company, after all."

"That I wouldn't have agreed to if you hadn't threatened to gum up my certification applications with the FAA and NASA." Butterfield had a high-pitched voice.

Overholt turned to him. "Rick, it wasn't a threat, just a friendly reminder that your aircraft hasn't yet been certified flightworthy, and that a word from me will cut a lot of red tape."

"You'd better not be yanking my chain."

"I think that my getting you a temporary certificate for this flight is proof enough of what I can do for you."

Butterfield's expression remained sour, but he seemed mollified. He asked Eric, "What time do we need to do this?"

"Using tracking data from NORAD, I calculate that to make an intercept I have to be in position at exactly eight-fourteen and thirty-one-point-six seconds tomorrow morning."

"I can't guarantee you that kind of time accuracy. We'll need an hour just to get to altitude, and another six minutes for the burn."

"A minute either way shouldn't make much of a difference," Eric said to reassure him. "Mr. Butterfield, I want you to understand the gravity of this situation. There are literally millions of lives counting on us. I know that sounds like a line from a bad spy novel, but it is the truth. If we fail, the people of the world are going to suffer in unspeakable agony."

He opened his laptop to show the aeronautical engineer some of the footage taken aboard the *Golden Dawn*. The scenes spoke for themselves, so Eric didn't bother narrating. When it was over, he said, "Most of the people killed were the ones responsible for manufacturing the virus. The men behind this murdered their own people just to keep them silent."

Butterfield looked up from the computer. His face was ashen under his farmer's tan. "I'm on board, kid. One hundred percent."

"Thank you, sir."

"You ever taken any serious g's, son?" Taggart asked.

"When I was in the Navy, I was launched off a carrier. That was about three, maybe three and a half."

"You barf easy?"

"It's why I'm here and another one of my associates isn't. I'm a member of ACE, American Coaster Enthusiasts. I spend my vacations riding roller coasters. Haven't been sick once."

"Good enough for me. Rick?"

"I'm not going to have you sign a bunch of insurance waivers and all that boilerplate. I can vouch for my bird so long as you vouch for your health."

"My company gives us physicals every six months. There's nothing wrong with me that these eyeglasses can't correct."

"Okay, then. We have a lot of prep work to get done before morning." Butterfield glanced at the big Rolex he wore on the inside of his wrist. "My team should be here in twenty minutes or so. I need to get you and your gear on a scale to calculate weights and balance, and then I think you should remain on your aircraft until the flight. Your pilots can stay at the hotel in town. I'll have one of my guys drive them."

"That works for me. Ah, Mr. Butterfield, I do have one request."

"Shoot."

"I'd like to see the plane."

Butterfield nodded and sauntered from the office, Eric, Taggart, and Overholt in tow. There was a handheld remote dangling from a long cord next to the shrouded plane. He hit a button, and a winch started to draw the tarp ceilingward.

Painted glossy white with little blue stars, the mother plane, called *Kanga*, looked unlike any other aircraft in the world. It had gull wings, like the venerable World War II Corsair, but they started high on the fuselage and angled downward, so that the airframe sat on tall landing gear. It had two jet engines above the single-seat cockpit, and twin spars under the wings that tapered back to a pair of delta-shaped tail assemblies.

But what was nestled under the larger plane was what held Stone's attention. *'Roo* was a rocket-powered glider with a single flat wing that could be hinged upward to impart drag after it had exhausted its load of fuel. Capable of speeds in excess of two thousand miles per hour, *'Roo* was a suborbital-space plane, and, while it wasn't the first privately funded craft, it already held the record for altitude, at nearly one hundred and twenty kilometers, or almost seventy-five miles, above the earth.

'Roo was carried to thirty-eight thousand feet by *Kanga*. The two would separate, and the rocket motor would be engaged so that *'Roo* screamed toward the heavens on a ballistic parabola that would carry it some sixty miles downrange. It would then glide back to its home base for refueling.

The intention of Butterfield and his investors was to take adventure seekers on a suborbital flight so they could feel the freedom of weightlessness at the very edge of space. Eric Stone was about to become their first paying customer, although he wasn't after thrills. His idea was to time the flight so that at its apogee he would be within range of the Russian weapons platform's damaged antenna. Using the codes Juan had gotten from Kerikov, Eric would reposition the satellite so it would launch one of its projectiles at Eos Island. The kinetic energy of the eighteen-hundred-pound tungsten rod striking anywhere on the island would obliterate the ELF transmitter.

"She's something godawful ugly, isn't she?" Butterfield said with pride. He rubbed a loving hand along the composite fuselage.

"What's it like flying in her?" Eric asked.

"I wouldn't know." Butterfield tapped his chest. "Bum ticker."

The test pilot, Taggart, said, "Son, this thing is going to ruin you for them roller coasters you like so much 'cause this is one ride that'll top 'em all."

Overholt cleared his throat. "Gentlemen, it wouldn't do for me to be here when Mr. Butterfield's people arrive, so I will bid my farewells." He shook hands all around, his grip firm despite his age. "Mr. Stone, please walk me back to my plane."

"Certainly, sir."

Eric had to stretch his stride to match the elder man's pace.

"I would like you to convey to the Chairman, the next time you speak to him, that I had a word with our friends at the National Security Agency. They also detected the ELF transmissions, one from your Mr. Hanley, I believe, and the other one a short while earlier. The very fact that someone has gone to the expense of building such a transmitter caused a bit of a stir, as you can imagine. Coupled with what you and your crewmates have been able to discern, almost all of it unsubstantiated"—Eric opened his mouth to protest—"I know you don't follow Justice Department rules, but there are legalities that must be followed if we're to prosecute Severance and his group.

"I helped grease the wheels for your little adventure tomorrow, so you know I am taking this threat seriously, but if we are going to expose the Responsivist movement for the monsters they really are I need facts, not second- and third-hand accounts. Do you understand?"

"Of course, Mr. Overholt. Just so long as you understand that without us acting the way we have, millions of people would be exposed to the virus by the time you found satisfactory evidence for said prosecution." Eric didn't believe he had the courage to speak so frankly to the veteran CIA agent.

Langston chuckled. "I can see why Juan hired you. Courage and brains. Tell Juan that things are in motion here that may help take down Severance once his transmitter is destroyed." They paused at the hangar door because the wind would make it impossible to speak once they stepped outside. "I wasn't told who thought up the crazy idea of using that Cold War relic the Russkies left littering space?"

"I did," Eric replied. "I knew Juan would nix my first idea of talking you into getting us a nuke."

Overholt paled at that. "Rightly so."

"I had to come up with an alternative, and when Ivan Kerikov mentioned Stalin's Fist and I researched it everything seemed to fit."

"You know it was Cabrillo who sabotaged the satellite, right?"

"He mentioned it briefly."

"Knowing him, he didn't tell you the full story. Juan spent seven months behind the Iron Curtain, living the life of one Yuri Markov, a technician at Baikonur. The pressure to stay undercover for that long, and under the tight security the Russians maintained there at the time, must have been pure hell.

"When he got out, it was standard practice for operatives to see an agency shrink. They met for just a short while. I saw the doctor's notes. His summary was just one line: 'That is the coolest customer I have ever met.' Truer words have never been written."

"Just curious, what happened to the real Markov? Juan didn't have to . . ."

"Kill him? Heavens no. We got Markov out in payment for first telling us about the Orbital Ballistic Projectile project. Last I heard, he works for Boeing's space division. But I know this: if he had been ordered to sanction Markov, Juan wouldn't have hesitated. He has the strictest moral code of anyone I know.

"The ends justify the means, for someone like Cabrillo. I

know in today's politically correct world that outrages a lot of people, but they live in the freedom men like Juan provide. It isn't their conscience that bears the burden. It's Juan's. They just get to enjoy a false sense of moral superiority without understanding the real costs.

"Toss an animal lover into a pen with a rabid raccoon and he'll kill it. He will feel bad, even guilty, but do you think he's going to consider his peers' outrage that he took that life? Not for a second, because it's kill or be killed. That is what our world is coming to, I'm afraid, only people are too horrified by that concept to accept it."

"Unfortunately, their acceptance isn't a factor to the forces arrayed against us," Eric said.

Overholt held out his hand to shake again. "That's what makes our jobs all the more difficult. I fought my war when we all knew it was black and white. Since then, someone convinced us there is gray out there. Let me tell you something, son: there isn't any such thing as gray, no matter what you hear." Overholt released Eric's hand. "It was a pleasure meeting you, Mr. Stone. Good luck tomorrow, and Godspeed."

CUTTING LIKE A KNIFE through blue silk, the *Oregon* raced across the Mediterranean. They avoided shipping lanes as much as possible so they could run her magnetohydrodynamic engines above the red line and not draw attention to her blazing speed. They slowed only once, when passing through the Strait of Messina, separating the tip of Italy's boot from the island of Sicily. Fortunately, nature was in a cooperative mood. The seas were calm, and there was no trace of a breeze, as they dashed across the Ionian Sea and entered the Aegean.

Juan spent nearly every waking hour in the Op Center, wedged into his chair with a continuously recharged mug of coffee. In the top corner of the main viewing monitor, a digital clock remorselessly counted backward. In a little over eighteen hours, Eos Island would be wiped off the face of the planet.

And Max Hanley would go with it if Cabrillo didn't think of something soon.

The ship didn't feel right to him. Eric and Mark should be

at the front consoles, navigating the ship and preparing its weapons systems for her defense. Max should be at the rear of the Op Center, hovering over the engine monitors like a mother hen. Linda should be here, too, ready to lend a hand to whatever section needed her. Eddie and Linc must have felt the same way. They rarely spent time in the Op Center, but, with so many of their friends in danger, there was no place else they would rather be.

"Nothing, Chairman," Hali said from his station along the starboard side of the high-tech room.

This was the third straight time that Linda and Mark had missed their appointed check-in time. Hali had contacted the cruise line and been reassured that there were no communications problems with the *Golden Sky*. He had even phoned the ship's communications center, pretending to be a passenger's brother with news of a dying parent. The helpful secretary had assured him that she would get a message to cabin B123, a number he had randomly picked. The passenger never called back, but that wasn't definitive proof of anything since he may have already lost both parents and thought it a cruel hoax. Juan had dismissed the idea of trying a few others with the same ruse, because the receptionist would have grown suspicious.

Even with the *Oregon*'s vast arsenal of weaponry and the best communications system afloat, there was nothing anyone could do but wait—wait until they were within range of Eos and hope that an opportunity presented itself. Max had figured out a way to elude his captors long enough to send the message, and the cagey old codger might come up with another trick or two yet. Juan had to be in position to help if he could.

Then there was the situation with Mark and Linda. Juan had no idea what events were unfolding on the *Golden Sky*. For all he knew, they had been identified as stowaways and were in lockdown someplace on a ship he had no doubt Severance had rigged with his virus. They still hadn't figured out what Max had meant, that the virus did something worse than kill, but it didn't matter. If they failed to knock out the transmitter, two of his top people were going to be among the first exposed.

Juan typed a command into his computer. On the monitor, the speeding seconds of the digital clock vanished. They had been reeling back depressingly fast, and he didn't want to watch them anymore. The minutes display was reminder enough that time was running out.

CHAPTER 33

"THE FBI RAIDED OUR PLACE IN BEVERLY Hills," Thom Severance said as he burst into Lydell Cooper's underground apartment. His voice nearly cracked with panic.

Cooper had been resting on a sofa and swung his feet to the floor. "They what?"

"The FBI raided my house, our headquarters. It happened just a few minutes ago. My secretary managed to call me on my satellite phone. The have a search-and-seizure warrant for all our financial records, as well as membership lists. They also have a warrant to arrest me and Heidi on suspicion of tax fraud. Thank God, Heidi is with her sister at our cabin in Big Bear, but it's only a matter of time before they find her. What are we going to do? They're on to us, Lydell. They know everything."

"Calm down! They don't know anything. The FBI is using their Gestapo tactics to intimidate us. If they knew about our plan, they would have arrested everyone in California and coordinated with Turkish authorities to raid this facility."

"But it's coming apart. I can feel it." Severance sat heavily on a chair and buried his face in his hands.

"Get ahold of yourself. This isn't a big deal."

"That's easy for you to say," Severance spat like a petulant child. "You're not the one under arrest. You get to hide in the shadows while I take the fall."

"Damnit, Thom. Listen to me. The FBI has no idea what we are trying to accomplish. They might have an inkling that we are plotting something, but they don't know what. This is a—what's that expression?—a fishing expedition. They issued a generic warrant to see our records in hopes of finding something incriminating. We both know there isn't.

"We've made sure from the very first that our records are clean. The Responsivist organization is a nonprofit, so we don't pay taxes, but we have filed our financials with the IRS like clockwork. Unless you and Heidi have done something stupid, like not pay your income tax on the salary you're paid, they have nothing. You've paid your taxes, right?"

"Of course we have."

"Then stop worrying. There shouldn't be anything at the house that could possibly lead them here. They might discover that we had an operation in the Philippines, but we can say it was a family-planning clinic that didn't attract any visitors so we closed it down. The Philippines is predominantly Catholic, so that wouldn't be out of the ordinary."

"But the timing of the raid, so close to when we release the virus?"

"Coincidence."

"I thought you didn't believe in them."

"I don't, but, in this case, I am certain of it. The FBI simply doesn't know anything, Thom. Trust me." When Severance's grimace didn't soften, Cooper went on. "Listen. Here's what we are going to do. You are going to issue a press release demanding these scurrilous charges be dropped immediately and calling the FBI's actions a violation of your personal and civil rights. This is pure harassment, and you are already preparing to file a civil suit against the Justice Department. You know the kind of thing I'm talking about. The helicopter we've been ferrying in personnel on is still here on the island. I will go to Izmir, where the jet is waiting. Tell Heidi that she should get out of California. I will meet her and her sister in Phoenix and bring them back. We hadn't planned on moving into the bunker until shortly before the virus manifests itself, but coming a few months early is no great hardship. Afterward, I guarantee that a bogus charge against you will be extremely low on the federal government's priority list."

"What about sending the broadcast?"

"It is an honor I leave up to you." Cooper crossed the room so he could lay a gnarled hand on Severance's shoulder. "It's going to be all right, Thom. Your man Kovac will eliminate whoever killed Zach Raymond on the *Golden Sky*, and, in a few short hours, all of our teams will be in position with the virus ready for disbursal. We're here. It's our moment. Don't let something like this ludicrous raid upset you, okay? And, listen, even if they seize the house and everything in it, our movement will have already achieved its greatest success. They can't take that away from us, and they certainly can't stop us."

Severance looked up at his father-in-law. It was disconcerting at times to look at his middle-aged face and know he was in his eighties. Lydell had been more than an in-law. He had been a mentor, and the driving force for all Thom's success. Cooper had walked away at the pinnacle of his career so he could protect what he'd created from the outside, tossing away his very identity in order to bring them to this point.

He had never doubted Cooper before, and, while errant thoughts niggled at the back of his mind, he would trust their relationship more than his gut. He stood, gently placing his hand over Cooper's arthritis-ravaged, gloved claw.

"I'm sorry. I was putting my petty fears above our goals. What does it matter if I am arrested? The virus will be released and will spread all over the globe. The scourge of overpopulation will end, and, as you've said before, humanity will enter a new Golden Age."

"In time, we will be seen as heroes. They will erect statues of us for having had the courage to find the most humane solution to our problems."

"Do you ever wonder if, instead, they will hate us for making so many of them sterile?"

"We will be hated by individuals, sure, but humanity as a whole understands that drastic change is necessary. They already see it with the global-warming debate. Things cannot go on the way they are. You may ask, by what right do we alone do this?" Cooper's eyes glittered. "And I say, it is by right of being rational rather than emotional.

"We do it by the right that we are right. There is no alternative. I wonder if Jonathan Swift was really being satirical when he penned *A Modest Proposal* in 1729. He saw then that England was being overrun by homeless urchins and that the country was going to be ruined. In order to save themselves, he said they ought to just eat the children and the problem would vanish. Eighty years later, Thomas Malthus published his famous essay on population growth. He called for 'moral restraint,' meaning voluntary abstinence, to reduce humanity's swelling numbers.

"Of course, that would never work, and now even after decades of cheap birth control our numbers multiply. I said that change was necessary, but we won't change. We haven't yet, so I say to hell with them. If they can't curb their instinct to procreate, I will give in to my instinct of self-preservation and save the planet by doing away with half of the next generation."

Cooper's voice became a strident hiss. "And, in truth, should we even care if the great sea of unwashed out there hate us? If they are too stupid to understand they are destroying themselves what does their opinion matter to us? We are like a shepherd culling a flock. Do you think he cares what the rest of the sheep think? He knows better, Thom. We know better."

CHAPTER 34

ERIC STONE'S STOMACH WAS TOO KNOTTED TO EAT the traditional astronaut's breakfast of steak and eggs. He wasn't nervous about the upcoming suborbital flight. In fact, he was eager for the experience. It was the fear of failure that cramped his body and turned his mouth as dry as the desert outside the hangar. He was all too aware that this was the single most important mission of his career, and, no matter what happened in the future, nothing would top it. He was facing a life-defining moment, with the fate of humanity resting in his hands.

And as if that weren't enough, he also couldn't get out of his mind the fact that Max Hanley was trapped on Eos Island.

Like Mark Murphy, Eric had been catapulted by his intelligence to early success without being given the time to properly mature. Mark hid it by playing at being a rebel, growing his hair long, blaring loud music, and pretending to flout authority. Eric had no such persona. He remained shy and socially awkward, so it was little wonder that he had always needed mentoring. In high school, the mentor had been a physics teacher, at Annapolis, an English instructor, who, ironically, he'd never had a class with. After he was commissioned, he couldn't find someone to take him under his wing— the military wasn't structured that way—and he was ready to leave after putting in his mandatory five years.

Eric hadn't known it, but his last commanding officer had gotten word to an old friend, Hanley, that Stone would make an excellent addition to the Corporation. When Max made the initial approach, Eric agreed to join almost immediately. He recognized in the former Swift Boat commander the same things he had seen in his old teachers. Max had this calm, steady demeanor and endless patience, and he knew how to nurture talent. He was slowly molding Eric into the man he always wanted to be.

This was the other reason Eric couldn't eat and had slept only fitfully the night before. Success today would mean he had killed a man who had been more of a father to him than the man who had raised him.

"You okay, son?" Jack Taggart asked as they were putting on their flight suits in a locker room behind the hangar office. The space plane's cabin was pressurized, so the suits were little more than olive drab overalls. "You look a little green around the gills."

"A lot on my mind, Colonel," Eric replied.

"Well, I don't want you to worry none about the flight," the former Shuttle pilot drawled. "I'll get us there and back, no problem."

"I can honestly say that the last thing I'm concerned with is the flight itself."

A technician stuck his head into the room. "Gentlemen, you'd better shake a leg. Flight director wants *Kanga* rolling in twenty minutes."

Taggart snatched up his helmet from his locker and said, "Then let's go light this candle."

There were two reclined seats behind the pilot's position in the sleek space plane, '*Roo*. Eric had spent the early morning hours securing his computer and the transmitter into one of them. He eased himself into the second and kept his hands away from his chest, as workers belted him in as secure as a Grand Prix driver. Above him was a pair of windows, through which he could see the underside of the mother ship. There were small windows on either side as well. Taggart was in front of him, talking to flight director Rick Butterfield.

Eric jacked his helmet into a communications port and waited for a pause in Taggart's conversation to do a radio check on the flight frequency, before switching over to another frequency, though he could still hear the pilot in one ear.

"Elton, this is John, how do you read me? Over." Hali Kasim had picked the code names from the Elton John song "Rocket Man."

"John, this is Elton. Reading you five by five. Over."

"Elton, prepare to receive telemetry on my mark. Three, two, one, mark." Eric hit a key on his laptop so that Hali could monitor the flight and the Russian satellite in real time aboard the *Oregon*. He'd even rigged a webcam so his shipmates could see what he was seeing.

"John, signal looks good. Over."

"Okay, we're about ten minutes from rollout. I'll keep you updated. Over."

"Roger that. Good luck. Over."

The big hangar doors rattled open, bathing the cavernous space in the ruddy light of a new day. There were enough workers on hand to push *Kanga* out onto the apron. On the edge of the runway sat a ramshackle mobile home that was the flight director's control center. Its roof bristled with antennae and a pair of revolving radar dishes.

"How you doing back there?" Taggart called over his shoulder.

Before Eric could reply, the two turbojets mounted on the top of *Kanga*'s fuselage roared into life. Taggart repeated the question over the radio, because it was too loud to speak comfortably.

"Getting a little excited," Eric confessed.

"Don't forget, I'll flash a red light on your console when we're ten seconds from the end of the burn. It'll turn yellow when we're at five and green when the rocket motor cuts out. At that moment, we'll be at an altitude of roughly seventy-five miles, but once the motor runs dry we start falling immediately. So do your thing fast."

"You got it."

"Here we go," Taggart announced as *Kanga* started to taxi.

The gawky mother ship, with its droopy wings, rolled onto the runway and turned sharply to align with the center stripe. It began to accelerate immediately, the engines keening at full power. Designed for the sole purpose of getting 'Roo up to its launch altitude of thirty-eight thousand feet, *Kanga* wasn't the most dynamic aircraft in terms of performance. It used up nearly the entire runway before transitioning into the air to start its long, stately ascent. Out the side window, Eric could see its bizarre shadow racing across the scrub desert. It looked like something out of a science-fiction movie.

It took an hour for the plane to spiral up to altitude. Eric spent the time double-checking his equipment. Taggart merely sat quietly in his seat, playing a Game Boy flight simulator.

They were ten minutes early, according to Eric's timetable, so the plane carved lazy figure eights in the sky. High above them, the Soviet satellite was fast approaching. Unlike the Shuttle or the International Space Station that orbited parallel to the equator, the Orbital Ballistic Projectile weapon swept over the globe from pole to pole. In this way, it crisscrossed every square inch of the planet in fourteen days, as the earth revolved beneath it. It was currently over Wyoming, coming on at almost five miles per second. In its present orbital track, it wouldn't arrive over Eos Island for another week, which was why one of the signals Eric had to send was to fire its maneuvering rockets and change its vector. If everything went as planned, the satellite would be in range to fire one of its rods in less than eight hours.

"Coming up on T minus one minute," Eric heard Butterfield announce. "All boards are green."

"Roger that, Ground. Sixty seconds."

A timer on Eric's console began to click backward, while the digital speed indicator mounted on the dashboard remained pegged at four hundred miles per hour.

"Thirty seconds . . . Ten . . . Five, four, three, two, one. Go for separation."

The pilot aboard the mother ship released a lever that held 'Roo clamped to the aircraft's belly. The space plane fell free for a few moments, to get distance from Kanga, before Taggart toggled the liquid-rocket motor.

To Eric, it felt as if every one of his senses were assaulted at the same instant. The roar of the engine was like standing at the base of a waterfall, a palpable sensation that beat on his chest. The airframe's vibrations forced him to clutch the armrest while he was slammed back into his seat, as if by a giant fist. His body shook inside his skin so much it felt like someone was rubbing him with sandpaper. His mouth had gone dry from the dose of adrenaline sent shooting into his veins. Focusing hard on the speedometer, he saw that, in seconds, they were nearing the sound barrier.

The g-forces kept him pressed into his reclined seat, as Taggart pointed the nose ever higher, the vibrations getting progressively worse, and Eric feared the airframe would come apart in midair. And then they burst through the sound barrier. The vibrations diminished, and while he could still feel the thrust of the engine they were traveling faster than its throaty snarl, and it grew noticeably quieter.

One minute after the motor kicked in, they burst above a hundred thousand feet, and Eric was finally coming to grips with the ride. His heart rate slowed, and, for the moment, he let himself enjoy the space plane's raw power.

The airspeed gauge hit two thousand miles per hour and they still accelerated. Looking over his head, he noticed the sky darkening rapidly, as they roared up through the atmosphere. As if by magic, stars began to appear, faintly at first but brightening. He had never seen so many so clearly. Gone was the twinkle caused by their light passing through earth's atmosphere. They held steady, and their numbers swelled, until it looked as though space were made of light rather than darkness.

He knew if he stretched out his hand, he would be able to touch them.

The indicator in front of him suddenly flashed red. He couldn't believe four minutes could pass that quickly. Straining against the g's, he moved his hand over to the laptop.

"Ten seconds," he said on the frequency the *Oregon* was monitoring. If Hali replied, it was lost in the rocket's din.

The altimeter was still reeling off numbers in a blur. They hit three hundred and ninety-four thousand feet when the light went yellow, and, in those last five seconds, they rose another mile. The indicator turned green just as they hit the four-hundred-thousand-foot mark.

Eric typed in the command, as the rocket motor consumed the last of its fuel and the cyclonic pumps that fed it went quiet. The g-forces that had hammered him into his seat suddenly released him, and the silence left his ears ringing. They had gone weightless. He had often experienced moments of it on roller coasters, and on a few flights with Tiny Gunderson, when they were fooling around, but this felt different. They were on the very edge of space now, not playing tricks with gravity but almost out of its reach.

In the cockpit, Jack Taggart activated the armatures that raised the entire wing so it was at an angle to the fuselage. The added drag, and the dynamics of the new configuration, kept the plane incredibly stable, as it started its long glide back to the airfield outside of Monahans, Texas.

"What did you think?" he asked.

"Just a moment."

Taggart thought Eric might be sick and he craned around to look, but Stone was concentrating on his computer. The kid had just been given the ride of his life and he was already working. Taggart admired the dedication, thinking back to his first Shuttle mission. He hadn't been able to do anything but stare out the window his first hour up here.

"Repeat that, Elton. Over."

"I said, we've got confirmation from the bird's onboard telemetry. She has fired her maneuvering thrusters and is changing orbit. Targeting computers are online, and it's going through its prefire checklist. Congratulations. You did it!"

Eric didn't know if he wanted to shout for joy or cry. In the end, he settled for simple satisfaction that his plan was going to work. He had to give credit to the Russians. When it came to their space program, they knew what they were doing. Where NASA was all about elegant finesse, the Soviets had gone for simplicity and brute force, and, as a result, they built to last. Their *Mir* space station remained in orbit twice as long as originally planned. Had it not been for lack of funds, it would likely still be up there.

"Roger that. Over and out."

"Well?" Taggart asked.

"It worked. We now have control of the Russian satellite."

"I wasn't asking about that. I want to know what you thought of the flight."

"Colonel, that was the most amazing thing I have ever experienced," Eric said, feeling weight slowly returning to his body. His stomach settled back into its normal position.

"I know it won't go into the books, but, just so you know,

we broke the altitude record. We're going to limit our paying flights to about three hundred and thirty thousand feet, so it's a record that'll be around for a while."

Eric chuckled to himself, thinking how jealous Murph was going to be—and how impressed Janni would be. But, no sooner had the thought crossed his mind, the smile died on his lips, and he once again considered Max Hanley's fate.

CHAPTER 35

Max HAD RACKED HIS BRAIN, THINKING OF A WAY out of the subterranean fortress, and he had only one solution. On a late-night foray, he had discovered triple guards on the stairwell leading to the garage, and he knew that he wasn't going to bluff his way past them. Kovac had left his face a swollen mess, and the guards would be suspicious the moment they saw him.

He wasn't getting out the front door, so he had to sneak out the back.

He left his hiding place in the closet of the executive wing and made his way to the generator room. He made sure to hide his face from the few people he passed in the hallways. He rounded a corner nearest the room where the jet engines spun the turbines that powered the facility and saw that Kovac had ordered a guard to stand watch here as well. Keeping his pace steady and measured, he walked down the corridor. The guard, a kid of about twenty wearing a blue police-style uniform and with a nightstick in his belt, eyed him as he approached.

"How ya doing?" Max called jovially when he was still ten feet away. "Yeah, I know, my face looks like hamburger. A bunch of antiabortion zealots jumped me day before yesterday at a rally in Seattle. I just got here. Hell of a place, huh?"

"This is a restricted area unless you have a clearance badge." The kid forced authority into his voice by deepening it, but he didn't seem overly wary.

"Is that so? Only thing I've been issued so far are these." Max pulled his last two bottled waters from the pockets of his overalls. "Here."

Rather than offer it and give the kid an opportunity to refuse, he tossed a bottle to the guard. He caught it awkwardly and glared at Max. Max grinned stupidly and twisted off the cap of his bottle. He held it up in a salute.

Etiquette and thirst overcame the young guard's limited security training, and he pried off the lid and returned Max's salute. He raised the bottle to his lips and tipped his head back to take a swig. Max lunged like an Olympic fencer, ramming the stiffened fingers of his right hand directly into the soft spot at the base of the kid's throat.

Water spewed from his mouth as his airway swelled closed. He couldn't cough. He managed a gurgling sound, as his eyes bugged from his head and he clutched for his throat in a desperate attempt to get air. Max laid the guard out with a haymaker to the side of the jaw and he fell at his feet. He bent to check on his breathing. Now that the guard was unconscious, he stopped hyperventilating and could draw a little air through his damaged larynx. His voice would be a husky whisper for the rest of his life, but he'd live.

"If I were you, I'd ask for a refund from whatever security guard training school you went to."

Max opened the door to the generator room. The control room was deserted, and, by the looks of the displays, only one of the jet engines was making power. Max stuffed the young guard into the kneehole of a metal desk and manacled his wrists to the leg with his FlexiCuffs. He didn't need to worry about gagging him.

Hanley had already considered the idea of sabotaging the engines and denying the Responsivists the means of transmitting the signal but felt it would be a waste of time. He knew they had a fully charged battery backup in some part of the facility he hadn't seen, so they would still be able to send it. If he managed to find and somehow disable the batteries, all he would accomplish was a short delay until they could repair the damage. He'd maybe buy a few hours or days while giving away his presence. The reason they hadn't found him lurking in their headquarters was because they thought he was either dead or eluding them outside. As soon as they knew a saboteur was inside the bunker, the security contingent would comb it inch by inch until they found him.

He could just imagine how painful a death Kovac would have in store for him.

Max was certain Cabrillo had gotten the message and trusted without question that the Chairman had come up with a plan to destroy the transmitter long before Severance sent the signal. So he discounted the idea of sabotage and had dedicated his time to an escape plan.

The four engines were laid out in a row, with fat ducts feeding them air on one end and large exhaust pipes venting the spent gases from the other. Just before the ducts exited the room through the far wall, the four pipes came together in a manifold so that a single large exhaust duct led outside. There was a heat exchanger located just after the pipes came together to cool the gases leaving the facility. The air intake worked the same in reverse, with a single conduit entering the power plant and branching off to the separate turbines. Max would have preferred that route, but the plenums were ten feet off the floor and inaccessible without a scaffolding.

"If it's good enough for Juan, it's good enough for me," he muttered, thinking back to Cabrillo's escape from the *Golden Dawn*.

He found tools and ear protectors on a workbench at the back of the control room and slid open the door to the power plant's main floor. With his ears covered, the engine's whine remained at a tolerable threshold. Before he got to work, he checked a distinctive red cabinet. Without its contents, his escape attempt would kill him.

There was an access port on each of the four exhaust pipes that was secured with a ring of bolts. He got to work removing the three-inch-long bolts, taking care that none rolled away from him. He had taken apart his first engine at age ten and had never lost his love of machinery, so he worked swiftly and efficiently. He left one bolt in place but had loosened it so he could pivot the inspection hatch away from the hole. Although the engine fitted to this exhaust duct was silent, the fumes rising up from the pipe made his eyes swim.

He grabbed a handful of short, fat bolts from a drawer of spares in the control room. They were a fraction too small for the threaded holes, but they would more than pass a cursory inspection. When the turbine was fired up, the pressure would blow them out of the hatch like bullets, but that wasn't Max's problem. He replaced the tools back in the control room and checked on the unconscious guard to make sure he was still breathing.

The red cabinet contained firefighting gear—axes, heat detectors, and, most important, air tanks with masks. Because any fire that broke out in the generator room would most likely be fed by the jet's kerosene fuel, there were also two silvery one-piece metallic suits with hoods that would protect wearers from the tremendous heat.

Max had noticed all of this on his first foray into the generating room, and the discovery had been the genesis of his escape plan. He cut off one of the suit's hoods and slid into it, pulling the second one over him so that everything but his head was double insulated. There was enough play in the boots for his feet, barely. He carried two of the air cylinders to the open access port. His movements were awkward, like a robot from an old science-fiction movie. The tanks were fitted with armored hoses that jacked directly into the suit at hip level through a valve. He would have preferred carrying more air, but he wasn't sure if his battered body could heft the extra weight.

He shoved the tanks into the duct and climbed in after them. The fit was extremely tight, but once he wriggled his way past the manifold he would have more than enough room. Lying on his back, he was able to rotate the hatch closed and partially thread one of the bolts he'd removed into its hole to hold it in position.

After securing the hood of his outermost suit, he cracked open the air tank and took a breath. It tasted stale and metallic. Max had no idea how far the duct ran before reaching the surface, nor what he would find there once he got there, but he had no choice but to start climbing.

Pushing the tanks ahead of him, he squeezed himself forward a couple of inches. The pipe was a black so deep it felt like a presence in there with him, while the roar of the running turbine filled his head with echoes.

The pain in his chest wasn't too bad, a background ache to remind him of the beating. It wouldn't last, he knew, and very soon he'd be in real agony. Pain was a distraction, Linc had told him, passing on some of his SEAL training. It's your body's way of telling you to stop doing something. Just because your body is sending you a message doesn't mean you have to listen. Pain can be ignored.

He scraped over the heat exchanger's fins and moved into the manifold, where all four exhausts came together. Even with the protection of the suit, he could feel a blast of heat, as if he were standing at the open door of a glassblower's kiln. It would get much worse once he entered the main duct. The exhaust gases originated thirty feet away and had gone through a cooling device, yet it felt as though he were lying directly at the back of the engine nacelle.

The force of the exhaust was like a hurricane. Without the suits and the oxygen, Max would have been poisoned by the carbon monoxide and his body burnt to a crisp. Even with the double-thermal protection, sweat erupted from every pore in his body, and it was as though someone were holding a hot iron to his feet.

The main duct was nearly six feet around and rose at a slight angle. He struggled into the air tank's flame-retardant harness, keeping low, so as not to get blown off his feet. As he was gingerly pulling the straps over his shoulders, the foot he had placed atop the spare tank slipped. The stream of hot exhaust took hold of the tank, launching it down the pipe like a bullet from a gun. He could hear it, banging against the side of the conduit over the jet's banshee scream.

Max tried to walk, but the pressure against his back was simply too great. Each step was a precarious balancing act that threatened to send him careening down the pipe like the errant air tank. He dropped to his hands and knees, and began crawling blindly out of the bunker. The intense heat blistered his knees and hands through the high-tech suit and gloves, and the weight of the tank on his back made it so his ribs felt like shattered glass grinding inside his chest.

As he lurched farther up the duct, the earth encasing it bled away a lot of the heat. The force of the exhaust pummeling his backside and legs never diminished, but at least the broken blisters had stopped multiplying.

"Pain . . . can . . . be . . . ignored," he repeated, saying each word as he moved a limb.

• • •

JUAN ORDERED AN AERIAL DRONE to be launched as soon as the *Oregon* was within range of Eos Island. George "Gomez" Adams piloted the UAV from a console behind Cabrillo's seat. Only the Chairman and Hali were members of the first watch, the watch Juan always used when steaming into a potentially dangerous situation, and it wasn't as if the replacements were any less competent. He just preferred to have his people with him at a time like this. Eric and Mark and the others could anticipate his orders as if they could read his mind, shaving seconds off reaction times, seconds that could mean the difference between life and death.

Eddie was down in the boat garage, prepping the RIB, the Rigid Inflatable Boat, with Linc and the gundogs. There was only one dock on Eos, and they suspected it was heavily defended, but it might be their only way onto the island. The real-time video feed from the flying UAV would give them an idea of the defenses they might face. Down in the moon pool, the dive team was prepping the Nomad 1000, in case they needed the larger of their two submersibles, and laying out tanks and equipment for a ten-man underwater assault. Weapons crews had gone over every gun on the *Oregon*, ensuring they were cleaned and the ammo hoppers were full. Damage control reported they were prepped, and Julia was down in medical, if the worst happened and her services were needed.

Gomez and his hangar team had pulled double and triple shifts since Kyle Hanley's rescue, trying to get the plucky little Robinson helicopter airworthy again. The chopper jockey wasn't too happy with the results. Without a proper test, under controlled parameters, he couldn't guarantee the bird would fly. All the individual mechanical systems worked; he just couldn't say if they all worked together. The elevator had raised the helo to the main deck, and a technician kept the engine warmed to flight temperature, so it sat on five-minute standby, but Adams begged Cabrillo to use it as the absolute last resort.

Juan glanced at the digital countdown on the main view screen. They had one hour and eleven minutes to find Max and get his sorry butt off the island. In truth, they had less than that, because when the Orbital Ballistic Projectile slammed into Eos there was a good chance it would spawn a massive wave. Eric's calculations said that it would stay localized, and the topography of the sparsely populated Gulf of Mandalay would severely dampen its effect, but any ship within twenty miles of Eos was in for a wild ride.

The *Oregon* was fifteen miles from the island when its image from the UAV slowly resolved on the main monitor like a gray lump on the otherwise-brilliant seas that gave this part of Turkey the nickname Turquoise Coast.

George flew the drone over the eight-mile-long island at three thousand feet, high enough so its engine couldn't be heard, and, with the sun beginning a rapid slide into the west, it would be near impossible to see. Eos was nothing but barren rock and the occasional scrub pine. He focused the UAV's camera on where the Responsivists had built their bunker, but there was nothing to see. Any entrance remained well camouflaged, from this altitude. The only way to know it was even there was the paved road that terminated at the base of a low hillock.

"Hali, capture a couple stills off the feed and enhance them," Juan ordered. "See if you can find any doors or gates at the head of the road."

"I'm on it."

"Okay, George, swing us around. I want to check out the beach and dock."

Using his joystick, Adams banked the remote-controlled plane back over the sea so he could approach the dock from out of the sun. The beach stretched for only a few hundred feet, and, rather than soft white sand, it was composed of waterworn rock chips. Sheer cliffs rose more than a hundred feet on either side of the beach, hemming it in completely. The cliffs themselves appeared unassailable without climbing equipment and a few hours.

The dock was situated at the exact center of the beach, an L-shaped jetty that thrust into the water a good eighty feet before the seafloor fell away enough for the small freighters that had brought the equipment to build the facility. The causeway looked sturdy, and was more than wide enough for the excavators and cement mixers that had once swarmed the island. A corrugated-metal building sat where the jetty met the road. A parapet wrapped around the flat roof, giving a wide-open field of fire for anyone up there. They also had an unobstructed view of the sea approaches. A pickup truck was parked behind the guardhouse.

They could see two guards with high-powered binoculars on the roof, automatic weapons at their sides. Another pair of guards was walking the jetty, while two more patrolled the beach.

Any communication lines they had with the main facility were buried, so there was no way to knock them out in order to isolate the guardhouse. Juan imagined Zelimir Kovac had laid out the security, and he would have left standing orders that, at the first sign of anything suspicious, the bunker was to be notified so it could go on immediate lockdown.

"Switch to thermal imaging," he said.

The scene on the monitor changed, so that nearly every detail dropped out, except for the body heat given off by the guards. There were teams of two atop each cliff they hadn't noticed on the visual scan.

"What do you make of those trace signals next to the guys on the cliffs?" George asked.

"Small engines cooling down. Most likely ATVs similar to the ones they had in Corinth. Heck of a lot of fun to ride, provided no one's shooting at you."

Cabrillo was more interested in the signal emanating from the road. It was waste heat from their power plant, just as Eric had said. They had done an excellent job of masking the heat signature. To even the most trained observer, it looked like the road was merely radiating heat built up during the day. The dull-orange line on the thermal scan continued out along the jetty, before spreading nearly the width of the dock.

It had to be a diffuser, he thought, to further mask their heat signature.

He saw no sign of the air-intake manifolds.

Cabrillo hit an intercom button, so he could speak to Eddie and Linc, who had been watching the aerial reconnaissance on a monitor in the boat garage. "What do you think?"

He knew the answer, before Eddie replied, "We're going to pay a hell of a butcher bill, and there are no guarantees. Have you gotten any detailed shots of where the road ends?"

"Hali's working on it now."

"They're coming up on screen," Kasim said.

The enhanced stills flashed onto the monitor, and everyone eyed them carefully. The road simply stopped at the hill. They knew there had to be doors to allow entrance, but they were too well hidden.

"Depending how armored they are, we might be able to blast our way in," Eddie offered with little enthusiasm.

"We don't know if it'll take a couple of ounces of C-4 or a cruise missile."

"Then we use the Nomad, to get us in close to shore, and try to find the air intakes. We'll need a torch to cut our way out of the pipe, once we get inside," Eddie said. "I just wish we had more time to let the sun go down."

The orbital track of the Russian satellite had dictated the time of their assault, and there was nothing anyone could do about it. Juan looked at the clock again just as the hour display clicked to zero.

"What are those two guards on the dock doing?" George asked, after flipping the drone's cameras back to visual.

"Laying down on the job, it looks like," Juan remarked absently.

"I think there might be something in the water. I'm going to swing the UAV around for a better view."

WITHOUT LIGHT, Max had no way to determine how much air remained in the tank, but he estimated he had been crawling for twenty minutes. As much as he had tried to keep his breathing as shallow as possible, he knew he was using up the precious air at a prodigious clip, and there was no end in sight. The tunnel ahead was as inky as the length stretching out behind him.

Another ten minutes and he could feel it growing more difficult to breathe. The tank was approaching empty. Soon, he would be breathing the last of the air trapped in his suit, and then he would begin to suffocate. Spending so much of his life at sea, Max had always thought he'd die drowning. He had just never considered drowning in a vortex of noxious jet exhaust.

Doggedly, he plodded on, gaining a foot with each four-legged pace. The outer suit was a charred ruin, and pieces of it were tearing away, especially at the knee. Fortunately, the single layer of protection remaining was more than ample.

Kyle will be okay, he thought. He was certain that, no matter what, Juan would rescue his son again. And because of the fiasco the first time, he would use a different shrink to help deprogram his mind. The Chairman never made the same mistake twice, even if he didn't know what had caused it in the first place. Max even believed that he would figure out that it was Dr. Jenner who had betrayed them, though he knew Juan would never guess Jenner's true identity. He could hardly believe it himself.

Dying to rescue a child, he mused. He couldn't think of a single greater cause to die for. He hoped someday Kyle would come to recognize the sacrifice, and he prayed his daughter would forgive her brother for their father's death.

"Pain . . . can . . . be . . . ignored."

It felt as though he were climbing Everest. He needed to breathe as deeply as possible to suck in enough air, but each time he did his ribs screamed. And, no matter how deeply he inhaled, or how much he ached, his lungs never felt full.

His hand smacked something in the darkness. His engineer's sensibilities were instantly insulted. An exhaust shaft like this should be completely clear of obstructions in order to get peak efficiency out of the turbines. He felt around the object and gave a giddy laugh. It was the spare air tank that had been sent tumbling down the duct. In its mad flight up the exhaust vent, it had finally come to rest with its more aerodynamic top facing into the flow.

Max hurriedly unplugged his nearly depleted tank and jacked in the fresh one. The air was just as stale and metallic, but he could care less.

Fifteen minutes later, he saw the proverbial light at the end of the tunnel. The duct widened and flattened into a diffuser, to help mask the hot exhaust from thermal imaging. The stealth bomber and fighter used something similar. The pressure of hot exhaust diminished when he removed his tank and got on his belly to crawl into the diffuser. There were thin vertical bars over its mouth to prevent someone from entering the duct.

He could see the ocean surging about eight feet below him. It had to be high tide. Otherwise, water would pour down the exhaust duct when it came in. He imagined the vent had a cover that could be lowered in the event of a storm. Forcing the bulky helmet through the vertical bars proved impossible, so he had no idea what lay to the right or left of his position. He would just have to rely on luck.

He spun around so that he could ram one of the bars with the air tank. Lying on his side, he couldn't get that much momentum, so he pushed himself back a bit and tried again. He could feel the impact through his hands as he hit the grille again and again. Weakened by the combined effects of salt air and corrosive exhaust, a weld on one of the vertical bars snapped with the fifth blow. He repeated his assault on a second bar and then a third.

Satisfied he had enough room to squeeze through, he gripped each thin metal bar and bent it outward. He poked his head outside. There was a narrow platform immediately below the diffuser, and a ladder to his right that led upward. He was just turning to look to the left when he was grabbed by the shoulders and yanked out of the exhaust shaft. It happened so fast he had no time to react before he was thrown onto a dock. Two guards stood over him, each with a submachine gun slung under his arm. Unlike the kid Max had knocked unconscious back in the generator room, these two had the look of professionals.

"And just what do you think you're doing, mate?" The guard spoke with a thick cockney accent.

With the helmet on and his ears ringing from so much time spent in the duct, Max saw the guard's lips moving but couldn't hear the words. As soon as he moved to pull his helmet off, their fingers tightened on the triggers. One guard stepped back to cover his partner, who tore the helmet away. "Who are you?" he demanded.

"Hiya, fellas, I'm Dusty Pipes from the Acme Chimney Sweep Company."

CHAPTER 36

"IT'S MAX!" HALI CRIED, AS SOON AS HE SAW the guards haul a figure wearing a silver suit out of the exhaust vent.

Juan snapped around to look at George Adams. "Last resort. Let's go!"

The chopper pilot threw a toggle on his console that put the aerial drone into a mile-wide circle. It would maintain that pattern until someone took over the controls or it ran out of fuel. He swung the camera so it pointed directly at the dock and hit a button so it would track, to keep the dock in frame. "Giddy-up."

Cabrillo launched himself across the room, heading for a stairwell to the aft deck, the long-legged Adams barely keeping pace. Juan's mouth was set in a tight line, but his body was loose and relaxed. He was wearing black fatigues, with one of the flex-screen panels sewn onto a sleeve. He carried a pair of FNs, Five-seveNs, in kidney holsters, and another two slung from his hips. With the chopper's stability in question, he wasn't going to risk anyone else on a flight, so he purposefully overloaded himself with weapons. In his thigh pockets were four stick magazines for the Heckler and Koch MP-5 machine pistol already stowed in the Robinson.

"How'd he do it, ya wonder?" George said.

"I keep telling everyone, he's a crafty one." Juan turned on his combat radio. "Comm check. Do you read?"

"Right here," Hali replied.

"Helm, Wepps, do you copy?"

The man and woman manning the weapons station and the ship's helm control responded immediately.

"Wepps, I want you to take over control of the drone from

your console and fire up its laser designator. I'm going to use its camera to call out targets. When I laze 'em, open fire with the one-twenty."

The *Oregon*'s fire control was nearly as sophisticated as the Aegis battle space computer aboard a Navy cruiser. The small laser in the chin of the drone would light up a target, the computer could automatically calculate its exact GPS coordinates, raise or lower the ship's 120mm cannon, and send any number of types of rounds downrange.

"We need to close in on the island. Helm is taking us in now."

Juan activated his flex-screen panel. He could see Max still sprawled on the dock, but it wouldn't be long before they tossed him in the back of the pickup truck and drove him to the bunker.

With the *Oregon* pounding through the sea at flank speed, the wind across the deck was like a hurricane. Juan and George raced to the Robinson, where crewmen were holding open Adams's door. Juan's had been removed. They had caught a break. The engine had just been shut down, so when George fired it up again he could immediately engage the transmission and start the rotor spinning. Only after the blades were turning did he pull on a headset and strap himself in.

"Helm, this is Gomez. We're ready to fly. Decelerate now."

The *Oregon*'s pump jets cut out immediately, and then they were fired in reverse. It looked as though a torpedo had struck the bow when a gush of water exploded from the front end of the ship's drive tubes, as she went into an emergency stop. While most vessels her size needed miles to come to rest, the *Oregon*'s revolutionary propulsion system gave her the braking ability of a sports car.

When an electronic anemometer, placed on one corner of the elevator platform, indicated the wind speed had dropped to twenty miles per hour, George fed the chopper power and lifted off the deck.

"We're clear," he radioed as the skids whizzed over the stern rail.

The propulsors were reversed once again, and the *Oregon* began to accelerate back up to flank speed. The maneuver had been so well timed that they lost less than a minute.

"Well done," Juan said.

"They say practice makes perfect. 'Course, I always believed starting out perfect never hurt."

Cabrillo grinned. "Ego, thy name is Gomez."

"Chairman, this is Wepps. Computer says the one-twenty will be in range in eight minutes."

"Fire off a triple salvo of flares," Juan ordered. "Let Max know the cavalry's coming." He turned to George. "What's our ETA?"

"I didn't file a flight plan or anything. I don't know, five minutes maybe."

Juan had synchronized his digital combat watch with the master countdown for the Orbital Ballistic Projectile's impact. He had fifty-five minutes to rescue Max and get the *Oregon* out of the danger zone.

"ON YOUR FEET," the English guard snapped, and when Hanley was slow to cooperate he was kicked in the hip.

Max held out his hands like a supplicant. "Take it easy, boys. You got me fair and square. I'm not going anywhere. Let me just get this tank off and get out of this suit."

Had he been thinking clearer, Max realized he should have rolled into the water. The suit was airtight, and the weight of the oxygen cylinder would have made him sink like a stone. Something out to sea caught his attention. He squinted into the setting sun and saw a tiny white orb hovering next to it. Another burst just below. And then a third.

If a hunter is ever lost in the woods, the internationally recognized call is to fire three evenly spaced rounds to attract search parties. The flares weren't a distress call from a ship in trouble; it was Juan telling him the *Oregon* was here to rescue him.

He had never given up hope, so he really wasn't that surprised, but it took effort to keep a smug look off his face.

Max slowly shed the heavy tank and peeled off the tattered remains of his thermal-insulation suits. While the front of the outermost suit remained shiny silver, the back was blackened by heat and soot.

One of the guards was on his walkie-talkie, getting orders from a superior.

"Nigel, Mr. Severance wants to see this bloke right away. They're going to open the outer doors only when we arrive." He poked Max in the back with his gun. "Move it."

Max took a halting step and collapsed onto the dock. "I can't go on. My leg's all cramped from crawling out here. I can't feel it." He clutched his knee with the theatrics of a soccer player hoping to draw a foul on an opponent.

The guard named Nigel fired a single bullet into the dock inches from Max's head. "There. Bet it isn't so cramped now, eh?"

Max got the message and hoisted himself to his feet. He made a show of limping ahead of them as they started for shore, and when he slowed too much for their taste he was shoved in the back.

The black Robinson helicopter suddenly thundered around the headland like a raptor chasing prey and dove straight for the dock. George kept the nose down so the blades chewed the air a few feet above the timber jetty. Max was already on his stomach from the push and was joined by the guards, throwing themselves flat, as the chopper roared overhead.

Gunmen in observation posts on both cliff tops overlooking the beach opened fire, but Adams danced the helo like a boxer avoiding a jab. The men didn't have tracer rounds, so they couldn't correct in time to hit the bird.

"We've got to wait until they get him off the beach," Juan said. "They'll kill us with that cross fire."

With shadows lengthening, the only way to spot the guards patrolling the beach was by the muzzle flash of their automatic weapons, as they added their weight of fire to the melee.

On the dock, each guard grabbed one of Max's arms and dragged him toward shore, trusting their partners in the guardhouse and along the beach to keep the helicopter at bay. Max tried to fight them, but after the ordeal he'd been through his struggles were ineffective.

RACING OVER GREENLAND like a vengeful demon, the Soviet Orbital Ballistic Projectile satellite was going through the last of its systems checks as it prepared to launch one of its eighteen-hundred-pound tungsten rods. Inside the external case, the telephone-pole-sized projectile had been spun up to a thousand RPMs to give it stability for when it hit the atmosphere. The targeting computer, archaic by today's standards but more than sufficient for the task, waited, with single-minded focus, as the satellite hurtled toward the proper coordinates.

A tiny burst of compressed gas vented from one of its maneuvering rockets when it detected the need for a minute course correction. The cover over the launch tube slowly peeled open, like the petals of a flower, and, for the first time in its life, the tungsten core was exposed to the vacuum of space.

It continued to streak over the earth, as the planet rotated below it, every second bringing it closer to its firing position with no regard to the drama playing out below.

"Chairman, Wepps," Juan heard over his tactical radio. "We are in range."

"Lay an antipersonnel round on the eastern cliff," Cabrillo ordered.

Eight miles out to sea, the autofeeder for the L44 selected the desired round from stores and rammed it into the cannon's breach. The gun was located in the *Oregon*'s bow, in a hidden redoubt, giving it a nearly one-hundred-and-eighty-degree traverse when its carriage was fully extended. The outside doors had already been lowered and the barrel run out. Deep inside the ship, the targeting computer recognized the laser pip beamed at the top of the cliff by the drone and instantly calculated its position relative to the cannon. The barrel came up to the right elevation, and, when the bow rose on a wave, the big gun bellowed.

The computer was so accurate, it fired an instant early to account for the microseconds it took for the round to leave the barrel and the distance the earth would rotate while the projectile was in flight.

Ten seconds after leaving the gun, the shell split open, releasing a metal storm of hardened pellets that hit the top of the cliff like a massive shotgun blast. Clouds of dust exploded off the cliff, and somewhere within the choking pall were the minced remains of the two Responsivist guards.

"Nice shot," Juan called. "Now the west."

The men carrying Max dropped him when the headland disintegrated, and he scrambled to his feet to start running. He only managed a few steps before he was hit by a flying tackle and smeared into the rough asphalt road. Cursing incoherently, a guard clubbed him in the back of the head, and, for a moment, it was as if the sun had been snuffed out. Max fought the curtain of darkness and willed himself to remain conscious.

A second explosion rolled across the beach as another round detonated. It hit just below the snipers' den and did nothing more than pock the stone with a thousand tiny pits.

"I know, I know," Wepps called, and, twelve seconds later, the western cliff was obliterated.

The guards threw Max into the back of a pickup, the one pressing Max's head to the floorboard with a submachine gun while Nigel jumped behind the wheel. They had gone no more than fifty feet when the guardhouse took a direct hit from a high-explosive shell. The corrugated-metal building blew apart at the seams, blossoming with orange fire like a deadly rose. The concussion rocked the pickup forward, and, for a moment, Nigel lost control, but he fought the wheel and kept on the road.

The two guards remaining on the beach must have thought a retreat had been called, because they hopped onto their ATVs and chased after the pickup.

George swung the Robinson around and came up behind the three vehicles, keeping to their right to give Juan a clear line of sight.

"Wepps, lay in an AP directly in the road ahead of that truck and keep firing ahead of them to keep them slowed." The reply was lost in a staccato burst as Cabrillo opened up with his HK.

The ATV driver he'd targeted swerved but kept going. Juan was an expert shot, but firing from a moving chopper at a moving target was next to impossible. The guy fired back, onehanded, and the stream of bullets came close enough to the chopper that George had to momentarily break off the chase.

The road a hundred feet ahead of the hurtling pickup suddenly vanished, as the depleted uranium core of an armor-piercing round slammed into the earth. Juan had specifically called for AP, because any other projectile in their arsenal would have torn the truck to shreds.

The driver slammed the brakes and cranked the wheel hard over. The road lay in a shallow defile, and the tires spun as he tried to claw the vehicle out.

Cabrillo saw his chance. "George, now!"

The pilot spun the helo and dove after the pickup. The guard holding Max went to raise his weapon, but Max kicked at him, forcing him to contend with his prisoner. With no time to ram a fresh magazine into his machine pistol, Juan tossed it into the back of the chopper and pulled off his safety harness.

Dust kicked up by the whirling blades partially obscured Juan's target, but he could see well enough, as George dropped their airspeed to match the pickup's as it neared the crest of the hill.

Juan didn't hesitate. He leapt when they were ten feet above the truck. The second guard had pounded on the pickup's roof to warn Nigel as soon as he saw a figure leaning out of the helicopter and Nigel turned the wheel.

Cabrillo landed on the edge of the pickup's bed, and as his knees bent to absorb the brutal impact, the momentum of the pickup's turn started throwing him bodily out of the vehicle. He scrambled to grab the guard but couldn't, and he just managed to snag his fingers over the bed as he tumbled back. His legs were left dragging against the ground as he attempted to pull himself back into the truck.

The guard's leering face suddenly loomed above him. Cabrillo let go with his right hand to draw one of his automatic pistols but wasn't fast enough. He had his hand on the weapon when the guard punched the tips of Juan's left fingers so hard that they opened automatically.

Cabrillo hit the ground hard and rolled with the impact, tucking his body into a ball to protect his head. He came to a stop as the pickup reached the top of the hill and started accelerating away.

He got to his feet with a curse, a bump to the back of his

neck leaving him momentarily stunned. He shook cobwebs from his mind and looked skyward to wave George in to pick him up. Flying up from the road came the two ATVs, their drivers needing both hands on the handlebars to keep the vehicles steady on the hill's rocky surface.

The range was extreme, but he couldn't risk them opening up at him with their automatic weapons. Juan drew the two Five-seveNs from the hip holsters and laid down a barrage at the driver coming up on the right. The guns barked as he torched off twenty rounds in less than six seconds. Eight of the rounds hit the guard, pulping his internal organs and blowing away half his skull.

Cabrillo dropped the two smoking pistols, drew his second pair from behind his back, and started blasting again even before the corpse of the first guard tumbled off the quad bike.

The remaining guard drove with one hand, as he reached for the AK-47 slung over his back. He kept charging, even with the air around him coming alive with bullets. He managed to get off a few shots before he took his first hit, a glancing shot that carved a trench through his outer thigh. He fired again, but it was as though his target didn't care.

Juan didn't flinch as rounds whipped past him. He calmly kept firing until he found his mark. Two rounds triggered in the time it takes to blink hit the rider in the throat, the kinetic impact tearing the last remaining bits of tendon and sinew so that his head fell off the stump of his neck. The ATV continued climbing the hill, like a modern version of Washington Irving's headless horseman. When it reached Cabrillo, he lashed out with his foot to kick the body off the saddle seat. The dead fingers still gripping the throttle released, and the machine slowed to an idle.

Cabrillo jumped aboard and took off after Max, hitting the crest of the hill so fast he caught air. The truck had gained a quarter mile on him, but when another armor-piercing sabot round blasted the rock ahead of it the driver veered sharply and gave Juan a chance to cut his lead.

CHAPTER 37

MARK MURPHY HAD NEVER FELT WORSE. HIS nose was red and painful to touch, but he kept having to blow it, so it felt like it would never heal. To make things worse, he was a serial sneezer. If he did it once, he'd do it four or five times in a row. His head felt stuffed to the bursting point, and every breath sounded like there were marbles rattling in his chest.

If there was one thought to give him comfort, it was that misery loves company, because nearly everyone on the *Golden Sky* was in a similar condition. Linda Ross's symptoms were only slightly less severe than his, but she hadn't escaped the viral infection that swept the ship like wildfire. Every few seconds, she'd shiver with a bout of chills. Most every passenger remained huddled in their cabin, while the galley pumped out gallons of chicken soup and the medical staff passed around handfuls of cold tablets.

They were alone in the library, sitting opposite each other, and holding books on their laps in the off chance anyone wandered in. Both had tossed wads of used tissues on the nearest coffee table.

"I now understand why they chose to release the virus on a cruise ship."

"Why?"

"Look at us. For one thing, we're basically trapped here like rats, stewing in our own juices. Everybody gets exposed and remains exposed until they catch the bug. Second, there's only a doctor and a nurse. With everyone getting sick at the same time, they're overwhelmed. If these terrorists hit a city, there are plenty of hospitals to help and therefore much less exposure time for people to infect others. An outbreak could be isolated and the victims quarantined pretty quickly."

"That's a good point," she said idly, too miserable to become engaged in conversation.

A few minutes later, Murph said, "Let's go over it one more time."

"Mark, please, we've done it a thousand times already. It isn't the air-conditioning or water systems, it's not in the food or anywhere else we've checked and double-checked. It's going to take a team of engineers, tearing this tub apart piece by piece, to find the disbursal device."

Murph had been unable to come up with the solution without the distraction of the cold racking his body, and he really held little hope that it would come to him now, but he wasn't one to give up.

"Come on, Linda. Think. This is basically a floating city, right? What does it take to run a city?" She gave him a look that said she wasn't interested in playing his game, so he answered his own question. "Food, water, septic, garbage removal, and electricity."

"Yes, they're going to poison the garbage."

He ignored her sarcasm. "Or let's look at this another way. A cruise ship is a hotel. What do you need to run a hotel?"

"The same things," Linda said, "Plus little mints on your pillow at night."

"You're not helping."

"I'm not trying to."

Mark suddenly shot forward in his seat. "You got it!"

"Poisoned mints?" she said archly.

"Who brings the mints?"

"A maid."

"And what is she doing in your room in the first place?"

"Cleaning up and changing the . . . Holy God!"

"I remember back in Greece when we rescued Max's kid. They had a bunch of industrial washing machines but no dryers," Murph said. "They were training. The virus is introduced in the laundry. Passengers get fresh sheets every day. And if that doesn't expose them to the virus enough, there are fresh napkins in the dining rooms as well as in the crew's mess. How perfect is that? Wiping your mouth with a tainted napkin is as effective as giving someone a shot of the stuff. I bet within twelve hours of it being introduced into the washing machines, everyone on board comes into contact with viral-laden linens."

He clamped his hands over his head. "Why didn't I think of this sooner? It is so obvious."

"It's only obvious after you think of it. Kind of like finding something in the last place you look," Linda teased, throwing Mark's words back at him. She slowly levered herself to her feet. "Let's go see if you're right."

THE QUAD BIKE WAS DESIGNED to handle rough terrain, with its extra-large shocks and springs, but Juan was pushing the four-wheeler to its very limits as he chased after the pickup. With shells impacting scant feet ahead of it, its driver was forced to keep an erratic track, and Juan made up the lost ground quickly.

"Chairman, it's Hali. This is the forty-five-minute warning. Repeat, impact in forty-five-minutes."

"I hear you," Juan said. They were now cutting into their margin of safety to clear out of the strike zone. "I just wish I hadn't. Wepps, I want you to hold fire. George, I need you to distract the guy in the back of the truck so I can get close. Buzz them."

"Roger."

With a knee pressing him to the pickup's bed and the barrel of an assault rifle jammed in his neck, Max had no idea what was happening around him. The gun was suddenly pulled away, and the guard fired a short burst. Max turned his head enough to see that he was firing into the sky. The Robinson suddenly flew over the truck, so low that the guard had to duck.

Max used the distraction to ram an elbow into the guy's groin. The blow was clumsy and awkward and didn't seem to slow the man at all. He whipped the gun around, and Max blocked it with his arm so that, when it discharged, the bullets sailed harmlessly into the darkening sky. Eyes burning from the spent gunpowder, Max saw his opportunity and punched the guard's exposed flank. The guard counterpunched Max in the face. The renewed agony seemed to goad Hanley and he went into a rage, swinging wildly, and slowly getting up to his knees to get more power behind his punches.

The pickup's bed was too confined for the guard to bring his assault rifle to bear, so he used it to shove Max off of him. Hanley went down, sweeping out his leg to knock the gunman on his butt. Max stood shakily, clutching the side of the truck to keep himself steady.

Juan was not more than two feet from the pickup's rear bumper, on an all-terrain vehicle. He was hunched low over the handlebars so the driver couldn't see him. Max could see Juan's lips moving, as he spoke to either George, still circling overhead, or someone on the *Oregon*.

Max jumped the supine guard like a professional wrestler, only the elbow he smashed into the man's gut wasn't for show. The guard's eyes bulged from his head, and his cheeks expanded as every bit of air in his lungs exploded out of his body.

A few seconds later, another round from the ship's main gun hit just in front of the pickup truck. The driver slowed and veered left, giving Juan a chance to pull up alongside the vehicle.

"Max, stop screwing around and jump!" Juan shimmied forward on his seat to give Hanley as much room as possible.

Max crawled over the rear gate to crouch on the bumper. He reached out with a leg, getting it over the saddle seat before throwing his weight. He landed solidly, clutching at Juan's waist to keep himself firmly planted.

Nigel, the English guard driving the truck, chose that moment to look in his rearview mirror. Realizing the prisoner was escaping, he swerved toward the ATV, forcing Juan to slam on the brakes. Nigel jammed on his, and then when the ATV started to scoot away he went after it.

With two big men astride the quad bike, the vehicles were evenly matched for speed over the rough ground. Juan couldn't pull more than a few feet ahead of the pickup, and, no matter how sharply he turned, the driver kept with him. The Responsivist had to have realized that if he stayed close to the fleeing four-wheeler, the big cannon targeting him wouldn't fire.

"He's toying with us," Juan spat, glancing over his shoulder to see the truck's flat grille less than five yards from their rear wheels. "And we don't have time for this. By the way, it's good to see you, and, boy, is your face a mess."

"Good to see you, too," Max yelled over the wind. "And it feels worse than it looks."

"Hold on," Juan warned, and sent the ATV over the hill that led back to the road. They roared down it at a breakneck pace, Juan turning the handlebars so that the bike skidded onto the macadam. He cranked the throttle, as the pickup fishtailed behind them.

They gained fifty feet, tempting Juan to call in a shot from the *Oregon,* but the pickup was much faster than the ATV on the smooth road and closed up the gap again before he could issue the order.

"Wepps, prepare to fire HE at the end of the dock."

"Standing by."

"What are you doing?" Max called anxiously.

"Plan C."

They flew down the road, although not at the ATV's top speed. Cabrillo needed to keep a little in reserve. They shot past the still-flaming ruin of the guardhouse, threading around smoldering sheets of corrugated metal. Juan hit the dock and opened the throttle as far as it would go, expertly judging speed, distance, and time.

"Fire."

The pickup's driver hung back, not understanding why the ATV would intentionally corner itself on the pier, but when he realized it wasn't slowing he hit the gas to keep close.

"George," Juan shouted into his radio. "Prepare to pick us up in the water."

The pilot replied something that was lost to the wind.

Juan and Max rocketed down the length of the dock, coming up on fifty miles an hour.

Max finally realized what Juan was doing and shouted, "You crazy son of a biiiii . . ."

They flew off the end of the dock, sailing out almost twenty feet, before splashing into the sea. An instant later, the pickup screeched to a halt in a four-wheel drift that almost flipped it on its side. Before the truck fully settled on its suspension, the door flew open and the guard raised his assault rifle, wanting nothing more than to kill the two men as soon as they surfaced.

The high-pitched whistle lasted less than a second, giving the guard no time to react.

The explosive shell actually hit the dock and not the truck, but it hardly mattered. Both were disintegrated by the blast, sending debris arcing across the sea.

Juan helped Max claw his way to the surface. He spat out a mouthful of water and surveyed the damage behind them. Half of the dock was simply gone, while the rest had become splintered timber and destroyed pilings.

"Was that strictly necessary?" Max grumbled.

"Remember me telling you about one of my first missions with the Company?"

"Something about a Russian satellite."

"An Orbital Ballistic Projectile weapon." Juan pulled his arm out of the water to check his watch. "It's going to obliterate this island in thirty-eight minutes. I, for one, want to be as far from here as possible."

The Robinson R44 was trailing smoke when it appeared over the cliff, beating its way to the dock. That must have been what George had tried to tell us, Juan thought, that their helo was damaged. Adams deftly swung the chopper over the two men, hovering just above them, the downdraft kicking up a choking mist of roiled seawater. He came down even lower, until the skids were awash. Juan reached up to open the door and helped Max clamber into the chopper. It dipped dangerously as his weight upset the center of balance.

He was about to follow Hanley when a stream of autofire bracketed the helo.

"Go!" he shouted, and clutched the skid.

George didn't need to be told twice. He revved the engine and tore away from the dock, where another pickup truck had appeared with two men in its bed, hammering away at them with AKs.

Hanging by his arms and legs like an ape, Juan clung to the Robinson's skid for all he was worth. The wind buffeting him was brutal, and his wet clothes felt like ice, but there was nothing he could do about it. The *Oregon* was only a couple miles out, and he didn't want George to slow down for him to climb into the cabin.

Adams must have radioed ahead about the situation, because every light on the ship was ablaze and extra crewmen were on deck to assist in the landing. The helmsman had already turned the bow away from Eos Island, and the old girl was under way.

George gave himself plenty of clearance as he came over the fantail. He ignored the warning lights flashing and horns sounding in the cockpit that indicated his beloved chopper was in her death throes. He imagined the oil burning away in the overheated transmission, as he gently reduced his altitude.

Juan let go of the skid when he was just above the waiting hands of the deck crew. They caught him easily and lowered him to his feet. They scrambled out of the way to give Adams the room he needed to set the Robinson on the deck.

"Helm, flank speed," Juan ordered the instant the skids kissed the pad. "Sound general quarters and rig the ship for collision."

Adams killed power as soon as he felt the skids bump down, but the damage was already done. Flames erupted from the engine cowling and around the rotor mast. Crewmen were standing by with fire hoses, and he and Max jumped from the chopper amid a torrent of spray.

George looked back when he was a safe distance away, his handsome face drawn. He knew the chopper was a total loss.

Juan clamped a hand on his shoulder. "We'll get you a shiny new one."

They went inside before the wind became too strong. In the *Oregon*'s wake, Eos Island crouched in the sea, an unsuspecting ugly lump of rock that was not long for this world.

CHAPTER 38

Thom Severance wasn't sure what to do. The guards at the dock had reported capturing Max Hanley as he tried to escape the facility through the exhaust vent, of all things, and then they said they were being attacked by a black helicopter. For a brief instant, he feared the UN was behind the assault, what with rumors of their squadrons of black choppers. He caught a few snippets of garbled conversation over the walkie-talkie and then everything had gone silent. The cameras mounted atop the guardhouse were out, so he finally ordered a vehicle to check out the dock.

"They escaped, Mr. Severance," the guard captain reported. "Hanley and another man in the chopper. The guardhouse has been destroyed and so has the dock. A lot of my guys are missing."

"Are there any more of them?"

"I've got patrols sweeping now. So far it appears as if it was just the one man."

"One man killed all your guards and destroyed the dock?" he said doubtfully.

"I have no other explanation."

"Very well, continue checking, and report anything out of the ordinary immediately."

Severance raked his fingers through his hair. Lydell Cooper's final orders had been very specific. He wasn't to send the signal for another two hours. But what if this had been the vanguard of a much larger assault? To delay might mean failure. On the other hand, if he sent the signal early it could mean that not all the virus had been attached to the feed lines of the laundry machines on all fifty cruise ships.

He wanted to call his mentor, but this was a decision he

felt he should make on his own. Lydell was en route with Heidi and her sister, Hannah. They wouldn't arrive until after the virus was released. He had had full control of the Responsivist movement for years, and, yet, like a son taking over a family business, he knew that he was under a constant microscope and wasn't truly in charge at all. He never forgot that Lydell could override any decision he made, without warning or explanation.

He had chafed at that a little, not that Cooper interfered much. But now with the stakes so high, he wished he had that safety net of being told what to do.

What would it matter if they missed a couple of ships? Lydell's calculations of the disease's vector only called for forty shiploads of people in order to infect everyone on the planet. The extra ten were insurance. When questioned why some of the ships escaped infection, he could claim the dispersal devices failed. And if they all worked, no one would ever know.

"That's it," he said, slapping his thighs and getting to his feet.

He strode into the ELF transmitter room. A technician in a lab coat was bent over the controls. "Can you send the signal now?"

"We aren't scheduled to send it for another couple of hours."

"That isn't what I asked." Now that his decision had been made, Severance's haughtiness had returned.

"It will take me a few minutes to double-check the batteries. The power plant is off-line because of the damage to the exhaust system."

"Do it."

The man conferred with a colleague deep beneath the facility using an intercom, speaking in arcane scientific jargon that Severance couldn't follow.

"It will just be another moment, Mr. Severance."

THE RUSSIAN SATELLITE'S electronic brain marked time in minute fractions as it streaked over Europe at seventeen thousand miles per hour. The trajectory had been calculated to the hundredth of an arc second, and when the satellite hit its mark a signal was sent from the central processor to the launch tube. There was no sound, in the vacuum of space, as an explosive gush of compressed gas blasted the tungsten rod out of the tube. It was pointed almost straight down, and it began its fiery trip to earth, descending at a slight angle, as its builders had designed, so it could be confused with an incoming meteor. Hitting the first molecules of the upper atmosphere created friction that merely warmed the rod. The lower it fell, the more the heat built, until the entire length of the rod glowed red, then yellow, and, finally, a brilliant white.

The heat buildup was tremendous but never approached tungsten's melting point of over three thousand degrees Celsius. Observers on the ground could see the rod clearly, as it hurtled across Macedonia and the northern Greek mainland, leaving sonic booms in its wake.

THE DIGITAL CLOCK on the main monitor was into the single digits. Juan had avoided looking at it before Max's rescue but now couldn't tear his eyes off of it. Max had refused treatment in the medical bay until after the impactor hit Eos, so Hux had brought her kit up to the Op Center and was working on his injuries. The seas were smooth enough for her to do her job, even though the *Oregon* was charging eastward at top speed.

Max usually had a sarcastic comment about Juan running his engines above the red line, but he knew full well what was coming and kept it to himself. They weren't yet at the minimum safe distance from the blast, and if the Chairman thought getting out and pushing would help he'd do it.

Hali Kasim tore his earphones off his head with a curse.

"What is it?" Juan asked anxiously.

"I'm picking up a signal on the ELF band. It's from Eos. They're sending the trigger code."

Cabrillo paled.

"It's going to be okay." Max's voice sounded nasal because of the cotton balls stuffed in his battered nose. "The wavelengths are so long, the full code will take a while to broadcast."

"Or they could release the virus at the first sign of an ELF signal," Hali said.

Juan's palms were slick. He hated the thought that they had come so far only to fail at the eleventh hour. He wiped his hands on his wet pants. There was nothing he could do but wait.

He hated to wait.

WEARING THEIR CUSTODIAL UNIFORMS, Linda and Mark prowled the lower decks of the *Golden Sky* once again, trying to remember where the ship's laundry was located. There were only a few crewmen roaming around, and each was too lost in his own suffering to question two unfamiliar faces.

The whine of dryers spooling up drew them to their destination. Steam billowed from the dimly lit room. None of the Chinese workers looked up from their duties when the two stepped inside the laundry.

A man leaning just inside the door that they hadn't seen grabbed Linda's arm in a tight grip.

"What are you doing here?" he challenged.

She tried to yank her arm free. Mark recognized the guy as one of the men who had arrived by helicopter with Zelimir Kovac. He should have known they would post a guard. He moved to intercede, and the man drew a pistol and pressed it against Linda's temple.

"One more step and she's dead."

The laundry workers were well aware of what was happening but went about their business of transferring clothes, folding sheets, and pressing shirts.

"Take it easy," Mark had backed up a couple of paces. "We have a work order for a busted clothes press."

"Show me your ID badges."

Mark plucked his ID from the front of his overalls. Kevin Nixon hadn't known the exact design the Golden Line used for their employee identification cards, but it was a good fake, and he doubted Kovac's henchmen would know the difference. "See. Right here. I'm Mark Murphy."

Kovac suddenly appeared, his bulky body practically filling the doorframe.

"What is this?"

"These two claim to be here to fix something."

The Serb pulled an automatic from inside his windbreaker. "I gave the captain express orders that no one other than the laundry workers are to enter this room. Who are you?"

"It's finished, Kovac," Linda said, her girlish voice icy hard. She could tell using his name had startled him. "We know all about the virus and how you spread it using the washing machines on cruise ships. As we speak, your people are being rounded up on ships all over the world. The devices are being removed. Give it up now and you might see the outside of a prison again."

"I doubt that very much, young lady. Kovac is not my real name." He mentioned another, one that had been all over the news during the Yugoslav war. It was the name of one of the worst mass murderers to ever come out of the conflict. "So you see, I don't believe I would ever be allowed out of prison."

"Are you totally out of your mind?" Mark asked. "You're willing to die for this stupid cause of yours? I was aboard the *Golden Dawn*. I saw what your virus does to people. You're a freak."

"If that's what you think, then you don't know everything. In fact, I think the two of you are bluffing. The virus loaded in those"—he swept his hand to indicate the massive washing machines—"isn't the same I used on the *Golden Dawn*. It was created from the same strain, but this one isn't deadly. We are not monsters."

"You just admitted killing almost eight hundred people and you say you're not a monster?"

Kovac actually smiled. "Very well. Dr. Lydell Cooper isn't a monster. The virus we are about to release will cause nothing more than a bad fever, only there is one small side effect. Sterility. In a few months, half of the world's population is going to discover that it can't have children."

Linda felt like she was going to throw up. Mark actually swayed on his feet when he grasped the insidious nature of their plot. Responsivists were always going on about how the planet was doomed because of overpopulation. Now they were planning on doing something about it.

"You can't do this," Linda cried.

Kovac leaned his face in inches from hers. "It is already done."

THE GUARDS SEARCHING Eos Island stopped their work and gazed heavenward. What at first looked like a particularly bright star quickly grew in size and intensity until it seemed to fill the entire sky. And what started as mild unease quickly exploded into panic, as the object plunging from space appeared to be aimed at the island. They ran, for when faced with danger it is what instinct compels humans to do, but it made no difference. There was no escape.

Down in the transmitter room, Thom Severance tapped his foot impatiently against a table leg as the display in front of him showed the agonizingly slow pace of the ELF signal being sent around the globe. In a few minutes, it would be done. The first of the virus would flood out of its vacuum-sealed containers and into the washing machines where it would contaminate the sheets, towels, and napkins. That precise amount of virus would be released into each load of laundry, thereafter, until the dewars were emptied.

A faint smile lifted the corners of his mouth.

The tungsten projectile hit Eos Island almost dead center, three miles from the subterranean base. Its tremendous speed and weight turned the potential energy of falling two hundred miles into the kinetic energy of a massive explosion.

The center of the island blinked out of existence. The rock was torn apart at the molecular level, so there remained virtually no trace of it at all. As the blast rippled outward, it sent a shock wave through the island that heaved hundreds of tons of rubble into the air. Much of the rock was melted into glowing globules of lava that snapped and hissed when they plunged into the cool sea.

The panicked guards were carbonized, their ashes mixing with the dust and debris.

When the shock wave hit the facility, the hardened ferro-concrete used in its construction cracked like fine porcelain. The building didn't collapse but rather was uprooted and thrown out of the ground. Walls, ceilings, and floors pancaked on themselves, crushing everyone inside. The destruction was

absolute. The miles of thick copper wire that was the ELF
antenna were ripped from the earth and melted into streams
of liquid metal that poured into the ocean.

The earth shook so fiercely that huge slabs of cliff face
sheared away, and cracks spidering out from the impact's
epicenter split the island into seven smaller ones.

A massive tidal wave surged off Eos in the direction the
Orbital Ballistic Projectile had been traveling. Unlike a tsunami, which travels below the surface and grows in height
only as it shoals, this was a solid wall of water with a frothing
crest that seemed to curl forever. It roared as though the gates
of hell had been thrown open and raced across the sea at as-
tronomical speeds. The wave wouldn't last. Friction would
eventually reduce its size until it wasn't even a ripple, but, for
as long as it lasted, it was the most destructive force on the
planet.

Forty miles away, the *Oregon* was racing with everything
she had. All her hatches had been doubly secured. Her two
submersibles had been lowered into their cradles and lashed
down. Every loose object the crew could think of had been
stuffed into closets and drawers. They knew they weren't going to get out of this without some damage, but they wanted
to keep it to a minimum.

"Time till impact?' Juan asked.

"I estimate five minutes," the helmsman reported.

Juan hit the button for the shipwide PA system. "This is
the Chairman. Everyone hold on tight. We're in for a wild
ride. Five minutes."

The mast-mounted camera was turned aft and switched to
night vision mode so they could watch the wave coming at
them. It filled the sea from horizon to horizon, impenetrable,
implacable. Its face was veined with emerald lines of phos-
phorus, and its crest looked like green fire.

"I have the conn," Juan said suddenly, and took command
of his ship.

He had noticed they were running from the wave at a slight
angle and gave the *Oregon* a bit of rudder by way of correction.
If they were going to ride this out, they needed to take the hit
directly on the stern. Any deviation and the five-hundred-plus-

foot ship would auger into the wave and roll a dozen times before being released from its grip.

"Here we go!"

It was like an express elevator. The stern came up so fast that, for a moment, there was no water under her middle. The sound of the hull's moaning was lost in the savage roar of the wave. The bow plunged into the sea. Juan cut power to keep her from burying her prow, and then the entire ship was dragged up the face of the wave. The acceleration sent everyone lurching forward. The ship climbed the wave, her bow pointing down at a dizzying angle. Juan glanced at their speed through the water, which was down to four knots, but their speed over bottom was nearly seventy miles an hour.

The stern burst through the wave's crest in an explosion of froth that swamped the decks. Water sluiced from the scuppers in sheets and blasted from the drive tubes in solid white jets. Thirty, forty, fifty feet of the *Oregon*'s stern hung suspended over the back of the wave before she began to tip. And then she went over, falling faster than when she'd been plucked off the surface.

Cabrillo fire-walled the engines, asking his ship to give him everything she had. When they hit the bottom of the wave, her stern would knife through the surface, and if the *Oregon* didn't have enough power she would simply keep going until the ocean closed over her bow.

With the ship at an almost sixty-degree angle, the fantail splashed into the rough water in the wave's trailing edge, and vanished. The sea climbed over the rearmost cargo hatch, and, had it not been for the thick rubber seals, the helicopter hangar under it would have swamped.

"Come on, girl," Juan cajoled, watching the water claim more and more of his ship. "You can do it."

The angle began to flatten out as the bow came off the wave, and the *Oregon*'s plunge into the abyss seemed in check. For a long moment, she neither sank nor rose out of the water. The vessel shuddered with the strain of her engines trying to deadlift eleven thousand tons from the sea's crushing embrace. And slowly, so slowly at first that Juan wasn't sure he was seeing it right on the monitors, the deck began to clear.

The leading edge of the stern hatch appeared as the magneto-hydrodynamics thrust her out of what should have been her watery grave.

Cabrillo finally joined the chorus of whistles and cheers when he saw the sodden Iranian flag hanging off her jack staff. He eased off the power and turned control back over to the helmsman.

Max sidled up to his chair. "And I thought you were crazy jumping an ATV off a dock. Any other ship would have turtled on a wave like that."

"This isn't any other ship," Juan said, and patted Max's arm. "Or any other crew, for that matter."

"Thank you," Max said simply.

"I've got one of my wayward children home. It's time to get the other two."

CHAPTER 39

Kovac knew there was trouble when he tried to reach Thom Severance from the *Golden Sky*'s radio room and got no response. He didn't even get a ring.

With the radios switched off, on Kovac's orders, it wasn't until twenty minutes later that word reached the ship from a satellite-news broadcast. A meteor had been spotted streaking across southern Europe. Estimated at weighing a ton, it had hit an island off the coast of Turkey. A tsunami alert had been issued, but there was only one report from a Greek ferry about a wave, and it was said to be only a few feet high and presented no danger.

He knew it was no meteor. It had to have been an atomic bomb. His two prisoners hadn't been lying at all. The American authorities knew about their plan and had authorized a nuclear strike. The light people had seen streaking southward across Europe must have been from the cruise missile that delivered the warhead.

Kovac hit the MUTE button on the television remote to cut out the anchorwoman's speculative blather. He had to consider his options. If they had sent operatives to the *Golden Sky,* they must have known he was on the ship. No, that logic wasn't right. He was here because he suspected they were aboard first. So they didn't know where he was. His solution, then, was simple: kill his two captives and leave the ship when it made its scheduled call on Iraklion, the Cretan capital.

"But they'll be waiting," he muttered.

Whoever sent the two Americans—the CIA, most likely, but what did it matter—would have operatives at the port to meet the ship. He wondered if he could slip through their dragnet. Then he wondered if it was worth the risk. Better to simply stop the cruise ship and escape in one of the lifeboats. There were thousands of islands in the Aegean to hide on until he planned his next move.

That still left the question of the prisoners. Should he kill them or take them as hostages? He wasn't concerned about controlling the man, who looked like a stoner to Kovac. But there was something about the woman that told him she could be dangerous. Better to kill them both than worry about them trying to get away.

That left one last detail. The virus.

It lived only for a couple of weeks in its sealed canister, so it wouldn't do him much good after his escape. Releasing it would infect the thousand or so people on the ship, and, with a little luck, they would spread it when they returned to their homes. But he didn't think there was much chance of that. The ship would be quarantined and the passengers held in isolation until they were no longer infectious.

It was better than nothing.

Kovac got up from his chair and walked onto the bridge. Night had fully descended, and the only illumination came from the consoles and radar repeaters. There were two officers on watch and two helmsmen. Kovac's assistant, Laird Bergman, was outside on the flying bridge, enjoying a cigarette under the stars.

"I want you to go down to the laundry and release the virus manually," Kovac told him.

"Did something happen to the transmitter?"

"Nothing that concerns you right now. Just get down to the laundry and do what I say. Then find Rolph and report back up here. We're getting off this ship."

"What's going on?"

"Trust me on this. We're going to be arrested as soon as we reach Crete. This is the only way."

One of the officers suddenly shouted, "Where the hell did he come from and what does he think he's playing? Call the captain up here and sound the collision alarm." He rushed out to the opposite flying bridge.

"Stay with me," Kovac said, and he and Bergman jogged after the ship's officer. A huge freighter was coming straight at the *Golden Sky*. She looked like a ghostship with all her running lamps extinguished, but she was cutting through the water at a good twenty knots.

The officer shouted back to the others on the bridge. "Didn't you see him on radar?"

"He was ten miles away, last time I checked," the junior officer replied. "And that was only a few minutes ago, I swear."

"Hit the alarms."

The *Golden Sky*'s bellowing horns had no effect. The freighter continued to aim straight for them, as if it intended to slice the cruise ship in half. Just when it seemed there was no avoiding a collision, the freighter's bow turned sharper than any ship the officer had ever seen, and she came alongside with only a few dozen feet separating them. It was an incredible piece of ship handling, and had the officer not been so angry he would have been impressed.

Kovac recalled that there had been reports of a large ship making an illegal passage of the Corinth Canal the night the Hanley kid had been snatched. He had always known that the two incidents were related, and now a freighter makes an appearance on this of all nights. With the feral instincts of a rat, he knew they were here for him.

He moved back inside and away from the crewmen. Their walkie-talkies didn't work well around so much steel, but he raised Rolph Strong, the third man who had choppered to the ship with him.

"Rolph, it's Kovac. I need you to clear everyone out of the engine room and lock yourself inside. No one is to enter, and kill anyone who resists. Do you understand?"

Unlike Bergman, Strong never questioned orders. "Clear the engine room and let no one enter. Copy."

Kovac pulled his pistol from under his windbreaker and said to Bergman, "Go out and find six or seven women. I don't care if they're passengers or crew. Bring them back here as quickly as you can. Also, go to my cabin and bring the rest of our weapons." Before Bergman could inevitably ask for an explanation, Kovac added: "Thom Severance is dead, the plan is ruined, and the people responsible for it are on that freighter. Go!"

"Yes, sir!"

The Serb locked the bridge door before threading a silencer onto the end of his automatic and dispassionately shooting the two crewmen and one of the bridge officers. The soft reports were drowned out by the blaring air horns, so the second officer didn't know what was going on until he stepped in off the flying bridge and saw the bodies. He had time to look to Kovac before two crimson blooms appeared on his starched white uniform shirt. His jaw worked silently for a moment, before he collapsed against a bulkhead and slumped to the deck.

Suspecting that the operatives on the freighter were going to throw a line onto the cruise ship to send over a boarding party, Kovac stepped up to the controls. There was a dial to order more or less speed from the ship's engines and a simple joystick to turn the rudder. Maneuvering such a massive vessel was as easy as steering a fishing smack.

He cranked the throttle to maximum and veered the ship away from the rusted-out freighter. The *Golden Sky* was only a few years old, and, while she was built for luxury more than speed, he was supremely confident he could outrun the derelict.

They started to pull ahead, easily outpacing the freighter, but only for a few moments. It, too, put on a burst of speed, and exactly mirrored his turn. Kovac was dismayed that a ship that looked ready to dissolve into a rust stain could move so swiftly. He checked the throttle control and noticed that if he pulled the dial upward, he could draw what was called EMERGENCY POWER.

He did, and watched their speed continue to increase. Looking across the bridge, he saw the freighter slowly falling back. Kovac grunted with satisfaction. It would take an hour or two to put enough distance between the two ships for them to stop so he could lower a lifeboat, but it didn't matter.

As if the freighter were toying with him, the big merchantman inexorably accelerated to match his speed and once again positioned itself no more that thirty feet off the *Golden Sky*'s beam. A quick glance confirmed the cruise ship was pounding across the flat sea at thirty-six knots. There was no way the freighter should be able to achieve that speed, let alone maintain it.

Kovac's frustration quickly morphed into rage. There came a sharp burst of automatic fire from the corridor behind the bridge, followed by a chorus of high-pitched screams. He rushed to the wheelhouse's sole entrance and threw back the bolt, his pistol at the ready. The ship's captain lay in a widening pool of blood on the carpeted deck, and four other officers cowered along the passageway. They must have tried to rush Bergman when he returned. Behind them, his assistant had seven women huddled in abject terror.

"Inside! Now!" Kovac snarled, and gestured with his weapon for the women to enter the bridge.

They moved in a tight cluster under Bergman's watchful eye, tears streaming down their cheeks.

"Stop this at once," the seniormost officer demanded.

Kovac shot him in the face and closed the bridge's thick metal door.

He grabbed one of the women, a dark-haired beauty he recognized was a waitress from the dining room, and raced back to the helm. He positioned her between him and the stalking freighter as a human shield, in case they had snipers. He noted that the merchantman had narrowed the gap even more.

"I believe the game is called chicken," he said to no one in particular, and savagely pushed the rudder control to port.

At this speed, the ship responded nimbly, and her bow came over. It slammed into the side of the freighter with a titanic scream of tearing metal. The impact heeled the ship to starboard, staggering Kovac, who had braced for it. The bow railing was crushed in, and the two ships grated against each other. A dozen balconies for the most expensive cabins were torn away, while, all over the ship, passengers and crew were thrown to the deck. There were injuries throughout the vessel, though nothing more severe than a few broken bones.

Kovac turned the ship away from the scene of impact. The freighter turned with him but kept a much wider separation this time, its captain obviously leery of another collision.

He wasn't sure what inspired him, but Kovac had a sudden idea to end this quickly. Leaving the helm position, he yanked one of the dead officers from the floor and walked the corpse outside, with one hand on the officer's belt and the other on the back of his neck so it appeared he was walking on his own. Kovac paused for a second, to make sure the men on the other ship had a chance to see him, before rushing the flying-bridge rail and heaving the body over.

He ducked behind the rail and couldn't watch the body fall the hundred feet to the sea, but he was certain his opponents had. Kovac knew they wouldn't let an innocent man drown, and it would take them at least an hour to rescue him. He liked the irony that they would be forced to give up their pursuit for a dead man.

"DAMAGE REPORT," Juan called, as soon as the two ships pulled apart.

"Crews are on their way," Max said straightaway.

When they hadn't been able to raise the cruise ship on the radio, their plan had been to get the crew's attention and hail them with loudspeakers. The owner of the Golden Line was most likely complicit in Severance's plot, but it couldn't involve all of his officers and crew. If they could get a warning to them about Zelimir Kovac's real reason for being aboard, they could put an end to this once and for all.

Cabrillo had fully expected the shipmaster to turn away, as he had, but never anticipated being intentionally rammed. No captain on earth would jeopardize his ship and crew with a stunt like that.

There was only one logical conclusion. "Kovac's taken over the Golden Sky."

Max eyed him and nodded imperceptibly. "Only thing that makes sense. How do you want to play it?"

"We'll lay up alongside again and fire over grappling hooks. I don't know how many men he has, but I think a dozen of us ought to suffice."

"I like your Captain Blood style."

"Avast, ye matey."

"If he tries to turn in to us again, you boys are going to be in a world of hurt."

"It's your job to make certain he doesn't." Cabrillo was about to call down to Eddie to prepare a boarding party when

Hali suddenly shouted, "Someone was just tossed off the wing bridge!"

"What?" Max and Juan said in unison.

"A guy in a dark windbreaker just threw what looked like an officer off the wing bridge!"

"Helm, full reverse," Juan snapped on the intercom. "Man overboard. Man overboard. This is not a drill. Rescue team to the boat garage. Prepare to launch the RIB."

"He's playing dirty," Max said.

"We can play dirtier. Wepps, aim the gun cameras on the *Golden Sky*'s bridge ASAP and put them up on the main screen."

A moment later, the images flashed on the monitor. Because the cruise ship was so much taller than the *Oregon*, the best angle came from the camera mounted on the ship's mast. When the camera was switched to low-light mode, they could clearly see into the bridge. There were women standing at all the portside windows, hostages placed there so a sharpshooter couldn't get a clean hit. There was a figure crouched at the helm, possibly Kovac, with another woman pressed tightly against him.

"He's no dummy, Juan. We can't risk a shot with him using those folks as human shields."

"Chairman, it's Mike. Doors are open and we are ready to launch."

Juan looked to see their speed through the water, waited a moment for them to slow to the maximum safe speed, and ordered Trono and his rescue team to go.

The Rigid Inflatable Boat flew down the Teflon-coated ramp and hit the seas hard. Mike turned the RIB immediately to port to ease the transition into the swiftly passing water.

"We're clear."

Using thermal-detection gear, they should have no problem spotting the officer. Mike Trono had been a pararescue jumper before joining the Corporation, and was cross-trained as a medic. There was no need for the *Oregon* to stand by.

"Helm, bring us to ninety percent of our former speed. If he turns, match him, and if he slows don't close the gap. I want him to think we can't catch up." Max shot Juan a questioning look. "We need a little time to get a boarding party organized, and I don't want him pressured into thinking he should keep throwing people overboard."

Cabrillo was changing in his cabin when he got word from Hali that Mike had found the officer and reported he'd been shot twice in the chest. Juan calmly gave his orders that the RIB should remain deployed in case Kovac tossed someone alive off the bridge. Inside, his emotions distilled down to a burning fury. He didn't care that they had wasted minutes searching for a corpse. With the *Oregon*'s massive speed advantage, there was no way they would ever lose the *Golden Sky*.

The anger was directed at himself. An innocent man was dead because he came charging in like a bull in a china shop. There could have been another way to capture Kovac and rescue his people. He should have come up with a better plan.

His phone rang and he snatched it up, barking, "Cabrillo."

"Knock it off right now," Dr. Huxley said.

"What are you talking about?"

"I just heard about what happened and I know you're blaming yourself for it and I want you to stop this instant. As soon as the news broke that Eos had been destroyed, Kovac went into trapped-rat mode. He's cornered and panicked. That's why that officer was killed, not because of us. You and I have been over this a hundred times before. You aren't at fault, so don't take blame that isn't yours. All right?"

Juan blew out a breath. "And here I am working myself into a world-record bout of recrimination and self-loathing."

"I knew you were. That's why I called."

"Thanks, Hux."

"Go take him down before he kills anyone else, and you'll feel much better."

"Doctor's orders?"

"Exactly."

Fifteen minutes later, Juan was on deck with his team. He divided them into two groups of six, with Eddie leading the first and him in charge of the second. In order to maintain control of the cruise ship, Kovac would need people on the bridge as well as in the engine room, to stop crewmen from killing power. That would be Eddie's responsibility. Juan wanted Kovac all to himself.

They all wore black formfitting outfits over Kevlar body armor that wouldn't snag on obstacles and impede their assault. Their boots had soft rubber soles, and each man carried a gas mask, because all sported tear gas grenades. The interior of the *Golden Sky* would be brightly lit, so only one man on each team carried night vision gear.

With the number of civilians aboard the ship, Cabrillo ordered half loads for their ammunition to avoid overpenetration killing someone beyond their target. He carried a Glock instead of his usual FNs, since even a half charge of powder would send the smaller bullets through a man.

Their grappling hooks were launched by a shotgun-type weapon. The lines they trailed were incredibly strong and light, which made climbing difficult. For that, each wore special gloves with mechanical pincers to grip the monofilament.

"Max, you read?" Juan said into his throat mike.

"You're live."

"Okay, take us in flank speed, and don't forget to tell Mike."

The acceleration was almost instantaneous. Juan slit his eyes against the brutal wind. The *Golden Sky* lay four miles ahead, her gleaming upperworks making her look like a jewel on the dark waters, while her wake glowed with an ethereal trail of phosphorescence.

The *Oregon* was moving some twenty-odd knots faster than the cruise ship, so they quickly cut the distance.

"Kovac must be going nuts," Eddie remarked. "We keep showing up like the proverbial bad penny."

"Chairman, he tossed another," Hali shouted over the radio. "It was a woman this time, and she was definitely alive."

"Alert Mike. Wepps, give 'em a squirt with the Gatling as close to the wing bridge as you can. Let Kovac know the next time he sets foot out there, we're going to shred him."

The armored plate covering the starboard-side Gatling gun folded back and the weapon peeked from its redoubt, as the motor spun up its six rotating barrels. When it fired, the sound was like a mechanical buzz saw tearing itself to pieces.

A tongue of flame shot twenty feet from the *Oregon*'s flank and a stream of two hundred depleted uranium rounds arced across the sky. They passed so close to the flying bridge that paint blistered off the metal railing. The bullets peppered the sea ahead of the ship in a multitude of tiny eruptions.

The *Golden Sky* immediately turned away from the attack.

"That rattled his cage." Eddie was grinning.

Max kept the *Oregon* a hundred feet off the other ship as they came abeam and when Kovac tried to turn into them again Max kept just out of reach, using the bow thrusters to keep the *Oregon* turning tighter than the *Golden Sky*.

"Max, get ready," Juan said, "Wepps, prepare to fire again on my mark, but don't hit the ship." He waited for his men to get in position on the *Oregon*'s rail, their grappling-hook guns at their shoulders. "Aim for the main deck. Max, go!"

The *Oregon* carved in on the liner, cutting the gap in half in just a few seconds.

"Fire," Juan said, and the Gatling shrieked again, as he and the assault team launched their grappling hooks.

All twelve hooks sailed across the gap, and when they heaved back on the lines all had caught firmly. The *Oregon* came in even tighter, almost brushing the cruise ship, so the men wouldn't injure themselves when they arced across, while the Gatling continued to spit a continuous stream of fire across the *Sky*'s bridge.

"Go."

Juan gripped the line tightly and leapt over the railing, swinging across the gap at an ever-accelerating pace. The *Oregon* cut away sharply behind him. He had intentionally aimed above a large row of windows and had judged the distance perfectly. His feet hit the glass, and he exploded into the deserted dining room, saving himself the tedious task of climbing up the line. His team knew to hook up outside the bridge if they got separated.

He unslung the MP-5 from across his back. Moving cautiously, the weapon tucked high on his shoulder so he had a constant sight picture, he weaved through the tables toward the exit.

He came out on the mezzanine level of the atrium. Passengers were milling around, still dazed after the impact with the *Oregon*. A man was lying at the bottom of a flight of stairs being attended to by a pair of women. An elderly lady screamed when she spotted him.

Juan raised the submachine gun's barrel in a nonthreatening manner. "Ladies and gentlemen, this ship has been hijacked," he said. "I am part of a United Nations hostage-rescue team. Return to your cabins immediately. Tell passengers you see that they must stay in their cabins until we have secured this ship."

A man in civilian attire with the aura of authority approached him. "I'm Greg Turner, second assistant engineer. Is there anything I can do to help?"

"Tell me the fastest way to the bridge, and see that these people get to their rooms."

"How bad is it?" Turner asked.

"Have you ever heard of a good hijacking?"

"Sorry. Dumb question."

"Don't sweat it."

Turner gave Juan the directions, as well as a magnetic pass card to get him into the off-limits spaces, and Cabrillo took off at a trot. When he reached the door marked NO ADMITTANCE, he swiped the card through the reader and propped the door open with a nearby potted fern for the rest of his team. By his estimates, they should be only a minute behind him.

He jogged past countless cabins and raced up two flights of stairs before emerging in the hallway that gave access to the bridge. He activated his laser sight as he slowly approached the door. Cabrillo paused when he heard voices muttering in a cabin a few doors back from the bridge entrance.

"Captain?" he called softly.

The voices stopped, and someone peered around the doorjamb. The single eye he saw widened in horror at his appearance.

"It's okay," Juan said softly. "I'm here to stop him. Can I speak to your captain?"

The person came fully around the corner. She was wearing a uniform, and, judging by the stripes on her shoulder boards, she was the *Golden Sky*'s first officer. She had jaw-length dark hair and perfectly tanned skin that set off her honey brown eyes. "That butcher killed the captain and our third purser. I am Leah Voorhees, first officer."

"Let's talk in there," Juan said, pointing to the cabin behind her.

He followed her inside. There were two man-size lumps on the bed with a sheet pulled over them both. Dark blood stained the chest of one and the head of the other.

Leah Voorhees tried to introduce him to the rest of the officers, but Juan cut her off. "Later. Tell me what you know about what's happening on the bridge."

"There are two of them," she said at once. "One named Kovac, the other I'm not sure. There is a third barricaded in the engine room."

"You're sure there's just one down there?" When she nodded, Juan radioed this piece of information to Eddie. "Go on."

"They came aboard by chopper not long after we left Istanbul. We were given orders from our head office to do whatever Kovac asked of us. They were supposedly looking for two stowaways who might have murdered a passenger."

"Those stowaways are part of my team," Juan assured her. "They didn't murder anyone. Do you know where they are?"

Given the circumstances, she accepted Juan's statement without question. "They were found a short while ago and are locked in the captain's day office directly behind the bridge."

"Okay. What else?"

"There were two ordinary seamen on duty, as well as two officers, when he took over. They also have female passengers as hostages. Who are you? Where did you come from?"

"This is a United Nations mission. We have been shadowing this terrorist cell for some time. Kovac shook us when he boarded your ship, so we had to act fast. I am sorry that you couldn't be informed, and I am sorry for the danger you've been put in. It was our intention to grab Kovac earlier, but, well, the UN's a bureaucracy like any other."

The rest of Juan's squad suddenly appeared, throwing dots of laser light around the room as they checked it.

"It's okay, boys," Juan called, and the weapons were lowered. While he filled them in on what he knew, he asked Leah to draw a diagram of the bridge, and called Max. "Give me a sit-rep."

"Mike fished the woman from the drink. She's fine, if a little hysterical. Kovac is still at the helm, surrounded by three of his hostages. We've spotted a second gunman, but he isn't in view right now. The three other women are still pressed to the windows."

"Pull ahead of the *Sky* and get directly in front of her so you have a clear view of everything going on. Mark and Linda are being held in an office behind the bridge. See if you can spot them."

"Aye, aye."

Eddie called in to say they were in position and that they would have to blast through the door to gain access to the engine room. Juan told him to wait so they could synchronize their attack.

Max radioed back, "I see a door on the back wall of the bridge, it's closed right now, but I bet that's the place. Kovac has shifted his three human shields to the main bridge windows. His chief goon is down a small corridor on the starboard side, standing at what I believe is the main entrance."

Cabrillo penned in the positions of everyone on the bridge on the diagram the first officer had drawn so his team knew what to expect. To date, they had never caused what was euphemistically called collateral damage, a record Cabrillo was immensely proud of and one he had vowed to keep.

In the wake of 9/11, not only had cockpit doors on aircraft been beefed up but a great many cruise ships had also installed reinforced doors to protect the bridge. Juan placed the plastic explosives on it himself and retreated back into the cabin. He called Eddie and Max to tell them it was a go in thirty seconds.

He kept his eyes glued to his watch and held up his splayed fingers when five seconds remained. He dropped a finger at every tick of the clock and pressed the button on the remote with his other hand.

The blast filled the hallway with reeking white smoke and was a brutal assault on their senses. Cabrillo was in motion less than a second after the shock wave rolled past the cabin door. The beam of his laser cut a ruby line through the coiling haze.

He raced onto the bridge with his men at his back, rushing past the red-hot remains of the door and ignoring the pile of gore that had once been Laird Bergman.

"Down! Everybody, down!" the men repeated as they swept the room with their weapons.

Kovac had reacted faster than Juan thought possible. As he pegged the Serb with his laser, Kovac had already pulled one of the women in front of him and pressed his pistol to her ear.

"Another step and she dies," he roared.

Juan was staggered to see that his hostage wasn't a stranger. Kovac must have known she was part of their team, because he had taken Linda Ross from the captain's day office and was using her as his shield.

"It's over, Kovac. Let her go."

"It is over for her if you move a muscle." To emphasize his point, he pressed the gun even harder to her ear. Linda fought the pain but couldn't manage to stifle a whimper. "Drop your weapons now or she dies."

"You do it and you'll follow her a second later."

"I realize now that I am a dead man, so what does it matter to me? But wouldn't you hate to see this young life extinguished needlessly? You have five seconds."

"Shoot him!" Linda cried.

"I'm sorry," Juan said, and let his machine pistol drop from his fingers. The incredulous look on her face crushed his heart. "Everyone, put them down."

The men let their weapons fall to the floor.

Kovac pulled his pistol away from Linda's head and aimed it at Cabrillo. "Smart move. You will now kindly jump over the rail and return to your ship. If you follow this vessel again, I will continue to throw passengers overboard, only from now on I will bind their hands."

He pushed Linda into Juan's arms.

A thousand yards ahead of the *Golden Sky,* Franklin Lincoln stood at the stern rail of the *Oregon,* watching everything unfold though the telescopic sight of his favorite weapon, the Barrett .50 caliber sniper rifle.

"Bye-bye."

While Kovac had been concentrating on the Chairman, his man had used subtle hand gestures to get the women he'd posted in front of the windows to lie flat on the floor to give Linc a clear field of fire.

On the bridge, they heard only a quiet ping as the bullet passed through the safety glass. The sound of it hitting Kovac between the shoulders was something altogether different, a thick meaty tone like a hammer striking carpet. Blood fountained from his chest, as the bullet transited his body with enough kinetic impact to toss his corpse a good five feet.

"Did you doubt me?" Juan smiled down at Linda.

"I should have known when I didn't see Linc," she said with a saucy grin, her composure fully restored. "I assume that was him."

"I can't think of anyone else when I need a million-dollar shot."

"Well?" It was Max.

"Congratulate Linc. He was dead on target. Linda's fine." Juan pulled away his earbud and put the radio on speaker mode so everyone could hear.

"Hi, Max," she said

"How are you doing, honey?"

"Other than this lousy cold, I'm fine."

Mark had been released from the office and the FlexiCuffs cut away from his wrists and ankles. He shook Juan's hand, smiling broadly.

"I've been thinking," Max continued. "You guys should probably check down in the laundry room. I think you'll find that is how they planned to disperse the virus."

Mark's smile fell until it had turned into a pout. His moment of glory had been stolen.

Juan read his emotions perfectly. Mark had figured it out, too, and was doubtlessly going to impress the nubile Miss Dahl with his insight. He didn't have the heart to tell him his competition for her affections was a bona fide astronaut now, and, in his book, that trumped just about anything in ways to impress a girl.

EPILOGUE

IN THE WEEKS SINCE THE DISASTER ON EOS Island, age had finally caught up to Lydell Cooper. He had spent decades and millions on reversing the process, having cosmetic surgeries and illegal organ transplants. However, it wasn't his body that was letting him down. It was his mind.

He couldn't accept his utter failure, and, because of that, he went through the motions of life in a daze.

It had been his daughter Heidi who had taken charge when they were still flying toward Turkey. She had told the pilot to alter their flight plan and had directed them to Zurich instead. There, she had drained several Responsivist bank accounts, converting the cash into stocks purchased by a dummy company she had the bank set up for her. She had understood that, with Eos destroyed, the authorities would arrest every high-ranking member of the organization, and her only chance to remain free was to go into hiding with her sister.

Cooper wanted to stay with them, but she said that he had loose ends to tie up back in the States, and since his Dr. Adam Jenner persona was a world-renowned critic of Responsivism he was above suspicion.

So he had returned home, mostly to empty a series of safe-deposit boxes in Los Angeles that the FBI didn't know about. When he'd taxied past the big house in Beverly Hills, there was crime-scene tape draped like a garland along the perimeter fence and uniformed police with cruisers camped in the driveway.

The dream was well and truly over.

Greek authorities had closed the Responsivists' compound in Corinth, and nations were kicking out Responsivist clinics all over the world. Even though there had been no mention in the media of the plot to sterilize half the planet's population, the corruption charges filed against the group had caused a backlash that continued to reverberate. Famous members, like Donna Sky, were turning their backs on the faith, claiming they had been brainwashed in order to financially support the group.

In a fourteen-day span, Cooper's lifetime achievement had been reduced to fodder for comics on late-night television. He closed up Jenner's practice, happily telling the other psychologists who shared the office suite that his work was done and he was retiring, while, inside, he was dying by degrees. He put his house up for sale, instructing the broker to accept the first offer.

Rather than live in glory as the famed Dr. Lydell Cooper in a sustainable world, he was forced to retire to obscurity as Adam Jenner.

He was returning to his house the day before he was to fly to Brazil, which has a notoriously lax extradition treaty with the United States. Because of the crippling arthritis in his hands, he had replaced a normal lock-and-key entry with a push-button pad. He pressed the sequence and stepped inside, using his elbow to close the door behind him. A moving company had packed the few possessions he wanted to keep, while the rest was to be sold with the house.

He crossed the foyer and made for his study to check the latest news on his laptop. The heavy wooden door closed behind him when he entered. He turned. A stranger had been hiding behind it.

Had he been in a normal frame of mind, he would have demanded the person leave, but he just stood there mutely instead, staring at the man who had invaded his home.

"Dr. Jenner, I presume?"

"Yes. Who are you? What do you want?"

"I paid you a great deal of money to help a friend not too long ago."

"I am retired now. All that is finished. Please leave."

"And how do you feel about that?" the stranger asked. "Responsivism is dead. You won. You must feel vindicated."

Cooper couldn't bring himself to answer. His identities blurred in his mind. He didn't know how to feel or act any longer.

"You know what?" the man continued. "I don't think you feel good about it at all. In fact, I think you're reeling inside because I know something that would surprise a lot of people."

Somehow, Cooper knew what was coming. He sat heavily on a couch, his artificially youthful face ashen.

"Even if you hadn't been overheard bragging to Kovac on Eos Island, I think I would have figured it out. You were the only person who could have betrayed us in Rome. We thought Kyle might have had an embedded radio tag, but now we know he didn't. He had no idea where he was being taken, so there was no way he could get a warning out to Kovac to snatch him back."

Now that the truth was out, Cooper sat straighter on the sofa. "That's right. I did make the call, getting Kovac to Rome and then telling him which hotel, once I had arrived and was left alone with that kid. You were behind the attack on Eos?"

The stranger nodded. "And we discovered the virus in the *Golden Sky*'s and all forty-nine other cruise ships' laundries you tampered with. The fifty containers are at a level-four biohazard lab in Maryland."

"Don't you understand that the world is doomed? I could have saved all of humanity."

The man laughed. "And do you know how many crackpots have been saying the world is doomed over the past couple hundred years? We were supposed to run out of food in the 1980s. We were supposed to run out of oil in the 1990s. The population was supposed to hit ten billion by the year 2000. Every one of these predictions was wrong. Heck, they wanted to close the U.S. Patent office in 1900 because everything that could be invented had been invented. I'll let you in on a little secret: you can't predict the future."

"You're wrong. I know what is coming. Anyone with half a brain can see it. Fifty years from now, civilization will be swept away in a tidal wave of violence, as nations realize they can't support their populations. It will be anarchy on a biblical scale."

"Funny you should mention that." The man removed a pistol from behind his back. "I've always liked biblical justice. An eye for an eye, and all that."

"You can't kill me. Arrest me. Put me on trial."

"And give you a stage to spout your demented ideas? I don't think so."

"Please!"

The gun spat. Cooper felt the impact, and when he moved to touch his neck he could feel something sticking in his flesh, but his clawlike hands lacked the dexterity to remove it.

Cabrillo watched for ten seconds as the tranquilizer from the dart gun coursed through Cooper's body. When Cooper's eyes closed and he slumped over, Juan brought a radio to his lips. Moments later, a big ambulance pulled up the drive, and two paramedics burst out the back doors, pushing a gurney.

"Any problems?" Eddie asked, wheeling the stretcher into the study with Franklin Lincoln.

"No, but after talking to him I feel like I need a shower. I've seen some loons in my life, but this one beats all."

Linc gingerly lifted Cooper off the couch and set him on the gurney. As soon as Cabrillo found Cooper's passport and a one-way ticket to Rio de Janeiro in a kitchen drawer, they rushed out of the house. A neighbor had come out of her house to see what was going on.

"He's had a heart attack," Juan told her, as he held open the ambulance doors so Linc could slide the gurney inside.

Forty-five minutes later, the ambulance arrived at LAX, and, ten hours after that, the Corporation's Gulfstream touched down at Gardermoen airport, thirty miles north of Oslo, Norway.

They had a brief reunion at an airport lounge with Jannike Dahl. She had permitted Eric Stone to escort her home. When Eric declined her invitation to show him the sights of Oslo, saying he had to return to the ship, Juan had taken him aside and explained that she wasn't that interested in him seeing her hometown. Eric had asked what she really wanted, and the Chairman had to explain it further. Red-faced with embarrassment and unbridled enthusiasm, Eric quickly accepted her offer.

It took another jet flight to Tromsö, in the far north of the country, and a helicopter ride, to finally arrive at their destination. Cooper was kept sedated the entire time and was closely monitored by Julia Huxley.

The glacier sparkled in the bright light of a summer afternoon, glittering as though it were the finest lead crystal. Outside the valley, the temperature hovered in the mid-fifties, but on the ice it was just above freezing.

George Adams had flown them in on an MD-520N, the replacement for the little Robinson. This chopper was larger than the previous one, and required some modifications to the hangar elevator, but it was also much more powerful and faster. And because it vented engine exhaust through the tail, to counter the main rotor's torque rather than rely on a second, smaller rotor, it was significantly more quiet. The *Oregon* was positioned just off the coast, and Adams would fly them out once they were finished.

Cooper was half conscious by the time they touched down but didn't fully comprehend where he was until another fifteen minutes had elapsed.

"Where are we? What have you done?"

"Surely you recognize where we are, Dr. Cooper," Juan said innocently. "But, then again, maybe not. After all, it's been more than sixty years since you were last here."

Cooper stared blankly, so Cabrillo continued. "The one thing that kept nagging at me this entire time was how a virus discovered by the Nazis and later given to their Japanese allies ended up in your hands. There was no record of its discovery, or of its transfer to the Philippines, nothing to give any indication of what was found here.

"Only one thing made sense to me. You discovered it yourself. There *are* quite detailed records of the Nazi occupation of Norway, and my team found something rather interesting. A four-engine *Kondor* reconnaissance plane was shot down on this very glacier on the night of April twenty-nine, 1943. Every member of the crew was killed save one, a gunner named Ernst Kessler."

Cooper winced at the mention of the name.

"What I find so fascinating is that Kessler is the German word for 'cooper.' Ironic, isn't it? And the publishing house you started to get your book in print—what was it called?

Raptor Press, I believe—is it coincidental that a condor is a kind of raptor? I don't think so."

Cabrillo threw open the chopper's door and shoved Kessler/Cooper onto the ice. In all his dealings with Cooper, Juan had kept his tone light, almost pleasant. But his anger suddenly boiled over, and he seethed. "We also discovered that after the plane crash, Ernst Kessler was accepted into the Gestapo, and was allowed to receive medical training at a lovely spot called Auschwitz. His final orders before war's end was a transfer to the German Embassy in Tokyo. I assume that was a cover for your going to work for Unit 731 in the Philippines.

"You should have died that night and saved the world a lot of misery, you sick freak. I have dealt with al-Qaeda assassins and Soviet torturers, and every perverted piece of slime in between, but you are the single-most-evil human being I have ever met. You could have shown the world one of the greatest discoveries of all time, perhaps the inspiration for a most beloved Bible story, but instead you only cared about reaping death.

"Well, Kessler, you have reaped what you've sown, and when I think about you freezing to death, tonight over dinner, I am going to smile." Cabrillo closed the helicopter door. "Let's go."

"What happens now?" Julia asked as the chopper shot past the edge of the glacier and over open water.

"He dies."

"I mean, with the ark."

"Oh that. I've already contacted Kurt Austin at NUMA. He told me they are going to find a way to convince the Norwegian government to let them do a detailed survey of that glacier. With her copper bottom, they should have no problem locating the ancient wreck."

"I wonder what they will find."

Juan gave her a dreamy look. "Who knows, maybe all the creatures of the world loaded two by two."

MAX HANLEY SAT ON A BENCH near the Griffith Park Observatory, overlooking downtown L.A. A shadow passed over his face, and when he looked up his son Kyle was standing over him. Max made a wordless gesture for him to sit. He could feel the anger radiating off the boy as though it were waves of heat.

Kyle was staring off into the distance, so Max studied his profile. There was a lot of the kid's mother in him, but he saw a few of his own features. As he watched, a single tear rolled down Kyle's cheek, and as if a floodgate had opened Kyle began to cry—deep, choking sobs that sounded like his soul was being torn apart. He clutched at his father, and Max took him in his arms.

"I am so sorry, Dad." Kyle sobbed.

"And I forgive you."

Because that's what fathers do.